THE VERSIPELLIS MYSTERIES

DEATH IN EAU DE NIL

RHEN GARLAND

Published in Great Britain 2025
by Amethyst and Greenstone

Copyright © 2025 by Rhen Garland
Illustrations by Adam Garland

ISBN 978-1-8384604-6-4 (Paperback)
ISBN 978-1-8384604-7-1 (eBook)

First Published 2025

Mum
1938 - 2023

Daisy
2022 - 2023

"We had no time."
Ergo the Magnificent

DRAMATIS PERSONAE

Elliott Caine/Versipellis	Private Enquiry Agent
Giselle Du'Lac/Angellis	Private Enquiry Agent
Abernathy Thorne/Shadavarian	Private Enquiry Agent
Aquilleia Aquilesi Thorne	Private Enquiry Agent
Veronique/Xenocyon	Labrador/Battle Hound
Captain Anthony Darling	An Other
Gabriel Masquelyne	An Other
Carandini Bey	Hotel Manager
Vanessa March	Carandini Bey's Secretary.
Evelyn Briar-Deveraux	A Young Honeymooner
André Deveraux	Her Husband
Jane Gagnon	Evelyn's Companion
Kiefer Devereaux	André's Brother
Marguerite Deveraux	André's Mother
Vincenzo Prezzo	Marguerite's Husband
Violette Donnadieu	Marguerite's Companion
Margaux van Sloane	André's Sister
Julius van Sloane	Margaux's Husband
Camellia van Sloane	Margaux's Daughter
Linden van Sloane	Margaux's Son
Heathers	Julius van Sloane's Valet
Sedgwyck	The Devereaux Family Butler
Gaston Cavet	French Author
Rex Nympton	American Gentleman
Thomas Breton	Unpleasant Artist
Amycus Mirylees	Archaeologist
Dr Jones	His Assistant
Caroline Jones	His Wife
Colonel Barrington	The Face of the Veiled Protectorate
Captain Abasi Sarhan	Egyptian Police Officer
Sergeant Jaziri	Egyptian Police Officer
Farasha	Simulandro Gynoid Maid
Maxwell	Simulandro Android Steward

With a supporting cast of Simulandros,
maids, stewards, and others.

PRONUNCIATION GUIDE

Versipellis - Ver-si-pell-is
Shadavarian - Shad-a-vair-rian
Angellis - On-jel-is
Aquilleia – A-kwee-lay-ah
Xenocyon - Zee-noh-sigh-on
Abditivus - Ab-dity-vus
Geminandras – Gem-in-and-ras
Fellithropos – Fell-eeth-rop-oss

Elliott's Cane

○

January
1901
London
Abney Park Cemetery
Midnight

High above the weaving, ivy-twined paths, damp mausolea, and fog-shrouded weeping angels that stood guard over the tombs of their wards, the weathered stone gargoyles of Abney Park Chapel gazed across the tree-covered expanse that lay beneath their perches. The odour of dank, damp vegetation mingled with the scent of burning coal from the fires of the City of London and filled the chill winter air that swirled in the silent graveyard with a rare miasma only found in the shadowy, overgrown, and overpopulated places of the world.

The stone guardians were not alone, for next to them, on the roof of their domain, stood the figure of a man; tall and dark, with bright-yellow eyes that gazed intently on the view before him; in particular, upon a procession of five men — the largest of whom was carrying what appeared to be a rolled-up rug — as they made their way, in silence and with only one shuttered lamp, towards a freshly dug grave tucked away in a dark corner of the foggy cemetery.

The eagle-eyed man placed one long, slender and pale hand on the Gothic crenelations that edged the building's roof and crouched slightly as he continued his observation of the small group. Wrapped in what appeared to be a long black cloak that kept the worst of the winter chill from his skin, the man's watchful yellow eyes seemed to glow in his pale, saturnine face as he continued his vigil from the roof.

Below him, the men arrived at the fresh grave and, at a gesture from one of their number, the man carrying the rug dropped it to the ground. The heavy length of material landed with a dull thud that was swallowed by the dampness of the earth. Slowly the beautiful Persian rug unrolled, spilling its unwieldy contents next to the grave. The observer on the roof watched in silence as the body of a man in late middle age, wearing a grey tweed day suit rolled out of the rug and came to a halt on the edge of the pit.

The group by the grave looked at the man who had given the order; a youngish man with dark-blond hair and a bored expression on his coldly handsome face. He snapped his fingers again at the man who had carried the rug and its contents to the graveside. "See to it."

The man bowed slightly. "Yes, Sir." He removed his black jacket and climbed into the grave. Lifting the shovel that had been left by the gravediggers for the next day's work, he began to dig the pit deeper still. After a surprisingly short space of time, the man stopped and placed the shovel on the graveside. As the yellow-eyed man continued to watch from the rooftop, the unprotesting body was manhandled into its final resting place. The obeisant man settled the corpse into its burial site, climbed out of the grave, then began to shovel earth on top of the corpse. As soon as the body was covered with a thin layer of soil, he leapt back into the pit and trod down the earth to better resemble its appearance when they had first arrived; that of the tamped floor of an empty, prepared grave. He climbed from the pit, dusted himself down, and pulled on his jacket.

One of the men; young and dark, consulted his pocket watch, grimaced, and spoke; his voice touched by a faint Italian accent. "We are running a little late. We could have dealt with this better had our sixth man been prepared to assist us." He looked at one of the others; an urbane but uncomfortable looking middle-aged man who seemed strangely averse to looking at the grave, and was instead devoting his interest to judging the damage the act of assisting with the rug-wrapped corpse had done to his neatly manicured fingernails. The young Italian noted his discomfiture and smiled. "Perhaps you should talk with your son about his loyalty to the family—"

The bored-looking man standing next to the target of his comment lashed out casually and back-handed the young Italian across the face, the supernatural force in the blow knocking the younger man to the ground with frightening speed.

In the deathly silence that followed, the bored man studied the blood welling from the back of his hand as the Italian stared up at him in shock, a bloody handkerchief pressed to his once aquiline nose. "You struck me! How dare you! I will inform Marguerite of this abuse!"

The bored man shrugged as he took his own handkerchief from his breast pocket and dabbed at the back of his hand. "Do as you will, although I believe my mother will support *my* reaction to your remark, rather than the attempts of her most recently acquired spouse to call her grandson's loyalty to our family into question."

The young Italian glared up at him. "You go too far! One day, you will go too far...even for your mother to protect you."

The bored man shrugged again. "That hasn't happened for several thousand years." He bent down and fixed his dark blue eyes on his much younger stepfather. "Remember this, human; we are older than your dreams, and more powerful than your nightmares. You need us – we don't need you! And it ill behooves you to bite the hand that feeds you." His eyes changed suddenly from dark blue to an opaque, milky white. "You married into our family and have been gifted what we were born to be. Do not make us regret that gift…you will find its rescinding painful!" He straightened, his eyes returning to their usual colour as he looked down at his step-father with a dismissive expression. "Remember your place." He took out his pocket watch, held it up to the moonlight and sighed. "You are, however, quite correct. We *are* running late." He turned and snapped his fingers at the large man who had buried the corpse. "Heathers, bring the carriage to the gate. It's time we returned home. There is much to do."

Heathers bowed again, rolled up the now-empty rug, and headed back towards the gates, rapidly followed by the middle-aged man who had found his nails so fascinating. As they disappeared into the gloom, the bored man looked at the one in their number who had been silent since they had entered the cemetery. "Well, brother, it's nearly time. Are you ready?"

The man, younger and darker than his brother, smiled lazily. "Yes, Kiefer…I do believe I am!"

They followed Heathers to the carriage as the Italian, swearing under his breath, clasped his bloody handkerchief to his broken nose, got to his feet, and followed them sullenly. The arrival of the silent group and the subsequent disposal of the body had taken less than twenty minutes.

As the group left, the man on the chapel roof rose from his crouched position, stretched, and flexed his shoulders. The long black cloak unfurled into thin, leathery wings which spread out as he stepped off the roof and glided to an elegant halt by the chapel door. As he walked towards the partly filled-in grave, his wings rewrapped themselves around his back and shoulders, and returned to their previous appearance as a form-fitting cloak.

Moving towards the most recent burial, he caught a

sudden movement out of the corner of his eye. Turning, he looked directly at a neglected grave shielded with a mortsafe and covered with glowing magical sigils that only his eyes could see. As he watched, the earth that covered the overgrown tomb rippled slightly as whatever had been buried there strained against the confines of the containing wards and was yet again prevented from escape. He frowned at the unquiet grave; the contents of that particular burial place would have to be dealt with...but there was something far more important on his mind that evening.

He continued to the most recently dug grave, knelt by its edge and looked within. As he did, he saw a faint movement, as of someone pushing against the weight of the earth above them. He stepped lightly into the pit and plunged his slender hand into the tamped soil. He rummaged under the damp soil then, with barely any effort, he lifted the recently buried man out of his shallow resting place, and with a sharp flex of his wings leapt from the grave. Landing next to the grave, he gently sat the disinterred man against the nearest gravestone, then knelt and studied the desperately pale and grimy face; it was the face of a man he knew all too well. He hissed as his sharp eyes took in the gaping wound in the man's stomach, and the bloodied mess where the man's right eye should have been.

As he studied the silent figure he had been following for several years, he caught the faint flicker of a pulse at the man's throat. He leant forward and gently patted the man's cheeks, taking care not to touch the terrible wound that had been wrought upon his face.

The man opened his uninjured eye and looked at the calm face of the stranger before him. He swallowed and rasped, "I'm dying."

The winged man nodded; his yellow eyes sorrowful. "Yes, you are. But before you leave this realm, I would like you to tell me what you know about those who attacked you. Then I shall tell you why they did this, and what I am prepared to do to prevent them harming the person we both care for."

An expression of hope appeared on the dying man's face. He took a deep breath and spoke in a whisper as the winged man leant forwards to hear his words.

The Pyramids

PART I

Wednesday 16th of January
The Isle of Wight
Osbourne House
Mid-Morning

In a quiet, heavily curtained bedroom that was lit by a single gas lamp, a grey-haired man sat in respectful silence and listened as he was given his instructions by the room's other occupant; an elderly, tired, yet determined looking woman, who lay, covered in blankets, and propped up against several feather pillows, in the massive four poster bed. As she finished issuing her orders, her voice weakly trailed off. There followed a silence that lasted for several minutes, before she spoke again; this time fainter, as though the mere act of talking had exhausted her. "But let judgment run down as waters, and righteousness as a mighty stream. See that my will is done. You may leave us."

The gentleman who was the sole audient stood, pulled the bell rope, and bowed deeply to the pale figure resting in the bed. As an elderly female companion entered the darkened room, he took his leave; never once turning his back on the now silent figure reclining in silence against the pillows. As he opened the door, she reached out a trembling hand to her bedside table and picked up a tinted photograph of two women; one much older than the other. Looking at the sepia image she clasped the photograph to her breast and closed her eyes. "My will be done."

Her visitor silently closed the door behind him, and made his way back to the office at the far end of the hallway. As he entered the wood panelled room, the austere-looking man waiting for him stood and raised a querying eyebrow. "I take it a certain person has been informed of the deaths? How did she take the news?"

The grey-haired man removed his glasses and rubbed his face. "As well as can be expected. Lady Melford was one of her most trusted confidantes. For her and her daughter to be murdered in such a way..." He shook his head. "She has expressed her deep sadness and loss, and she has insisted that we send for the official intermediary between us and the Espion Court..." He paused. "She wants an official document drawn up requesting their assistance in discovering the perpetrators."

The other man frowned. "Why? And how on earth did she hear of our occasional...ah, confederates?"

The elderly man looked at his associate pointedly. "She wants those responsible dealt with...unofficially. As to how she found out about the Espion Court, I have absolutely no idea...but she *does* know of them. Therefore, I have no choice but to send for Lapotaire. And I must hope that he can get here before this evening." He looked at the other man and slowly shook his head. "I don't think this will end very well for those responsible; making a personal enemy of the Queen of the United Kingdom of Great Britain and Ireland could well be construed as the singularly most catastrophic mistake of their murderous careers!"

February
London
The Grunewald Hotel
Early Evening

In a large suite situated on the sixth floor of the palatial Grunewald Hotel, a guest paused in their pre-cocktail hour ablutions as a knock sounded at the door. Wandering back into the sitting room, they saw a small envelope that had been forced through the narrow gap of the threshold. They picked up the envelope with a frown and opened the door; the corridor beyond was empty in both directions. Their eyes narrowed as they turned their attention to the envelope – good quality stock with no watermark. They opened the envelope and examined the contents; a short note and two photographs. One was a daguerreotype dated 1856, the other a tintype dated 1890, but both showed the same people; unaged and unchanged.

The guest closed the door, sat in one of the comfortable armchairs by the window, and unfolded the piece of paper. As they read the few words inscribed on the note, a vicious smile appeared on their lips. They replaced the document and photographs in the envelope and sat back with a look of triumph; so, they were once again returning to their lair. Finally, after so many years, the revenge they had long sought was within their grasp!

○

Sunday 17ᵗʰ March
Venice
The Teatro Goldoni
Late Evening

Marizza Dimitrova, doyen of the ballet world, raised her hands in gracious acceptance of her audience's rapturous applause, smiled at her adoring public, blew a kiss to the packed boxes and took her final bow. She flew offstage and into the wings, where she was met by her beaming manager, Georgi Sokolov, who grasped her hands and kissed her cheeks with continental flair. "A perfect performance, my darling Marizza! You were spectacular, as always."

He escorted her past the other dancers, who were also leaving the stage and scurrying towards their cramped changing rooms as the star of the show was guided with rather more care and attention towards her expansive, and expensive suite, several floors above the stage, deep in the heart of the Teatro Goldoni.

Arriving at her suite, Georgi took in the ornate brass doorplate, emblazoned with the legend 'Marizza Dimitrova, Prima Ballerina'. He threw the door open with a bow and a smile that did not quite reach his eyes as Marizza swept in and sat gracefully in her favourite armchair with a happy sigh. Georgi caught sight of a bottle of Champagne sitting in a bucket full of ice. He lifted the bottle and cast a judgemental eye over the label before opening it with a flourish and pouring two full coupes, one of which he presented to the most prized asset on his company's books.

Marizza accepted the drink with a smile, looked at her manager and leant forward. "What did you think, Georgi? Was I as good as ever?"

Georgi smiled. "You were quite wonderful. But then, you have never been anything other than perfect." He took a sip from his glass and shot a glance at her before clearing his throat. "There is something…just a little favour that I wish to ask…"

Marizza arched one elegant black eyebrow. "You always say that, Georgi, right before you ask me to do something that may be a little dangerous. What is it this time?"

Her manager smiled; again, it did not touch his eyes. "I have been approached by a certain admirer of yours. He wishes you to dance for him…privately."

Marizza's smile froze; a muscle under her left eye began to twitch. She sat back in her chair and skewered Georgi with a narrowed gaze. "That does not sound like an evening of ballet, Georgi; that sounds more like an assignation." She took a deep breath and placed her glass carefully on the table next to her; her hands had begun to tremble. "You dare ask me to do this after what happened the last time someone requested a private meeting with me? How can you—"

Georgi held up his hand. "My darling, I would be there, and your dresser Anya will also be by your side…there is no impropriety, I assure you. My dearest Marizza, would I endanger my most beloved golden goose?"

Marizza's face looked pinched. She shook her head, her voice nearly a whisper. "You did once before." Her manager's face darkened as she continued. "I am not interested, Georgi. This appointment is not for me."

Georgi blinked; she had never turned down one of his suggestions before. He spread his hands. "But my angel—"

Marizza shook her head violently. "No!" She stood up and stalked behind the changing screen. Her ornately embroidered tutu was flung over the top of the frame as she raised her shaking voice. "Anya!"

The door leading to Marizza's bedroom opened and an

elderly woman entered. She shuffled to the screen. "I am here, my child."

Marizza's head reappeared above the discarded tutu. "Anya, my red peignoir."

The elderly dresser nodded and went back into her mistress's bedroom, reappearing with a scanty piece of red silk that floated like air. She walked behind the screen and fastened the dainty gown around her mistress.

Marizza stepped out from behind the screen, picked up her Champagne and looked at her manager, her eyes still narrowed. "We will talk about this in the morning, Georgi. As it is, I am tired. I shall rest for a while, then take a late supper at Dante's. Anya, see to it."

As Anya nodded, Georgi rose, his anger still apparent in his face. "But, my dear—"

Marizza threw the Champagne coupe at his head; he barely had time to duck as she screamed. "I said no! Get out, Georgi! Get out! Get out!" He hurriedly backed towards the door as the dancer, her face twisted in anger and fear, threw open the door Anya had entered by and slammed it shut behind her.

After a silence, Anya turned to Georgi with a raised eyebrow. "I believe the answer was no!"

Georgi finished his glass of Champagne and refilled it. "As you heard."

Anya nodded. She took the full glass from Georgi, drained it, and handed it back to him. She cast an eye at the closed bedroom door before she spoke. In the few seconds that had elapsed since her mistress had left the room, her elderly-woman act had disappeared; though the expertly applied aging make-up was still there, the stoop was gone, her eyes were bright, and her voice fuller as she returned to her usual, much younger appearance. She crooked a finger at Georgi, who leant in slightly as she spoke in a husky whisper.

"I said it was a mistake to tell her…we should have just taken her there and she would not have been any the wiser. By the time we arrived it would have been too late for her to refuse. It worked before, remember?"

Georgi shrugged, looking uncomfortable. "Well, we have lost the element of surprise. How do we proceed now?"

Anya smiled faintly. "No, Georgi; we have lost the opportunity of silence, but we can still take her to the address." She looked at the manager. "The sum offered is far too great to be lost simply because the item for sale has thrown a tantrum!"

Georgi refilled his coupe, took a sip, and nodded slowly. "What do you suggest?"

Anya sat down in the seat her mistress had vacated. "I shall accompany her to supper at Dante's, as I always do. You know the route we take. After we leave, send word to the buyer that we will be walking down the Calle del Lovo away from Campo San Salvador and Dante's restaurant…"

As Georgi and Anya continued to make their revolting but highly profitable plans, the subject of their greed stood by the bedroom door, her ear pressed against the ornate wood. An expression of utter horror appeared on Marizza's face as she listened to the two people she thought she could trust discussing how best to conspire with a wealthy patron of the arts to once again brutalise her for money. She reached out a trembling hand and quietly locked the door, walked to the window and gazed down at the narrow alley that ran behind the theatre as thoughts of escape tumbled through her mind. She turned, squared her shoulders, lifted the telephone receiver, and placed a call to New York City.

As she held the receiver to her ear and listened to the ringing, she cast a worried look at her door; hopefully neither Georgi or Anya would attempt to open the door before she had had the chance to speak to her dear friend.

There was a click on the other end of the line and a woman's voice spoke. "Centralinista."

Marizza hunched over the telephone and murmured, "I need to place a call to a number in New York, America… please hurry." She gave the operator the number and waited.

The line clicked and whirred before a clipped male voice spoke. "The Riva Residence."

Marizza gripped the receiver hard. "This is Marizza Dimitrova, calling from Venice. Is the Dona there?"

"Yes, Mlle Dimitrova. I shall inform the Dona that you have called."

Marizza swallowed. "It is an emergency. Please inform the Dona that I…I do not feel safe. I need to speak with her, urgently!"

4157 miles away from the gothic splendour of Venice, in the opulent vestibule of a suite on the top floor of one of the plushest hotels in New York, the imperturbable English butler who accompanied the suite placed the receiver on the table, walked to his mistress's private rooms, and knocked at the door. After a few short moments, the door was opened by Dona Carla's companion, Lilith, who raised an auburn eyebrow at the manservant.

"A telephone call for the mistress…a Mlle Dimitrova, calling from Venice." He paused. "The lady said it was urgent, and that she does not feel safe. Does the Dona wish to accept the call?"

Lilith blinked. It was nearly time for Carla's pre-dinner bath and the cocktail hour, but Marizza was one of Carla's oldest friends…and Carla had told her what had happened the last time Marizza had been worried about a situation. She nodded at the butler. "Yes, Reece. Put the call through to the Dona's room immediately."

The butler nodded. "Yes, Ma'am."

As the butler returned to the vestibule, Lilith closed the

door and walked towards the private telephone line in the somewhat ostentatious sitting room; puce and gold were quite an eye-catching combination. She arrived at the telephone just as it started to ring and lifted the receiver. "Hello, Mlle Dimitrova, it's Lilith___" She paused as Marizza began to talk; her words coming in breathless waves of panicked, staccato bursts.

As Lilith listened, Dona Carla appeared at the bedroom door. The Brazilian dancer raised an immaculately drawn eyebrow at her lover. "My darling, it's nearly bath-time!"

Lilith cupped her hand over the receiver. "It's Marizza, she sounds frightened!"

Dona Carla Riva, who had been reclining in her bedroom with the latest scandal sheets until she had heard the telephone ring, frowned. She dropped the newspapers next to the telephone and took the receiver from Lilith. "Marizza? Whatever is the matter?" She listened with growing concern to the words tumbling down the line. At a pause in the storm, she interjected. "Do you feel he is trying to do what he did before?"

There was a pause, then a single word was whispered down the line. "Yes."

Carla gripped the receiver. "You know what I shall say, Marizza, about leaving him. Do you still want my help?"

There was another, longer pause, then a faint sob. "Yes."

Carla cupped her hand over the receiver and looked Lilith. "Use the other telephone. Call Phillipe immediately. Tell him to book a suite in the Danieli for Marizza under my name, and organise tickets for us to Venice on the next available airship — the fastest he can find!"

Lilith turned and headed into the vestibule where she hurriedly put a call through to Carla's manager, Phillipe Renoir.

Carla turned her attention back to her friend. "Marizza, I

am booking a room for you in the Danieli. I want you to go there tonight and wait for us to arrive. Do not open the door to anyone but us; do you understand?"

Marizza nodded. "Yes. Please help me, Carla — I am afraid of what he has planned!"

"My darling, we will be there as soon as possible. Now, have you dined yet?"

"No — the idea of food makes me feel sick!"

"Good! Take your reticule with some money, go to the Riva del Carbon and get a góndoła to the Danieli; the room will be booked under my name. Ask at the desk for the keys, go straight there and lock the door. We shall see to the rest. Go now, Marizza, and may the Madonna protect you."

Many miles away, in the still of the Venetian night, Marizza gently placed the receiver on its cradle and turned to the door that led to her sitting room. Sidling over, she pressed her ear against the gap between the cold oak and the wall. Her eyes widened again as she heard Georgi and Anya continuing to discuss their plans for the money they would make from selling her to the admirer who had approached them.

Marizza backed away, her fear threatening to spiral out of control. She took a deep, shuddering breath and thought rapidly. She looked at her wardrobe, full of beautiful gowns impossible for her to fasten by herself. She knew she could no longer trust Anya, but she couldn't leave the theatre in her peignoir!

Her eyes turned to Anya's little room. Moving quickly, she entered the tiny bedroom and opened the small wardrobe. A dark-blue outfit caught her eye; it was simple, but still a far grander outfit than the average dresser could afford.

Marizza set her lips, dropped her peignoir to the ground, and hurriedly pulled on the outfit; designed for a woman who needed to dress herself without assistance, the outfit was surprisingly easy to don. She collected her reticule and threw her warmest cape across her shoulders before quietly opening the door that led into the bathroom. On the other side of the opulent, marble-filled space was the spare bedroom, currently empty. However, also in that room was another door that opened onto a private staircase leading to the back door of the Teatro Goldoni, and that led in turn to the Calle Bembo, and the Riva del Carbon.

Marizza hurriedly locked the bathroom door from inside. Taking a deep breath, she entered the spare room, unlocked the door to the stairs and removed the key. Opening the door with care, she glanced around the silent hallway beyond. She closed the door behind her and locked it before tucking the key into her reticule and hurrying down to the door she knew would be open. The door that led to the Calle Bembo, and her freedom.

Reaching the ground floor, Marizza paused to look behind her. The corridor leading to the storage rooms was empty and the stairs to the basement were silent.

As she paused to catch her breath, a distant crashing sound came from the stairs above her. Her breath stuttered in her throat as she realised it was the sound of someone breaking down the door to the stairs. As she stood in fear, she heard Georgi's voice travelling down the stairway. "Marizza? Marizza…are you down there? My darling, we need to talk. You know I do not take kindly to you locking doors! Your admirer wishes to see you tonight, and neither he nor I will not take no for an answer!"

Marizza threw the door open and ran into the dark, narrow Calle beyond. Turning left, she rushed towards the Riva del Carbon; even at that time of night, there would be osterias, pensions, and tavernas full of people. As she fled, she turned to look behind her — and ran straight into an immovable object that had suddenly appeared in the alley. She fell backwards, her head smacking against the ground with a sharp crack that caused a flash of bright lights behind her eyes before everything faded into darkness.

The immovable object; a short but powerfully broad man dressed in black and wearing a black top hat that covered his face in shadow, gazed at the young woman lying at his feet, then slowly turned to look down the alley as Georgi and Anya appeared in the alley. The movement of his neck was accompanied by a strange humming as he looked at the approaching couple.

Georgi, who had seen Marizza run into the large man, plastered a smile on his face and hurried to Marizza's side. "My darling, what have you been doing to yourself? Anya, help me with your mistress."

The dresser hurried to his side and the two of them tried to lift the unconscious woman. Georgi looked at the silent figure before him. "Would you help us? We need to get her back into the theatre."

The tall man looked at Georgi, then bent forward and lifted the comatose dancer in one smooth motion...seemingly with no effort at all. Georgi frowned; the man's movements had been accompanied by strangely muffled clicking and whirring noises.

Georgi exchanged glances with Anya before turning back to the dark man. "If you would please bring her into the theatre, we will look after her. She must be well enough to dance for a private patron tonight."

The tall figure paused, and there was another series of clicks and whirrs before he spoke. His voice was low and breathy, like air passing through weak bellows. "She is a...dancer?"

Georgi drew himself up with a look of pride. "Yes: she is the Prima Ballerina, Marizza Dimitrova, and I am her manager, Georgi Sokolov. Please be careful; she is very precious to me."

The dark man was silent, but the whirring sounds increased. With a sudden, sharp movement, he threw Marizza over his left shoulder and made a twisting motion with his right forearm. The whirring was joined by a smooth, metallic hiss as a blade appeared in his right hand and was plunged neatly into the centre of Georgi's chest.

The deathly silence was rent by sudden, pealing screams as Anya realised what had happened. She turned to run, but her cries were cut short as the blade that had killed Georgi swept down and severed her head.

○

Tuesday 19th March
England
The London Aetherdrome
6:45am

In the soft, misty light of a crisp March morning, a private air-carriage bearing the markings of the Anglo-International Remington-Smythe Aether Company drifted across the vast green expanse of Richmond Park towards the Londinium Tower, home to the largest aetherdrome in the Northern Hemisphere. Within the plushly upholstered, dark-stained oak góndoła that hung like a sparkling jewel beneath the blue and gold balloon, a young man with dark, Macassar-smoothed hair and startlingly blue eyes looked hopefully at the young woman next to him. Hers was a simple beauty; a classic English-rose complexion with golden hair, rosy cheeks, and soft grey eyes.

André Devereaux took his bride's hand and pressed a kiss

against the soft skin of her pale wrist. "Well, my darling…are you pleased?"

Evelyn Briar-Devereaux smiled at her husband of less than three days. "Egypt?"

André smiled in return. "I know it's long been your dream to travel there, my dear, and what better time than our honeymoon?"

Evelyn's grey eyes glowed as she looked at her husband. "But how did you know? I've never mentioned…"

André's smile faltered. "Your father told me—" He stopped as Evelyn's face began to crumple. "My darling, I'm sorry…I didn't mean to cause you more pain." He pulled out his handkerchief and gently blotted his wife's tears before continuing. "Your father told me that travelling to Egypt had always been a dream for you." He pressed his lips against her hand again. "Now that your dear papa is no longer with us, I consider it both my duty and my honour to give you all that you desire, my darling wife."

Evelyn blinked through the bitter tears that stung her grey eyes and gazed at her husband with a tremulous smile. "Thank you, André. To honeymoon in Egypt! Oh, but what of our packing? I have only my reticule, and surely we need to say goodbye to your mother and family?"

As the air-carriage began its descent to one of the many jetties lining the ground floor of the opulent and massively tall Londinium Tower, André glanced out of the window. As their carriage landed, he caught sight of what he was looking for and smiled gently. "No, my darling. Look at the two air-carriages just across the way."

Evelyn looked through her window at the two smart carriages nearest them. As their passengers disembarked, she felt an immediate sinking feeling as she recognised them. An elegant and impossibly beautiful woman of middle years was assisted from the first carriage by a much younger man, whose classically handsome face was somewhat marred by a slightly petulant expression. The lady was her mother-in-law, Marguerite Devereaux, accompanied by her most recent husband, Vincenzo Prezzo. Next out of the carriage was Margaux van Sloane, André's only sister; beautiful, blonde, and sartorially flawless in a periwinkle blue House of Worth travel gown that suited her colouring perfectly. She was assisted from the vehicle by her husband, Julius van Sloane, who very nearly outdid his wife in the tall, blond, and elegant stakes; a stunningly beautiful woman and a debonair and handsome man…the only problem being that Margaux was — as Evelyn had to admit to herself — selfish, mercenary, and utterly vacuous. And Julius, though attractive and urbane, was sadly as dense as a brick; a very becoming and rather charming brick, but a brick nonetheless. They were followed by their twin children, Linden and Camillia; in their early twenties, both carried the unmistakable familial imprint of their beautiful and stylish parents; Camillia was as avaricious, vacuous, and absorbed in jewellery, fashion, and her own appearance as her mother, while Linden could be as charming as his father, but with slightly more intelligence — and a sometimes disconcerting habit of not engaging in social intercourse at all, but simply sitting in silence and observing.

They were joined by the last member of the family, André's older brother Kiefer; tall, with dark-blond hair kept firmly under control by well-applied Macassar oil, and with eyes several shades darker than his brother's, Kiefer had been highly prized by various society hostesses as an attractive and much sought-after addition to their soirees. However, his invitations to certain social occasions had been placed on temporary hold after a rather unpleasant incident in France had led to a duel which had left Kiefer badly injured. His recuperation had required a lengthy period of seclusion and rest at the family's home on the banks of Lake Garda. In addition, the sudden violent death of his opponent and the young man's second several weeks after the duel in Marseilles had provoked rather more than the usual idle gossip amongst those who had previously thought him a worthy addition to their society events.

As Kiefer assisted his niece from the air-carriage, a sudden wave of almost visceral dislike hit Evelyn's stomach. She suppressed a shudder; she had no knowledge of Kiefer's past, but she truly couldn't stand her brother-in-law, and no matter how hard she tried, she couldn't find a way to tell her husband that she felt ill when she was near him. She swallowed hard, forced a tremulous smile onto her lips and turned to look at her husband. "Everyone! How...lovely."

The family was joined by the passengers from the second carriage, made up predominantly of the household servants; Marguerite's companion, Violette Donnadieu; Julius' solid but silent valet, Heathers; the ancient but still serving family butler, Sedgewyck; and the newest addition, Jane Gagnon, who had been hired as Evelyn's companion...the family having decided that a companion was far more suitable than a maid for a woman of Evelyn's increased stature. Evelyn sighed. She had been rather upset at the loss of her maid, Barber, who had been her mother's maid before Evelyn had been born.

Jane Gagnon approached the young couple, flashed a pert smile and made a faint bob of her head to Evelyn before turning her glowing brown eyes to André and speaking in a soft French accent. "Monsieur, the trunks have been packed as you requested. Madame Devereaux requests that we hurry; the airship to Venice leaves shortly."

André nodded, then turned to Evelyn and smiled. "It's been many years since Mother was in Egypt." He cast a sharp look at his mother before muttering under his breath.

"Rather a lifetime, actually! I thought it would be a good idea to make it a family event. We shall travel first to Venice and spend a few days seeing the sights, then take to our cabins aboard the Airship *Cartouche*, which will carry us to our destination; the Eridanus Hotel Eau de Nil"

Evelyn blinked at the name of one of the greatest and most luxurious hotels in the known world. She flicked a glance at the Devereaux family, who had gathered like a fabulous collection of the finest, brightest gems by the entrance to the aetherdrome and bit her lip; expecting her husband to do anything without the constant presence or approval of his family was turning out to be rather difficult. However, they *were* both new to marriage. Perhaps, when he realised that it was perfectly acceptable to do things without the presence or input of his mother, brother, or sister, things would improve.

As André took Evelyn's arm with a smile, Jane caught his eye. She held his glance as they made their way towards the aetherdrome entrance and the journey to come.

○

Londinium Tower Departure Lounge
7:00am

"Ah, there you are, Caine! You have no idea how happy I am to have found you! Good morning, Mlle Du'Lac, Madame Aquilleia, Thorne…ah, Veronique."

Elliott and the others turned at the sound of the urbane but unwanted address. Lord Vyvian Lapotaire smiled at them with a genial and somewhat smug expression; there were times when he loathed his work, and then there were times when his enjoyment of his chosen profession was almost spiritual…this was one of the latter. He still hadn't forgiven

Caine and Thorne for the vast amount of paperwork he'd been obliged to disseminate in order to smooth over a certain issue in New Zealand…not to mention the wider social and political ramifications their investigation had caused. The beauty of the immediate situation and its timing conspired to make him feel rather happy. He knew it was childish, but he was definitely enjoying himself.

Lapotaire doffed his hat to Giselle and Aquilleia, and skirted around Veronique with a frown at the faint growl that came from the usually docile Labrador. He arrived at Elliott's side and handed him an official-looking and ominously thick envelope. "For you, Caine; the Empire once again has need of your assistance."

Elliott took the proffered envelope with bad grace, noting with a scowl that it bore the seals of both the British Empire Office and the Espion Court. He ripped open the thick vellum envelope and read the lengthy missive, his dark eyebrows lowering with every line until he could barely see past them. Thorne watched his friend's reaction, then sidled over and read the document over Elliott's shoulder. His own eyebrows shot into his hairline as he read the request for assistance. By the time he saw the seal and the signature at the end of the document, his eyebrows could travel no further, and instead his mouth dropped open. He stared at Lapotaire. "I didn't think she knew of our existence!"

Lapotaire smiled. "Some things are too important for the use of plausible deniability, Thorne." His expression became less amused. "Shortly before Queen Victoria's death, two British subjects, a mother and her daughter, were found dead in Egypt. That was not so much of an issue…many British travellers die whilst abroad. However, these two ladies were, in fact, the victims of murder…murder most foul! The elder of the two was one of Queen Victoria's most trusted friends and confidantes. So, the Queen herself, God rest her soul, demanded that the Espion Court be brought in to investigate matters. And investigate we have. The situation is of such grave danger and import to the Empire *and* the West that both the Espion Court and the Empire are in desperate need of your...special abilities, and they have formally requested your assistance in this case."

Elliott looked at the letter, handed the missive to Giselle, and turned back to Lapotaire with a dark look. "But plausible deniability still applies to us and our investigations, of course?" Lapotaire nodded with a smile. "Of course. Every government on the face of this earth utilises the ability to pretend things have never happened...especially if they are the ones responsible, or are the ones impacted the most by things going wrong. Just make sure that things *don't* go wrong, and you'll be absolutely fine!"

Giselle looked sharply at Lapotaire before turning her attention to the document. One of her eyebrows shot up as she read the document. She was joined by Aquilleia, and Veronique, who snuffled at the document before deciding it was not suitable for lunch and dismissing it. The starving Labrador turned her brown eyes to Thorne, who caught the look with a smile and gestured to her to sit down. The Labrador turned her back on them and sat with a humph.

Giselle handed the document back to Elliott and turned to Lapotaire. "This document was signed on the evening of the 16th of January...why are you only informing us of this request now?"

Lapotaire's face stilled. "The request from Queen Victoria was issued the day before her health truly began to fail. Luckily for us, her insistence on our presence led to her government providing us with the necessary permissions to begin our investigation that very evening. After we received those documents, we thought it best to utilise the people that the Espion Court, the Empire, and the Veiled Protectorate, already had on the ground in Egypt to start the initial investigation. What we discovered made us realise that we needed a far more experienced company of agents who were prepared to see that the case would be resolved with, if not discretion, then at least with finality and speed. So, as a matter of desperate urgency and in response to the Royal decree, all four—" He hastily corrected himself as Veronique growled at him again. "I do, of course, mean all *five* of you… will take our fastest airship and head straight to Cairo."

Elliott dropped his valise with a thump and glared at the offending document, then turned a burning eye that flickered with swirling green lights on the beatifically smiling peer. Lapotaire's own eyes widened at the sight of the green swirls. He took a nimble step out of Elliott's reach and cultivated a genial humour he did not quite feel; it was always a shock to see their Other nature when it was roused. He ventured a smile. "Now, now, Caine…this hasn't come from me; this is an order from Queen Victoria herself! His Majesty's Government and those even higher than me in the Espion Court support this — a heartfelt request made from her deathbed! I'm afraid that your belated honeymoons will have to wait a little longer. We've booked you on one of our military airships to Egypt. After you've had a chat with our man in Cairo, Colonel Barrington, and dealt with this little mess, you can journey on to your respective honeymoons. Your investigations should only take a few days; a week at the most. That isn't too much to ask, is it?"

Elliott ground his teeth. He was loath to tell Lapotaire that, although they were ostensibly on their way to their honeymoon, they were also travelling to Venice in a private capacity. In the end, though, the choice was not his to make. He turned as Giselle gently touched his arm and looked at Lapotaire. "We're going to Venice because a friend of ours has asked us to find someone who has gone missing." She blinked back tears as she spoke, remembering the awful telephone conversation she had had with Dona Carla. The Brazilian dancer had become hysterical as she begged Giselle to help find her friend, the renowned ballet dancer Marizza Dimitrova, who had disappeared from the Teatro Goldoni. Dona Carla and Lilith had travelled from New York to Venice to meet with her at the Danieli, but when they had finally arrived at the hotel, Marizza was not there.

As Giselle finished her explanation, she dabbed a tear from her eye with a delicate handkerchief. Lapotaire stared at her, his dark eyes blinking rapidly. "I'm very sorry to hear that, Mlle Du'Lac. I wonder..." His gaze flickered back to Elliott. "Perhaps there's a way of bringing this situation to a mutually beneficial conclusion?" He looked at Elliott and Thorne with a hopeful expression. "I shall make you an offer. Our rapid-strike military airship, HMA *Arketurion* is standing by to take you to Egypt; she's capable of travelling at nearly one hundred miles an hour. Accept the deathbed request of Queen Victoria to seek out these villains in Egypt, and you may use the *Arketurion* to travel to Venice first to help your friend. I can give you two days. I *know* you; that should be all the time you need to help find Mlle Dimitrova." He raised a dark eyebrow. "What do you say?"

Elliott looked at Giselle, who thought for a moment, then nodded. Elliott turned to Thorne and Aquilleia who also gestured their acceptance. He turned back to Lapotaire and flourished the document. "We shall accept the Empire's kind offer of assistance in return for our help in hunting down the villains who are causing trouble for the Empire and the Veiled Protectorate." He paused and looked at Lapotaire, and the swirling green lights in his eyes intensified. "But after we have dealt with our investigations in Venice, we shall go directly to our hotel to begin our honeymoons and Colonel

Barrington can come to *us*. Now, Lapotaire, what do *you* say?"

Lapotaire let out the breath he was all too aware he'd been holding. "Capital! I shall get our man in Cairo to meet you at the aetherdrome and confirm when Colonel Barrington will be able to visit you." He Looked at Caine. "I understand that you will be travelling on to the Eridanus Hotel Eau de Nil?" At Elliott's nod, Lapotaire placed his attaché case on the ground and rummaged within it, taking the opportunity to break eye contact with Caine. He pulled out a large, very thick envelope, which he handed to Elliott. "These documents will bring you up to snuff on exactly what the named operatives have been up to — Well, the things we know they have done, at any rate! There are at least three of them that we know of at the top of their little organisation; they call themselves Prussian Blue, the Black Eagle, and Rouge Noir — fantastical names, I grant you! The people using them probably think they sound frightening or inspiring, but they sound more like characters from a penny dreadful to me. Enjoy your reading." He looked at Giselle. "I truly hope you find this missing lady, Mlle Du'Lac. Godspeed, ladies, gentlemen...Veronique."

Lapotaire doffed his topper and walked jauntily away. As he turned the corner, he leant against one of the ornate wrought-iron columns, closed his eyes and took a deep, shuddering breath; perhaps using his official clearance to read about who and what the Others actually were had been a mistake...simply being in their presence was enough to cause him deep concern. He straightened, passed through the massive doorway and out into the chill March morning. Walking to the nearest jetty, he hailed an air-carriage, gave the address of his club, and settled into the plush interior with a relieved sigh; after the morning he'd had, a smallish cocktail might well be in order. It was early, certainly, but the sun was over the yardarm somewhere!

Back in the aetherdrome, Elliott turned to Giselle and took her hand. "My darling, I *am* sorry."

Giselle smiled gently. "It's quite all right, Elliott. We have the *Arketurion* at our disposal, so we'll arrive in Venice several hours earlier than we thought. We'll be able to start our search for Marizza far sooner."

Thorne nodded. "Well, we need to find the *Arketurion* first. I have two questions. Firstly, are there any directions on those documents Lapotaire gave you that say where the airship is? And secondly, Veronique is more than ready for her breakfast, and, quite frankly, so am I. Is it now breakfast time?"

Elliott laughed and took his wife's arm. "Yes, I do believe it's breakfast time. Let's find the airship and see if they are prepared to serve us our first meal of the day."

As they walked towards the embarkation lounge, there was a sudden shouting from one of the booking desks. They turned to see a group of porters struggling with a large, tightly strapped steamer trunk. One of the porters lost his grip and one corner of the solid item of luggage hit the floor with a crash. A tall man with dark-blond hair angrily strode across the lounge and pushed the porter to the ground. "That's an expensive trunk with precious contents, you bloody idiot!" He looked up, caught Elliott's eye, and scowled. As he took a menacing step towards them, an older woman standing with a group called sharply, "Kiefer! See that the trunk is undamaged."

Kiefer turned away from Elliott and ran a surprisingly gentle hand across the steamer trunk before addressing the older woman. "It seems to be fine, Mother, in spite of the best efforts of the useless halfwits they employ here!" He glared at the porter. "Bring it to the jetty. If you drop it again, this will be the last job you ever have!" He turned his back on the angry porter and stormed back to his mother's side.

Thorne cast a professional eye over the family group which was made up of several well-dressed people, two of whom looked distinctly embarrassed by the spectacle their kin was causing. As the ill-tempered man returned to his family, the group made their way through the door leading to their airship, followed by their servants, a large selection of luggage that was carefully wheeled behind them, and lastly, the undamaged steamer trunk.

As the trunk moved past Veronique, the Labrador gave the iron-bound wood a cursory sniff; her hackles rose and a deep growl rumbled from her throat.

Thorne gave her a sharp look. "Something wrong with the trunk, old girl?"

Veronique turned to him, a faint red light in her usually limpid brown eyes.

Thorne frowned as he gently stroked the agitated dog's head. He leant towards Aquilleia with a raised eyebrow. "Precious contents, hmm? I'm intrigued...Veronique doesn't usually behave like this. I want to know what resides within that trunk."

Aquilleia smiled. "There will be no need for you to do anything involving curiosity during our honeymoon, husband...unless it's discovering what your wife wants!"

O

Venice
That Evening
7:15pm

The stately lines of HMA *Arketurion* slowly descended into the dark waters of the jetty at the Stazione Etere. The wave created by the sleek airship's displacement swept along the length of the Bacino Etere, swelled over the walkway and splashed against the highly polished patent-leather shoes of Marcello Belluno, Direttore of the Stazione Etere, who danced backwards and threw a pained look to the heavens before making his way back along the Calle Etere to his office, where he closed the door forcefully behind him. Walking to his desk, he lifted the file with the day's tally of airships and ran an immaculately manicured fingernail down the list to the final ship of the day. Picking up his fountain pen, he placed a neat tick next to the name 'HMA *Arketurion*', placed the file in a tray marked 'Archivio', and checked his pocket watch; another day nearly over with minimal fuss. He shot the bolt on his office door and sat at his desk with a satisfied smile as he waited for the last few minutes of his working day to pass; the less he had to do with the people who actually used his station, the better. Paperwork was far preferable to people, in his humble opinion.

Beyond the closed door, the góndoła of HMA *Arketurion* settled snugly into her berth as several young men in the smart blue, white, and gold uniforms of the Royal Airship Fleet leapt to their stations and began the task of tying the massive vessel to the jetty.

As they saw to their duties, Elliott, Giselle, Thorne, and Aquilleia emerged from the cocoon-like góndoła sitting beneath the massive blue, white, and gold envelope that held the airship's hydrogen-gas ballonets and began the task of finding their travel documents, whilst also extricating their luggage from the hold, and attempting to remove the remains of the unhappy captain's roast pheasant dinner from a very happy Veronique who categorically refused to 'drop'. After some time had been lost in ineffectual faff and fuss, the four enquiry agents, and a rather displeased Veronique, who still had the last vestiges of the captain's fowl gripped between her jaws, were finally guided into the passport office.

A bored-looking young man gave Elliott and Thorne a dismissive glance before nearly falling out of his chair at the sight of Giselle and Aquilleia. "Mi scusi, belle signore!" He shot out from behind his desk and almost prostrated himself at a smiling Giselle's feet as he tripped over Veronique. Absentmindedly patting the startled Labrador's head in apology, he grudgingly accepted Elliott and Thorne's paperwork, gave it a cursory skim, then practically flung the documents back at them as he continued to inundate both ladies with his youthful charms.

Elliott looked at Thorne, who raised an irritated eyebrow then picked up his valise, manoeuvred himself alongside his smiling wife, and addressed the young official. "If you are quite finished with our paperwork, we have an important appointment. Thank you very much!"

The young man looked at him with an equally irritated but slightly quizzical expression. Thorne realised that English was not one of the young man's strengths and pulled himself up to his full, not inconsiderable height. "Abbiamo un appuntamento urgente." The young man blinked, hastily smoothed his shirt, and stepped away from Giselle and Aquilleia, nearly falling over Veronique again as he returned to his desk.

As they left the booth, Giselle looked at Thorne. "I didn't realise you could speak Italian."

Aquilleia smiled at her husband. "I've been teaching him; I was born here."

Giselle blinked. "I keep thinking of us as Others…I sometimes forget that we were reincarnated here and have human lives as well. Where in Italy are you from?"

Aquilleia placed her hatbox on the ground. "The town I was named for, Aquileia. It's strange how things work; I was born in the Italian town that was my original name in Astraea. It's not far from here; only a hundred miles or so to the East." She looked out over the lagoon, a wistful expression on her pale face. "I haven't seen Nonna, my father, or my brother, Berengar, for quite some time…and I never will."

Giselle frowned. "What do you mean?"

Aquilleia smiled sadly. "My family here are devout Catholics. When my gifts became too obvious for them to hide from the Church, I was banished. They consider me a curse on the family."

Giselle looked horrified. "Why?"

"They're very pious. The Bible says 'Thou shalt not suffer a witch to live'…and they are firm adherents to its teachings

Giselle's mouth dropped open. "So, they cast you out?

"Oh, yes. When my father decided that it was time for me to leave, I was ordered out of the family home that same day. Nonna was upset…but Father insisted. My mother here had died bearing my brother, so she couldn't speak for me…and he was all too willing to get rid of me." She smiled at the stunned look on Giselle's face. "Berengar is very much our father's son. As far as he was concerned, when I was thrown out of the family, it was one less person to take a share of his inheritance." She paused, thinking back. "When I left the house, Nonna was waiting for me at the bottom of the hill.

Father had refused to even offer me a few coins to help me on my way…but Nonna gave me my mother's jewellery. It was all she could do. I hope Father wasn't too angry with her…" Aquilleia's voice trailed off; her lavender eyes thoughtful.

Giselle looked outraged. "Have you spoken with them since?"

Aquilleia shook her head; her lavender eyes reflecting the glittering sunlight on the water. "It's been over ten years. One can never truly tell with family, but I believe that particular bridge was reduced to ashes that day…and with very little input from me."

Thorne took his wife's hand and pressed a kiss on her palm; his green eyes gentle.

They all turned at a sudden crunching sound behind them. Veronique looked up with an expression of enjoyment as she finally finished the mortal remains of the pheasant, licked her chops, and looked at Thorne expectantly; as a starter it had been pleasant, but now she was ready for her main course.

Thorne shared a look with Aquilleia and smiled. "I do believe that Veronique is informing us that it's past her dinner time." He checked his pocket watch, and pulled a face. "It's quite late! Perhaps we should have taken the captain up on his offer of dinner aboard the *Arketurion*?"

Elliott shook his head. "There are things we need to do. Waiting aboard the airship for another hour or two would lessen the time we have here."

Thorne nodded glumly. "Very well. Shall we adjourn to our hotel and hope they can accommodate our need for a meal?"

Aquilleia, relieved that the conversation had turned away from her earthly family, smiled at her husband. "That sounds like a very sensible idea. We're staying at the Fenice Palace Hotel. It's on the Calle Fenice, just off the Bacino di San

Marco. I don't think dining will be a problem…here in Italy, we tend to eat quite late; after nine o'clock is not unheard of."

Thorne nodded, put down his valise, poked his head into the booth and addressed the young official. After a few minutes he withdrew and smiled. "There's a pier on the Canal de ła Zueca where we can hire a góndoła to take us to the hotel. It's a few minutes that way." Thorne gestured past the slowly bobbing mass of HMA *Arketurion* to the canal beyond.

Elliott looked at their luggage. "I think we should leave this here and send a porter from the hotel. We can bring the most important items with us."

Giselle nodded. "If we organise a góndoła to take us to our hotel, I'll send a message to Dona Carla and Lilith to let them know we've arrived." She looked at Elliott and grimaced. "That may well be a very unpleasant meeting!"

○

The Fenice Palace Hotel
9:00pm

Giselle accepted her drink from her husband and took a sip. "Perfect." She sat back in her chair with a sigh and glanced at the ornate Louis XIV clock on the green marble mantle. "She's a little late."

Elliott sat down opposite her with his drink. "Is that usual?"

Giselle shook her head. "For events and such — no, not really. The Dona adheres to the school of 'dramatic entrance.' But considering the reason she asked us here—"

Giselle paused as the lift doors opened and Lilith and Dona Carla appeared. The Dona, clad in jet-black silk, with a black fox stole slung across one shoulder, and trailing clouds of expensive perfume, bore down on them in a flurry of diamonds, furs, and tears.

Thorne and Elliott hurriedly stood up. Thorne caught Elliott's eye and raised his hand to the waiter, who disappeared behind the bar and returned with another bottle of Champagne and two extra coupes.

Giselle gently settled the weeping dancer in a chair and turned to Lilith, who stood by her lover's side. The Frenchwoman looked at Giselle with a steady expression. "Giselle, I apologise for nothing…she needs me!"

Giselle nodded. "I ask for no apology. I shall always be here for you, Lilith; always."

The two women embraced as Elliott filled the two coupes of Champagne and handed them to the late arrivals. He sat next to Giselle and looked at Dona Carla. "Dona, I can't say that it's a pleasure to see you again, given the circumstances. But please, tell us everything you know about the disappearance of Marizza Dimitrova." He paused. "And omit nothing."

Dona Carla took a deep breath; she looked at the coupe of Champagne and drained it before handing it back to Elliott, who refilled it without a word. She pressed a thin, black handkerchief of lace-trimmed silk to her eyes, accepted the refreshed glass and began.

Several coupes of Champagne later, after another tearful outburst in Portuguese which Thorne was quite sure was unsuitable for mixed company, the Dona sat back in her seat, again pressing the handkerchief to her red-rimmed eyes. Thorne finished taking notes and tucked the now full notebook in his breast pocket.

Giselle gently clasped her friend's hand. "I promise you, Dona, we *will* find out what has happened to Marizza. It's too late to start tonight, so we'll dine together, and tomorrow morning we'll begin our investigations."

Dona Carla nodded, sniffed, and pressed her little handkerchief against her eyes again before tucking it in her reticule and rummaging for her powder. She opened the little compact, looked at her reflection in the small mirror and pulled a face at the state of her complexion. She looked at Giselle as she dabbed at her face with the powder puff, and her gaze hardened. "There is...something else I must tell you."

Giselle nodded slowly. "I thought there might be. Go on."

Dona Carla replaced the compact in her reticule and picked up her coupe; Elliott noticed that her hand was trembling. She took a deep breath. "When Marizza spoke with me, she told me that her manager, Georgi, had tried to send her to a...a private appointment with an admirer."

Giselle's eyebrows shot up. "Is it possible that she went?"

"No, never!" Dona Carla gazed at them all, and Elliott and Thorne in particular. "Gentlemen, I am about to betray a trust. Please do not let this knowledge go any further. It would destroy Marizza if she knew I had told anyone...especially two men."

Elliott and Thorne nodded and the Dona took a deep sip from her coupe. "Do you remember, Giselle, two or so years ago, Marizza took an extended leave of absence from the ballet?"

Giselle frowned. "Yes...I seem to recall it was for personal reasons."

Dona Carla gave a harsh bark of laughter. "Very personal reasons! Georgi had arranged for her to attend a private meeting with an admirer...an admirer who believed he had paid for her undivided attention and who refused to accept no for an answer!" Dona Carla fought back tears as she continued. "Marizza was in hospital for weeks...they did not think she would ever dance again." She took a deep breath and continued. "Georgi swore he had no idea what the man had been planning. But the night Marizza telephoned me, she told me she had overheard Georgi, and her dresser Anya, laughing about sending her to that Bastardo!" Dona Carla gritted her teeth. "They were gloating about how much money they would make from doing the same thing again that evening…the evening Marizza went missing!"

There was silence as the Dona finished speaking. Thorne refilled her coupe and looked at her, his green eyes cold as ice. "Where are Georgi and Anya now?"

Dona Carla accepted the glass with a brittle smile. "They were discovered in the Calle Bembo, an alley at the back of the Teatro Goldoni. Georgi had been stabbed through where his heart would have been, if he'd had one! As for Anya, her body was found next to Georgi's…" Dona Carla took a sip of her champagne, savouring the bubbles. "Well, they think it was Anya…they are still looking for her head!"

○

The Isola di Maschere
11:00pm

A few short miles to the south-west of Venice, a tiny, tree-covered island sat like a jewel in the velvety, cerulean blue of the Venetian Lagoon. Reachable only by private boat or air-carriage, the Isola di Maschere was dominated by an ornate tower; a half-sized replica of the Campanile di San Marco just a few miles away. At the foot of the soaring tower, nestled into its surroundings like a sleeping cat, sat a garish but incredibly luxurious crenelated building; the Palazzo di Maschere. Painted a vibrant pink that glowed in the flickering lights of the blazing fire pits, the island and the Palazzo were owned by the reclusive, but equally luxurious and garish, Conte di Maschere; a man known, in spite of his advanced age, for his quite spectacular parties.

The Palazzo itself was renowned for its exquisite art collection and magnificent rose gardens, as well as for being the domicile of the Conte's most spectacular, most prized, and most scandalous collection; thirty attractive young ladies who lived in the palazzo and who were his constant companions. Most lived permanently on the island, whilst others stayed, at his expense, of course, in several other fabulous palazzos along the Italian coast, all waiting for the summons to accompany him on his travels.

There was quite a rapid turnover within the collection, due to the Conte's ever-changing tastes. During one eye-opening season alone, all his ladies had been blondes; another year, they were all from Spain. The ladies jostled to be the one he would ask the all-important question…but after more than forty years of his chosen lifestyle, the Conte showed no inclination for tying himself to just one woman. If anything, he seemed more disposed to broadening his horizons further; a recent visit to Japan had made him wonder whether his previous predilections had been rather tame and lacking adventure.

The soft strains of classical music surrounded the palazzo like a gossamer veil as its fabulous owner and several of his attractive and attentive companions welcomed invited guests to yet another of his splendid and notorious masked balls. In the gilded opulence of the ballroom, nearly eighty of Europe's great and good arranged themselves along the walls and watched a handful of brave souls attempting to dance to Mozart's *Divertimento*.

At the midway point of one of these walls, Evelyn pulled a face behind her ornate feathered eye mask as her husband accepted his niece's request for yet another dance. She sipped her glass of punch and turned her attention to the rest of the revellers in the massive ballroom. As Evelyn watched the throng of masked men, women, fire-eaters, and dwarves, her eyes widened as she caught sight of one man, barely dressed as a loincloth-clad gladiator, making his way to the bar, accompanied by a tiger on a lead. Evelyn hurriedly pulled her eyes away from the startling sight as the orchestra abandoned Mozart and began their next piece.

Evelyn blinked as the harpist, an elegant woman dressed in black, her eyes covered by a silver and black feathered domino mask, plucked her harp's D string twelve times. As the twelfth note faded, the chattering guests fell silent. Then a solo violinist began to play, and the strains of the *Danse Macabre* filled the opulent room.

Evelyn felt a sudden strangeness in her stomach and placed her hand on the front of her gown. A dull, almost gnawing ache was spreading from her middle. She frowned; perhaps the rich Italian food was not to her simple English taste? Perhaps three croissants with apricot jam for breakfast, Risotto al Granchio e Gamberi for lunch, and Bigoli in Salsa for dinner had been a menu choice too far?

As Evelyn stood in quiet contemplation of the temptation offered by Venetian cuisine, a man suddenly appeared at her side. He was tall, slender, and immaculately dressed, his mask depicting the face of an eagle. As she looked into his eyes, her mouth dropped open; surely it was a trick of the light, but the stranger's eyes appeared to be a brilliant shade of yellow.

He held out his hand and, in a husky, low voice said, "Madame Briar...Devereaux? Allow me to introduce myself; I am Gabriel Masquelyne. May I have this dance?"

Evelyn blinked. His eyes were strange, but both they, and his voice, were very, very familiar. She saw the sudden frown that appeared on her mother-in-law's face across the ballroom; feeling a sudden desire to do something quite scandalous, Evelyn set down her glass of punch, accepted the man's hand and walked with him into the dance.

On the other side of the room, Marguerite watched her daughter-in-law under her lowered, perfectly drawn eyebrows. As André and Camillia spun past, Marguerite tapped her youngest son's shoulder with her fan and gestured angrily at Evelyn. "Go and dance with your wife, André — we can't risk losing her now!"

André shot his mother an equally angry glare before glancing at his wife and her partner. "Don't be hysterical, Mother! It's a ball; Evelyn is just enjoying herself." He leant down to his mother's ear and murmured, "It's not as though she'll be with us much longer. Let her enjoy what time she has left, hmm?"

Marguerite glared at him. "I shall speak with your father about this, André!"

He laughed. "Well, he won't be able to do anything about it for a few more days, will he? Have you explained to dear Vincenzo that in very little time he will be superfluous to your marital requirements?"

Marguerite's full lips thinned as she looked at her son. "What my husband and I talk about is none of your business, André, and don't you forget it!"

André shrugged as he prepared to sweep Camillia back into the dance. "Whatever you say, Mother. Father is always quite accepting of the arrangements you make in his absence, most of which he discards with smiling indifference once he returns to us." With that parting shot, he swung his giggling niece back into the crush of bodies on the dance floor.

○

**Venice
A Private Palazzo
Midnight**

The solid door swung open and hit the wall with a clang as the whirring, clicking man carried the unconscious Marizza from the room where she had been kept for several days, to a new, more salubrious suite of rooms, and carefully deposited her on the bed. He settled her head onto the pillow and paused before reaching out with a trembling hand to touch her face.

A sharp staccato tapping rang out on the floor behind him. He spun around; the clicks and whirrs from his body increasing as his dark, deep-set eyes met those of the elderly man standing in the doorway.

The older man leant on the walking stick he had used to get the dark man's attention and shook an admonitory finger. "Luca, you know she is not for you. If the Toymaker finds out that you have been entertaining yourself with the liveware again…well, I am sure you remember what happened last time?"

The whirring man stared at him in silence, his dark eyes unnaturally large in his pale face. He walked away from Marizza's still form, pushed past the elderly man, and stalked out.

The older man paused, looking at the unconscious woman on the bed. He slowly crossed himself before limping from the room and locking the door behind him.

○

The Fenice Palace Hotel
Midnight

In a private suite at the Fenice Palace Hotel, Aquilleia began to run her bath. Pouring a large quantity of jasmine-scented bath salts into the water, she turned to the large mirror and carefully pinned up her thick blue-black hair. As she pushed the last of the pins in, a sudden coldness began in the base of her spine, crept up her back, and settled in her scalp. Recognising the signs of an imminent vision, she sat on the edge of the rapidly filling tub and waited. Her lavender eyes became unfocused as swirling silver lights formed in the purple depths, and she started to hum gently under her breath as myriad black, white, and grey images slowly appeared in her minds eye; a wide town square, a theatre door, a flight of stairs, and then an alley she did not recognise, its stone walls covered in blood; the deep crimson colour a stark contrast to the monochrome imagery. Aquilleia turned slowly within the vision and saw the body of a man, lying on its back, shock still distressingly visible on the twisted face. Beyond him lay the body of a woman, truncated by its missing head.

Aquilleia allowed her eyes to move over the scene, taking in the position of the bodies, their clothing, and the arcs of crimson that had sprayed on the walls before collecting in glistening, garnet-coloured pools on the stone flags.

As she studied the images, Aquilleia became aware of a movement in the alley behind her. In her mind's eye she turned slowly and tried to focus on what was there.

Beyond the bathroom, in the bedroom of the suite Aquilleia shared with Thorne and Veronique, the black Labrador snuffled and blinked as she woke from her nap. Her brown eyes narrowed as a sharp scent came to her sensitive nose. Veronique raised her head and faced the room where Aquilleia was preparing for her bath. The black Labrador's hackles rose as she started to growl.

Thorne looked up from his study of the hotel's menu card. "Veronique, what's wrong?" He stood up rapidly as a high-pitched keening sound came from the bathroom.

Thorne hurried into the room as Aquilleia slid to the floor. Kneeling beside her, Thorne gathered her into his arms. She looked up at him, an expression of utter horror on her desperately pale face, tears falling from her lavender and silver eyes. "He has her, Shad — Marizza! The Toymaker has her!"

○

Wednesday 20th March
Morning

Aquilleia's discovery that the Other known as the Toymaker was behind the disappearance of Marizza was a deeply unpleasant surprise. Giselle knew the Dona would never leave Venice without discovering what had happened to her friend, but trying to tell her the truth was not an option... Dona Carla herself would almost certainly be taken too if she tried to fight the Toymaker alone. The ugly truth was that the Toymaker was as interested in breaking people down to their basic components as he was in rebuilding them. Death was preferable by far to what the Toymaker offered those he kidnapped for use as raw material in his workshop.

Aquilleia detailed what she had seen in her vision; the alley, the bodies of Georgi and Anya, and the looming presence of Luca; the Clockwork Man, one of the Toymaker's oldest creations. He had been human...once. A sentinel for the Borgia family, his abilities had been recognised by the

Toymaker several years before he was finally kidnapped and turned into one of the Toymaker's first human creatures, his turning destroying what little humanity and sanity he had left.

The Espion Court had been searching for the Toymaker and his accomplices for centuries, after evidence of his vile torments was brought to their attention by an Other whom he had used cruelly. She had fought his attempts to break her, and succeeded in using her Otherness to escape…but not before he had begun to alter her. It was her refusal to submit that had persuaded the Toymaker to use humans instead of Others in his experiments, as they were far easier to break, debase, and control.

Wherever the Clockwork Man was, there too was the Toymaker. He never allowed his creations to travel too far from his side, which meant that he must be very close. The others agreed with Giselle's suggestion that the Espion Court should be informed of the Toymaker's presence in Venice, and that Dona Carla should be told that it was too late to save Marizza — for in truth, it was.

They took their painful leave of a distraught Dona Carla and Lilith, watching as the women boarded the private air-carriage that would take them to London, and then back to New York. As the craft rose from the jetty, they made their way to HMA *Arketurion* in subdued fashion, boarding the airship and standing in silence on the poop deck at the rear. As the góndoła rose from the Bacino Etere and the Grand Canal appeared before them, Giselle gripped the railings and turned tear-filled eyes to her husband. "I can't believe we told her that Marizza's dead! We don't know for sure…"

Elliott covered her twisting hands with his own. "We know that if she isn't, she very soon will be. If the Toymaker has her, may the Gods make it sooner!"

Aquilleia looked distressed. "I remember the testimony

from Mystici; she told the Espion Court everything..." She shook her head, tears coursing down her cheeks. "What he did to her — how he kept her alive!" She covered her face.

Thorne wrapped his arms around her. Veronique looked up with a soft whine and leant against Thorne's leg as the five of them remembered the hideous investigation into the Toymaker and his cohorts so many years earlier.

Elliott frowned as one particular memory came back to him. "Aranea was part of that investigation...he was found guilty of procuring victims for the Toymaker; that was why he was thrown into the Boundary."

Thorne nodded, then pulled out his handkerchief and pressed it into Aquilleia's hand. "He admitted it and gave evidence against him. That's why he was sent to the Boundary instead of being sentenced to the Unmaking, like the Toymaker."

Aquilleia wiped her eyes. "But the Toymaker escaped justice and was sentenced in absentia. That was nearly a thousand years ago, and he's been hiding ever since. But he created the Clockwork Man during that time. Who knows what other horrors he's created from living flesh?"

○

Thursday 21st March

Egypt

Day One – Cairo Aetherdrome and a Journey Past the Pyramids

Very Early Morning

The night had passed much as Elliott and the others had expected. Having discovered that the Toymaker had reappeared and resumed his cruel practices, they had been unable to rest; their painful memories of the terrible aftermath of the case in Astraea ensuring their reluctance to sleep. Instead, they settled themselves in the officer's mess with a pot of tea, two bottles of champagne, and a selection of sandwiches and biscuits, and went through the documents that Lapotaire had so kindly furnished for them about the Espion Court's investigations with the Empire and the Veiled Protectorate in Egypt.

Thorne sat back in one of the comfortable armchairs and flipped open his ever-present notebook. He licked the end of a brand-new pencil, looked expectantly at Elliott, and nodded at the thick packet of documents on the table. "Story, from the beginning, begin!"

Elliott smiled faintly as he opened the thick envelope. He separated the enclosed documents into three piles, picked up the first, lengthy missive they had been given and skimmed the text he had read with irritation at Londinium Tower. "It would appear that the issue is quite severe. Multiple atrocities have been committed in various towns across Egypt. The first was just over a year ago; an attack on an English missionary school in the upper Aswan area. The school was run by three missionaries from a church in the East End of London..." Elliott's voice trailed off; he looked at Giselle and Aquilleia with a guarded expression before continuing. "The attackers set the building alight, murdered the two male teachers, and all the boys, who ranged in age from six to twelve years." He grimaced. "The teachers were crucified and their bodies left on display. The one female missionary and the girls, of similar ages to the boys, were kidnapped, taken across the Nubian Desert and sold in the slave markets of Anglo-Egyptian Sudan." Giselle covered her mouth with her hand and bowed her head.

Aquilleia looked at Elliott, silver lights swirling in her eyes. "Children? They murdered, kidnapped, and sold children?"

Elliott nodded grimly. "The nearest British garrison crossed the desert and launched a raid on the slave market. Because it was in Anglo-Egyptian Sudan, they used the kidnapping of the female missionary to justify their incursion; there's been a ban on the selling of white women in that part of the world since 1884, so, it was well within their remit to do so. They killed most of the attackers and managed to rescue the teacher and several of the girls, but for some it was too late…they had already been sold, and their whereabouts are still not known."

Giselle reached out a trembling hand for her cup of tea and took a sip, the china cup rattling as she placed it carefully back on the saucer. Elliott reached out and gently touched her hand before continuing. "From the investigation that followed and interrogation of the surviving attackers, they discovered that the men responsible were Islamists, made up from various countries, determined to overthrow the Veiled Protectorate and reestablish hardline Islamist rule. The group called themselves al-khalafa al-rasheda, or in English, the Rashidun Caliphate; named for the Caliphate which led the invasion of Egypt in 639."

Thorne looked up from his notes with a cold eye. "In my experience, religious fundamentalists who endorse murder and slavery never make for the most stable of governments!"

Elliott nodded, his face equally stoney. "Indeed."

Aquilleia took a sip of her tea. "You've just summed up the history of the human race in one word. What a mess!" She looked at Elliott. "I assume there's more?"

Elliott leant forward and picked up the next sheaf of paper. "But of course…there always is! The Islamists who escaped bided their time, regrouped, and continued their work. There have been many more attacks in much the same vein; missionary schools and the like. But most recently they have started a line of attack that is the reason for our presence here; multiple attacks on British, European, and American civilians, mostly travellers in the same region. They target only the very wealthy; those carrying large amounts of money and jewellery. Their modus operandi is killing the men and older women, kidnapping and selling the younger women and any children, and stealing their victim's money and possessions. The belief is that they are using the money to buy arms to aid their cause."

Aquilleia frowned. "I thought you said that the selling of white women has been banned here since 1884?"

"It has — but since when has making something a crime stopped those bent on committing the outrage?"

Aquilleia sat back in her chair, the silver lights still active in her angry eyes. "And what of the selling of African women and children? Is that not also banned?"

Elliott shook his head. "Slavery itself is not banned in Anglo-Egyptian Sudan. But the slavery of white women and the *import* of slaves are banned. There *is* a ban on the sale of existing slaves, but the markets must be seen and reported. Those slavers who raid villages and sell their victims on the markets hidden deep in the mountains or deserts...they're far beyond the Empire's reach."

Aquilleia sat back angrily as Giselle frowned. "Going back a touch; how did the Islamists attack the travellers? Surely, if it happened in or around the hotels the staff would have seen or heard *something*?"

Elliott flicked through the documents he was holding. "Yes, you're right. It would be far too difficult to take someone forcibly from the hotel they were staying in...there would have been multiple witnesses. They would have to get them out of the grounds first." He placed the files on the table and tapped the black-bordered document. "Here's the reason for our presence; Lady Rosamund Melford, seventy-six, and her daughter, Devora, fifty-four. They were travelling to their hotel by airship. The airship docked at Kom Ombo, and they decided to go for a walk around the temple. When they failed to return by the cocktail hour, a steward from the airship was dispatched to find them. He discovered their bodies on the banks of the Nile" — Elliott's lips twisted — "partially eaten by the temple's resident crocodiles. When the officers went to their suite on the airship, they discovered the Melford's money, jewellery and other items had been taken."

Elliott perused the other documents. "Mr Edward Johnson-Blake and his wife Matilda, both in late middle-age. Mr Johnson-Blake was apparently an ardent amateur ornithologist. They went for an unguided walk to the temple of Abu Simbel very early one morning to see the blue-cheeked bee-eaters. Their bodies were discovered by the next group of travellers, who arrived less than an hour after the couple had arrived on their privately-hired felucca. On entering their hotel suite, officers discovered that all the jewellery and money the couple had brought with them was gone." He scanned through the information. "Yes, it's here in black and white. All the travellers had left the safety of their hotels or airships to visit remote Egyptian sights." He sat back. "But how did they get their victims to leave the safety of their hotels...and how do they know about the money and jewellery in their rooms? People are careful about such things these days."

Aquilleia sipped her tea. "Someone on the inside of the hotel or airship, perhaps?" She sat forward. "A suggestion; the guests meet with someone who arranges a tour that is never 'put through the books' and made official. They could inform the guests that they have organised the excursion, and then empty the rooms when the guests are out... knowing that the guests will never return." She frowned. "A maid, or a steward wouldn't be in a position to make bookings for a guest…it would have to be someone higher up in either the hotel or airship management."

Giselle looked at her husband, a thoughtful expression on her face. "Are there any descriptions of the jewellery and other items taken?"

Elliott turned over the document he was reading. "There are. The Johnson-Blakes had over a thousand pounds in notes and Mrs Johnson-Blake's family jewels; a platinum and emerald set consisting of a necklace, earrings, bracelet, and tiara."

Giselle poured herself another cup of tea. "From my dealings with the Fox, I can safely say that a set like that would be very difficult to sell in its complete state. Unless it was stolen to order for a particular buyer, it would be broken up, the stones sold on, and the platinum melted into bars or coins for ease of transportation."

Elliott nodded as he continued down the list. "Lady Melford and her daughter were travelling with a large amount of money and a rather lovely chess set that had belonged to the late Lord Melford; ivory chess pieces with mother-of-pearl and brass inlays and an ebony and ivory board. Apparently, the daughter was a gifted player."

Giselle sipped her tea and mused. "That could not be broken up. It would have to be sold to a collector or kept as a trophy by those who killed them." She looked at her husband. "Shall I send a message to Dona Carla, asking for her assistance? It might help take her mind off losing Marizza if she has something else to focus on."

Elliott nodded. "That's a very good idea. She has connections who could well aid us in discovering just where these items have disappeared to; dealers, private buyers, and those who can get around the customs agents. If we can find the buyers, the Empire might be able to trace the funds procured from their sale." He ran a finger along a line of totals and winced. "Looking at the money, jewellery, furs, and objet d'art these villains have taken from their victims, they could fund their campaign for a decade based on what they stole in the last year alone!"

He replaced the document on the table and picked up the black-bordered file on Lady Melford and her daughter as Thorne leant forward to filch a biscuit. Taking a bite, he waved the remains of the biscuit at Elliott. "What I don't understand is why *we* have been asked to investigate this. Aside from the fact that Lady Melford was a friend of the late Queen, this is nothing a local office in the Veiled Protectorate couldn't deal with, so why are we here?"

Elliott read through the document and sighed. "I think this explains why. As Lapotaire said, Lady Melford was one of the Queen's most trusted confidantes. She had access to the Queen's day-to-day arrangements; meetings, appointments, and security information that also applies to the rest of the Royal Family." He continued to read the document and winced. "And in spite of the hideous damage wrought by the crocodiles, it would appear that many of the injuries suffered by Lady Melford and her daughter could not have been caused by a crocodile attack. They were inflicted *before* they died, and their bodies thrown into the water to try and hide the damage."

Giselle blanched. "They were tortured?"

Elliott nodded grimly. "It would appear so. More than likely to gather information about Queen Victoria and the Royal Family's security arrangements."

Silence fell as the four friends tried not to dwell on the last moments of the two women whose deaths had caused such fear and loss in the heart of the Royal household. Elliott looked at them. "And *that*, my friends, is why we're here." Because Queen Victoria ordered the British government to invite the Espion Court to investigate the murders of her trusted confidante and her daughter. The Espion Court, in turn, came to the only people they knew could help; us." A faint smile appeared on his lips. "They knew we would seek out the information they sought with skill, thoroughness, speed, and finality...and with the added bonus of plausible deniability for the Empire's sake." Elliott handed Thorne the copies of the covering letter that had been sent to the British government, and the Empire's response. "All His Majesty's security has since been strengthened, but the threat of someone having access to information about the day-to-day running of the palaces has rattled quite a few of the great and good. They want us to discover who, why, where, and how. And they leave it to our discretion as to the 'finality and speed' with which we wish to make our final judgement on the named leaders. They will then use their greater manpower to take down the armed groups."

Thorne's eyebrows arched as he read the letter; a gleaming recommendation from Lapotaire confirming that the Espion Court would be honoured to send their very best agents to assist in the discovery and dismantling of the Islamist group responsible for the murders of Lady Melford and her daughter, and the many other outrages perpetrated on British, European, and American travellers in the Veiled Protectorate...with absolute discretion guaranteed. The Empire's response to the Espion Court was also effusive... and blunt. Thorne's green eyes widened at the passage that Elliott had quoted. He held out the document. "Finality and speed? They *are* worried! Judge, jury, and executioners...if we deem it necessary." He gestured at the list of names. "These are only the British victims. As the documents also refer to European and American victims, I take it there are more?"

Elliott pushed another piece of paper across the table. "At the last count, there have been over a hundred further attacks on various buildings and more than ninety separate attacks on British and European travellers, following the modus operandi of the Johnson-Blake and Melford cases." He frowned as he ran an eye down the list of names. "There was also one attack on an American traveller; a Mr Filippo Senape. He managed to fight off his attackers, but died from his injuries later that day."

Giselle scratched Veronique's head. "I'm amazed that the American government haven't sent an agent of their own; they're usually quite protective of their citizens."

Aquilleia broke a biscuit in half, gave half to Veronique and nibbled the remainder. "They may well yet send someone." She settled back in her chair. "But what of these names Lapotaire found to have a touch of the penny dreadfuls?"

Elliott rummaged through the papers and pulled out the salient document. "According to the civil servants given the task of translating the documents discovered on the dead Islamists, the names are indeed Prussian Blue, Black Eagle and Rouge Noir." He looked at the others. "They are a trifle childish, aren't they?"

Giselle stood up and stretched. "They sound Occidental, not the least bit Arabic; more like a touch of the Baltic and French, with a healthy dollop of English schoolboy. May I see?" Elliott handed the file to his wife, who frowned at them. "These are the translated files. Do we have the original documents?"

"Not the originals, no…but we do have copies of them."

As Elliott passed them across the table, Thorne grinned. "Never let it be said that Lapotaire doesn't give us the information we need!"

Giselle held the two documents side by side and scanned the contents. When she arrived at a particular passage, she gave Elliott a triumphant smile. "I knew it! The translators were slipshod in their work. It isn't Prussian Blue — the name in the original document is 'Caeruleum'!"

Thorne frowned. "Isn't cerulean just another shade of blue?"

Giselle smiled at his expression. "Remind me never to ask you to buy any paint, Thorne." Aquilleia giggled faintly at her husband's wounded expression as Giselle continued. "Not cerulean but 'Caeruleum'; that's what the Romans called it. But in the ancient world it had another name; Egyptian Blue."

Elliott raised his eyebrows. "Caeruleum?" He leant back and looked at Thorne. "That name is very familiar, but I can't for the life of me think why." He turned back to Giselle. "You say it means Egyptian Blue?"

"Hmm. The two colours are quite different in appearance; Egyptian blue is much lighter. The original recipe has been lost to time, but it can still be seen on pottery and jewellery found in archaeological sites here in Egypt."

"Well, it certainly fits the situation better than Prussian Blue!" said Elliott. He pointed at the other names on the list. "Just check those are correct, please."

Giselle looked at the names. "From what I can see, the translators were correct with the first; Black Eagle is as it sounds. The second one...wait a moment." Giselle stared at the document. "It's been a while since I read Arabic — especially Arabic with a touch of French! But this is also wrong. I don't think it's 'Rouge Noir', I think that it's 'Rouge *et* Noir'."

Elliott frowned. "Isn't that a French novel?"

Giselle shook her head. "That's *Le Rouge et le Noir*. Rouge et Noir is a game of patience played with two decks."

Thorne looked at her and raised his eyebrows. "Two decks? Could that mean two different people under one name?"

Giselle considered. "Possibly."

Elliott pulled a face, stood up, and stretched with a groan.

"So, what do we have? Three, possibly four people who are the leaders behind these atrocities?"

Giselle nodded. "And at least one of them will be in charge of the others." She looked at the document and tapped it with a manicure nail. "I think Caeruleum might be the leader of this little clique."

Thorne raised an eyebrow. "Why do you think that?"

She smiled. "Black Eagle is a little too childish for a leader; it sounds like someone trying to be far grander than they are. Rouge et Noir will be two people, I'm sure. Sharing a name marks them as lower in the hierarchy, and no self-respecting leader of a murderous band of villains would share their codename with another! They might be the ones passing information about the money and jewellery. So that leaves Caeruleum, a name which is poetic, unique, and speaks of a classical education."

Thorne gazed thoughtfully at the biscuit tray as he tapped his now-blunt pencil against his chin. "So, we have the Black Eagle, a flunky with delusions of grandeur. The Red and the Black...I really can't pronounce French, so I'm not even going to try! The Red and the Black, who might be two people watching the travellers and passing information to these bandits. And Caeruleum, the leader. Going by the name alone, definitely a touch pretentious. They all have no difficulty with murder, slavery, arson, or theft, and they have a great love of other people's jewellery, money, and other possessions." He looked at the others with a grimace. "Well, don't they sound like the type of stable and reliable people you want running your country?!"

Elliott eyed the documents, his face grave. "This could well be one of our more dangerous cases. We need to discover who these people are while keeping each other safe."

Thorne closed his notebook. "We'll be meeting with

Colonel Barrington at some point. Hopefully, he'll be as open to our assistance as Lapotaire suggested."

Elliott held out one of the letters. "According to this, he's not only open to our assistance but extremely grateful for any help we can offer him and his officers. Now, Lapotaire said that one of his men in Cairo will meet us at the aetherdrome tomorrow — or perhaps I should say, later this morning — and we'll be informed approximately when Colonel Barrington will present himself. At that point, the game begins!"

○

Cairo
Midday

HMA *Arketurion* descended gracefully from cruising altitude into the dusty, heat-hazed skies over Cairo and slid into her berth at the British Military jetty on the fifth landing floor of the Ash al-Tair Aetherdrome. As she came to a majestic halt alongside the gleaming limestone and oak quay, she was met by several uniformed young men who tied her firmly to the cantilevered jetty that jutted out some one-hundred feet above the sprawling city below.

Elliott, cane in hand, and dapper in a cream linen three-piece suit, stepped onto the gangplank and held out his arm to Giselle, who took it with a smile. Clad in a stunning eau-de-nil travel dress with matching hat, reticule, and parasol, she was followed in equally stylish fashion by Thorne and Aquilleia. Thorne was resplendent in a salmon-pink linen suit that had caused at least two outbreaks of hushed sniggers from some of the younger lads serving aboard the airship, while Aquilleia was clad in a beautifully simple confection of cream poplin. Veronique finished the gathering's sartorial elegance in her own inimitable fashion by presenting herself at the top of the gangway with a bow of bright-yellow silk tied on her collar. Aquilleia had done this at the Labrador's own insistence; Veronique had pawed at the pouch of ribbons in Aquilleia's vanity case until the yellow one had fallen to the floor. When Aquilleia tried to return it to the pouch, Veronique had snuffled at it, and so Aquilleia had tied it to her collar, much to the Labrador's delight.

As they alighted from HMA *Arketurion*, Thorne turned to the others and nodded towards Veronique. "If you'll excuse us for a few minutes?"

As Thorne and Aquilleia wandered off with the determined looking Labrador, Elliott turned to his wife. "We need to know where we 'e going next." He paused as a young man in the dark blue and gold uniform of the Royal Airship Fleet appeared before them, handed Elliott a thick envelope, saluted, and swung away before they had time to respond.

Giselle raised an amused eyebrow. "A very brisk young man!"

Elliott opened the envelope and read the missive, his eyebrows knitting. As he finished reading, he folded the letter with a muttered expletive and glared out across the city below them.

Giselle looked at him with an arch expression. "Is it from Lapotaire? That's the face you usually pull when he's involved!"

Elliott scowled. "It *has* come from the Espion Court, but not from Lapotaire. It's confirmation that Colonel Barrington will meet with us at the hotel the day after we arrive."

"So why do you look so irritated?"

Elliott ground his teeth. "This order has come direct from Geminandras!"

Giselle's eyes widened. "The Commander?"

"The man himself."

Giselle narrowed her eyes. "There must be greater things afoot when the man in charge of the Espion Court takes an interest in a case."

Elliott waved the letter. "Not just an interest; he's taken charge of the overarching investigation. He'll inform us of the current state of the investigation, personally…alongside Colonel Barrington. But because the Espion Court is acting sub rosa, he's to be referred to by his human title and name; Captain Anthony Darling."

Giselle looked at her husband with a concerned expression. "It'll be interesting when Thorne finds out!"

Elliott gave a short bark of laughter. "You can say that again!"

Giselle turned to look at the view from the jetty. "He'll have to be told…"

"Yes, I know! It's just that the last time they saw each other it ended…badly! I can't see another meeting between them going well at all."

Giselle bit at a manicured fingernail. "Where is Geminandras…I mean, Captain Darling, now?"

Elliott studied the missive. "He is currently working undercover as the captain on the *Eridanus Cartouche,* the airship that will take us to our hotel." He looked at Giselle with a pained expression. "It's a three-day journey…we don't arrive at the hotel until Sunday morning!"

Giselle winced. "Three days! Bearing in mind that we're boarding that airship shortly, Thorne will find out sooner rather than later! Should we tell him before they actually see each other?"

Elliott paused and shook his head. "No…it'll probably be better if we avoid the issue completely and simply run when they finally set eyes on each other. Speaking of which, they're back!"

Elliott and Giselle turned to greet Thorne, Aquilleia and Veronique, fresh from Veronique's necessary after-lunch perambulation. Aquilleia took in Elliott and Giselle's expressions with a questioning look. But as she opened her mouth, a young man bearing the uniform of an Aetherdrome officer came up and informed them that their air-carriage was waiting, saving Elliott and Giselle from any uncomfortable questions.

As the porters began to deal with their luggage, the smart young officer led them across the jetty and into the main building. The cool marble interior shielded them from the worst of the heat as they were guided to one of the private jetties. The officer paused by a small kiosk and tapped sharply on the closed door, which was opened by an older, darker man in a similar uniform, bearing a clipboard. The young man turned to Elliott. "Officer Hammad will need to see your documentation, Mr Caine."

Elliott reached into his breast pocket and Giselle and Aquilleia opened their reticules. Thorne looked at his wife. "Darling, do I know where my passport is?"

Aquilleia smiled and held up the papers she had just retrieved. "Yes, husband, you do!"

The documents were handed to the Officer who checked their names on his paperwork. He gestured at their trunks and travel cases and held up a small card. The card, neatly printed in English, stated that the officer needed to check the contents of their luggage for contraband. After several minutes of patting, rummaging, and embarrassed glances, followed by several more minutes of discreet repacking, the officer made a few unintelligible notes in thick, dark pencil and stamped their papers with a florid entry stamp in a garish shade of purple. He walked back to his kiosk, lifted the communications tube, and blew down the mouthpiece. After a few brief moments, there was an answering whistle. He turned to Elliott, bowed, and waved a hand at the end of the jetty, where a suitably ostentatious air-carriage awaited them.

The air officer reappeared, opened the door of the air-carriage, and gave them a sharp bow. "Ladies, gentlemen, if you will please board. Your luggage will be taken to the *Eridanus Cartouche* shortly. Bon voyage."

The five entered the sleek carriage, settled themselves into the plushly upholstered seats and prepared for take-off…the nature of which always depended on the pilot; sometimes it was smooth, sometimes it was more like sitting on an angry horse. Luckily, this time was the former rather than the latter.

Elliott took a steadying breath as the air-carriage rose smoothly into the air. Giselle gave his hand a gentle squeeze. She knew why he disliked airship travel and she agreed with most of his complaints, but it had been exceptionally helpful to travel to Venice so quickly. And that reminded her — not only did she need to send a message to Dona Carla about the names of possible buyers, she still needed to find a maid! As amusing as it was for Elliott to assist her in dressing — and indeed, undressing — her hair was beginning to fight her every attempt to civilise it. In truth, she desperately required a lady's maid who had experience in dressing, discretion, and the coiffing arts of style, arrangement, and containment. As she smoothed her heavily pinned hair self-consciously, the air-carriage swept them away from the main quay and towards the Eridanus Hotel Corporation's private pier on the eighth floor of the aetherdrome.

As their air-carriage alighted on the high jetty, they saw for the first time the vessel that would be their home for the next three days; the *Eridanus Cartouche*. The massive cigar-shaped envelope of material that held the gas ballonets was resplendent in gold and eau de nil, the hotel's colour scheme. The dark wood góndoła hanging beneath the balloon was built along the lines of the twin-decked Egyptian boats known as dahabiya. The second floor was surmounted on the quarterdeck by the bridge, where the Eridanus Corporation was proud to have one of the world's first Simulandro android pilots...and where, unbeknownst to Thorne and Aquilleia, Captain Anthony Darling warily awaited their arrival.

Giselle eyed the balloon and cast a wry glance at her matching outfit. "I think I need to reconsider my choice of colour!"

A young man in the corporation's uniform appeared before them. "Good afternoon, ladies, gentlemen; I'm Chief Officer Martock. I trust you've had a good journey?"

Elliott smiled in an urbane fashion. "As well as can be expected, Chief Officer Martock. My name is Elliott Caine. This is my wife, Mlle Du'Lac, and our friends Mr Abernathy Thorne and his wife, Madame Aquilleia." There was a slight gruffing noise from the floor. Elliott smiled. "And of course, Veronique."

"A pleasure to greet such a distinguished guest, Mlle Du'Lac; your vocal gifts precede you." He bent over Giselle's hand and pressed a light kiss near her thumb. Giselle smiled at the earnest young officer, ignoring the amused expression on Elliott's face.

Chief Officer Martock released her hand and gestured behind him. "If you would please board the *Eridanus Cartouche*. We're waiting for the rest of the guests. As soon as they arrive, we shall depart for the first stage of our journey."

Aquilleia turned from her contemplation of the airship. "And what is the first stage?"

He handed her a large, flamboyantly illustrated brochure.

"We will sail for the settlement of Giza, where we shall spend a few hours taking in the sight of the Pyramids. Tomorrow, we visit Thebes, Karnak, Luxor, and Kom Ombo. On Saturday, we arrive at Abu Simbel, and on Sunday, we arrive at the hotel." He turned his head sharply to one side in a birdlike movement as he pointed to one of the paragraphs in the guide. "All you need to know about the next few days of your journey is detailed in this guide. If you would please board now, you can settle in and prepare for your first night. He smiled and gestured to the vessel.

Elliott took Giselle's arm and guided her across the roped gangplank onto the deck of the *Eridanus Cartouche*, followed by Thorne, Aquilleia, and Veronique, who was immediately intrigued by various new and interesting smells.

As they waited on the deck, voices came from the jetty as the other passengers were met by Chief Officer Martock. Thorne rolled his eyes as he spotted the angry young man who had threatened the porter at Londinium Tower; hopefully they wouldn't be placed at the same table! He darted a sharp glance at Veronique as she growled at the reappearance of the large steamer trunk that accompanied the family. Thorne knelt beside the grumbling Labrador and stroked her silky ears. "It's all right, old girl. Now, how do you fancy a wander around the airship after dinner? We might accidentally pop into the wrong cabin and check the contents of a certain trunk. What do you say?"

The black Labrador looked up at Thorne as her long, pink tongue lolled in an approximation of a conspiratorial smile.

As Thorne stood up, he scanned the faces of the other travellers. Apart from the large family and their assorted servants, there was a solidly built man of early middle years with greying, curly hair, and a genial expression on his deeply tanned face. He wore a light-blue travel, the trousers of which were cut so short and so squarely, that they almost exposed his ankles. Thorne shook his head; American tailoring…they always cut the trousers too short.

Slightly behind the American stood another solo traveller; a well-dressed, but very thin, dark-haired man bearing an artist's easel, a small portmanteau covered with patches of oil paint, and a well-practised sneer as he surveyed the other passengers with obvious contempt. Thorne hid a sardonic smile; a young man in an expensive suit who obviously did not know the people around him, but who knew automatically that he despised them. Thorne nodded to himself; definitely a product of Cambridge!

Another man approached the group, stood beside the artist, and leant nonchalantly upon his cane. He was in his early forties, with a perfectly manicured dark beard and a moustache almost on a par with Thorne's. He was elegantly attired in a chartreuse linen day suit that even Thorne found a touch too much. Thorne's green eyes narrowed as he summed up the man in one word; popinjay. As Thorne contemplated the most recent arrival, the elegant man's expression slowly changed to a look of horror. He turned his eyes to the artist next to him and with much ceremony, removed a delicate silk handkerchief from his pocket and pressed it to his aquiline nose.

As the young man noticed his actions, a dark scowl crossed his face. "What?"

The popinjay grimaced and edged away from the belligerent artist as the irate young man dropped his easel with a thud and again barked, "What?"

The man lifted the handkerchief and spoke, his voice touched with a slight French accent. "My dear young man, while you are aboard this splendid vessel, I beg you to make use of *all* the facilities provided — especially the bathing equipment!"

The artist's eyes widened in outrage, but before anything could come of his anger at the popinjay's bluntness, strange whirring sounds came from the deck above them as the Simulandro pilot appeared on the stairs. An adult human male in appearance, the android was dressed in the eau-de-nil and gold livery of the Eridanus Hotel Corporation. He paused before them, his strangely vibrant blue eyes glowing in his unnaturally pale face. "Good afternoon, ladies and gentlemen. Welcome to the *Eridanus Cartouche*." His voice was low and breathy, each intake of air into his bellows clearly audible. "I am your pilot, Mr James. The captain sends his regards. He will meet you for the cocktail hour, which begins at eighteen hundred hours. Please follow the stewards, who will escort you to your rooms." Mr James gestured towards the stairs, where several stewards appeared and began herding the passengers towards the upper deck.

As Elliott, Giselle, Thorne, and Aquilleia were led to their suites, a Simulandro gynoid maid appeared in the doorway before them; built by the same company who had designed the android pilot and stewards, her countenance and figure was that of an adult human female. The maid's wide ice-blue eyes stared at them in an unnerving fashion before she moved swiftly aside and bobbed a curtsy.

As the others filed past the silent maid, Veronique approached the gynoid and gave her pale, still hands a questioning sniff. She sat back on her haunches and tilted her head to one side as she contemplated the maid with mild confusion in her brown eyes.

As she gazed at the gynoid, Thorne reappeared in the doorway above. "Veronique! Come along, old girl — biscuits!" The Labrador hurriedly stood up and padded after Thorne and the others.

The maid slowly turned to follow the dog's retreat. The gynoid's glowing blue eyes suddenly turned a vibrant yellow as the Other impersonating the maid mused on the possibilities of coincidence, and the likelihood of Versipellis, Angellis, Shadavarian, Aquilleia, *and* Xenocyon being on the same vessel as they. Hopefully, the presence of the five would not interfere with their plans *too* much.

○

**The *Eridanus Cartouche*
Thorne and Aquilleia's suite
6:10pm**

Thorne glared at the offending burnt-orange and amethyst-purple cravat that stubbornly refused to puff up in the necessary fashionable manner, pulled it apart with gritted teeth, and began the painful and wholly one-sided process again. Aquilleia smiled at him from her chair by the balcony. "If you continue to attack that most obstreperous of articles, we'll be more than fashionably late for cocktails. Concede defeat now, my darling, and punish it later."

Thorne scowled at the offending article, angrily looped it round his neck, tied it, and jabbed the emerald tiepin into the folded material with vigour. He stepped back and glowered at his reflection in the ornate mirror. "Perhaps I need to get angry with the damned thing more often! Look at it — I slave away trying to tie the thing neatly and it looks terrible! I tie it in anger, and the bloody thing looks superb!" He sighed, smoothed an eyebrow, and turned to his wife with a frown. "Am I the only one to think it odd that the captain didn't greet us when we boarded?"

Aquilleia nodded as she pushed an escaping jewelled silver pin back into her thick, blue-black hair. "It *was* strange. Perhaps he was busy with other things—" She stopped as a shiver crept up her back. Silver lights swirled in her lavender eyes as an image appeared in her mind; the back of a man, and standing next to him, replicated as though in a mirror, stood a perfect duplicate. Aquilleia's eyes glazed as she focused on the figure. The man was tall; easily as tall as her husband, lean, and immaculately dressed in fine evening wear, his short, dark-blond hair finished with a gleaming, jet-black silk topper. As the figure slowly turned, Aquilleia shivered; where the figure's face should have been, there was instead a smooth, blank visage with no visible features.

As her eyes regained their outward focus, Thorne took her hand. "What did you see?"

As she described the fleeting image, Thorne frowned. "Tall, lean, with blond hair…and no face? Hmm. The only person I can think of who is my height or taller is Aranae, but his hair is quite dark — like his soul! And why see two of him?"

Aquilleia looked at her husband. "I don't know… But I think he's somehow known to us, and I believe he may be on this vessel."

Thorne's frown deepened. "I can't recall anyone on board who resembles this man."

Aquilleia shook her head. "He's very important. That's all I can see."

"Then if you are well enough, my darling, let's adjourn to the bar for cocktails and get the best seats. Then we can ogle the other passengers and see if we can spot this important interloper!" Aquilleia smiled as her husband offered her his arm.

He turned to collect his gloves and saw Veronique, indifferent to the sounds around her as she lay on the bed, her faint snoring ensuring that Thorne and Aquilleia knew she was asleep and not feigning her tiredness.

Thorne placed a biscuit on the pillow next to the sleeping dog before they left their suite and made their way down to the salon, where the cocktail hour was in full swing. Thorne guided Aquilleia to a comfortable velvet settee upholstered in the hotel's signature shade of eau de nil and scanned the room. There was no sign of Elliott or Giselle — well, they could get their own drinks when they deigned to arrive.

He smiled at Aquilleia. "Champagne?" She nodded with a smile as he headed for the bar.

○

The Bridge
6:30pm

Captain Anthony Darling, Commander of the Espion Court and the Other known as Geminandras; a being who struck fear into the hearts of the most hardened and terrifying criminals in the Astraean prison known as the Boundary… most of whom he had sent there, raised an immaculate but irritated blond eyebrow high over a somewhat jaded green eye, ran a smoothing finger across his moustache and sighed in a deliberately exaggerated fashion. Taking a deep breath, he spread his hands in a placatory gesture and addressed his audience of one. His voice, rich and velvety, increased in both ire and volume as he spoke to the irate and quivering man before him.

"My dear François, far be it for me to interfere in the running of your kitchen. I wouldn't dream of telling you how to create your delectable menus for our expectant clientele, who most certainly pay through the nose for the privilege! All I ask is that when you retire for the evening, you ablute in the bathroom in your grossly oversized suite, and not in the pristine kitchen sink whose sole purpose is for cleaning the dishes — not your bloody feet!"

The Chef de Cuisine, his moustache bristling and his

plump face almost puce, responded in kind by launching himself into a full-throated and increasingly operatic display of histrionics that rivalled Dame Nellie Melba at her most theatrical. At a particularly obscene and rather squeakily delivered personal insult, Darling held up an admonitory finger and fixed the corpulent chef with a withering glare. "Enough! Your personal hygiene should be dealt with in the privacy of your own rooms, not in the kitchens. That is all. You may go." He waved his hand in the general direction of the door, turned his back on the irate Frenchman, and focused his attention on the charts scattered across his desk.

The incandescent chef, realising that he had been dismissed without any attempt to bribe or cajole him into a more pleasant demeanour, stormed out of the bridge and back to the sanctuary of his sacred domain in the kitchens.

As the door slammed with Gallic violence, Darling closed his eyes and sighed; of all the most frightfully irritating things to have onboard ship, hysterical Frenchmen, hysterical chefs, and hysterical women were on his list; finding two out of the three wrapped up in one person had to be a record!

He walked to the still-vibrating door, opened it cautiously, and peered out; the coast seemed quite clear. He made his way down the ornate cast-iron spiral staircase and poked his head through the door at the bottom to see if the incandescent chef was waiting for him, but the keel corridor beyond was empty. He closed the door, returned to the bridge, took his seat in the captain's chair, and stared blindly at the maps as he thought about the case the Espion Court had been invited to investigate in Egypt, and, in particular, the imminent arrival of the Espion Court agents. He sighed and rubbed his eyes; that, of course, meant Thorne. He had known for centuries that they would eventually cross each other's paths again. Darling leant back in the oversized brown-leather chair. He had no idea what Thorne's reaction would be on seeing him after so many years. Perhaps his hope that Thorne's anger might be pushed to one side until after the case was a touch naïve? He shook his head; it was something the two of them would have to deal with as it arose, and not before.

He turned away from the maps, opened a small drawer in the desk, removed an ornate metal box that bore the legend *Madame Marvelosa's Chocolates*, and popped a chocolate-coated strawberry cream into his mouth. As he savoured the bonbon, there was a discreet knock on the door behind him. Darling hurriedly swallowed the remains of the chocolate, threw the box back in the drawer, slammed it shut, and cleared his throat. "Come."

The door opened and his navigations officer, Cade, entered the room, carrying a large leather tube and a thick folder. He saluted smartly. "Good evening, Sir. I have the charts for tomorrow's journey. Would you like to see the route?"

Darling hid a smile at the sharpness of Cade's salute. The company always hired from the vast ranks of retired or pensioned-off men and women of the British Royal Airship Fleet, and some military habits were far too difficult for them to break. "Yes, thank you, Cade. I would also like to see the weather reports for the next few days, please."

Cade handed him a large file. "I took the liberty of getting the report sent as a matter of urgency, Sir — what with the colour of the sky, and all."

Darling's smile broadened. "I knew you would, Cade. You're very good at reading the weather." He took the file and placed it on his desk without opening it. "I was reliably informed by my predecessor that I should trust your judgement on this matter more than I should the Royal Meteorological Society. Now, what are you thinking?"

Cade gestured out of the huge window that spanned the front of the bridge. "In my opinion, Sir — and it *is* only an opinion, mind — we may be in for a spot of bad weather."

Darling frowned. "How bad?"

Cade looked at him with a slightly worried face. "The worst kind down here, Sir."

"A sandstorm?"

Cade nodded slowly. "Aye, Sir."

Darling opened the file and scanned the contents. "You are indeed quite correct, Cade. The Royal Meteorological Society suggests that the elements are ripe to foment a sandstorm. They believe it's likely to hit the first cataract of the Nile late in the evening of the 24th, and they project that it will last for up to three days. Damn and blast! It's going to land right on top of the hotel while we're there! That's all we need."

Cade smiled. "These travellers will just have to pop back again when the weather's better, Sir. God knows they can afford it."

Darling nodded absentmindedly. He was not thinking about the wealthy elite aboard the *Cartouche*. Rather, he was pondering the planned meeting between Versipellis, Shadavarian, Angellis, Aquilleia, Xenocyon, Colonel Barrington, and himself — and in particular, the utter hell of having to rearrange it through the interfering civil servants and courtiers who littered the Espion Court, the British government, and the Veiled Protectorate, like so much discarded confetti. The logistics of trying to rearrange such a meeting simply didn't bear thinking about. He handed Cade the file. "See to it that this information is passed on to the second officer, will you, Cade? All necessary precautions must be taken, in case the bloody thing decides to arrive early."

Cade accepted the file. "Yes, Sir!"

Darling sat back in his chair. "After all that, are we on schedule?"

Cade nodded as he opened the large leather tube, unrolled the chart within, and placed it on the desk. "Yes, Sir. We should arrive over Thebes shortly before dinner."

"Excellent, excellent. Our guests have certainly paid enough for the stunning view that awaits them. Right, I am off to tidy myself for the cocktail hour…I'm running a little late. If there are any problems, find me."

Cade saluted again. "Yes, Sir."

○

The Viewing Walk
6:35pm

Elliott brushed a minuscule piece of lint from his immaculately clad shoulder, picked up his cane and smiled at Giselle. "Ready?"

Giselle returned his smile and nodded. She caught up the heavily beaded jet and malachite reticule that matched her most recent acquisition from the House of Worth; a stunning evening gown in green and black silk, and accepted her husband's arm. They left their suite and made their way towards the spiral staircase leading to the salon, where the cocktail hour had already begun for several of the guests.

As they walked past the entrance to the bridge, the door opened and Darling appeared on the threshold. The three of them stared at each other in a tense silence for some time before Darling tentatively offered his hand. "Mr…Caine, I believe?"

After a pause, Elliott took it and nodded. "Geminandras."

Darling winced. "Would you mind awfully keeping that

on the q.t, old chap? It's Captain Anthony Darling on board this ornate rust-bucket."

Almost against his will, Elliot smiled. It'd been many years since he'd last seen Geminandras, and that had been under deeply unpleasant circumstances, but it was nice to see that he hadn't changed much. Elliott nodded. "Very well; Captain Darling."

Darling smiled back. "I take it Lapotaire has informed you of certain issues we've been having out here in the Veiled Protectorate?"

"Enough to whet our appetites."

Darling smoothed a slender hand across his oiled blond hair. "Tomorrow, perhaps after lunch when the passengers are otherwise engaged, we might meet in your suite and discuss it?"

Elliott shared a look with Giselle. "Have you seen Thorne yet?"

Darling's smile fell away. "No, not yet. I think our reunion will be rather — obvious to anyone nearby!"

"Understood. It might be best to see how your reconciliation goes. We need to talk about the goings-on here in Egypt, but Thorne and Aquilleia must be a party to this from the beginning. If there are still issues between you and Thorne, it may take a day or two to bring him round."

Darling nodded slowly. "It's been many, many years since our falling out…I'd hoped things would change, but I haven't heard from him for nearly a thousand years."

Elliott studied him, a green light in his dark-brown eyes. "Your actions caused him great pain."

Darling shot Elliott a sharp look. "Yes, I know. I had my reasons, but then…ah, never mind!" He turned to Giselle. "I remember you, Angellis, but we have not yet been introduced in this world. Perhaps a reintroduction is in order?"

Elliott noted the abrupt change of tack. "As you say,

Darling, not in this world. Giselle, allow me to reintroduce you to Geminandras, also known as Captain Anthony Darling; Commander of the Espion Court…and Thorne's brother. Darling, this is of course my wife, Angellis, known in this world as Mlle Giselle Du'Lac."

Giselle smiled at Darling as he took her hand and pressed a gentle kiss against her wrist. He smiled back, a faint twinkle in his bright-green eyes. "Charming, quite charming! I was very pleased and relieved to hear that you'd been returned to us."

Giselle returned his smile. "I'm delighted to say that it's not only us, but Shadavarian and Aquilleia have also been reunited."

Darling's smile widened. "Yes, I understand that they finally found each other. I can only hope that will mitigate my brother's sensibilities towards me, somewhat — although I have my doubts!" He straightened up and looked at his pocket watch with a grimace. "And on that note, I am afraid I must leave you, at least until dinner." He hesitated. "It may well be unpleasant, but I do believe that the time has come for my brother and I to bury the hatchet."

Elliott took Giselle's arm. "Hopefully not in each other!"

Darling gave a bark of laughter. "As you say!" He bowed to Giselle. "Good evening."

As Elliott and Giselle watched Darling disappear down the staircase to the captain's quarters, Elliott shook his head. "That will be a deeply unpleasant conversation for both of them."

Giselle shook her head. "I can't remember what happened. What went so terribly wrong?"

Elliott sighed. "It was something that occurred shortly after you and Aquilleia were murdered by Chymeris."

Giselle stilled at the expression on her husband's face. "What happened?"

Elliott gently disengaged his arm from hers and leant against one of the handrails by the stairs. "It concerned a case in Astraea...involving Filicidae."

Giselle blanched at the mention of the creature that had made such an unwelcome return in their previous investigation. A faint golden light appeared in her blue eyes as she looked at her husband. "Go on."

Elliott shook his head. "I think it best for Thorne to tell you, my love. It was a very bad time for him; it came not long after you and Aquilleia were killed. He was already in a very dark place, and then what happened with his parents and brother..."

As Elliott's voice trailed off. Giselle nodded tremulously. "You're right, I'll wait for Thorne to explain. He's probably already told Aquilleia."

Elliott took his wife's arm. "I am sure he has. And now, my darling, cocktails!"

○

The Salon
6:45pm

Elliott and Giselle entered the salon just in time to hear the second gong, indicating that dinner was a little over a quarter of an hour away. Elliott scanned the room and caught sight of Thorne and Aquilleia sitting by one of the large viewing windows. Elliott grimaced — airships and a dislike for heights made uncomfortable travel companions!

He waved at Thorne, who raised his glass as Elliott and Giselle made their way through the packed room towards the comfortable settees Thorne and Aquilleia had reserved.

Giselle settled herself into one end of the settee and

looked at Elliott with a bright, slightly forced smile. "Champagne, darling?"

"I'll be right back." Elliott turned to Aquilleia and Thorne. "Can I get you another?"

A Simulandro maid suddenly appeared behind Elliott, a tray heavily laden with Champagne coupes held at a jaunty angle before her. Her vivid blue eyes stared at him. "Champagne, Sir?" Elliott paused for a moment before nodding. The gynoid held the tray in one hand and handed him two glasses, then passed another two to Thorne.

Aquilleia accepted the offered coupe of Champagne from her husband with a smile which she also conferred on the Simulandro maid. She knew the creation wasn't human, and therefor, by some people's reckoning, exempt from the niceties of human interaction, but she had been raised to be courteous and respectful to those who were polite to her. She took a sip from her coupe; it was a very pleasant Champagne — Thorne would be pleased.

Aquilleia cast her lavender gaze across the room, which buzzed with conversation and laughter. As she took in the various guests, she shivered suddenly; something was wrong…very wrong. Among the bright and cheerful conversations was a faint sound…an underlying, unintelligible, monotone murmuring that caught the lowest edges of her hearing. Aquilleia's eyes narrowed as she focused on the sound; it was a man's voice, but it sounded strange — hollow and faint — as though it were travelling a great distance before being heard. She closed her eyes as she tried to pinpoint where it was coming from; it seemed to be quite close, but the voice didn't seem to be coming from any of the men in the room.

She looked at the guests seated on the settees nearest to her; the Devereaux family. The matriarch, Marguerite, dressed in a sublime House of Worth creation in deepest oxblood that framed her dark-eyed beauty, was seated almost next to her, her ornate and rather large reticule sitting between them on the velvet settee. Aquilleia frowned as she focused on the bag; it seemed unusually bulky and rounded, as though a cat had curled up inside for a nap. The sounds seemed to come from within the embroidered reticule — and they were not quite human…

Aquilleia's eyes widened; she turned to Thorne just as the Simulandro steward appeared at the entrance to the bar. "Ladies and gentlemen, may I present, Captain Darling."

Thorne and Aquilleia turned to face the doorway, missing Elliott and Giselle's mutual wince as Darling appeared at the door, a charming smile on his handsome face. Thorne's green eyes widened as he stared in open-mouthed shock at his brother.

Aquilleia's jaw dropped as she darted a rapid glance at her silent, staring husband; she too recognised the captain. She also suddenly realised the reason for her earlier vision of a blond man doubled in a mirror image; Thorne and Darling were identical twins. Aquilleia took a healthy gulp of her champagne; she, like Giselle, had died in Astraea shortly after Filicidae had been caught and sentenced to the Unmaking, but before the hideous estrangement between Thorne and Darling had occurred. Since they had found each other again, Thorne had hidden nothing from her; she knew everything that Thorne did about what had happened the day he and his brother had become estranged.

But there had been other powers in play during the many months it had taken to hunt down and destroy Filicidae in Astraea; her own mother had been a part of the search for the creature and had paid the ultimate price with the loss of her sanity. Many had fallen under the spell of the creature, up to and including the King's Chief Concubine, who, as a member of the ruling class, could not be sentenced to the

Unmaking for her crimes, and so had instead been sentenced to eternity in the Boundary. Aquilleia shivered; the Unmaking would have been a far more lenient and forgiving sentence.

She turned her attention back to the scene before her as Darling smiled at the gathered guests. "Ladies and gentlemen, my name is Anthony Darling and I shall be your captain for the duration of your journey aboard the *Eridanus Cartouche*. Please rest assured that your safety, enjoyment, and pleasure are my highest concern. Aboard the *Eridanus Cartouche* you will find every possible means of entertainment known to man — and a few that are unknown!" His green eyes scanned the faces of the guests before finding Thorne.

There was a deathly pause as Thorne glared at his brother, purple lights appearing in his eyes with frightening speed. He shot a dark look at Elliott, turned, and stalked from the room. Aquilleia hurriedly placed her coupe on the table and followed her husband; she knew he would need her.

Darling blinked rapidly as his brother and sister-in-law left. Then he collected himself and turned to one of the Simulandro stewards standing to attention directly behind him. "I believe two of the guests will not be joining us for dinner," he murmured. "Mr Abernathy Thorne and his wife, Madame Aquilleia. Please see that a supper tray is sent to their suite. With regard to the table, see that their places are removed and the other settings are adjusted accordingly. Please also remove both Madame Aquilleia's name from the list of ladies requiring an escort into dinner, and Mr Thorne's name from the roster of escorts."

The Simulandro bowed slightly before replying in a breathy, hollow voice. "As you request, Sir." He turned, silently opened the door into the dining room, entered the room, and closed the door behind him. The Simulandro stewards were exceptionally swift at fulfilling an order, and their programming would ensure that the settings were rearranged and placed to the exact sixteenth of an inch in very little time.

Darling turned his attention back to the guests in the room. "You have already enjoyed your first day aboard the *Eridanus Cartouche* with views of the Pyramids and, in some cases, your first glimpse of the majestic Nile."

Marguerite shared a smile with several members of her family; it certainly was not *their* first time in Egypt! She sipped her Champagne with a satisfied smile as Darling continued.

"Tomorrow, you will have the opportunity to experience the sights and sounds of Thebes, Karnak, Luxor, and Kom Ombo. On your final day aboard, we shall stop at the sublime temple of Abu Simbel, before turning back and carrying you to your final destination; the Eridanus Hotel Eau de Nil. The journey will afford you two nights aboard this magnificent vessel, where you will enjoy exquisite food and wine, cooked to perfection by our resident chef de cuisine, François Le'Friteuse." He tried not to dwell on his last exchange with the airship's gifted, but somewhat unhygienic chef, as he continued. "A few moments ago, we dropped anchor just north of Thebes of the Hundred Gates. The view of this incredible site will be the setting for this evening's dinner. The setting for tomorrow's dinner will be the Temple of Sebek at Kom Ombo, where the sacred crocodiles still mass in their pools in the Nile, in the hope of offerings from both the worthy, and the unworthy, alike." He smiled at the guests. "Crocodiles were worshipped there. The remains of over three hundred mummified crocodiles were discovered in the ruins of the temple. Several had the gold jewellery they wore in life wrapped into their bandages."

At this remarkable piece of information, Camillia turned her limpid blue eyes from the platinum and diamond bracelet that glittered on her slender wrist and raised her clear voice. "Jewellery?"

Darling nodded with a slightly hard smile; the mention of gems attracted the attention of a certain type every time. "Yes indeed, Miss Devereaux. A great deal of jewellery, mostly bracelets and earrings."

Camillia took a sip of her champagne. "They were not yet discovered when last we were here."

Marguerite shot her granddaughter a sharp glance. Camillia caught her look and in a flustered, breathy voice mumbled. "Gold jewellery for an animal? What a waste!" She darted a glance at her grandmother and a strange note entered her voice as she looked back at Darling. "Is the jewellery still there?"

Darling nodded again. "Indeed, it is. It's on display in the museum…and very well protected by glass covers and guards."

Camillia pouted and turned her gaze back to her diamond bracelet. "What a pity."

Giselle, about to take another sip of her champagne, blinked at the young woman's strange response. She cast her eyes over the Devereaux family and frowned as her gaze took in those closest to her; the newly-wedded couple, and the bride's companion. The young bride, a perfect English rose, was talking to her husband, who looked rather bored. He also seemed to be paying rather *too* much attention to his wife's companion, who was smiling at him in a far too familiar fashion. As the bride turned away to pick up her drink, the companion leant forward and brushed a piece of lint from the groom's shoulder. Giselle's eyebrows shot up at the very public display of such an intimate gesture.

As the guests sat, the sudden melodic sound of the dinner

gong echoed around the room. Darling smiled; saved by the bell! "Ladies and gentlemen, dinner is served!" He gestured to the massive double doors, which were thrown open by the two Simulandro stewards standing by the heavily gilded doorway. The Simulandro maid walked around the room, handing each gentleman a card with the name of the lady he was to escort into dinner.

Elliott shared a smile with Giselle as she was enthusiastically collected by Thomas Breton, the sneering artist who, luckily for Giselle, had followed certain rather blunt advice he had received at the jetty, and who had indeed availed himself of his suite's bathing facilities.

Elliott took his card with a smile of thanks and read the name printed on it; *Marguerite Devereaux*. He made his way to the elegant matriarch's side and bowed. "Madame Devereaux? Allow me to introduce myself — Mr Elliott Caine, at your service. May I escort you to dinner?"

Marguerite looked up with a gracious smile. She carefully collected the large reticule and stood up, extending her arm to Elliott. "Thank you, Mr Caine."

As the maid continued around the room, handing cards to the gentlemen, she came to the solidly built American whose tailoring had earlier been dismissed by Thorne. He stood; smoothed the lapels of his dinner jacket, accepted his card, and read the name on it with a slightly bemused expression. He leant in and in a deep Southern drawl, whispered. "I don't know which lady bears this name, Ma'am... could you kindly point me in the right direction?"

A faint whirring sound came from behind the maid's painfully blue eyes as she calculated the correct response to his request. She leant forward, and with the strange wheezing sound that always accompanied a Simulandro's voice murmured, "Mrs Evelyn Briar-Devereaux is the young lady in the cream and rose gown, Sir."

The American straightened up and touched his forelock. "Thank you kindly, Ma'am."

As he turned to address Evelyn, Kiefer, lounging by the bar near his brother and sister-in-law, gave a short bark of laughter, knocked back his whisky and drawled, "They aren't human, old boy — you don't have to be polite!" He held his glass out to the maid. "Whisky! And make it a treble."

The maid's eyes flickered as she took the glass and stepped behind the bar. She poured the drink and placed it in front of him, Kiefer took it without a word and turned his back to her; an insolent smirk on his smooth face. Rex looked at the young man with a faint smile that didn't quite reach his eyes. "The worth of a man can be read not in the way he treats those he perceives to be his equals, but in how he treats those he perceives to be his inferiors. My mama raised me to be polite. After all, who knows when we might have entertained angels unawares?"

Kiefer's face darkened. He slammed his glass down on the bar and was advancing towards Rex when the Simulandro maid moved between them. He glared at her in incredulous anger and hissed. "Get out of my way, slave!"

There was a flash of movement and the maid's hand was suddenly inches from Kiefer's nose. "The name of the lady you are to escort to dinner…Sir."

Kiefer glared at the Simulandro, who gazed back at him blankly. He snatched the card from her slim white fingertips and scowled at the name, then turned and approached his sister. "Margaux!" he snapped.

His sister looked up with mild defiance as she savoured the last of her champagne. As she finally stood up to accept her brother's arm, she remarked to her husband, "He offers his arm with such good grace!"

Julius smiled at his wife as the maid handed him a card. As he read the name that was printed on it — *Violette*

Donnadeiu — his smile widened. He turned to his mother-in-law's constant companion with a smile. "It would appear that I am your escort this evening, Violette." The sultry-looking brunette returned his smile and accepted his arm. Julius' smile widened as he tucked the card into his breast pocket and escorted Violette into the dining room.

Rex approached Evelyn and held out his arm with a smile. "Mrs Evelyn Briar-Devereaux? My name is Rex Nympton. May I escort you in to dinner?"

Evelyn smiled back as she stood up and took his arm. "I'd be delighted, Mr Nympton." She turned back to her husband. "André, I'll see you at dinner?"

André tore himself away from Jane's knowing smile and looked at his wife with a distracted air. "Yes, yes, I suppose so." The Simulandro maid handed him a card. He read the name and turned to his niece. "Camillia, shall we?" His niece once more peeled her attention from her sparkling bracelet and gave him a vague smile. He took her arm and walked past his wife without a second glance.

Evelyn watched her husband go in silence before turning to Rex, who looked at her with an understanding expression. "Shall we go in, Ma'am?"

Evelyn blinked, then nodded. He gently folded her arm into his as he escorted her towards the dining room.

As Evelyn and Rex disappeared, the elegant man who had been so offended by Thomas Breton's scent at the jetty appeared by the settee Jane was seated on and smoothed his moustache. "Mlle Gagnon, it is a genuine pleasure for me to say that I am to escort you into dinner." He paused and looked around them, making sure no one could overhear before leaning in with a slightly more familiar air. "It is most opportune, meeting with you again, Mademoiselle."

An expression of irritation flashed across Jane's smooth face before it was replaced by a sultry smile. "Why, Monsieur

Cavet, fancy seeing you here! Whatever brings you to this part of the world?"

Gaston Cavet smiled, his neatly trimmed moustache flattening against his thin top lip. "I am very lucky, Mlle Gagnon. My…how do you say…work? It has taken me to some very interesting places, and introduced me to some very interesting people. Why, only the other week I was in Marseilles, talking with some extremely knowledgeable people, and now I am here!"

Jane's smile hardened slightly. "A very interesting life, indeed, Monsieur."

Gaston beamed. "Oui, I am blessed. And now, shall we dine?" As Jane allowed him to take her arm and escort her to the dining room, a calculating expression appeared on her face.

The Simulandro stewards bowed as the massed ranks of guests walked past them and entered the richly decorated dining room. As the last guests left the salon, the Simulandro maid who had borne the brunt of Kiefer's rudeness glared after them; her eyes turning from their usual brilliant blue to a deep golden yellow as the Other within their disguise fought their anger.

In the dining room, the usual polite scrum was taking place as the guests searched for their place cards on the table. As the last of the guests stood by their chairs, Darling, at the head of the table, raised his Champagne coupe. "Ladies and gentlemen, to a good journey!"

The guests raised their glasses and sipped their champagne. The gentlemen waited as the ladies sat and arranged their skirts to minimise creasing, then took their seats as the Simulandro stewards refilled their Champagne coupes to accompany the first course; turtle soup.

As the guests settled into their seats, one guest sipped their Champagne and pondered the moment when the captain had arrived and one of the guests had stormed out, followed rapidly by his wife. In particular, they thought about the strange purple lights they had witnessed swirling in the tall man's green eyes. The guest moved forward and smiled politely at the Simulandro steward as their soup was served and shook out their napkin; so many intriguingly strange people on board…and so little time to find out who and what they were. As they lifted their spoon, they surveyed the gathered guests — perhaps a restful evening or two was in order before beginning their work? They were all travelling to the same destination, after all, and the true reason for their very personal trip to Egypt could be dealt with after they arrived at the hotel, when most of the guests would be at their most relaxed; busily searching the local souks, investigating the surrounding ruins…and less likely to notice one or two disappearances! As the table chatter began to swell, they turned their attention back to the soup and listened to the conversations buzzing around them.

Giselle patted her lips with her napkin and smiled at the young man who had escorted her to dinner. "I understand that you're an artist, Mr Breton?"

Thomas Breton, who had just taken a large bite of his bread roll, turned puce as he hurriedly tried to swallow it. He took a swift gulp of his Champagne and coughed as he nodded. "Yes, yes, I am. I've been engaged by the Eridanus Corporation to create a painting of the Eau de Nil hotel."

Giselle sat back in her seat as the Simulandro steward refilled her Champagne coupe. "How marvellous!" She turned to Rex Nympton, who was sitting on her left. "And you, Sir? What do you do?"

Rex smiled. "Well, Ma'am, my name is Rex Nympton and I have been many things; a sailor, a rancher, and a businessman. But most recently, I was a Texas Ranger."

Silence fell around the table. Marguerite and Kiefer

shared a sharp glance as everyone turned to look at the genial American.

Rex's smile widened as his bowl was removed and replaced with a gold-trimmed plate. "Did I just make what you might call a *faux pas?*"

Giselle smiled and shook her head, but before she could say anything Thomas spoke. "Yes, you did! How dare you take a seat at this table! You, Sir, are a cad and a murderer!"

The silence became deathly as Rex raised his calm blue eyes and looked into those of the angry artist. After several long moments, the older man responded, his Southern accent somewhat thicker than before. "I have never murdered anyone in my life, young man. That is a slanderous remark, and I urge you to recant and apologise."

Thomas leant forward in his seat and glared at Rex, a muscle in his narrow jaw twitching angrily. "I will never apologise! We know all about your kind, *Mister* Nympton!" Thomas looked daggers as he spat the American's name. "It's reported in all the newspapers in Britain and Europe! You are a self-confessed Texas ranger; a killer with a badge! You see yourself as judge, jury, and executioner!" He sat back in his chair and looked around the room; his expression a strange mixture of fear, enjoyment, and self-righteous fervour.

Rex smiled as he sipped his champagne. "And of course, we all know that newspapers never lie, don't we?"

At the older man's remark, Thomas's face turned an even deeper shade of purple. As he opened his mouth to respond, Rex held up his hand. "I was indeed a Texas ranger. It was my job to find, arrest, and bring the accused in for questioning, young man; nothing more. If it went to the judge — well, better judged by twelve than carried by six, as my old grand-pappy used to say." His tanned face hardened. "Many people don't like their behaviour to be judged or shamed, especially if it's illegal. They try to twist their willful transgressions, their choice of a life of crime, and use it against those who arrest them and present them to the courts for trial. It's always someone else's fault, never theirs. 'Why me?' is a very familiar cry in the cells. They never have a thought for the real victims — those they choose to prey on. No Sir, I saw, and still see myself as a detective. I searched out those who destroyed lives, and I very much enjoyed my work. But I have always believed that the accused should have their chance to prove their innocence. If the evidence is there to support their claims, it should be brought to the attention of the judge and the case decided thus. *If*, however, the evidence shows their guilt..." He sat back in his chair and slowly shook his head. "Well now, I would have to say that I agree with that fine Scottish philosopher, Adam Smith, who said 'Mercy to the guilty is cruelty to the innocent'. In truth, I do enjoy seeing a murderer swing for their crime."

The silence continued as the lawman smiled gently at the angry artist. Thomas leapt to his feet and gestured angrily at Rex. "I will not sit at the same table as a murderer!"

Rex continued to smile as he shook his head. "Now, young man, I have just said that I am no murderer. It was my job to bring actual murderers to justice. If someone you loved — perhaps someone you loved even more than you love the sound of your own opinions — was murdered, wouldn't you want justice to be done?"

Thomas stared at Rex in shock; in all his life, through boarding school, the finest art schools his parents could afford, and his adult crusade to bring art to the down-trodden proletariat, no one had ever spoken to him in that manner! A muscle twitched under his left eye as Rex continued. "Besides, can we ever really know who we are dining with, can we? There could well be murderers, thieves, pederasts — beggin' your pardon, ladies — and possibly even worse sharing this table with you tonight. We can never truly know who we're sitting next to. Why, if you adhered to your own rules, young man, you would never speak to anyone, or share your table with them, just in case."

Thomas opened his mouth, then closed it with a snap. He stood up, flung his napkin on the table, and stormed out, making sure to slam the door as he left.

Rex looked round the table. "Well now, ladies and gentlemen, I do apologise for any upset the young man's reaction to my previous employment has caused."

Giselle smiled at him. "That's quite all right, Mr Nympton. Mr Breton's behaviour is not your fault." She took a sip of her champagne. "You said that was your previous employment. May I enquire as to your current employment?"

Rex sat back in his chair, a lazy smile on his genial, tanned face. "Why of course you may, Mlle Du'Lac. I found the harsh Texas sun a mite damaging to my fair skin, so I returned to my hometown of Baton Rouge and found a position that suited my sensibilities perfectly. I am now the chief Pinkerton agent for the great state of Louisiana."

An even more deathly silence descended. Rex sipped his drink, his grin widening as he looked at his dining companions. "We all have our little secrets. My job is to uncover those secrets that the law of the land, and certain private citizens, need to know to ensure that justice is seen to be done."

○

The Salon
8:45pm

As the guests made their way into the salon, Elliott leant towards Giselle. "That was an interesting meal!" Giselle smiled and nudged him lightly in the ribs as Rex and Evelyn walked past.

Thomas glared at the blithely unconcerned American from his seat at the bar, then slammed his empty glass on the walnut counter and stormed out. His exit would have been rather impressive, had the toe of one of his highly-polished patent-leather shoes not caught the edge of the exquisite Persian rug. Giselle choked back a laugh as the angry artist disappeared through the door in a furious windmill of arms, legs, and strangled swearwords. She turned to her husband, who was failing to stifle his laughter. Giselle covered her own grin with her gloved hand. "Oh dear! Now he'll be in an even fouler mood!"

Elliott grinned back. "Well, I doubt we shall see much of him for the rest of this evening." His face darkened as Darling walked past, chatting with Julius. "Perhaps we should see how Thorne is taking this somewhat forced reunion with his brother. I don't think it went very well!"

Giselle shook her head. "Perhaps it would be best to leave Thorne to his thoughts for tonight. If he needs anyone, it will be Aquilleia."

Elliott paused. "Yes, of course. More Champagne?" Giselle nodded as they headed for a small settee and settled themselves in for the evening.

◯

Thorne and Aquilleia's Suite
8:45pm

In the golden glow of the gaslight, Veronique raised her muzzle from the floor with a faint whine and looked at her master and mistress. Thorne had been sitting by the balcony windows almost since they'd returned, his green eyes staring at nothing. Veronique's nose twitched; neither of them had eaten before they had returned…she could smell when they had.

Her worried thoughts had been confirmed when, shortly after Thorne and Aquilleia returned, two Simulandro maids had arrived bearing a supper tray for two, and a chilled bottle of champagne. The supper tray sat untouched, but the Champagne was long gone.

The worried Labrador's soft brown eyes flicked to Aquilleia, seated next to Thorne; her watchful lavender eyes fixed on her husband as the three of them sat in silence.

○

Marguerite and Vincenzo's suite
9:45pm

André smiled at his mother and leant in to kiss her cheek. "Goodnight, Mother."

Marguerite smiled up at her son. As she pressed her cheek against his, she murmured, "Use your gift to make sure she sleeps."

André turned to Jane and smiled, a wolfish expression in his eyes. The use of one of the families more unusual gifts, that of the art of enchantment, was something he had been very grateful for over the last few weeks. It not only ensured Evelyn's somnolent captivity, but freed his evenings for far more pleasant and entertaining company. He walked over to his wife, who was standing by the large viewing window in his mother's suite, and held out his arm. "Time to retire, my dear."

Evelyn didn't register his appearance, her cornflower-blue eyes gazing into the inky blackness of the desert night.

André frowned. "Come, darling. We have many beautiful ruins to see tomorrow…we must get some rest."

Evelyn blinked. "Yes, yes, of course. Goodnight, everyone. Goodnight…Mother." As she lent to press her cheek against Marguerite's, the older woman smiled slightly. "Goodnight, dear child. Sleep well."

Violette gave a faint snort of laughter. Marguerite gave her a dark look and she hurriedly turned her attention back to Vincenzo, who was sitting beside her, studying his nails in a bored fashion.

As Sedgewyck, the elderly butler, closed the door behind André, Evelyn, and Jane, Kiefer looked at his mother with a sour expression. "Is the American after *us*, do you think?"

Marguerite held out her empty Champagne coupe to Julius and rolled her eyes in an exasperated fashion. "How on earth should I know?" She accepted the refilled coupe from her son-in-law without thanks and took a healthy sip, then sighed and pinched the bridge of her nose. "I doubt it. What could an American possibly know about us? We've never been to the Colonies, and we've never reassembled our family using New World stock. It's a little too…" She paused, searching for the right word.

Margaux looked up from her drink with a hard expression. "Mixed, Mother? Is that the word you're looking for? Rather too much like small beer for our rare and refined tastes, hmm? Only the purest and finest Old-World eau de vie for us!"

Marguerite frowned at her daughter, her jet-black eyebrows knitting over her dark eyes. "You've had a little too much to drink, child! Perhaps it's also time for *you* to seek your bed. Bearing in mind the reason why we're here, a good night's sleep is required for all of us. Julius, take my daughter back to your suite." She paused and glared at him. "And make sure you *both* stay there!"

Julius opened his mouth, then caught his mother-in-law's eye. "Of course, Marguerite. Come along, darling."

Margaux stood up angrily and lifted the bottle of Champagne from the bucket next to her. She shrugged off her husband's proffered arm and with careful steps wove her way from the room. Julius gave the family a slightly embarrassed glance as he followed his tipsy wife to their suite.

As the door closed behind him, Camillia looked at Marguerite with a raised eyebrow. "You didn't really answer the question though, Grandmama, not really. Do you think the American knows?"

Marguerite turned and threw her Champagne coupe at the wall. Her dark eyes turned a frightening, blinding white as she hissed. "How in the name of Nekroshema should I know!"

Linden jumped to his feet and moved in front of his cowering sister as Marguerite stalked across the room towards them. "The American is taking the same journey as us, like all the others on board this vessel. The artist, Breton; does he know? The opera singer, Du'Lac; does she know? I. Do. Not. Know!"

Marguerite pushed Linden to one side as though he were made of gauze and gripped her flinching granddaughter's face; her pale, slender fingers digging painfully into the younger woman's flesh. She gazed into Camillia's terrified eyes as the rest of the family watched in silence. Vincenzo sipped his whisky with a bored expression as Kiefer smirked at the scene playing out before them.

Marguerite took a deep breath as she lessened her grip and gently stroked Camillia's smooth, wide-eyed face; her eyes returning to their usual colour. "Child, there are things that even I don't know. We shall simply have to wait and see. If the delightfully southern Mr Nympton needs removing, I'm sure one of us will be able to deal with him." She released her granddaughter and stepped back. "I doubt we would have to rely on Heathers' special abilities. Even Sedgewyck would be more than capable of running that particular lawman out of Tombstone!" Her remark brought a sudden bark of laughter from Vincenzo.

As the situation eased, Kiefer looked rather disappointed. He drained his coupe, turned to the butler standing silently in the corner and gestured at the remains of Marguerite's glass. "Sedgewyck, Mother has dropped her drink. Clean up the mess and pour her another."

The butler bowed and shuffled towards the small bar. Kiefer rolled his eyes as Marguerite sat down. "Any time this week, Sedgewyck!" As the butler continued with his painfully slow movements, Kiefer growled. "For God's sake; I'll get the drinks! You deal with that bloody mess."

As Kiefer pushed past the butler and started to pour drinks, Linden turned to his sister. "Are you all right?" he murmured.

Camillia turned her bright-blue eyes on her brother. Her throat and jaw, where her grandmother's hand had gripped her, showed deep red welts. "Of course I am. I shouldn't have angered her; it's nearly time for Grandpapa's resurrection. I should have thought before asking such a foolish question."

Kiefer handed her a full Champagne coupe. "Do you want something to drink, Linden?"

Linden looked at his uncle and shook his head. "No thank you. I believe Grandmama is right…an early night might be in order for me, too." He stood up and bowed to Marguerite. "Goodnight, Grandmama." He kissed her cheek and cast a look at Sedgewyck, who was picking up individual pieces of broken glass. "I'll show myself out."

As Linden closed the door, Kiefer turned to Marguerite. "I have a suspicion that our dear Linden may have lost his taste for the immortal life."

Marguerite shook her head. "He's only just five hundred and twenty years old, Kiefer. The first few deaths are always the worst. After he has participated in more of the necessary sacrifices, he will find it second nature, just like the rest of us." She smiled at her eldest son. "And besides, he's a good boy; he will do exactly as he's told." She sat back in her chair and looked at her companion, Violette. "My dear, is everything prepared for the ritual tomorrow?"

Violette nodded. "Yes, Marguerite. All is in readiness for the choosing."

An unpleasant smile appeared on the matriarch's face. "Perhaps the choice is already made. I believe it's time for Julius to prove his mettle once more; it's been quite a while since he played a hands-on role in a sacrifice, and I think it would be good for Linden to see his father actively participate in the gathering of an offering…it's been quite a while since Julius was involved as anything other than a mere spectator." She took a sip of her champagne, savouring it. "Yes… Julius will be our choice of weapon for the gathering of Evelyn's heart's blood and life force. Use your legerdemain, my dear, to ensure that he receives the correct stone in the blind ballot." Her eyes turned a dull, opaque white. "Then my beloved Reynaud will once again walk upon this earth."

Vincenzo shifted in his seat at this allusion to his wife's previous husband. Marguerite smiled. "Don't worry, Vincenzo. As agreed, you will continue to be rewarded for your service to us; eternal life, eternal youth, and an unending supply of money and social position will be yours for ever. That was Reynaud's promise to you, and I shall keep it. You are of this family, Vincenzo…you have been for many years now, and we never allow one of our own to fall. Once Reynaud returns to his rightful place at my side, you will remain a much-loved member of our family. Remember, my dear, that Reynaud is a generous and kindly master…just as I am a generous and kindly mistress."

Vincenzo looked at his wife with an unreadable expression, then drained his drink. He studied the intricate pattern of the Persian rug as Marguerite held her coupe out to Kiefer, who topped up the glass with a knowing smirk.

○

Friday 22nd
Day Two - Thebes, Luxor, Karnak, and Kom Ombo
Thebes
8:00am

The arrival of the *Cartouche* and her consignment of wealthy travellers had been eagerly anticipated by the many expectant merchants who pushed their varied wares at the souk. Affluent visitors could usually be relied upon to part with a few Egyptian pounds or piastre for a piece of genuine, gaudy, Egyptian tat. However, from the point of view of the local traders, their early-morning trip into Thebes had been a complete failure.

Very few of the guests had bothered to venture forth at such an obscenely early hour of the morning, so the sum total of customers from whom the locals could beg, steal, and barter, consisted of a sleepy Elliott, an intrigued Giselle, a subdued Aquilleia, a very bouncy Veronique, who remembered the smell of Thebes from many, many years earlier, and short-tempered Thomas Breton; yawning hugely and bemoaning the weakness of his coffee at breakfast.

Aquilleia walked down the gangplank and joined Elliott and Giselle on the *scarab*, the small airship launch that would ferry them from the *Cartouche* to the jetty, three hundred and fifty feet below them. As the airship began her descent, Giselle touched Aquilleia's hand. "How is he?"

Aquilleia bit her lip, her lavender eyes glistening. "I've never seen him like this, Giselle. He's silent. He hasn't spoken since he saw his brother last night."

Elliott nodded slowly. "That sounds very familiar. When you were murdered, he didn't speak for over a month."

Aquilleia nodded, her slender fingers plucking at the edges of her sky-blue parasol. "When we were returning from New Zealand, he told me about what had happened… with his parents and brother. I felt the pain it caused him." She looked at them. "I had a vision, last night before dinner, of a tall blond man who was doubled in a mirror." She shook her head. "I should have known it meant Geminandras!"

Giselle looked at her friend. "Have you no idea what Thorne will do about his brother?"

Aquilleia gazed into the distance. "I think they *will* speak…but I can't see the outcome."

Elliott frowned. "As long as they talk with each other long enough for us to deal with this issue in the Veiled Protectorate, that's all we can ask." He shook his head. "We can't do anything more until after we meet with Colonel Barrington, so I suggest that we give Thorne and Darling a little time. They may surprise us!" He paused as the *Scarab* finished her descent and landed smoothly in the water by the jetty. The Simulandro pilot, who looked very much like Mr James, the pilot of the *Cartouche*, lent out of the wheel-house and gave the order for the airship to be moored, and her gangplank deployed. As they began to disembark, Thomas Breton pushed past them rudely, bearing his easel, his bag of charcoal, and a blank canvas, before him like a shield as he pushed his way past the desperate merchants and walked briskly down the jetty, leaving the others at the mercy of the various ware-pushers and dealers who touted for trade by one of the many entrances to the City of a Hundred Gates.

Elliott frowned at the back of the rapidly disappearing artist. "May I suggest we enjoy a walk around one of Egypt's greatest treasures? The Mortuary Temple of Hatshepsut is that way." He pointed to the dusty, earthen road that Breton had taken; the well-trodden path leading away from the jetty and into a selection of jumbled buildings.

The watery early-morning sun bathed the stone and mud-brick houses in a golden, buttery light as the travellers left the jetty and were immediately accosted by the merchants, ragged children, assorted dragomen, and determined donkey traders that the long-vanished artist had pushed past. Elliott frowned at the ragged gaggle of donkey-wranglers; all seemingly determined to equip them with one or several of the silent and emaciated creatures that stood dejectedly next to their owners. As they fended off the more insistent merchants, Aquilleia looked at one poor donkey, fresh whip-marks still bleeding on her side. She turned her burning lavender eyes on the wrangler; silver lights swirled in the depths as her utter anger at the treatment of the animals rendered her incapable of controlling her Otherness.

On seeing the swirling silver lights in her eyes, the owner backed away rapidly, his hands making the sign against the evil eye. She called the nearest dragoman over, taking care to keep her eyes averted from the polyglot, and pointed at the abused donkey. "Tell this man that if he harms another of these creatures again there will be no refuge from my wrath!"

The tall dragoman cast an appraising eye over Aquilleia, made a deep bow, and snapped a bullet-like stream of Arabic at the cowering wrangler, who threw his hands into the air with an exclamation and ran from the jetty as though the hounds of Hell were on his tail.

The dragoman turned to Aquilleia with a smile and spoke

in heavily accented English. "He has relinquished his owner-ship of the animals." He gestured at the three thinnest of the donkeys that stood despondently by the jetty. "They are now yours."

Aquilleia blinked. Veronique sat down and whined as she looked from the donkeys to her mistress and back. Aquilleia nodded sharply, the silver lights subsiding in her lavender eyes as she looked at the dragoman. "Then I require your services to find someone who will look after them here."

The dragoman tapped a finger against his lips in thought. "There is an Englishwoman who might help. She is…ekken-trikós. I am sorry, what is the word in English?"

Giselle raised an immaculate eyebrow. "Eccentric?"

"Yes. A little strange, but she takes in animals." He smiled. "And occasionally people who have also been harmed by the evil of others. She owns a house in Luxor…on the other side of the river. I can take you there; it is only an hour's journey if we take a boat across the Nile. Livestock is allowed on the larger vessels."

Aquilleia nodded. "Thank you. Yes, I think that will do very well."

Giselle looked at Elliott, who was gazing longingly down the road that led to the Mortuary Temple. She jammed her elbow into her husband's ribs and turned to Aquilleia and the dragoman. "We'll come with you. The airship will collect us from the Luxor side of the river this afternoon, anyway." She turned innocent eyes on Elliott, who was surreptitiously rubbing his bruised ribs. "We can organise a day trip to see what we have missed easily enough on our return journey. Won't that be marvellous, darling?"

Elliott took her arm and shot her a pointed look; a twinkle in his brown eyes. "Perfectly marvellous, my dear!" He turned to the dragoman. "I am known as Caine. This is my wife, Mlle Du'Lac, and our friend Madame Aquilleia."

The polyglot nodded. "The lady who now owns three donkeys." Elliott nodded with a smile. "Yes, that lady. How are you known?"

The dragoman bowed again, his red and gold turban gleaming in the rapidly warming sunlight. "I am Akakios Kyriaku, a Greek a long way from home."

Elliott nodded. "A pleasure to make your acquaintance." He turned and looked at the donkeys with a concerned expression. "I think it might be sensible if we pay a visit to this lady now; we need to get these poor creatures out of the sun before it becomes unbearable."

Kyriaku walked over to the donkeys and untied them. "The jetty for the boat across the Nile is a little further down the river. Please follow me." Elliott, Giselle, Aquilleia, and a snuffling Veronique walked in companiable silence as the Greek led them and the uncomplaining donkeys down the dusty road that ran alongside the Nile, and on towards the ferry to Luxor.

○

The *Cartouche*
The Bridge
8:35am

Darling settled into his captain's chair and ran a finger along the list of guests who had put their names down for the various tours the *Cartouche* were offering. He handed the document back to the Simulandro steward. "That seems to be in order, Mr Phillips. Count them out, and count them back in again. Just make sure the numbers tally...we don't need any repeats of the previous unpleasantness!"

Mr Phillips, identical in appearance to all the other male Simulandro stewards, save for the gold flashes on his lapels that marked him as the head steward, nodded as he accepted the paperwork. "Yes, Sir, of course." As he turned to leave, the door to the bridge opened and Thorne walked in. There was a strained silence as the two brothers looked at each other.

Mr Phillips looked at Thorne; a quizzical expression in his bright blue eyes. "May I help you, Sir?"

Thorne shook his head, his eyes fixed on Darling. "No, thank you. I have come to see…" He gestured at his brother.

Darling stood slowly. "It's quite all right, Mr Phillips. That will be all." The steward made a sharp salute and left the room, closing the door behind him as he left.

Darling looked at Thorne with a guarded expression. "It's been a long time, brother."

Thorne nodded slowly; his eyes equally guarded. "But still not long enough for me." His tone was steely. "I understand that as you are the Commander of the Espion Court, and I am in its employ, our paths will occasionally cross. I have managed nearly one thousand years without having to endure either your face or your company. Those long years have not changed my opinion of you or what you did." He stared at Darling with cold green eyes. "I do however understand that there is clear danger to the British Empire, His Majesty, and His Majesty's subjects, and we both need to bring our skills to the battle. For that reason alone, I am willing to put our shared past aside…temporarily, and bring my not insubstantial gifts to bear on the case."

Darling looked at his brother with the faintest hint of a smile. "I agree, brother. Thank you. This case is worrying, as it concerns the deliberate targeting of British subjects for the most nefarious of purposes. It's perhaps best to discuss it with the others in greater depth, but I am sure they won't mind if we…ah, open negotiations here." Darling sat at his desk and waved at the empty first mate's seat opposite him.

Thorne hesitated slightly before sitting down as his

brother continued. "I understand that Lapotaire furnished you with the necessary documents, but to summarise; from what we can see, it involves the targeting of mostly British travellers, a small number of French and Italians visitors… and one very unlucky American. They arrived in Egypt, and they and their luggage were taken to their airships or hotels. At some point in their journey or stay, while they were not in their suites, their luggage was ransacked and various items were stolen. In the case of several of the more unfortunate travellers, they too were attacked and disposed of, with two of the deaths a little too close to the British monarchy for comfort. We believe the items that were stolen were traded for money and used to purchase armaments for the Islamists and their cause."

He paused and plucked at the neatly-trimmed Van Dyck that covered his chin. "To be honest, it's an absolute bloody nightmare!" He settled back into his chair with a sigh. "There have always been those who would prefer the British Empire to pack up and leave the various parts of the world they govern, and a few of those people are quite prepared to use any means at their disposal to see the Empire gone. But the Islamists here in Egypt have taken things in a very new and very ugly direction…particularly in the way they prefer to target civilians — rather than armed troops — to achieve their ends. So much so that the Empire realised that they couldn't approach the issue as they usually would; with talks and deals. When dealing with terrorists who seek the eradication of those who are not like them, one cannot negotiate, one must eradicate, otherwise they and others like them will sense weakness and rise again, and again, and again…like some grotesque hydra. The Empire needed to find the leaders responsible for the outrages, while also guaranteeing plausible deniability in case things became untenable, or in case we need to end the investigation with finality and speed." He paused and looked at his brother. "I believe those *were* the words they employed in their letter to you…'finality and speed'."

Thorne nodded faintly. "But only if required."

Darling tapped his lips. "Indeed. When Queen Victoria was informed of the murders of Lady Melford and her daughter, her demand that they send for us led to a great sigh of relief in Whitehall. Employing people without any visible links to the Empire to investigate and deal with the issues arising was the best and most satisfactory way forward for everyone. Thus; enter the Espion Court. The one thing they have insisted upon, however, is an intermediary; a go-between who is also on the inside of the Veiled Protectorate; step forward Colonel Barrington. He's known as being a fair and just man — if a little too fond of curry. He has the support of the Empire, the Veiled Protectorate, his men, and the locals. I've arranged a meeting with him at the hotel; I am just waiting for him to confirm the timings."

Thorne nodded slowly as he stood up. "I think we should continue this discussion with Elliott, Giselle, and Aquilleia, before you say any more about this case."

Darling nodded. "Yes, of course." His face became uncertain. "There's a great deal for the two of us to discuss also, brother. Most of it you already know, but there are things I must tell you that may alter your feelings towards me and my actions so long ago. The Empire's request was serendipitous, as it's forced us to speak again." Darling appeared apprehensive; he swallowed and continued. "Now might be the right time for me to explain what happened…the night our father died."

Thorne stared at Darling; his jaw clenched. After several strained seconds that seemed like hours, his lips curled in a snarl. His green eyes showed twin pools of spinning purple light as he allowed his rage to manifest. Darling saw Thorne's expression and drew back in his chair as he witnessed the depth of his brother's fury.

Thorne ground his teeth as he looked down at his brother's face; a face that was so like his. When Thorne spoke, his voice was frighteningly calm and steady, something Darling recognised as his reaction to being pushed to the very edge of his limits. "Our father murdered our mother. When you found him, instead of arresting him, you enabled his escape from justice by allowing him to kill himself. For that, Geminandras, I will never forgive you." He stalked from the room, slamming the door violently behind him.

Darling looked at the quivering woodwork with a blank expression, then whispered softly, "He didn't escape, brother — truly, he didn't."

○

Luxor
9:30am

Having managed to transport the three donkeys across the Nile with minimal fuss, Kyriaku led Elliott, Giselle, Aquilleia, and Veronique down many narrow and winding streets that led deeper and deeper into the fragrant, bustling city of Luxor. After working their way through one particularly packed and interesting souk, Giselle handed Elliott a small, beautifully formed figurine of a black cat which she had purchased from a charming but insistent merchant. "He said that it's third Dynasty — I wonder if that's true?"

Elliott smiled. "Possibly from the lesser-known Bagatelle Dynasty, and freshly imported from the finest warehouse in Whitechapel!"

Kyriaku held out his hand. "May I see, please?" Elliott handed the figurine to the dragoman as they walked into a street that was more like a square; the buildings festooned with colourful rugs, and wall hangings. Kyriaku stopped and ran his finger across the fine carving and hieroglyphs covering the small space between the cat's paws. He handed it back to Giselle. "It is a genuine find. I believe it is third Dynasty; you can tell from the markings here and here."

Giselle threw Elliott a smart glance and tossed her head. "Bagatelle Dynasty from Whitechapel, hmm?"

Elliott smiled ruefully as Kyriaku led them down another meandering street, where the merchant stalls and shop fronts had been replaced by what appeared to be residential dwellings. The thickly plastered, mud-brick walls bore large, ornately carved, iron-studded doors, and the sound of splashing water could be heard coming from the hidden courtyards beyond. With each turn, the roads became narrower and the walls higher, until the street tapered to a sudden end at a high wall, into which was set a large, elaborately-carved but shabby double door.

Kyriaku pointed at the door. "This is the dwelling of the lady who may help you."

Aquilleia peered at the small brass plaque embedded in the wall at eye height. "*Miss Francesca Barrington's Home for Abandoned Beings.*" Elliott's eyebrows shot up as she continued. "*No hawkers, dealers, or fakirs. Any who cause harm to others will be roasted and fed to the pigs.*" She looked at Giselle with an approving nod. "I've never met the lady, but I like her already!"

Elliott gestured to Giselle and Aquilleia. As they leant towards him, Elliott murmured. "Barrington is the name of our contact here in Egypt; Colonel Barrington. It was on the documentation we received from Darling."

Giselle shot a quick look at Kyriaku, who was approaching the small bell pull. "the sign says 'Miss Barrington'…daughter of, do you think?"

Elliott shrugged. "I haven't the foggiest! Perhaps we'll find out once we're inside."

Giselle nodded as Kyriaku gave the brass bell pull a strong tug. A distant bell began to peal on the other side of the wall. After some minutes, they finally heard a bolt being withdrawn. As the heavy portal swung open, they found themselves staring at a woman covered from top to toe in a white gauze shroud, the flimsy material of the shroud glowing in the bright sunlight that filled the unexpectedly massive garden on the other side of the wall. The figure stared at them and in a harsh voice barked. "What?"

Aquilleia blinked. "I...we were told that the English lady who lives here could assist us."

The figure pulled the white material from their head, revealing a middle-aged face with strong cheekbones and an unapologetically Roman nose framed by a wealth of haphazardly pinned and greying red hair. She waved the white gauze headdress at them. "Dealing with wasps. Nothing like bees. Vicious little bastards!" Her sharp, hazel eyes glared at the four humans in turn before she saw the donkeys. Her eyes softened as she immediately stepped outside and approached the nearest of the three. A gentle hand was slowly held out to the donkey, who flinched slightly, but gave it a guarded sniff before moving closer to the spare-looking woman who gently stroked the long, scarred ears. "Oh, so it's been like that, has it, my little one? No matter now. You're here and you're safe, and that's all that matters." As she spoke, the other two donkeys pricked up their ears and moved closer. She stroked their ears and removed their fetters before looking at Aquilleia. "You took them from someone who was not worthy of them?"

"Yes."

"And now you give them to me, to be cared for and treated well, yes?"

"I do."

The older woman nodded sharply. "Good! Any other answer simply would not do." She straightened up and held out her hand to Aquilleia, who accepted the firm grasp with a smile. "I am Francesca Barrington. You are welcome in this place. Come in. Cook has just made a seed cake, and I can offer you tea and whisky. Close the doors behind you." She turned without waiting for an answer and walked through the door, followed without hesitation by the three donkeys.

Kyriaku bowed. "I believe this invitation does not include a poor dragoman." He turned to Aquilleia. "If you would kindly pay what you believe my services were worth, I shall take my leave of you."

Francesca's harsh voice rang from the other side of the doorway. "My invitation was definitely extended to you, Kyriaku; I know much about you. Come along, before the cake gets cold. It's far better hot from the oven."

Kyriaku looked at the others with a confused expression as they entered and closed the door behind them.

At the sound of the bolt being shot echoed down the narrow alley, three men stepped out of the shadows at the far end of the street and glared at the door. The older of the three shrugged. "They will have to come out some time. And then...we will help ourselves to whatever wealth they have with them."

The smallest smirked as he fingered the edge of an ugly-looking blade. "A waste about the women."

The man in charge scowled at him. "Your defiling of the women led to the police paying far too much attention to what we do! That is why the women are now only for robbing, killing, or selling. Do I make myself clear?"

The small brigand's lip curled in anger as he jammed his knife back into its sheath.

The older man nodded coldly. "Good. Now...we wait."

○

The *Cartouche*
Marguerite and Vincenzo's Suite
Midday

Heathers closed the sitting room door and stood with his back to the cold wood; his expressionless face almost as stiff as the oak the door was made from. He lowered his gaze to the floor as Marguerite stood and smiled at her gathered family. "The time is near when we shall once again welcome back our most beloved patriarch; my husband, Reynaud."

She ignored the irritated movement from Vincenzo and continued. "You know what must be done, and with that in mind…" She gestured at Violette, who approached the group with a smile. She stopped by her mistress's side; a small black velvet bag held loosely in her left hand.

Marguerite looked at her children and their servants with a raised eyebrow. "You know what happens next. Let the choosing begin."

An unpleasant smile appeared on Violette's face as she walked to each family member – including Heathers and Sedgewyck, and held out the velvet bag. One by one they each put their hand into the bag and selected one of the smooth stones within, hiding it from view until Violette had taken the last stone and returned to Marguerite's side.

The matriarch looked at her family and raised her hand to show them the stone she had chosen; it was plain white. One by one the others revealed theirs until there were eleven white stones…and one black.

Julius grimaced at the dark stone in his hand. "Oh, damn it!" He looked at his mother-in-law with a plaintive expression. "Do I have to?"

Kiefer's smile was as ugly as Violette's. "This is how it's

always been done, Julius. You should know that by now, old chap!"

His brother-in-law stood up with a muttered swearword, stalked to the drinks cabinet in the corner, poured himself a treble scotch and drank it in two gulps. He looked at André, who was sitting next to Jane. "Are you quite sure that you are — well, after all, Evelyn is your wife!"

André shrugged. "As Kiefer says, this is how it's always been done. Don't worry, Julius, I won't hold it against you. To be honest, I find Evelyn's burgeoning individualism and genuine niceness rather tedious. Her blood will return father to us. I am more than willing to proffer my bride as an offering to bring him back." He sat back and smiled at his brother-in-law. "I'm looking forward to seeing him again… thirteen moons is too long a time."

Marguerite smiled and waved her hand at Sedgewyck. The silent butler shuffled up to the matriarch and waited, his deep-set eyes gazing at the floor.

Marguerite looked at him with an exasperated expression on her coldly beautiful face. "Oh, good Gods, Sedgewick! Champagne!"

The butler nodded ponderously, his cadaverous head bobbing on his thin neck as he shuffled to the drinks cabinet and laboriously began to open and pour Champagne into a suitable number of coupes. He slowly placed them on a tray and began to make his way around the room. After several tedious minutes had passed, he returned the tray to the cabinet, faced Marguerite and bowed. She shot him a dagger-like look and waved her hand. "Leave us, Sedgewick."

The silent butler bowed again and doddered slowly from the room, carefully closing the door behind him. Kiefer turned to look at Marguerite with an irritated expression. "It's high time Sedgewick was put out to grass, Mother."

Marguerite took a sip from her coupe and shook her

head. "After everything he's seen, and what happened to him the last time we resurrected him, that could only be done in the most permanent of manners." She paused and rolled her eyes. "And there *is* the little problem of his other half to be considered."

As Kiefer opened his mouth to respond, the door to the keel corridor crashed open; Julius choked on his Champagne as a swirling ball of dark-red energy barrelled into the room, knocking over the half-empty Champagne bottle, and spilling the contents over his immaculate linen suit. Julius leapt to his feet with a curse, pulled out a pristine handkerchief and began to mop his damask waistcoat. He glared at the spinning ball that pulsed in the upper corner of the room and shook his fist. "Damn you, Sedgewick! It wasn't our fault!"

A sound that was unmistakably that of a descending raspberry filled the room as the mass of energy shot back through the door as rapidly as it had entered, the door slamming shut behind it. Kiefer looked at his mother with a raised eyebrow. "You were saying?"

Marguerite took another sip of her drink. "I see what you mean. Yes; he is getting a trifle...unstable."

Linden gave a derisive bark of laughter. "I'd be unstable if the family of necromancers I worked for had promised me eternal life, attempted to resurrect me on my death, then buggered it up and left me in two parts; a revenant and a poltergeist!"

Julius glared at his son. "Mind your language, young man; there are ladies present!"

Linden smiled at his father. "You swore too, Papa...and it was rather more uncouth than the word I chose!"

Marguerite shook her head sadly. "He's been with us for over three hundred years, and we've resurrected him several times with no ill-effects. Oh well...perhaps a light refresh of the staff might be in order. Now, to other business." She sat forward in her chair and looked at André with an expression of avarice on her beautiful face. "An important question before Julius carries out his duty; are you quite sure that Evelyn has made her last will and testament?" Her lips twitched slightly. "I wouldn't want her dear father's plentiful capital to go to waste."

"Yes, Mother. I saw to it the day before our marriage." André settled himself in his armchair. "In order not to worry her, I too created a new will at the same time, leaving her the entirety of my estate in the event of any personal unpleasantness." He smirked. "I shall of course change my will as soon as we return to London — sadly, without my dear Evelyn. Everything is legally binding, Mother; I ensured both wills were suitably witnessed by our lawyers; Messrs Chortle, Higgins, and Blackthorpe, of Marylebone, London."

Marguerite's smile widened as she leant back in her chair. "Ah yes, lawyers…one can't live with them, and one can't die without them!" She raised her coupe with a smile. "Now, a toast to our future, and then a visit to Karnak. À votre santé!"

○

A Visit to Karnak
1:30pm

The massed ranks of the Devereaux family trooped down the gangplank for their trip to Karnak and were immediately set upon by the swarm of merchants, dealers, and grubby children who had waited by the airship jetty in the hope that a few coins would come their way. Kiefer paused by the quayside and watched as Vincenzo handed out a handful of piastre to the younger children while deftly slapping away the merchants attempts to press rugs, idols, and cheap glass trinkets on the gathered clan. Kiefer stepped away from the throng and watched as, trailed by a cloud of babbling children, his family disappeared down the well-worn route that would bring them to the Avenue of Sphinxes, the First Pylon, and the gateway into Karnak.

Kiefer shook his head; he had been to Karnak many times before, and in his opinion, it had certainly declined since the first time he had seen it…well over three thousand years earlier.

A discreet cough came from behind him; Kiefer turned and looked at the uniformed man with an irritated expression. "You're late!"

The middle-aged Egyptian standing behind him nodded. "I am. The aetherdrome only allows us so much time away from our work. I had to tell them I had a family funeral to attend."

Kiefer's expression soured even more. "I really don't care for your excuses, Hammad. Do you have the list?"

Hammad nodded, looked around furtively, and handed Kiefer an envelope. As Kiefer opened the envelope and cast his eye down the list of jewellery, money, and other expensive items that the guests on the *Cartouche* had in their luggage, Hammad grinned and pointed at one of the names. "Three of our men are already following this man, his wife, and the other woman who travels with them. They should be in possession of several nice pieces of jewellery before this evening. The rest can be taken by our operative at the hotel after their luggage arrives. I have already sent a copy of this list to our man in Aswan, and I will of course ensure that the customs list is altered so that certain expensive items are never confirmed as having been brought to this country in the first place."

Kiefer nodded impatiently. "Yes, thank you, Hammad. Now, I need one of your men to do something rather special

for me. A certain person travelling with us needs to be...
removed, while we are at the hotel. Can you arrange it?"

Hammad looked at him with an ugly smile. "Of course.
For the usual fee, I will arrange for the Bedouin, Budaiwi,
to be at your disposal." He paused. "But he will not be
allowed near the hotel...for obvious reasons! May I suggest
a trip to Abu Simbel. I have the dates and the tour information; I shall book it for you. Will the rest of your family be
there?"

Kiefer thought quickly and nodded. "Yes. I think it would
be best if all of us go to Abu Simbel. But, if Budaiwi sees to
the matter in hand, it sadly appears that one of us will not be
returning!" He turned his attention back to the list of valu-
ables, a mercenary light glinted in his eye as he noted one or
two pieces of jewellery. "Very nice indeed. Well done,
Hammad. Though you should use some of your share to buy
yourself a fountain pen — this thick pencil is bloody difficult
to read!"

Hammad bowed with a smirk and held out his hand. "As
you say, Excellency. I shall buy one from my share of the
proceeds before I send the rest on to my Amir."

Kiefer glared at him, removed a thick envelope from his
breast pocket, and threw it to the official, who opened it and
checked the contents. He looked at Kiefer with an avaricious
light in his eyes. "Is it all here?"

Kiefer's expression darkened further. "What the hell do
you take me for? Of course it's all there! Bloody ungrateful
—" He took a deep breath and clenched his jaw. "Yes! It's all
there."

Hammad smiled and placed the envelope in his breast
pocket. "It will be put to good use. My Amir will use this to
buy what we need to chase the British and those who
conspire with them out of our lands." A fanatical light
appeared in his bloodshot brown eyes. "We shall burn the

Veiled Protectorate into ashes, enslave their children, and take our pleasure with their women!"

Kiefer grimaced as a strand of drool appeared at the corner of Hammad's mouth. He tucked the list in his breast pocket. "Yes, yes…you do that. And remember, old boy; rape before burning; that's what my dear old papa used to say, and it's a lesson I live by." He clapped the rabid Islamist on the shoulder. "Must go — ruins to see!" He left the distant-eyed fanatic standing by the jetty as he walked past the watching sphinx and entered the First Pylon in search of his family.

○

Luxor
Miss Francesca Barrington's Home for Abandoned Beings
3:20pm

Elliott checked his pocket watch with a sigh and looked at his wife. "I *am* sorry, but we have to go. The airship moves on to Kom Ombo in less than an hour's time, and we must be on board."

Giselle looked up at her husband with a wistful expression. She was sitting in a comfortable and well-stuffed armchair with a small black kitten sleeping belly-up on her lap. "Must we?

Elliott nodded ruefully. "I'm afraid so."

Giselle sighed, then gently picked up the kitten and held her out to Francesca, who smiled and shook her head. "She's taken a shine to you, my dear, and she gets on rather well with your friend's Labrador…keep her and give her a good home." A sharp light entered her eyes. "Mind; if you don't look after her, I *shall* find out!"

Giselle held the kitten to her cheek, her blue eyes glistening. "I wouldn't have it any other way, Francesca."

Francesca sat back. "Good! Now, you need to get back to the airship jetty." She looked at Aquilleia. "I take it the craft will leave from this side of the river?"

Aquilleia nodded as she sipped her tea. "Yes. If we walk back the way we came, it would take far too long." She sighed as she placed her cup on the table. "Perhaps I shouldn't have stayed so long. I need to see if Thorne is all right, and if he managed to bring himself to speak with his brother."

Francesca shot her a sharp glance. "I can't help with the issues your husband is facing, but I *can* help with travelling back to the jetty." She leant across her the arm of her somewhat threadbare but comfortable armchair and tugged the bell pull on the wall. The door was opened almost immediately by the white-gowned safragi who had served them tea earlier. The imposing man stood in the doorway and bowed. "Yes, Madam?"

"Sadek. My friends need to reach the airship jetty on this side of the river as swiftly as possible. What would you suggest?"

The Egyptian butler frowned. "Madame could use the horse and carriage…" He paused. "But if Madame wanted speed, there is Madam's automobile; the Panhard et Levassor M4E."

Francesca hit the arm of her chair, sending a faint plume of fine, dusty sand into the air. "Of course!" She smiled. "It was gifted to me by Émile Levassor himself. I don't use it very often because…well, it brings back memories." She tapped her lip thoughtfully. "Perhaps it was a good thing that Kyriaku had to leave; I can only fit five people in the automobile, and Veronique is large enough to require a seat in her own right." She looked at the butler. "Please make the automobile ready, Sadek. We shall leave as soon as possible."

The servant bowed again. "Of course, Madam."

As he left the room, Giselle finished her tea and raised an

amused eyebrow. "How on earth did you manage to get an automobile down those streets?"

Francesca laughed. "Oh, it wasn't brought in on that side of the house. We brought it in through the northernmost wall. Had to smash a hole in the damn thing — caused the most frightful bloody mess! My dear brother was here during one of his fleeting visits at the time and was quite miffed at the damage to his prized azaleas, I can tell you!"

Elliott caught the allusion. "Your brother?"

She nodded. "Yes. Colonel Barrington. He's the face of the Veiled Protectorate in these parts. Though he lives here, de jure, he's very rarely in residence," She turned as the door opened. "Yes, Sadek?"

The safragi bowed again. "The automobile is ready, Madam, and I have taken the liberty of bringing your driving hat, gloves, and goggles."

Elliott shot to his feet as Francesca stood up. "Marvellous man! Thank you, Sadek." She looked at the others with a smile. "Shall we go?"

○

**The *Cartouche*
Thorne and Aquilleia's Suite
4:15pm**

After a short but hair-raising journey through the winding, narrow streets of Luxor, at the whim of Francesca's heavy-footed use of both the accelerator and brake — with more emphasis on the former than the latter — Elliott, Giselle, Aquilleia, Veronique, and the as yet unnamed kitten arrived at the airship jetty. With a none too quiet sigh of relief, they bade farewell to the formidable Miss Barrington, who waved her gloved hand and sped off in a squeal of tyres, sand, and coarse swearing from the merchants who were lounging by the short pier in the hope of making more sales before the *Cartouche* continued her journey.

They boarded the *Scarab* and sank wearily into the well-upholstered seats as the small, Simulandro-piloted airship moved away from the jetty and prepared to ferry them back to the *Cartouche*, some three hundred and fifty feet above.

Beyond the jetty, amidst the scrum of merchants, dragomen, and beggars, three irritated men, one fingering a small, sharp knife, suddenly appeared in a speeding carriage pulled by a whipped and sweating horse. The merchants scattered as the carriage pulled up almost on the edge of the jetty and the three men tumbled out. They glared at the *Scarab* as she rose from the green waters of the Nile and made her way towards the massive airship above them.

The oldest of the three spat on the jetty then turned to the others. "I will send a message to the Black Eagle informing him that the package was not collected. He will have to pass it to one of our brothers further down the river." The men turned and climbed back into the carriage. The sweating horse was again whipped into movement and the carriage disappeared back into the bustling city.

Having taken several minutes to lure Veronique across the narrow gangplank from the *Scarab* to the safety of the *Cartouche*, Elliott, Giselle, Aquilleia, Veronique, and the rather intrigued kitten finally arrived at the door to Thorne and Aquilleia's suite, Aquilleia gave them an uncertain smile. "I don't think we'll be down for dinner…Thorne is finding this situation very difficult."

Giselle took her friend's hand. "I don't know what happened between them, Aquilleia…it happened after we died, and Elliott won't tell me; he says that it's best for Thorne to explain. But we're here for you both; if you need us, please talk with us."

Aquilleia nodded, but as she reached out to open the door, she felt a deep chill move down her spine. Veronique's leash fell to the floor as she turned to face Elliott and Giselle, silver lights swirling in her wide, lavender eyes. When she spoke, her voice was hollow and strange. "The time has come to tell what you know of that night, Versipellis. Now is the time for things to be held up to the light, cleansed, and made whole." She blinked rapidly as the silver lights dimmed; her eyes rolling back in her head as she slid to the floor. Elliott caught her as she fell and carefully rested her head against his shoulder as Giselle hurriedly pushed the door open for her husband.

Veronique bounded into the suite with a whine and sniffed the air; Thorne was not in the sitting room. As Elliott and Giselle settled Aquilleia on the settee by the balcony door, Veronique snuffled her way into the bathroom. His scent was there, but Thorne was not. She followed the marker into the bedroom, where Thorne lay fast asleep on the bed, an open bottle of whisky in one hand. Veronique pressed her black nose to his face, her jowls wrinkling at the strong smell of whisky on her master's breath. She leapt on the bed and put her muzzle inches from Thorne's face as Elliott appeared in the doorway, looked at his friend and sighed. He walked to the bed, removed the bottle and placed it on the bedside table, next to the empty tumbler and small jug of water.

One green eye opened and looked at him blearily. "Why did it have to be him?" Thorne's voice was hoarse. "Of all the agents the Espion Court have at their disposal, why did he choose to come himself?"

Elliott sat in the chair beside the bed and poured himself a drink. "I think he wants to talk with you, to explain why he made the choice he did—"

Thorne held up a warning hand, purple lights flashing in

his bleary but hard green eyes. "I don't want to hear it, Elliott! Not from you, and certainly not from him!" He groaned and shut his eyes. "I know I must do this. I know that I'm bound to assist in solving the case. But I think it would be best if I only meet with my brother on a professional basis. I will investigate the terrorist outrages, but I will not socialise with him!"

Elliott rubbed his face as he sat back in the chair. "Giselle has asked me about what happened. The...event occurred after she and Aquilleia were murdered. I told her it's best if it comes from you."

Thorne pushed himself into a more upright position and shook his head. "I can't, Elliott. I just can't face talking about..." He closed his eyes as tears fell down his cheeks.

Veronique whined and licked his face. He wrapped his arms around the Labrador and looked at Elliott with a tired expression. "You tell her. You know everything that happened; the case we were investigating at the time — and the outcome. Tell her for me, please, Elliott."

Elliott nodded wearily. He stood up and finished his drink, then walked to the door, taking the bottle of whisky. He looked back at Thorne. "As we arrived, Aquilleia had a vision. She said; *Now is the time for things to be held up to the light, cleansed, and made whole.* She's in the sitting room. You might want to go to her. She's a little shaken, as she always is after a vision."

Thorne stared at him, then hurriedly swung his legs over the edge of the bed and stood; he gripped the chair by the bedside as a wave of dizziness hit him. Veronique sat up with a whine as she watched him sway. Elliott hurried back to his side and gripped his shoulder. "Are you all right?"

Thorne grimaced as he poured water into the tumbler and took a gulp. "I've been better!" He smoothed the front of his rumpled shirt and pulled at his mustard coloured cravat.

Elliott smiled as Thorne licked his hand and ran it over a stubborn cowlick that refused to lie flat. "Will I do?"

Elliott nodded. He gestured to the door. "After you."

Thorne walked into the sitting room where Aquilleia sat by the balcony, a small glass of red wine in one hand and a biscuit in the other. As Thorne knelt by his wife's side, Giselle looked at him with an apologetic smile. "I thought a little something to help settle her was a good idea." She looked at Elliott and spoke in a low voice. "Perhaps we should leave."

Elliott looked at Thorne and Aquilleia and nodded. They turned and left the suite, closing the door quietly behind them as Veronique curled up by Thorne's feet and settled her muzzle between her jet-black paws; her watchful brown eyes fixed on her master and mistress.

In the sumptuously carpeted corridor, Giselle turned to Elliott with a worried look. "Will Thorne be all right?"

"I think so. He's finished most of a bottle of whisky, but he's drunk a damn sight more than that in one sitting and been perfectly fine. It's nothing a good night's sleep won't cure."

Giselle arched an eyebrow. "But what of the issue with Darling? I doubt that will be remedied by a good night's sleep!"

"I agree...that particular problem will take more effort to deal with!" He paused. "Thorne gave me his permission to explain why he and Darling are estranged."

Giselle stilled; her blue eyes wide. "I think we should go somewhere more private for such a conversation."

Elliott nodded. "I agree."

Giselle took his arm as they made their way back to their suite. Giselle sat by the balcony door and carefully placed the reticule, complete with sleepy kitten, on the seat next to her.

She arranged her skirts and looked expectantly at her husband.

Elliott gazed out of the window, but his vision was turned inwards, to the past. "You know of our investigation of Filicidae in Astraea…what it did before it was caught." At Giselle's nod, he continued. "When Filicidae first appeared and began its reign of terror against children, it had many supporters. Men and women who were both high and low-born, all connected by a desire to gain power and inflict pain. After Filicidae was captured and destroyed by the Unmaking — or rather, what we thought had been the Unmaking — we were ordered to find all its supporters and bring them to the King's Court; the Espion Court, for punishment. They had to face the law of the land and be tried for their collaboration with Filicidae, regardless of who they were, how highly placed they were…or if they were friends — or family."

Giselle looked at him in horror. "You don't mean…"

Elliott sighed and rubbed his eyes. "Thorne and Darling's father was one of Filicidae's supporters. Thorne and I went to his house to arrest him; Thorne insisted on seeing that justice, without fear or favour, was done. But when we arrived, his father was dead in the bathroom and Darling was sitting next to him. He'd offered him what the English refer to as the 'gentleman's way out', and their father had taken it. Thorne never forgave Darling for preventing their father from facing justice along with the others."

Giselle's blue eyes were huge in her deathly pale face. "But Filicidae fed on pain. Was their father…" She bit back a sob. "I can't even say it!"

Elliott's eyes filled with green lights. "Was he a sadist, like the others who followed Filicidae? Yes, I am afraid he was. Did he harm Thorne and Darling when they were children? Yes, he did. It stopped when they became old enough to protect themselves and their mother and could fight back with their own abilities. She died in strange circumstances shortly after Filicidae began its reign of terror in Astraea. Thorne believed that she too was a victim. An offering from a willing follower — a tribute of blood!"

Giselle reached towards her reticule, gently nudged the kitten out of the way, pulled out a lace handkerchief and patted her eyes. "How could Darling have done such a thing? How could he allow their father to escape justice for what he did?"

Elliott took the handkerchief from her trembling hand and gently dabbed the tears from her cheeks. "I truly don't know…Thorne swore never to speak to him again, so I've never found out."

Giselle swallowed. "They need to talk."

Elliott tucked the handkerchief in the reticule and kissed her forehead. "As you say. We can hope this adventure will lead to a reconciliation between brothers. If not, it may well end in a war the like of which even the ancient world has never seen! And now, my darling, I suggest a bath and brush-up, then a much-needed cocktail…or four!"

○

The *Cartouche*
5:15pm

The door to one of the many private suites opened, and a man, furtive yet confidant, stepped into the silent keel corridor. Pausing to make sure that he was alone, he made his way to a small room at the far end of the richly carpeted hallway. He looked up and down again before knocking a strange tattoo on the carved wooden door. The door swung open almost immediately. Jane smiled at the man and held out a glass of wine. "Well, my love?" André smiled in return, accepted the glass, and entered, closing and locking the door behind him.

As Jane turned to embrace him, the little bell on the wall behind her suddenly rang. Jane glared at it; glowing white lights appearing in her eyes as she hissed. "That bloody woman!" She turned an arch look on her lover as she took back the glass of wine and sipped it, running a slim finger along his black silk cummerbund. "You surely know that I love you, my darling André, because I allow myself to be debased enough to travel in the servants' quarters, and be on call to that mewling cretin you married!" The bell rang again. Jane swore and drained the contents of the glass, an ugly light in her eyes. "I yearn for the moment her heart's blood is spilt!"

André's smile widened, his white teeth flashing in the golden gaslight. "Patience, Jane, patience. They fitted the bell in this room especially for you; as Evelyn's companion, you must be at her beck and call...for a little while longer, at least." He laughed as Jane tried to pull away. "You know I only have eyes for you, my darling. Go and see what she wants...it probably has something to do with an outfit for dinner." He retrieved his glass, refilled it, and took a sip, a thoughtful look on his handsome face. "May I suggest nothing too memorable? If Julius kills her *after* she's changed, she'll be found in that gown, and we don't want people to remember her *too* much."

Jane tossed her head with a dismissive sniff. As she walked past him, André caught her wrist and pressed a kiss against her palm. "Hurry back, my love. Julius needs to carry out his duties in privacy, and we haven't much time before the cocktail hour. I'll be waiting."

Jane left the room, a faint smile on her full lips as she stalked down the hallway towards the cabin André shared with his unsuspecting bride. Jane's smile widened, becoming crueller as she approached the door that led to her lover's wife. There were many things of which Evelyn was unaware. They would keep it that way until the right moment, after which it would be too late for little Miss Naïf to escape their clutches. She took a deep breath, and calmed her temper before she tapped on the door with her sharp fingernails and entered.

Evelyn was sitting by the door leading to the little balcony, which now overlooked the magnificent temple complex of Kom Ombo. She looked up as Jane entered. "Jane, I would like to bathe and change for dinner. Will you lay out an outfit and run a bath for me, please?"

Jane nodded brusquely and entered the small bathroom that Evelyn and André shared. She placed the rubber plug in the bath and turned on the ornate tap, before turning to regard the bottles that sat next to the tub.

Evelyn called from the other room, "Not the lavender tonight, Jane…the rose, I think."

A spiteful look appeared on Jane's face. With a mulish set to her jaw, she took the bottle of lavender bath salts and poured most of it into the bath with a smirk before calling out. "I'm sorry, Madame; I have already used the lavender. Shall I empty the bath and begin again?"

In the sitting room, Evelyn cast a sharp look at the bathroom door; there was something about Jane that she simply did not like. She sighed; she wished she had been able to keep her former maid, but her husband's family had insisted on employing a companion instead; perhaps that was something she could bring to André's attention, once they returned home from Egypt.

She stood, walked to the door, and regarded Jane, who was standing by the bath reading the label on the bottle of *Madame Rosemerta's Attar Bath Scent*. "That will be fine, thank you, Jane. Please lay out my blue velvet gown for this evening, and then you may return to your room. I shall call you when I need you to help me dress."

Jane bobbed a curtsy that was barely a curtsy at all and walked past her with a pertness that made Evelyn's usually nonexistent temper flare. "That will do, Jane! I have had quite enough of your impertinence. After we arrive at the hotel, you will leave my employ. I shall seek a temporary maid from the staff there. Lay out my gown, return to your room, and stay there until I send for you."

Jane's jaw dropped. Evelyn swept past her into the bathroom, slammed the door and pressed her forehead against the cold glass of the mirror. She looked at her reflection with a rueful expression; this could well cause some problems with her husband's family!

On the other side of the door, Jane stood and seethed; who the hell did that simpering bitch think she was? She gritted her teeth until they squeaked as she fought to suppress her anger; her eyes filling with a blinding white light. She took a deep breath and closed her eyes. After a few moments, she opened them and smiled an ugly, twisted smile; if Evelyn thought she could remove her from André's life and from the family, not only was she very much mistaken, but given the lots that had been drawn earlier, she was in for the worst evening of her sheltered, pampered life!

Jane's mind turned to the last order Evelyn had issued. The blue velvet gown? She didn't think so! Jane entered one of the two tiny bedrooms that led off the sitting room; it contained a double bed, a few other pieces of furniture, and several items that were all feminine in nature; nothing to suggest a man had ever been in the room. Jane smirked; it was nice to see that André was keeping his promise to sleep in a separate room when he was forced to spend time with his wife.

Jane opened the wardrobe and scanned its contents

before removing the dullest, darkest, most unbecoming evening gown from Evelyn's trousseau, before dropping it in a dishevelled mess on the neatly made bed. She left the suite, slamming the door behind her with force. André would be amused to hear what his dear wife thought she had a right to do to *her*, his true love! As she made her way back to her room, Jane paused; perhaps telling André what had happened would be a mistake. It would be better heard in the morning, when it would not interrupt their evening plans. Jane's lips curled; if Julius was already on his way to see to his familial duty, Evelyn would die before she had a chance to be humiliated in that hideous gown…what a shame!

Back in the suite, Evelyn opened the door and peeked around it. She walked into her bedroom, looked at the dishevelled heap of pewter grey taffeta on the bed and silently rehung it in her wardrobe. She walked back into the sitting room, sat on one of the upright chairs, and gazed at the far wall in silence. She shook her head and reached for the bell pull; her desire for cocktails and dinner had vanished.

As she waited for the steward, Evelyn lent back in her chair, rested her chin in her hand, and faced the worrying thought she had been trying to avoid for the last few days; she had been a married woman for nearly a week, and André still hadn't made any demands upon, or even polite requests about, her wifely duties. A sudden, unpleasant thought entered her mind; was André perhaps…was there someone else? She frowned; it seemed unlikely…he spent nearly all his time at work, and in the evenings went directly to his mother's house before returning home quite late. Indeed, since their marriage he seemed to spend more time than ever in the company of his mother and his older brother, Kiefer. She shivered and rubbed her arms; no matter how many times she reminded herself of her dear father's maxim that she should love her fellow man without question, she simply couldn't stand being in the same room as her brother-in-law. Something about him made her skin crawl...especially the way he turned his eyes on her when André wasn't looking.

Evelyn's mind turned suddenly to the man she had danced with in Venice; the man with the golden eyes. She shivered again...and for entirely different reasons. She *knew* him; he was both a stranger, and yet so familiar. Her eyes suddenly widened — she *had* seen him before! Many years earlier, at her mother's funeral. She had run from the line of mourners outside the church, hidden herself in the bell tower and wept, feeling as though her heart would break for the loss of her gentle, loving mother. As she wept in the still, dusty room, a dark figure had approached her. She'd thought that her father had come for her, but instead she saw him; the man with golden eyes. He'd knelt before her and whispered a name...one she had never heard before, but which she knew; *Calliandra*. He'd taken her hand and told her that everything would be all right — different, strange, but that she was safe and all would be well.

Her father's voice coming from the stairwell had startled them both, and the man had disappeared, seeming to dissolve into the wall itself. Her father had appeared in the doorway, looked at her with gentle, sad eyes. He'd taken her by the hand and gently led her out of the tower. But instead of taking her back to the church, he had ordered their carriage to take her home.

Evelyn's aunt, a moral shrew who used the shield of scripture to denounce those she disapproved of, had taken being abandoned in the churchyard with her sister-in-law's coffin badly, and had been vociferous about Evelyn's perceived lack of breeding and manners in running away; insisting that a spell in a nunnery would be the making of the girl — or the breaking, as she personally hoped. When

Evelyn's father had soundly rejected her advice, the sour old zealot had thinned her already narrow lips into nonexistence and decided to deal with her niece in her own good time. Over the next few years, she had tried repeatedly to crush Evelyn's spirit, and had singularly failed on every occasion. Not least because Evelyn's father had dedicated himself to the game of foiling his sister's rancorous malice towards his beloved daughter with his own form of gentle derision that had matched his sister's spite and enraged her further. The game between them only ending when his sister had died after being struck by lightning. The irony of such a death had not been lost on the two surviving members of the family.

Evelyn pursed her lips as she rifled through her memories. Was that the only time she had seen the man with the golden eyes? She thought hard. There had been a distant figure watching her at her debutante ball...he'd not requested a dance, but had instead simply watched her from afar.

She wandered to the French door leading onto her balcony and opened it. The chill night air swept around her and left her shivering. She hurried back to her wardrobe, pulled out her warmest dressing gown and wrapped herself in the patchworked folds; it had belonged to her father, and it reassured her to smell the familiar scent of his pipe tobacco on the thick material.

Evelyn walked onto the balcony, sat in the little wicker chair, and stared at the incredible view; far below her, the Temple of Kom Ombo shone in the purple and orange dusk. Rays of golden light from the setting sun causing the stone to glow with a lustre that touched the soul...but Evelyn's eyes were blind to its beauty. Her mind had turned inward to ponder the unfortunate possibility that she had made a terrible error of judgement in marrying into the Devereaux family.

As she sat, her mind dabbling in waters she was sure her father would consider with both horror and gentle reproach, she was unaware of a shadowy figure creeping towards her from the other side of the balcony.

Clad in black with a jewelled blade gripped firmly between his teeth like a jaunty pirate, his extreme distaste and embarrassment visible even through the black domino mask that covered half of his face, Julius van Sloane was also considering whether he had made a mistake in marrying into the Devereaux family; the money was marvellous, the social position irreproachable, and the ability to repel death beyond belief…however, the constant stream of murders required to keep the family in body parts for resurrection purposes could be rather depressing. He willed his lips not to come into contact with the hideously sharp blade as he lifted himself to the edge of Evelyn's balcony…and then froze as he found himself looking straight into her face.

But Evelyn's eyes were closed — Julius grinned around the blade; this might turn out to be easier than he thought! As he began to pull himself over the rail, he stopped dead at a sudden knocking sound from the sitting room beyond. He hurriedly lowered himself back down as Evelyn's eyes opened. She got up and walked into the suite, pulling the door to the balcony shut behind her as Julius berated himself for not moving faster.

Evelyn opened the suite door to find the airship's chief Simulandro steward, Mr Phillips, who apologised in his wheezing voice for the time it had taken to respond to her bell. Evelyn smiled. "Oh, that's quite all right, Mr Phillips. I'm afraid I have the beginnings of a migraine. Would you please send my apologies to the captain and ask him to excuse me from his table this evening? After that, would you bring me a simple supper tray, please?"

Mr Phillips nodded. "Of course, Madam. Is everything acceptable with your suite?"

"It's absolutely lovely, thank you."

As the steward bowed, and left, Julius pulled himself back over the balustrade with a pained groan and removed the blade from his teeth; of all the ridiculous ways to kill someone! The next time the family wanted a killing done, unless it was a simple poisoning, he would stand back and allow one of the others to claim the trophy. It was high time their nonsensical method of choosing the slayer was replaced with the simple question, 'which one of you would like to kill the next victim?' Kiefer was far more capable of the grand physical performance required to climb like a Sherpa around the sides of an airship tethered three hundred and fifty feet above the Nile, stab a virgin in the heart, and empty the blood into a sacred vial—

He whipped round sharply, his eyes darting from side to side; he could have sworn he'd heard...but no, there was nothing there. He swore under his breath; he was obviously imagining things. The quicker this was dealt with, the quicker their Patriarch would be returned to them — which meant a return to far more enjoyable duties, and a welcome decrease in the amount of strain he had been living under for the last year. Having to find, meet, entertain, and cultivate false friendships with the necessary number of suitable victims required for the resurrection had caused him a great deal of personal stress...asking him to actually kill one after all the hard work and effort he had already put in was quite simply beyond the pale! He peeked round the curtain; Evelyn was alone and standing by one of the settees in the private sitting room. Julius shook his head; a shame, really, such a pretty girl, and good-humoured, too...but they needed blood from a virgin's heart, so blood from a virgin's heart was what they would get.

He realised that Evelyn was walking across the sitting room. He moved to the side of the French door and waited… and waited. He peeped again; Evelyn was nowhere to be seen. He hissed an exasperated expletive; this was rapidly becoming a farce!

Julius carefully opened the French door and crept into the sitting room where he heard the sound of running water coming from the bathroom. Wonderful! Now she was taking a bath! He swore under his breath and stalked back to the balcony, taking great care not to slam the door behind him. He stood by the wicker chair Evelyn had been sitting in, folded his arms across his chest and angrily tapped his foot against the dark-stained deck; if, as it appeared, he would be spending most of the night there, he would simply have to make himself comfortable until the blasted girl reappeared. He threw himself sulkily into the little wicker chair Evelyn had recently vacated and used the jewelled blade to clean his nails as he went over his plans for the evening; he had to kill his sister-in-law, collect a few drops of her heart's blood, set the scene for a staged suicide, return to his own suite, bathe, and be ready for the cocktail hour that started at seven o'clock. He removed his pocket watch, checked the time, and scowled; it was nearly six o'clock already…if he adhered to the plan, he would probably miss the cocktail hour; damn! He sat forward in the chair and pondered how he could shave a few minutes off the timeline; perhaps, instead of setting up a suicide scene, he could simply throw Evelyn off the airship? Julius stood and leant over the edge of the rail, mulling over the idea as he gazed at the distant blue ribbon of the Nile looping sinuously through the ruins of Kom Ombo beneath him; yes, it might just work! Once he'd taken what he needed from Evelyn, he could simply throw her over the side of the craft and into the Nile; the followers of Sebek would hopefully accept his offering and clear up any possibility of the authorities discovering any evidence of stab wounds. If the beasts of Kom Ombo were particularly hungry that evening, it might even do away with the possibility of the discovery of her body and a formal identification entirely.

Julius moved away from the rail and sat back in the wicker chair with a complacent smile; yes…it had definite possibilities. As he sat in smug contemplation of his plans, Julius heard the sound again; a sort of…slithering was coming from the other side of the rail. He frowned, glanced at the empty sitting room behind him, then got up and walked to the edge. Nothing there. He smoothed his mask with a scowl and turned away. But as he did, a powerful hand appeared from the other side of the balcony, grasped the astounded man by the front of his collar, and dragged him over the rail. The jewelled blade fell from his nerveless fingers and clattered across the deck as the golden eyes of Gabriel Masquelyne met those of the terrified Julius. Masquelyne held Julius' wild-eyed gaze, allowing his rage to pour into the terrified man's eyes, before with a contemptuous expression, he dropped Julius van Sloane to his death.

Several yards away, there was a sudden strangled expletive as one of the airship travellers, enjoying a pre-cocktail hour drink on their balcony, witnessed the defenestration of the screaming Julius. They shot out of their steamer chair and gripped the rail as the shrieking man plummeted towards the winding, teal-coloured river below. The shocked traveller, mesmerised by the screaming, windmilling figure, gazed in open-mouthed silence as Julius' rapid vertical journey came to a sudden halt on the distant surface of the Nile. They watched, almost hypnotised, as, visible even from the *Cartouche*, long, slender shapes began to enter the river, each moving sinuously towards the body. There was a brief moment of stillness in the water, followed by a sudden frenzied disturbance, then a pinprick of blood bloomed in the water below, as the denizens of the Temple of Kom Ombo settled in for their supper.

The stunned passenger tore their eyes from the distant, disturbing scene and looked back towards the balcony, as Masquelyne, dispassionately watched the death of Julius, then stepped backwards, seeming to dissolve into the side of the airship.

The shocked guest hurriedly re-entered their cabin, locked the door and drew the curtains. Surely, they couldn't have seen...it was unreal — incredible! But then, they had seen things which had made people threaten them with a permanent address in Bedlam. Turning to the drinks cabinet, they poured a generous double, paused, then made it a treble. Knocking the drink back, they poured another, sat in the little armchair by the drawn curtains and thought about what they had witnessed; a dark figure, clinging like a limpet to the outside of an airship hovering hundreds of feet above the ground, lifting a man with one hand and dropping him over the side before dissolving into the wall like a — well, it wasn't like anything they had ever seen in their life! they took another gulp of their drink and rested the glass against their cheek; they'd recognised the victim, even at that distance and with that ridiculous mask, as Julius van Sloane...which raised some interesting possibilities.

A faint smile appeared on their lips as they sat back, took a more leisurely sip of their drink, and considered the possibility that more than one predator was hunting members of the Devereaux clan.

As they dwelt on the scene they had just witnessed, a thought presented itself. their faint smile grew into a vicious grin as a plan formed in their mind; as Julius had landed for his unexpected supper date at the Temple, the waters of the Nile had turned red; what a delicious idea!

Crocodile Head

PART II

**The *Cartouche*
Thorne and Aquilleia's suite
5:45pm**

Aquilleia pushed the last pin into her mass of blue-black hair and took a step back from the bathroom mirror to survey her work; yes, that would do nicely! She turned and froze as a chill began at the base of her spine and worked its way up to the nape of her slender nec. Sitting on the edge of the bath, she shivered as a rushing sound filled her ears. Several monotone images appeared in her mind's eye…each image lasting no longer than a second; a balcony, a woman's back, a black-clad figure, a sudden flash of water…then nothing.

As the images faded, Aquilleia pressed a hand to her temple; someone had disappeared from her sight — someone had *died* — but a remnant was still there; a strange, distant murmur on the edge of her hearing that slowly faded into silence. She took a deep breath; she had heard a similar sound before…coming from Marguerite Devereaux's reticule.

Turning away from the mirror, she hurried from the bedroom and entered the small sitting room where Thorne stood before the door to their balcony, a glass of red wine in his hand. He turned as she approached him and gave her a slightly self-conscious smile. "I'm afraid I don't feel much like dining with the others tonight, my love. Would you mind if we dined here instead?" Aquilleia looked at her husband; the urgency to convey the images from her vision disappeared as she reached out and gently stroked his face. "Of course not. I'll call for the steward." She walked to the bell pull and gave it a tug as Thorne poured another glass of wine and handed it to her. She smiled as she met her husband's eyes and took a sip of the light red wine; what she had seen in her vision could wait.

○

Saturday 23rd
The *Cartouche*
Margaux and Julius' suite
2:30am

Margaux woke with a start. She sat up in her silken, pillow-laden bed, turned up the gas lamp on her bedside table, and looked around the room; there was still no sign of Julius. She checked the gold travel clock next to the lamp, plumped up her pillows, settled herself back into her down-filled nest, and bit her lip worriedly; it didn't take that long to kill an offering— and she should know, having dispatched many over the last five thousand years of her life.

She thought back to the events of the previous evening; the rest of the family had arrived in the salon for cocktails to find neither Evelyn nor Julius present, and there had been smug smiles all round at the belief in a job well done. But when Julius hadn't appeared with the vial required for the ritual, the family had become irritated. As André and Jane were busy elsewhere, Kiefer had gone to his brother and sister-in-law's suite to check on Evelyn, but his repeated knocking roused no response. He had been preparing to force the door, when the sudden appearance of Rex Nympton in the corridor had foiled his attempts, so, he'd returned to the dining room and explained his thoughts; Evelyn hadn't answered him, so Julius must have succeeded. Everyone knew what Julius was like; not too keen on the bloodier side of the family's work, but prepared to fulfil his side of the bargain in exchange for the gifts the family would bestow. Kiefer had taken a glass of Champagne from a passing Simulandro maid and laughed as he issued his verdict; Julius would be found in a stupor somewhere in the morning — hopefully alone, and with the vial of Evelyn's blood ready for the ritual.

Margaux's eyes narrowed as she recalled her mother's strong language about her husband's occasional disappearances during the years of their marriage. She chewed her lip; he had better not be up to his old tricks! He knew that if any attempt to return to his old ways occurred, she would leave him. And bearing in mind what he knew about the family, his survival quotient without her would be less than that of a dandelion clock in a hurricane!

She reached for the ornate little glass next to her diary. If Julius *had* failed in his attempt on Evelyn, why hadn't he simply returned to complain, as he usually did when things went badly? He nearly always managed to see things through on the second or third try. She took a sip of her Sazerac and settled back on her pillows; either way, her mother and father would not be happy!

○

The *Cartouche*
Marguerite and Vincenzo's Suite
8:30am

Marguerite placed her empty teacup on back on its saucer, looked pointedly at the clock above the table and tapped her fingers in an irritated fashion on the table. "If we wait any longer for Julius and Margaux, our breakfast will be cold." She sat back with a sigh as André refilled her cup. "I had hoped they would be here with the vial by now." She looked at André with a smile. "With Evelyn dead, we can begin the ritual to resurrect your father as soon as we arrive at the hotel."

Camillia sat at the table and sipped her tea. "Don't forget, Grandmama…I get her jewels!"

"Ahem, whose jewels?"

Camillia's cup of tea fell from her suddenly nerveless fingers and smashed on the polished wooden floor as she stared in shock at Evelyn who looked back at her from the doorway with a quizzical expression. "Whose jewels, Camillia?"

André leapt to his feet and stared at Evelyn with an equally stunned expression, which was swiftly replaced with a look of blasé good humour. "Our dear grandmama's jewels. Camillia has always loved the family diamonds." He paused. "Did you…did you have a good night, my darling?"

Evelyn nodded. "Yes, I did. I had the beginnings of a migraine, so I decided to have a light supper and retire to bed with a sleeping powder." She looked at her husband with an expression he couldn't quite decipher. "You didn't return to our suite…did you have a good rest, André?"

Her husband blinked. "Uh, yes. I…that is, Kiefer and I

were playing cards. We missed dinner, and by the time we were done, I realised it was far too late to return to our suite, so I slept in Kiefer's room…I didn't want to wake you, my darling."

Kiefer rolled his eyes at his mother. They all knew exactly where André had spent the night!

Evelyn gave her husband a steady look. "You should know that I've given Jane notice. When we return home, I shall write to my previous maid, Barber, and ask her to return to my service."

André blinked. Jane had said nothing to him of an argument with Evelyn; indeed, after she had returned to her room, they hadn't done much talking at all. But this firmness was a side of his wife which he hadn't seen before; it was unexpected…and quite unwelcome. His eyes narrowed. "May I ask why?"

Evelyn looked at him calmly. "Pertness, insubordination, recalcitrance, and conceit."

André's face darkened at the exceptionally well-rounded denouncement of Jane's finer qualities. He ignored Kiefer's faint snort of laughter and looked at Evelyn, who looked back at him silently, her grey eyes unwavering in their contemplation of his set face.

As André opened his mouth to issue a rebuke, his mother spoke. "Of course, my dear. If Jane is guilty of such behaviour, one simply cannot accept such an abuse of her position. I'm sure Jane will make a perfectly good companion, once she has accepted the rule of law in the family home…and her place in its hierarchy. We shall tell the hotel to furnish you with a companion of sorts while we are there, and see about reuniting you with your maid — Barber, I believe you said — when we return to England." Marguerite settled back in her chair with a bright smile. "Now, to the day ahead. Kiefer has had a marvellous idea! He suggested going on a trip to the Temple of Abu Simbel. It was discovered by the Italian strongman, Giovanni Battista Belzoni, and is said to be one of the greatest archaeological discoveries in Italy's history. Would you like to accompany us?"

Evelyn nodded. "That sounds lovely. I would be delighted."

Marguerite beamed at her unsuspecting daughter-in-law and sipped her tea. "Wonderful! The *Scarab* leaves here at eleven thirty. Now, my dear, head back to your suite and make ready. We'll meet you by the gangplank at, oh…shall we say a quarter past eleven? Have you had breakfast?"

Evelyn smiled. "Yes, I have. A quarter past eleven sounds fine. I'll see you by the gangplank." She nodded at the family, her gaze holding André's, before she turned and left.

As the door closed behind her, André exploded from his chair, his eyes glowing a brilliant, blinding white. "That jumped-up little bitch! How dare she speak of Jane like that? I'll rip her heart out!"

Marguerite calmly placed her cup on its saucer, stood, walked towards her son, and slapped him across the face. The sound echoed around the breakfast room with shocking violence; André nearly folded in half as his mother's immortal strength forced him to his knees.

Marguerite bent, gripped her son's chin, and forced his head up, the glowing whiteness in his eyes matched by her own. "We need her heart to resurrect your father, you idiotic brat! I've always had my reservations about Jane playing Evelyn's companion…she completely lacks the necessary humility to be a domestic." She released her son and returned to her chair. "Which is one of the many reasons why you married her four thousand years ago, and why, as a wife bound by blood, she fits in so well with the rest of us. Now, Julius has obviously failed and we need to find him. Send Heathers and Sedgewyck — they can spend this morning searching the *Cartouche*." She sighed and hit the arm of her chair. "He has to be *somewhere* aboard."

As she took another sip of her tea. Kiefer saw his chance. "I have an idea, Mother." As Marguerite turned to look at him, Kiefer settled himself into his chair and wondered just how much to tell them about his meeting with Hammad; perhaps a little information and a few small lies might be enough to season the pot...but not *too* much! He cleared his throat. "Before we left Thebes, I had a meeting with Hammad about the list for this trip. There are one or two guests who are worth our while; the Caines and the Thornes. They're travelling with quite a large collection of jewellery and cash. Hammad had already set his men on their trail. However, I received a telegram from him last night, informing me that his men in Thebes missed them, so I had a word about util-ising Budaiwi to gather that particular package at Abu Simbel. I thought that perhaps we could use his presence to cover an 'accident' with dear Evelyn. So many occur in the wilds of North Africa; Bedouin tribesmen can become quite inflamed at the sight of a pale-skinned Englishwoman. My suggestion is that, after they have robbed and killed the Caines and Thornes, we can kill Evelyn and blame them. If we say that we were bothered by the Bedouin while we were there, the authorities won't pay much attention to anyone or anything else. They'll take our word that Evelyn must have been killed by wandering tribesmen — especially as there *will* be Bedouin in the vicinity. What do you think?"

Marguerite looked at her son silently, before her full lips curved into a wide smile. "Superb! Yes...a superb idea, Kiefer. As we still haven't found Julius, I think gathering this partic-ular offering is now in your hands. I'll leave the manner of her death to you...just make sure you get that vial."

Kiefer grinned; he hadn't informed his mother of his little discussion with Hammad about Budaiwi carrying out the actual deed…what she didn't know about his plans wouldn't hurt him. But one way or another, Evelyn would die that day.

As Kiefer congratulated himself, on a job well done, Marguerite turned to André. "After you have finished your breakfast, return to your suite. You will need to change before we descend for the morning's entertainment."

Her youngest son nodded sulkily as the rest of the family tucked into their breakfast; their expressions showing every emotion from pleasure to sheer vicious enjoyment at the thought of the sacrifice to come at Abu Simbel…all save one. Linden sat and frowned at his coffee cup in silence as his family made their plans for the rest of the morning.

○

The Abu Simbel Jetty
11:30am

In the painfully bright mid-morning light, the small airship *Scarab* separated from the *Cartouche* and descended into the glassy green waters of the Nile. As she came to a graceful halt by the large stone jetty, the Simulandro staff lowered the gangplank and tied the airship firmly to her moorings as the milling guests were marshalled for their trip to the Temple of Abu Simbel.

Elliott, Giselle, and the entirety of the Devereaux family made their way down the jetty, again running the familiar gauntlet of sellers, donkey-wranglers, and ragged children. Marguerite smoothed their passage by gesturing to Vincenzo, who pulled a flat leather purse from his breast pocket and handed out coins; several piastre to the smallest children and a pound each to the adults.

As they walked along the short path to the temple, Giselle was uncharacteristically quiet. Elliott's explanation for the rift between Thorne and his brother had affected her deeply; the harm Filicidae had caused continued to poison lives even after its Unmaking.

They had called upon Thorne and Aquilleia that morning, to see if they would be interested in the jaunt to the temple. The door to their suite had been opened by a tired-looking Aquilleia who had politely rejected their offer. Even Veronique had shown no interest in leaving Thorne's side. So, Elliott and Giselle, accompanied by the small kitten they had yet to name, had decided to go on the trip alone.

Several yards behind them, Evelyn and André walked side by side with Marguerite and Vincenzo, while Jane scowled from the back of the group, her sharp eyes spitting venom at Evelyn.

As they walked, Kiefer slowed until he was a fair way behind his family, then stopped altogether by a boulder a little off the well-trodden path. A short, dark-haired man wearing the dusty garb of a Bedouin emerged from behind it and grinned at Kiefer, his broad smile exposing his lack of front teeth.

Kiefer nodded to him. "Budaiwi, I have two propositions for you that are well within your abilities." He pointed at his family. "Do you see the young woman in blue?"

Budaiwi turned and saw Evelyn wandering alongside her husband; her pale-blue frock and matching parasol glowing against the golden stone of the temple. He nodded as Kiefer continued. "Take this blade and this vial; I want you to stab her in the heart and catch some of her heart's blood in the container. The blood is very important, do you understand?"

The small man nodded again as Kiefer handed him a small black crystal vial, and a viciously sharp but unusually thin knife with a jewelled hilt...the twin to the blade Julius had failed to use on Evelyn. The multi-faceted surface of the bottle glittered in the sunshine as the Bedouin took both items and tucked them within his garments. He then held out a grubby paw with an expectant expression.

Kiefer scowled, withdrew a small pouch, and threw it at him. Budaiwi caught it and poured the contents into his dirty hand; three small but brilliant diamonds sparkled in the sunlight. He looked at Kiefer and grinned, then pointed at Evelyn. "You want her body found, or not?"

Kiefer shrugged. "I personally don't care. You can do whatever you choose with her remains." His eyes narrowed. "However, you must return the vial to me before we board the airship at two o'clock. I'll make sure that she's in the Chapel of Thoth, alone, at midday; I want you there at that time and no later...do you understand?" Budaiwi nodded. "Good. That will give you two hours to do whatever it is you're thinking of. We'll go directly to the Chapel now, and I'll make sure she's left there, in time for your arrival. Now, the second proposition; three of our men missed a package in Luxor...I want you to collect it." He gestured to Elliott and Giselle who were walking hand in hand down the path. "The couple several yards ahead of my family are the target. Kill them, take their possessions, and leave their bodies for the dogs. It doesn't matter if you kill them before the girl...my family are more than aware of our business arrangements, and any mess will be ignored. The payment you've just received will be more than adequate to cover your fee." He walked past Budaiwi without waiting for a response, an ugly smirk on his face as he strode along the dusty track; his mother would undoubtedly disapprove of his methods, but surely now she understood the need for rapid results? Hiring someone to kill an offering was not what the family usually did, but sometimes it was necessary to get the job done with a minimal amount of fuss...and, more importantly, a minimal amount of damage to a good linen suit! Why she'd insisted on Julius carrying out the sacrifice was beyond him when it had been obvious for several centuries that Julius couldn't be trusted to find his backside with both hands, a fully illustrated map, and diagrams!

Kiefer's grin became almost feral; when his dear brother-in-law finally returned from the bed of whoever had taken him in, he would take great delight in informing Margaux that they would be replacing Julius with a far more useful addition to the clan — possibly a pet ferret! It would serve her right for daring to reject his choice of husband for her.

Kiefer took a deep breath as he headed towards the temple; it was time to bring Father back, and no one would be allowed to prevent that — certainly not a boulevardier with delusions of adequacy, and much less the naïf, whey-faced brood-mare André had married to secure her virginity and fortune. Kiefer rubbed his hands as he thought of the sizeable sum Evelyn had inherited upon the death of her father; a handsome addition of extra capital would be of great benefit to their coffers.

As Kiefer disappeared down the path, Budaiwi slapped his hand against the boulder. Two men, similar in appearance and size to Budaiwi, stepped out and stood with him as Kiefer reached his niece's side. Budaiwi gave the two men an ugly smile and spoke in rapid Arabic. "He wants us to steal from the couple at the front of the group, kill them, then kill the woman in blue. He has given us two hours, and he doesn't care what we do with her body!"

The younger of the two grinned. "Two hours is plenty of time!"

The three men sauntered after the unassuming travellers — unaware of a strange, shadowy outline moving under the ground behind them, a shadow that followed them down the path, and towards the distant temple.

○

Abu Simbel
11:50am

Elliott and Giselle approached the Temple of Abu Simbel and stopped in wonderment at the magnificent scene before them; the dry, desert air was heavy with the calls of the blue-cheeked bee-eaters that darted around the four Colossi of Ramesses II; the massive figures continuing their millennia-long watch by the doorway to the Large Pillared Hall. The golden stone glowing with almost painful intensity in the vibrant sunshine as the travellers from the *Cartouche* approached the temple built to honour the long-dead Pharaoh.

As Elliott and Giselle stood in awed contemplation, the Devereaux family overtook them and walked past without any acknowledgment. Elliott looked at them, his dark eyebrows knitted. "They appear to be one short. Where's the delightful Julius?"

Giselle frowned. "I don't recall seeing him at dinner yesterday evening." She paused. "It's rather difficult for a gentleman to simply disappear…especially from an airship. It's not as though he could just walk off. I wonder where he is?" She tucked her arm into her husband's and watched the Devereaux family wander past the temple's ornate façade, towards the Chapel of Thoth.

As the family followed Marguerite into the smaller temple, Evelyn caught her breath at the first sight of the colossi of Ramesses II. She clutched her husband's arm and made an expansive gesture with her blue parasol. "Oh, André! It's as beautiful as I'd imagined…no, more so!" She turned to her husband, her grey eyes bright. "Can we enter the temple?"

Kiefer darted a sharp look at his brother, then relaxed as André shook his head. "Not yet. I suggest we start over there, at the Chapel of Thoth, and then continue to the larger temple." He took her arm and guided her past the colossi, steering her to the doorway that lay on the far side of the temple's watchful guardians.

As the family disappeared through the dark doorway, Elliott glanced at his wife. "Giselle, you're very quiet...are you all right?"

She gave him a reassuring smile. "Yes, darling, I am. I really need to train my thoughts better! I truly hope that the issues between Thorne and his brother will resolve without any interference from us. We have another day to ourselves before our meeting with Colonel Barrington; perhaps we should use it to enjoy the sights and sounds of Egypt. We'll have to be our professional selves again soon enough."

Elliott smiled as he cast a swift eye around; they were alone. Giselle caught his expression and shared his smile as the two of them leant towards each other for a kiss.

The romantic moment was broken by an ugly snigger behind them. The black kitten, who'd been blissfully asleep in Giselle's reticule, poked her head out and hissed angrily as Elliott and Giselle turned to face the three heavily armed Bedouins standing behind them. The eldest removed a dagger from his belt and held it before him; the Jambiya's razor-sharp edge glinting in the sunlight. "We have need of your wealth. Give us what we want, and you will come to no harm."

Elliott drew his sword stick; the silky hiss of the Damascus steel cut through the Bedouin's confidence as he realised they were attacking a foe far more capable of protecting himself and his wife then they had believed.

The leader again waved his dagger and grinned at them; Elliott grimaced at the sight of the man's missing front teeth.

"There are three of us, and only one of you. Now, we will kill you both and leave you to the vultures!"

Giselle pulled her pearl-handled revolver from her reticule and pointed it at his chest. "Two of you will be dead before the third can do anything more than run!"

The youngest Bedouin glared at her and spat something in Arabic. Giselle looked at the angry young man with an arched eyebrow and tutted. "That was a *very* unpleasant thing to say to a lady!" As the five stared at each other, silence fell; Elliott and Giselle recognised the calm before the storm as they watched the Bedouins for the telltale signs of an attack.

The youngest Bedouin suddenly lunged towards Giselle, his jambiya raised high over his head. As he came within touching distance, and before Giselle could pull the trigger, there was a strange, shuddering movement in the rocky ground beneath them as a winged figure suddenly erupted from the earth; the violence of his entrance showering them in sand and stones. Huge black wings billowed around him like living silk as he landed between Elliott, Giselle, and the attackers, and with a snarl, reached for the youngest Bedouin with razor-sharp claws.

Elliott pushed Giselle behind him as Masquelyne, rage evident in his glowing yellow eyes, rapidly dispatched all three in a frighteningly fast display of anger, blood, and terror.

In the shocked silence that followed, Masquelyne withdrew the claws of his right hand from where they were embedded the chest of the eldest attacker, stood, and gently flexed his shoulders; his wings rustled like silk as they moulded themselves to the line of his back and changed colour, taking on the appearance of a long, pale linen duster covering his day suit. He took a large handkerchief from his breast pocket and mopped the worst of the blood from his hands. Casting an irritated golden eye across the red spatters that speckled the front of his cream waistcoat, he tucked the sodden handkerchief into the garments of one of the dead Bedouin at his feet, then paused as he felt something in the man's pocket. Reaching into the bloody material, he removed a pouch and opened it; it contained a black crystal vial, a sheathed blade that looked very familiar, and a smaller pouch. He tucked the items into his own pocket before he approached Elliott and Giselle, arms outstretched. "Pel! It's been far too long."

Elliott stared at him in stunned silence before wiping and sheathing his sword and accepting the proffered embrace. "Father! What on earth are you doing here?"

Masquelyne paused; there was no way he could hide what he had discovered from his son. He looked at Elliott with a tremulous smile. "I've found her, Pel — I've finally found her!"

Elliott shook his head in confusion. "Found who?"

Masquelyne's smile softened as a deep glowing light filled his yellow eyes. "Your mother."

○

The Chapel of Thoth
11:58am

Evelyn stood in the doorway of the dimly lit chamber, delight on her face as she gazed at the hieroglyphs covering the walls. As she walked past her brother-in-law, Kiefer pulled out his pocket watch and hissed an uncouth word under his breath; where the bloody hell were they? He had been quite clear in his instructions. He darted a glance around the chapel before walking towards the doorway that led back to the small courtyard, and the main temple complex beyond.

As he walked past his mother, she turned and tapped him sharply on the wrist with her ivory and silk fan. Kiefer winced as she turned the full force of her attention on him. "What are you up to, Kiefer?"

He attempted a charming smile while massaging the lump that was already appearing on his wrist. "Whatever do you mean, Mother?"

Marguerite fixed him with a look. "I know you, child! I know when you have secrets…you've never been able to hide them from me!" She cast a look at Evelyn, who was standing at the far end of the chapel, and lowered her voice. "Is it to do with the offering?"

Kiefer scowled, glared at his shoes, and nodded.

Marguerite's lips thinned; she knew that look all too well! She raised an immaculate black eyebrow. "What did you do?"

Kiefer's scowl deepened, but a touch of trepidation crept into his eyes. "We lost valuable time because of that useless dolt, Julius. So, I thought it would be sensible to…to hire a professional to take the tribute."

Marguerite's eyes widened in shock. When she finally spoke, her voice was flat with anger. "You did *what*?"

Kiefer swallowed and continued in the same flippant vein, hoping his mother would not sense his unease. "I paid Budaiwi to kill her and collect her blood, but he's late. I told him to be here by midday…."

Marguerite stared at him. "The offering must be taken with one of the sacred knives and the blood kept in a crystal vial to retain its purity…how could a human do this?"

Kiefer took a deep breath. "I gave him one of the knives and a spare vial from the trunk. That bloody idiot Julius took the other knife and vial and he hasn't brought them back yet!"

Marguerite closed her eyes and ground her teeth; the brittle cracking sound making Kiefer flinch. She shot her son a withering look and spoke as though addressing a child. "The Blades of Nekroshema are not trinkets to be given away lightly, you fool! They can be used not only to give us life, but to take it away...permanently! They are the only weapons that can kill us, and you gave one to a paid assassin?" She took a deep breath and glared at her son. "As for using a human to gather the blood...you know that the offering must be taken by a family member, Kiefer. The one who kills the offering *must* be bound to our family by blood or marriage. I shudder to think of the possible outcome of a mortal performing this essential ritual."

Kiefer shook his head mulishly. "I've done it before!"

There was deathly silence as his mother looked at him, a strangely frozen expression on her face. When she finally spoke, her voice was almost a whisper. "For whose resurrection did you hire an outsider?"

Kiefer caught the look in her eyes and realized he had gone too far; he swallowed hard. "Sedgewyck."

Marguerite's breath hissed between her teeth as she looked at her son in rage and disgust. "Now we know why his resurrection failed...why he was separated into a revenant and a poltergeist! You half-witted__" She caught herself as her voice began to climb in anger. She fixed him with a withering glare as she hissed. "You could have inflicted that hideous outcome on your own father!"

Kiefer opened his mouth to reply, then saw the white lights fill his mother's eyes. He snapped his mouth shut as she struck him across the collarbone with her fan; tears sprang into his eyes as he felt the bone snap under the firmly applied ivory and silk. Marguerite leant in to her son's face and hissed. "Whatever you have organised, cancel it. Pay them out of your own purse — do whatever you have to do — but see that the offering is kept safe. Get the blade and vial back from Budaiwi; they are sacred items that should never be wielded by the hands of a mortal!" She took a deep breath and cast a glance at Margaux who was wandering at the far end of the chapel, a distant look on her face. "When we get back to the *Cartouche*, if they haven't already found him, assist Sedgewyck and Heathers in locating Julius. I don't care *whose* bed you have to drag him from — there are things we need to do, and the family must be quorate…at least until after your father has been returned to us. At that point, Julius may rue the day when he allowed Margaux to save his life during the Crusades! Now get out of my sight, you pathetic, cretinous little child!"

Kiefer's face took on a mulish, sulky expression as his mother pushed him out of her way and returned to Vincenzo's side. He glared after her as she gave him one final hard look before deliberately turning her back on him. Kiefer scowled; damn her! Nothing he did was ever good enough. He turned and stormed out of the chapel. As he walked through the small courtyard beyond, he paused at the narrow doorway that led to the main steps to allow his eyes to reaccustom themselves to the light.

As his vision returned, he recoiled in disgust; the bodies of at least three men lay in several bloody pieces in front of the steps before the colossi. The scene a viscous, gory tableau describing the hideous violence that had occurred while he and his mother had been talking on the other side of the doorway.

Kiefer glanced around the immediate area, but the area was empty, and the only sounds his keen ears could detect were those of his family in the chapel. He walked towards the nearest material-swaddled piece and nudged it with his patent-leather shoe. His eyes narrowed as he recognised the blood-soaked over-garment as that worn by Budaiwi when they had made their agreement. A hideous thought entered his mind as with a strangled curse he bent and reached into the bloodied mass of material. His fingers searched inside the remains of the torn cotton, but to no avail; the vial and the blade were gone…as were the diamonds.

Kiefer bared his teeth as he smashed his fist into the blood-soaked earth beside Budaiwi's remains; Mother was certain to blame him for this! Unless he came up with a suitable plan to assuage her wrath, he just knew that when he next needed resurrecting, he would be spending quite a long time in the liminal space between the worlds, waiting for her to bring him back.

He pulled out a handkerchief and wiped his suddenly tremulous hands, his mind spinning through the situation he found himself in; how could he walk away from the utter mess before him with his standing intact? Perhaps he could say these were not the men he had hired? Perhaps he could inform the authorities that he had seen another group of Bedouin riding from the scene? He stood up and looked about him; the area in front of the temple was silent.

Kiefer shook his head, fear and unease on his face; he could pull the wool over the eyes of any authority…but never his mother! He looked at the doorway leading into the Chapel of Thoth and winced; this could well be the singularly most painful experience of his life. As he began to walk back, he cast another look at the torn remains of the Bedouin; who or what could have carried out such a violent act in so little time, and in absolute silence?

He walked back to the courtyard, stood in the doorway, and waited until his mother noticed his presence. The dim white light reappeared in her eyes as she left Vincenzo's side and approached her son with an irritated expression. "What?"

Kiefer's eye twitched. "We have a little problem."

Marguerite fixed him with another glare, her eyes returning to their usual colour. "Explain."

Kiefer made a slight motion towards the outside of the building. "Perhaps it's best if you see for yourself, Mother."

Marguerite stepped through the doorway and walked into the sunshine. She took in the eviscerated bodies, blood, and gore, in silence before turning to her son. Dull white lights filled her eyes as she took a deep breath and spoke in a voice pitched so low as to be almost silent. "Did you do this?"

Kiefer shook his head. "No."

Marguerite's eyes bore into her son's face. "Where are the vial and the blade?"

Kiefer flinched. "Gone."

There was a faint cracking sound as Marguerite again ground her teeth. When she spoke, her voice was a sibilant hiss. "Witnesses?"

Kiefer hurriedly shook his head. "None that I could see or hear."

Marguerite's slender white fingers gripped the handle of her ever-present reticule as faint murmuring came from inside the padded confines of the embroidered bag. She lifted the reticule; her eyes distant as she listened to the sounds coming from within before shaking her head. "No, Reynaud, I don't think we could get away with drawing and quartering Kiefer, even here. I shall deal with this, my love." She turned her attention to her trembling son. "I take it one of these men was Budaiwi?" Kiefer nodded shakily as his mother pressed him further. "I also take it that you saw no one else?" He nodded again. Marguerite paused; her eyes narrowed. "Where were the couple who were ahead of us?"

Kiefer blinked and shook his head. "I don't know, Mother."

He hissed in pain as Marguerite gripped his chin; her unnaturally strong, sharp fingernails digging into his flesh as she spat. "Then find out! Must I do everything? They were ahead of us. Are they in the main temple, or have they returned to the jetty? Find them, and find out what, if anything, they know. Now!" She threw him roughly to the ground, then turned her back on him and began to walk back to the chapel.

Kiefer clasped a hand to his bleeding face. "But Mother... how do we explain this." He gestured to the dead Bedouin.

Marguerite paused and turned to face him. "I shall tell André what has happened and press upon him the need to keep Evelyn close. We shall walk out of this chamber together...all of us. We shall exclaim with horror at the sight, and assist the authorities as best we can, given that we neither saw nor heard anything." She gestured to the chapel. "Join your brother and Evelyn, and keep your mouth shut. I shall deal with this mess, as I always do!"

Kiefer got to his feet and approached the doorway, then flinched as his mother placed her hand on his jaw. Marguerite frowned. "Don't be ridiculous!" As she lightly stroked the torn skin it began to heal, the bloody marks fading into a smooth, healthy surface. She stood back and nodded. "There."

"Thank you, Mother."

Marguerite glared at him, her dark eyes flashing with anger. "I didn't do it for you, Kiefer! When the authorities talk with us, it's better they see no injuries that could be attributed to a fight between you and the dead Bedouin. Now, let us go and see to our alibi...and the awful discovery the authorities are yet to make on the steps of this Temple."

○

The *Cartouche*
Midday

Navigations Officer Cade entered the bridge and approached the captain's seat. He dropped a folder on the chair and moved the paperwork on the too-small desk to accommodate the travel information for the next day's return flight to Cairo. Unrolling a large map, he positioned it carefully, weighing it down with two of the brass rulers that lay on the walnut desktop. As he turned from the desk, he cast a casual glance out of the window and stopped dead, an expression of incredulity appearing on his deeply tanned face. Cade leant on the rail and pressed his face against the thick glass. His jaw dropped as he realised exactly what he was looking at. He seized the communications tube from the desk and blew down it. After a short pause, a tinny voice sounded at the other end, "Communications Officer."

"This is Navigations Officer Cade. Call the captain! I believe he's in his cabin. Tell him to come to the bridge — urgently!" He slammed the tube into its rest, turned to the window, and stared at the scattered, bloody remains and crimson splashes clearly visible in the pale-yellow sand, two hundred feet below.

○

The Abu Simbel Jetty
12:05pm

Before anyone in the temple could bear witness to what had occurred…or discover their part in the bloody violence that had taken place outside the temple, Elliott, Giselle, and

Masquelyne had left the corpse-strewn steps and had hurried back to the distant jetty. As they scurried down the pathway, Giselle gave her husband a worried look and waved her hand towards the bloody detritus behind them. "How on earth are we going to explain *that* to the authorities?"

As Elliott opened his mouth to respond, Masquelyne shook his head. "I wouldn't worry about it, my dear. Once we inform Geminandras of these events, he'll deal with it. It is, after all, the reason for his presence here in Egypt."

Elliott shot his father a dark look as they arrived at the edge of the river and advanced towards the jetty. "What the Hell is going on, Father? What do you mean about finding Mother? And what exactly do you know about the reason for Geminandras being here?"

Masquelyne looked at his son with a slightly embarrassed expression. "Ah well, now, hmm…yes, there are some things I do need to tell you. I think we're far enough away from the remnants of our attackers to deny all knowledge of their existence — and how they met their demise! But first things first." Masquelyne's pale, raw-boned face softened in a tender smile as he embraced his daughter-in-law. "Angellis, it has been many, many years. I am so very happy that you have found each other again." Giselle smiled back; her blue eyes bright with tears as she returned her father-in-law's embrace.

As they stood on the stone platform, the limpid waters of the Nile lapping at the stanchions, Masquelyne looked at his son. "To answer your questions, Pel; Evelyn Briar-Devereaux…*she* is your mother. There are no doubts in my mind."

As Elliott and Giselle listened, Masquelyne explained when and how he had ascertained Evelyn's true identity, and how his plans to reveal himself had been dashed after his discovery that she had become engaged to another man."

Elliott's brown eyes swirled with vivid green lights as he listened to his father's words. "But are you sure, Father? Mother has been gone for so long…" He saw the expression on Masquelyne's face and nodded slowly. "Of course you're sure; I knew as soon as I saw Giselle. I'm sorry."

"There's no need for you to apologise, Pel. You have no memory of your mother; she died giving you life…" Masquelyne paused, a deep golden light appearing in his eyes. "I have seen her face in my dreams every night since that day. A day both terrible and beautiful, for two very different reasons."

Elliott gripped his father's arm, the memory of many years of searching for Giselle etched into his own mind. He looked at Masquelyne. "I've tried to find you for the last few years, Father. There's so much to tell you — not just about finding Angellis, but also about Phoenixus…and Chymeris."

Masquelyne looked at Elliott for a long moment. "I already know."

Elliott stared at him. "How?"

His father sat on the edge of the railing and sighed as he rubbed his face. "In following Evelyn, I also found myself following the Devereaux family. If I was losing her to another man, I had to know that he would be a good husband, and care for her at least as well as I." The golden lights in his eyes deepened in anger. "Instead, I discovered that André Devereaux was neither kind nor worthy, nor even fully human!"

Elliott stared at the golden-eyed man. "What are you saying?"

"We Astraeans are colloquially known as 'Others'; similar in appearance to humans, but not *of* the human race. There are also humans who are neither Others nor completely human. The Devereaux family are one such evolutionary niche; they are of the line of the Children of Nekroshema; they are necromancers."

Elliott stared at his father, an expression of incredulity on his face. "Death Dealers?"

Masquelyne nodded. "It's one of the many terms used to describe them."

Elliott and Giselle shared a look; of all the many variations of humanoid life known within the Espion Court as Crypto-Anthropos, necromancers were by far the most unstable. Their ability to resurrect, reanimate, enslave, and utilise the body, mind and soul of the dead required a callous disregard, an indifference to suffering, and a lust for power, that was looked upon, even by the ancient vampiric Blood Lords of Aldenhithe, as an abomination. Although in the case of the Blood Lords, their objections were mostly due to the embarrassment that arose when attempting to feed on a victim who was already dead.

Masquelyne leant against the jetty and continued. "From what information I've gathered, this particular family has existed in various guises for well over five thousand years."

Giselle looked at Masquelyne with curiosity. "We are immortal; humans are not. If they are a type of human, how can they live for so long?"

Masquelyne's lip curled in disgust. "When a member of the family dies, the surviving necromancers kill humans of the corresponding sex and use their body parts to resurrect the departed family member."

Giselle's eyes widened in horror. "If they've lived for over five thousand years, they must have killed thousands of people!"

"Easily! The ritual to resurrect a necromancer is very rigid; they have to assemble thirteen separate body parts, and to harvest those pieces, they must kill one person for each full moon of the year. They take the pieces in a set order, and the final offering must be from a virgin, of either sex, whose heart's blood completes the requirements. This resurrects the dead necromancer, and their existence on this earth continues."

Giselle shook her head. "But how does the ritual know which dead necromancer to resurrect?"

Masquelyne grimaced. "Because when a necromancer dies, the family always take possession of the one item that carries their personality, knowledge, and persona; their skull. Without it, they cannot be resurrected."

The black kitten raised his head from Giselle's reticule, gazed at Masquelyne with her huge, violet-coloured eyes, let out a small squeak, and retreated back into her cosy den.

Elliott stared at his father. "How did you discover this?"

A muscle spasmed in Masquelyne's jaw. "A few months ago, I followed the Devereaux family and witnessed them commit cold-blooded murder."

Elliott's eyebrows shot up. "Did you go to the police?"

Masquelyne looked at his son with an equally raised eyebrow. "And tell them what, exactly? That at an obscenely late hour I just happened to be sitting on the chapel roof in Abney Park Cemetery and witnessed the arrival of four members of the Devereaux family and one of their servants, bearing a body, which they then proceeded to bury in an open grave." Masquelyne sighed and again rubbed his pale face. "I disinterred the corpse and discovered that the body was not quite dead. He was a gentleman by the name of Emmerson Briar — Evelyn's own father." Masquelyne's eyes darkened. "Of all the ways I had hoped to meet my beloved's father here on earth, meeting him shortly after he had been stabbed was not an ideal situation. I asked him what had happened, and he told me."

Masquelyne paused, thinking back to that cold night in January. "Briar had hired an enquiry agent to check on his son-in-law's family. The information he had received supported his fears about the Devereaux clan. In an act of extreme stupidity, he went to their house in Mayfair to confront them with what he knew. Whereupon, he was attacked without warning; there was no preamble, no discussion, it was simple murder! After stabbing him, the attacker removed his eye. Briar identified the men as Kiefer, André, Julius—" He darted a ruffled look at his son before continuing. "— and Vincenzo. Kiefer was the man who stabbed him. They were assisted by Julius' manservant, Heathers." He paused for a moment and shook his head. "There's something odd about Heathers — I don't know what, but there's more to him than just a human familiar offered a gift of long life." He took a steadying breath. "Briar told me of his fears for his daughter..." Masquelyne's eyes filled with a deep, golden light. "I promised him on my immortal soul that I would protect his child from harm, even if it meant my death — or the death of every member of the Devereaux clan!" A muscle twitched in his jaw. "He could have survived the loss of his eye; the brutal wound in his stomach was what killed him."

Giselle winced. "You said that Heathers is 'a human familiar offered a gift of long life...what do you mean by that?"

Masquelyne shifted against the rail, his pale wings rippling around him. "Their gift is that of resurrecting the dead, if one can call it a gift. A necromancer can live a massively extended life — many thousands of years — but they can still die by violence, injury, or neglect."

Giselle raised her eyebrows. "Neglect?"

Masquelyne nodded. "If for some reason the resurrection ritual is not carried out, they can't return...they are trapped in the liminal space between the living and the dead. They can wait there for thirteen times thirteen moons; that's a little over fourteen years. If they are not brought back within that time, they die completely and can never return. but if the ritual is carried out and completed in time, they can be resurrected by another necromancer and their life continues. The same rules apply whether they are killed by accident or design, or even by their own hand. Now, A human can join a necromancer family one of two ways; they can marry a full-blooded member and in so doing they become blood-linked to the family...they themselves become full-blooded necromancers capable of resurrecting others. Or, they can offer to work for a necromancer, and in so doing, they become a familiar. This is very similar to those who work for the Blood Lords of Aldenhithe; in return for their service, they are given the gift of long life, similar but different to their master."

Giselle's frown deepened. "What do you mean 'similar but different'?"

"Upon death, a human who has married in can be resurrected and will live for the same amount of time as any full-blooded necromancer. A familiar can also be resurrected, but for a drastically reduced length of time...their bodies will only last for a few years, a decade at most, before the ritual must be repeated...whereas a necromancer, once resurrected, can live indefinitely. This is because necromancers are supernatural beings, much like us. When they marry, this magical state is conferred on their spouse in a blood-bond, the human familiar is not granted that connection; their bodies lack the necessary magic to hold on to the ritual. In short, a necromancer may live for several thousand years between resurrections, as will their once-human spouse, but a human familiar has a finite number of resurrections before Mother Nature takes over, as she always does, and death finally comes for them. Familiars can be brought back many times — some have lived for over a thousand years — but they will never have true immortality. Put rather brutally, human familiars are animated corpses with their will intact;

liches or revenants, if you will. They are dead, and dead things rot…that is why they only last a few years before they must be resurrected."

Giselle looked appalled. "They know that, and they do it anyway?"

Masquelyne shrugged. "Some humans will do anything for a taste of immortality." He turned his golden gaze on the deep green river before them. "They desire something they can never understand. If they had any idea of the price we pay for our immortality…" His voice trailed off before he shook his head and continued. "One other thing to remember is that when a necromancer dies fully; I mean utterly dies, those he resurrected also die; spouse, children, familiars, and servants…all perish with their creator."

Giselle looked nervous. "I have a feeling that I shall regret asking this, but…how is the ritual performed?"

Masquelyne looked at his son. "You know more about the order of the ritual than I, Pel."

Elliott nodded slowly as he answered Giselle's question. "Across a period of thirteen moons, they must take thirteen body parts from victims of the same sex as the necromancer who is to be resurrected. The body parts must be taken in a set order; lower left leg, lower right leg, upper left leg, upper right leg, lower torso, upper torso, upper left arm, upper right arm, lower left arm, lower right arm, left eye, right eye, and finally, the heart's blood from a pure, virginal source. They then perform a ritual where they use the dead necromancer's skull as…well, glue, for want of a better term, to bind the pieces together and create a new body that will bear the necromancer's mind, and original appearance. That creation is what they then resurrect."

Giselle gazed at her husband in silence for some time. "You've had to deal with something similar?"

Elliott nodded. "Many years after you were killed, Thorne

and I were tracking a necromancer by the name of Caeruleum—" Giselle blinked as Elliott suddenly smacked his hand down on the rail. "Yes! That's why it was familiar!" He looked at his wife and father, who were staring at him as though he had grown another head. "Remember, Giselle? When you were reading the Arabic translation of the code-names you queried 'Prussian Blue; you said it was actually Egyptian Blue…"

A golden light appeared in Giselle's blue eyes. "Of course! It was the wrong translation…Caeruleum means 'Egyptian Blue'." She looked at Elliott. "But…does that mean the Devereaux family are a part of the attacks here?" She frowned. "If you and Thorne were after this Caeruleum, surely you know what they look like?" She looked at Masquelyne. "Unless they can change their appearance when they resurrect?"

Her father-in-law shook his head. "They appear as they were in their very first incarnation. The body parts that are taken from their victims change to become those of the necromancer; hair colour, skin tone, even birthmarks on the body parts will change during the ritual. They do have the ability to slightly alter the appearance of their familiars, but only their familiars."

Elliott dragged a hand through his dark hair. "It's been well over a thousand years since that particular case, but if it's the same Caeruleum, I don't think it's any of the Devereaux clan we have seen so far…if it's one of them at all. We simply don't know yet!" He looked at Masquelyne. "Please continue, Father."

Masquelyne nodded. "I realised that I needed to let someone in a position of authority know who Evelyn really was, and what the Devereaux family were capable of. So, I contacted the Espion Court. They put me in touch with one of their agents, a young woman called Remedae; she oversees the various Astraeans who are reborn here. After she had made her investigations, she put me in touch with Geminandras. It was quite a surprise seeing him again..." Masquelyne shot his son a look. "I can't begin to imagine Shadavarian's reaction upon seeing his brother again, but I digress. I informed Geminandras of all I knew about Evelyn and the Devereaux family. The information I provided is part of the reason why Geminandras is here." A faint smile appeared on Masquelyne's face. "I managed to discover a great deal about the Devereaux family before I decided it was time to pass on the information. After a few days, I was finally given an audience with Abditivus." Masquelyne's face softened and became even paler. "After I informed him of my fears, he reintroduced me to my son, Phoenixus." His jaw clenched. "Pel...the damage Chymeris inflicted on him is too great to be fully removed without the assistance of an Unmaker."

Elliott nodded slowly. "Mellior?"

"He's already there, with Phoenixus and Abditivus. He's hopeful that Phoenixus can be healed, as is Abditivus." Masquelyne swallowed hard. "There is a possibility that some of who he is will be lost...but he's prepared to try."

Elliott gripped his father's arm. "Then he's with people who can help him."

Masquelyne looked up at Elliott, tears on his cheeks. "When Phoenixus was explaining what had happened to him, he seemed to separate — to become three different people. Both Mellior and Abditivus agreed that this was to protect the real man within from the torment and harm Chymeris had caused. The three are Phoenixus, my son and your brother; a boy called Harrow, damaged and afraid; and the last..." Masquelyne's voice sank to a whisper. "Hellion." He turned his gaze on Elliott. As he saw the look on his father's face, Elliott took an immediate step towards him. "What, Father? Who is Hellion?"

Masquelyne shuddered. "A pool of darkness lay behind his eyes. I pray I will never have to meet with that side of him again."

Silence descended as they thought of Phoenixus and the harm Chymeris had caused him for so long. The silence was broken by a sudden noise above them as the *Scarab* separated from the *Cartouche* and sped towards the jetty.

Elliott looked at his father with a grimace. "I have an unhappy thought that the approaching vessel might have something to do with a certain collection of body parts strewn across the steps of the temple behind us! It's obviously visible from the *Cartouche*." He looked at the others. "In the event of Geminandras not being among those descending, we need a plan — and quickly!"

Giselle bit her fingernail as she thought. "I have it! We walked to the temple, you began to feel the effects of the heat, and we decided to return to the airship. However, the launch had already returned to the *Cartouche*, so we had no choice but to stand here and wait for them to return. We saw and heard absolutely nothing of the goings-on at the temple. What do you think?"

Masquelyne smiled. "Pel always did get a little unwell in direct sunlight."

Elliott rolled his eyes. "Thank you very much, Father! Oh, by the way...here, in this time, my name is Elliott Caine, and Angellis is Giselle Du'Lac...it might be sensible to use it in company." At Masquelyne's nod he turned to look at his wife. "Why can't *you* feel the effects of the sun?"

Giselle grinned. "Because you can remove one or two items of clothing without fuss. If I were to remove one or two garments to relieve the heat, I would be down to my corset — and that would never do!"

Elliott grinned back. "Noted! Very well, if I must succumb

to the ill-effects of the afternoon sun, I had better remove my cravat and jacket before the *Scarab* arrives."

As Elliott began to undo his cravat, the launch reached the jetty. This time, its arrival was neither gentle nor graceful as the vessel slapped down firmly into the green waters of the Nile; the bow wave swelling over the wooden planks and heading towards them at speed.

Elliott, Giselle, and Masquelyne hurriedly stepped onto higher ground as the gangplank was speedily deployed and to their great relief, Darling appeared. He strode towards them, followed by several earnest looking young men bearing the latest weaponry from the Eridanus Corporation's non-lethal suppression armoury; aether-wands... designed to render an aggressor unconscious within seconds, but gentle enough to keep them alive for trial.

As Darling approached, he saw Masquelyne. His eyebrows shot up and he stopped dead, then held up his hand. The men behind him immediately came to a sharp halt, their military training glaringly obvious to those watching. Darling turned his head towards the men, but kept his eyes on Elliott, Giselle, and Masquelyne. "Gentlemen; you know what to do." The young men turned as one and began an easy march towards the temple beyond the rocks.

As his men marched along the pathway, Darling glared at Elliott and Giselle before turning his snapping green eyes on Masquelyne. "Please don't tell me the mess near the temple has anything to do with you!"

Masquelyne shrugged; a faint smile playing on his lips. "As you wish."

Darling gritted his teeth. "May I politely remind you of our discussion in London some weeks ago?"

Masquelyne's mouth curled in a hard smile that was somewhat lacking in humour. "How could I possibly forget,

Geminandras? You told me in no uncertain terms to let the family do what they would, without any recourse to the law."

Darling frowned. "That is not what I said, Masquelyne, and you know it!"

Elliott raised his hand. "May I ask exactly what you *did* say about my mother and the Devereaux family?"

Darling glared at him. "Ah, so he's informed you of his belief about Evelyn's identity? I said that he should keep an eye on the young lady in question…but he was not to go off half-cocked and do anything rash!"

Masquelyne pulled a face as he recalled the rather speedy way in which Julius had descended from the airship the other evening. Realising Giselle was looking at him curiously, he assumed a carefully blank expression as Darling continued. "I understand the orders from the Espion Court were not to your taste, Masquelyne, but—"

Masquelyne leant towards Darling. "Not to my taste? They suggested that I should ignore the possibility of Evelyn being my Other, because of the faux immortality the Devereaux family can offer politicians and businessmen. Do you really believe that I would sit by and allow them to murder my wife in the name of expediency?"

Darling stared at Masquelyne, whose pale face was unusually blotchy. The pale covering on his shoulders shifted of its own accord; the silken skin shimmering with faint colours and patterns as the immortal fought to keep his volcanic temper under control. Darling slowly shook his head. "No, Masquelyne, I can't ask you to turn a blind eye to murder. I personally believe that the Espion Court is wrong here. All I can ask is that you give me more time to try and convince the Court of the danger this family poses. Will you allow me that?"

Masquelyne stared at him in silence, a muscle twitching in his jaw. "You ask me to give you more time? You expect me to wait while the Devereaux family continue their plot to murder my wife?"

Darling took a step back at the expression on Masquelyne's face. "Masquelyne, please! We both know that what the Court said was so much nonsense, designed to prevent you from doing whatever it's that you plan to do anyway! I'll approach the Court and ask them to rethink their previous judgement. But I beg you, until I receive word from the them, please keep your distance. Don't approach any members of the Devereaux family, and if they try to harm anyone, let me know and await orders!"

Masquelyne straightened up; a decidedly wolfish smile appeared on his face. "My dear Darling, I don't work for the Espion Court. I shall do whatever it takes to protect my Other, with or without your help...and I intend to enjoy every minute of it!" His eyes filled with a golden glow as he looked at Darling. "Have you bothered to check the contents of the steamer trunk that travels with them? Of course you haven't! You might like to start there." He turned back to his son. "Now, if you will excuse me, Elliott, Giselle, I'll head back to the temple and continue my watch on Evelyn."

As he started back towards the temple, Darling called out, "You should consider yourself lucky that none of the guests witnessed your bloody parley on the steps." A sudden look of concern appeared on his face. "Good Gods! Tell me you didn't—"

Masquelyne came to a halt. "No, Darling, it's not one of the Devereaux family. The elder son, Kiefer, hired three Bedouin to kill Evelyn in the Chapel of Thoth. I overheard their plans and arrived in time to witness the three men attacking my son and daughter-in-law instead." He turned his yellow eyes on Darling. "My presence was quite opportune." He continued along the path and disappeared around the corner.

Darling turned to Elliott, deep concern on his face. "Elliott, please…if you have any form of control over your father, I urge you to wield it!"

Elliott looked at Darling, a faint green light in his eyes. "If Evelyn Briar-Devereaux is my mother — and my father is very rarely wrong — what on earth makes you think that I would try to prevent him from protecting her?"

Darling stared at him in consternation. "Elliott, if your father kills any member of the Devereaux family without good reason, the Court will send agents after him…and if you assist him, they will add you to their list. I could do nothing to prevent it."

Elliott nodded and took Giselle's arm. "Then let us hope that Father continues his vigil and ensures that Mother isn't harmed, because if she is, I will not rest until the Devereaux family and their gifts to the unquestioning great and good are vanquished. Now if you will excuse us, it's been an emotionally draining morning, and I feel the need for several glasses of Champagne."

○

The Chapel Of Thoth
12:15pm

As Marguerite and Kiefer reentered the chapel, Marguerite stood in the doorway and looked around the room. She finally caught sight of Evelyn who was standing at the far end of the chamber; an expression of rapt enjoyment on her young face as she gazed at the hieroglyphs that marched across the wall. Marguerite narrowed her eyes, and turned until she spied her youngest son standing with Jane in a dark corner of the dimly lit chamber. She made her way to André's side, prodded him sharply with her fan and hissed.

"We have a problem! Go to your wife and stay with her."
André turned his attention from the pouting Jane and glared
at his mother. "Do you mind, Mother? Jane and I are talking
—" He stopped as white lights suddenly appeared in his
mother's eyes. Marguerite leant towards him and bared her
teeth. "The Bedouins your brother hired are dead. They have
been torn to shreds and their remains left on the steps of this
temple. We need to come up with a coherent story for the
authorities. The best I can think of is that we saw nothing,
heard nothing, and cannot help them further. Tell the others
and go to your wife now." She paused as Kiefer joined them.
He leant in to his mother's side and murmured. "The *Scarab*
has just launched from the *Cartouche*...I think the bodies
have been seen."

Marguerite's lips thinned. "The remains of three men are
on those steps...that amount of blood could be spotted from
a damn sight further away than the *Cartouche*!" She turned
back to André. "Tell Evelyn that the authorities believe there
has been a fight between rival Bedouins, that the authorities
are on their way, and that we are safe here."

André nodded and made his way across the room,
pausing to speak with Margeaux, Linden, Camillia, Violette,
and Vincenzo. He arrived at Evelyn's side and leant in to her
side. "My dear?" Evelyn tore her gaze from the markings on
the wall and turned to him. She took in his expression and
frowned. "What is it? What's wrong?"

As they spoke, the airship's guard, led by Darling
suddenly appeared in the doorway of the chapel. Darling
approached Marguerite and bowed slightly. "Mrs Devereaux.
I must inform you that there has been an...incident. I must
respectfully ask you and your family to return to the
Cartouche immediately."

Marguerite opened her eyes wide as Vincenzo slid from
Violette's side to stand next to her. "Why, whatever has

happened, Captain Darling?" Darling, his face carefully blank, continued. "I am afraid there has been an attack on the steps of the temple, Mrs Devereaux. Several men are dead. Did you and your family hear anything...unusual?" Marguerite shook her head and turned to look at her family. "I heard nothing...but I have been in deep discussion with my husband at the far end of the chapel." She smiled faintly. "Ancient Egypt is a passion of my family's. The rest of my family were with us; we saw and heard nothing. Isn't that so?" This final question was thrown to her family who had gathered around her. At their nods of agreement, Darling pressed his lips together. As he opened his mouth, a soft voice spoke from behind Marguerite. "I heard something."

There was a sudden silence as everyone turned to look at Evelyn. She flushed and lifted her chin. "It was around ten or so minutes ago...I thought I heard raised voices...coming from outside."

Darling nodded. "Did you hear what the voices were saying, Mrs Briar-Devereaux?"

Evelyn looked at the family who were staring at her in silence before she shook her head. "No. All I heard was the sound of voices...mostly men's voices, but also, I think, a woman's voice."

Darling nodded and made a mental note to have a further chat with Elliott and Giselle. "Thank you, Mrs Briar-Devereaux. If you will please follow me back to the jetty, the *Scarab* will return you all to the airship for the remainder of our journey to the hotel." He paused and then turned back to Evelyn, and allowed his gaze to take in Marguerite, Margaux, Camillia, Violette, and Jane. "It's not a pretty sight, ladies...I suggest keeping your eyes averted."

Marguerite lowered her eyes with a gracious nod as the family allowed themselves to be escorted from the temple complex without argument.

As they left the chamber, a shadow moved across the hieroglyphs before Masquelyne stepped out from within the stone wall. He removed the crystal vial from his pocket and scowled at it contemptuously before dropping it to the floor and grinding it to dust beneath his heel.

○

The *Cartouche*
5:25pm

Six-hundred feet above the rocky desert, the silken balloon of the *Cartouche* lazily followed the blue-green curve of the Nile, as in the hazy distance, the dim outline of the airship's final destination gradually appeared.

In the bridge, Darling stood by the wheel and glared at the faraway island through narrowed eyes; his mind on the messy issue he had been forced to deal with back at Abu Simbel. Luckily, aside from the unfortunate presence of the Devereaux clan and Evelyn's claim to have heard raised voices, there had been no other guests present at the temple, either from the *Cartouche* or any other vessel, to bear witness to Masquelyne's fit of pique. Equally luckily, none of the guests aboard the *Cartouche* had seen the attack or the copious quantities of blood and gore that had drenched the ground outside the temple.

Darling closed his eyes and rubbed the bridge of his nose; again, fate had been in his favour, as the former military men who had accompanied him to the site were fully conversant in the process of cleaning away evidence of a hard day's entertainment. The temple complex had been completely cleansed of any evidence of foul play, and, indeed, had actually ended up looking far tidier than it had in years!

He opened his eyes, sat in the captain's seat, and again

glared at the rapidly approaching island as he thought back on his somewhat one-sided conversation with the Devereaux family matriarch who had agreed all too readily with his polite suggestion that they draw a veil over the events at the temple and leave it to the relevant authorities to investigate. Darling shook his head; Marguerite hadn't taken much persuading to hold her tongue. Whether her acquiescence on behalf of her family was to assist him or her kin was anyone's guess; he had a deep suspicion it was the latter, rather than the former.

He sighed deeply and leant back in the leather chair as around him, his crew made ready to land at the ornate stone jetty that served the Eridanus Eau de Nil hotel.

The Eridanus Eau de Nil Hotel
5:30pm

The late-afternoon sun shone upon the winding green ribbon of the Nile with a blasting heat that imbued most of the airship's passengers with a desperation to arrive at their destination and adhere to the Spanish habit of the siesta just as soon as was politely possible.

Mr James brought the circling airship lower and lower before finally making a gentle landing in the calm waters of the Nile. Several deckhands appeared as the boat glided through the river towards the private jetty that served the hotel. Waiting on the jetty, the multitudes of hotel staff — human and Simulandro — stood in regimented lines, their eau de nil uniforms glowing in the vibrant sunshine. While before them stood the tall and terrifyingly slim figure of the hotel's manager; Carandini Bey.

Italian, by way of Turkey and one of the more salubrious

parts of London, Carandini Bey had inherited a great deal of money from his father, who had been one of the earliest investors in the Eridanus Corporation. Sadly, due to an unfortunate mishap several years earlier involving a cashier's cheque, a lady of questionable virtue, and a horse that wasn't quite as fast as he had been led to believe, Carandini had been left with nothing but the clothes on his back and what few shares in the company remained in his possession.

Upon his request to sell those shares, the company had instead offered Carandini the position of manager in one of their hotels, whereupon Carandini realised that his father's insistence on learning the languages of his many forebears had been his saving grace; his knowledge of English, Italian, Turkish, Arabic, and French, and his ability to smooth even the most ruffled of feathers was considered a blessing by the company. Carandini had looked at what little remained of his fortune and accepted the offer of employment at the company's Egyptian flagship with good grace — if not a little ire at his loss of personal standing.

Carandini watched the approach of the opulent airship with a thin-lipped smile; Papa would not have been pleased to see a Bey working to keep a roof over his head, but he would have appreciated the fact that in an ocean of poorly paid work, his son had found employment in a place where his father's teachings could still be adhered to; allow the rich their play, but never the bourgeoisie! He, Carandini Bey, might well be nouveau pauvre, but parvenus would be allowed in his hotel over his dead body!

Carandini heaved a deep sigh. His life hadn't quite worked out as Papa had planned...but it was still better than it might have been. His long fingers plucked at his neatly trimmed Van Dyke as he forced his mind from the embarrassments of his past to the richness of the present.

Some of the new intake of guests had already arrived and

were safely ensconced in their suites; Dr Amycus Mirylees, the elderly, respected, and rather querulous archaeologist who had directed the excavation of the ruins within which the hotel had been built, had arrived the previous day with his assistant and the younger man's wife and child. He had immediately stated exactly which suite he wished to stay in; his overriding specification was that he be at least four rooms away from his assistant's young son, who woke early, demanding sustenance, and continued in much the same vein for the rest of the day. Carandini had charmingly acquiesced to this request, and had placed Dr Mirylees, and Dr Jones and his family at opposite ends of the Osiris corridor.

The Contessa de Mostada had been a little more difficult to accommodate. Carandini's grasp of English, Arabic, Italian, Turkish, and French had all been wasted on the elderly and extremely wealthy lady, who insisted on speaking her own strange language with a small amount of heavily accented English thrown in. They had finally managed to understand each other, and Carandini had obligingly furnished her with one of the larger suites on the Isis corridor.

As the bright Egyptian sun blazed down on the golden landscape before him, Carandini smiled. His Mephistophelian moustache twitched as he watched the new guests disembark; their outfits, jewellery, and attitudes exuding the very scent of wealth. He smoothed one immaculately shaped eyebrow as he ran a sharp eye across the guest list his secretary, Miss March, had furnished for him: The Devereaux family once again, with two names that were new to him; Evelyn and Kiefer. The opera singer Mlle Du'Lac and her husband, Elliott Caine; the world-famous psychic Madame Aquilleia, her husband Abernathy Thorne...and their Labrador. Both Carandini's jet-black eyebrows rose; unusual, most of the dogs brought to the hotel were small, crabby, snappy toupées on leads. A dog of a decent size was quite a novelty. He continued to contemplate the list: Thomas Breton, the artist commissioned to create a painting of the hotel; the French author, Gaston Cavet; and the American businessman, Rex Nympton. Carandini's finger tapped the last name on his list; Miss March always checked the backgrounds of their guests before accepting a booking, to ensure social acceptability, and the background of Mr Nympton, though impeccable, was still a trifle disconcerting.

As the guests continued to disembark, he folded the list, tucked it in his breast pocket, and removed a second piece of paper; this one a private telegram that had arrived a few hours earlier from Captain Darling aboard the *Cartouche*, informing him of a slight contretemps between rival Bedouin at Abu Simbel that had left at least three dead at the temple complex. Luckily, no guests had been injured but a certain family had been forced to walk past the remains of the dead on their return to the airship. The telegram stated that the family had not witnessed the attack, so they would not be required to talk to the authorities about the event. Carandini replaced the telegram in his pocket and frowned; tribal politics could be quite concerning. Luckily, he rarely had to deal with such issues due to the geographical position of the hotel, situated as it was on an island surrounded by crocodiles. Certain warring factions within the local population were quite easily ignored by simply denying them access to the island and, if they were particularly insistent, repelling them by use of the hotel's Simulandro stewards.

He raised his eyes, took in the rapidly advancing patrons, and snapped his fingers at the first line of bellboys, who leapt into service. As the new guests walked down the left side of the jetty, the bellboys made their way along the right-hand side and began their task of collecting the trunks, valises, and packages of various shapes and sizes that had been purchased from sellers at the Pyramids, Thebes, Karnak, Luxor, Kom Ombo, and Abu Simbel.

As Elliott, Giselle, Thorne, Aquilleia, and Veronique appeared and walked down the deck. There was a slight pause as one of the doors opened and Thorne and Darling came face to face. The two men stared at each other in silence before Darling waved his hand at the jetty. "After you, Mr Thorne." Thorne turned, took Aquilleia's arm and escorted her and Veronique onto the jetty; the black Labrador turning several times to look back at Darling then turning to look up at the stoney-faced Thorne.

As the bellboys carried the luggage and various packages down the jetty, one sizeable trunk was being dealt with under the watchful eye of a man with dark blond hair and an unpleasant disposition. Carandini looked at him and frowned as he realised that he had taken a sudden and instant dislike to that particular young man. He turned to Miss March, who was standing beside him with her ever-present clipboard. Elegant and tall, with unusual light-auburn hair pinned in a severe bun at the nape of her neck, Miss March's black and cream linen outfit matched her appearance; tasteful, understated, yet expensive and subtle. Hiring Miss March had been viewed by the company as a step too far for women's rights, until they had seen her employment records and grudgingly accepted her as the best possible candidate. She had worked alongside him with professionalism, grace, and skill for several years.

Carandini gestured at the family. "Who is that gentleman, Miss March?"

Miss March studied the young man. "That is Mr Kiefer Devereaux, Mr Bey. He's staying here with his entire family, including his younger brother's new wife. They are here for their honeymoon."

Carandini nodded slowly; those were the names he hadn't

recognised. Then he blinked as Miss March's words sank in. "The entire family? A rather peculiar honeymoon!"

Miss March smiled faintly. "As you say, Mr Bey."

They watched as the new guests were marshalled into a manageable gaggle and escorted into the hotel through the massive gates leading past the Halls of Nectanebo I, before turning sharp left into the Outer Court. They walked past the Chapel of Mandulis and the Temple of Asclepius towards the First Pylon and the reception, which was located in what had been the temple's forecourt.

The guests, followed by the bellboys carrying their luggage, paused every now and then to take in the beauty of the hotel which would be their home for the next week. So intrigued were they by the sight that none of them noticed the strange shadow that slid down the side of the airship and which seemed to move under the sand behind them.

As the last guest entered the reception, the uniformed figure of the head steward, Henson, appeared at the door to the Kiosk of Trajan. His attention was on Carandini who, after a moment, languidly raised a hand. Hassan nodded, made a similar gesture to the room behind him, and walked towards the jetty, followed by the numerous guests who had concluded their stay at the hotel. These guests, as fabulously dressed, coiffed, and bejewelled as those who had just arrived, wafted onto the airship, followed by yet more uniformed bellboys bearing their luggage.

As the last of the homeward bound guests made their way on board, a figure waved from the bridge of the *Cartouche*, signalling that the process of making ready for the return flight to Cairo had begun. As Bey and Miss March watched, the Cartouche rose from her berth and began her return trip to Cairo.

○

The Temple of Kom Ombo
5:45pm

Akeem Jalal glared at the empty barrel aboard his father's dilapidated dahabiya and sighed; hopefully, the last net of the day would bring enough fish to sell at market, Allah willing! He waved at his little brother. "Atif, yallah!" The young boy, barely eight years old, obediently moved to his brother's side and helped him pull in the net.

After several minutes of dragging in sodden, empty netting, both paused as they realised the net had suddenly grown heavier; they had finally made a catch! The brothers redoubled their efforts, hauling reams of netting on to the small boat. Their eyes widened in disbelief at the mass of fish writhing within — they had never seen such a haul! Then the thrashing river fish fell away from the centre of the nets...and the thing they had been feasting on.

Akeem's eyes widened in horror. He made the sign to ward off evil as he gaped at the hideous sight, before dragging his wide-eyed little brother away from the revolting mass in the net. He sat the trembling little boy down beside him.

"Atif, do not look...do not go near it! Do you understand?"

At Atif's wide-eyed nod, Akeem placed his hand on the tiller and guided the boat towards the riverbank to report their appalling discovery to the authorities.

○

Aswan
6:45pm

Some thirty miles away, within the gleaming stone police station of Aswan, a telephone rang. The shrill sound echoed through the empty office for several minutes before a man in the uniform of the Egyptian National Police appeared in the doorway. He was stocky, and of medium height, with thick black hair that was trimmed with military precision. Wiping his wet hands on a towel, he glared at the ringing telephone, lifted the receiver, and snapped. "Nim? Captan Sarhan, hanna!" His black eyebrows lowered as he listened to the voice on the other end of the line. "Antazari!" He clapped his hand over the receiver and swore violently under his breath.

He straightened, pressed the telephone to his ear, glared at the pile of manila envelopes on his already heaving desk and swore again, this time silently. "No... No, tell me again, and in English, please. Whoever is listening on this line needs to understand us." He smiled as the sound of a receiver being hung up sounded somewhere on the line. "Right, go on. Yes, a body...where? Kom Ombo? Who discovered it? Fishermen? Ah, abandoned in the Nile." He listened with an irritated expression. "I do not understand. Why are you telling *me* this? You need to contact the police there — it is not in my jurisdiction." He rearranged the envelopes on his desk as the voice droned on interminably before he took a deep breath and shook his head. "No...the fact that I am thirty miles away is not the issue; the issue is that this is not my problem, as it is out of my jurisdiction!"

As the distant voice continued to talk, he frowned. "A foreign gentleman? Are you sure? The crocodiles and fish of the Nile are not averse to a little fresh meat in their diet, and that will make them difficult to identify." He gripped the side of his desk. "Oh, he still had his identity papers in his pockets…" He muffled the receiver and muttered, "What a shame the fish did not start with those!" With a sigh, he uncovered it. "So, again, why are you telling me this?" Captain Sarhan closed his eyes and pinched the bridge of his nose at the next words. "I see…his papers identify him as a British traveller…" He gripped the side of his desk again and hissed down the line. "Have you any idea how many robbed, dead, or simply complaining travellers I must deal with, here in Aswan? I am swamped with British travellers, living *and* dead! Not to mention the other issues that— Never mind! With respect, you say he was not robbed? He still had his wallet and watch?" Captain Sarhan winced slightly as the voice on the line shared an unpleasant piece of information about the state of the gentleman in question. He shook his head. "The fact that his right arm is missing does not mean his watch was stolen…it simply means that the crocodiles ate it! Is he still wearing any rings on the hand that remains?" As the voice confirmed the presence of what appeared to be a wedding ring on the body's left hand, Captain Sarhan slammed his hand on his desk. "Then that proves it! Because his documents and personal possessions were still on him, they prove that he cannot be a part of my current investigations. All the victims in my case were robbed of their identity papers and jewellery. So, this looks like a case of either death by tragic happenstance or — and this is my official suggestion — death caused by the stupidity of a foreign traveller walking beside a crocodile-infested stretch of the Nile without due care and attention! So, you can investigate this case in Kom Ombo."

He swallowed hard as the voice became sharper, and nodded begrudgingly. "Yes, I understand. As a British citizen, his death needs to be investigated…but I am already seconded to the Veiled Protectorate; I cannot—" He rolled his eyes as the voice droned on. "But I have already...no, you need to— " He ground his teeth, then waited until the voice paused for breath before leaping back into the mostly one-sided conversation. "No! Do not send the corpse here! What do you mean, it is already on the way'? No, I do not need to know where his family are staying, because this is not my—"

The voice on the line cut across his protestations, as, switching from English to Arabic, and in a tone that brooked no further argument, they detailed the orders that they expected Captain Sarhan to carry out immediately. As Captain Sarhan seethed, the voice reiterated the current state of the corpse; half-masticated, missing the right arm at the shoulder, and with the skull attached to the body by a few threads of muscle. They rattled off the name of a well-known, highly exclusive hotel where he could find the deceased's wife and family; Sarhan gritted his teeth...it was a hotel he knew all too well.

There was a sharp click on the line. Captain Sarhan jerked the receiver away from his ear as his Sergeant, Mahmood Jaziri walked into the room, carrying a tray with two glasses of thick black coffee and a plate of dates. Captain Sarhan slammed the receiver into its cradle and glared at his sergeant. "He hung up on me! That pettifogging little..." He took a deep breath and looked at the items his sergeant had just brought in. He pointed at the second cup. "Who is that for?"

Sergeant Jaziri smiled and stepped away from the door as a voice boomed out in the corridor beyond. "As I have always said, curry is far better with apple, parsnip, and sultanas... can't find a blasted parsnip for love nor money in this bloody desert!"

Captain Sarhan closed his eyes and groaned. "Not now, please, not now!"

A large figure appeared in the doorway. Sergeant Jaziri hid his smile and saluted sharply. "Colonel Barrington, Sir."

The solid figure of Colonel Boldre-Penn Barrington, scion of the Hampshire Barringtons, brother to Francesca Barrington, sufferer of flattened azaleas, and stern but fair face of the Veiled Protectorate, entered Captain Sarhan's cluttered office and immediately made his presence felt.

Exceedingly tall and ramrod-straight, his face tanned to the colour and appearance of saddle-leather, and with a bristling salt-and-pepper moustache which could have dropped from his upper lip and commanded its own regiment, Colonel Barrington was the epitome of the English colonel abroad; no-nonsense, blunt to the point of rudeness and occasionally beyond, a surprisingly agile polo player, and a dedicated adherent to the joys of a well-made curry, the hotter the better. Indeed, his manservant, Srinivasan, considered it a matter of pride that he had once managed to make his colonel a curry so hot that he had been forced to drink a pint of yoghurt to suppress the afterglow. The colonel had rewarded his manservant with a generous bonus, an extra day off per month, and an order to serve the same curry on all future bridge evenings with his brother officers.

Colonel Barrington sank into a chair by the overflowing desk and flapped vigorously but ineffectually around himself with an ornate ivory fly-whisk which appeared surgically attached to his hand. In his attempts to destroy the winged minions that seemed intent on plaguing him, he managed to hit everything within a three-foot radius, including the long-suffering Captain Sarhan, while missing every single member of the multitudinous and determined flying irritations. He took another swipe at the air before him. "Bloody flies!" He looked at Captain Sarhan and his bristling eyebrows snapped down over his nose. He pointed at him with the fly-whisk. "You look like a man with a problem — talk!"

Captain Sarhan waved a hand at Sergeant Jaziri, who bowed and left the room, pulling the door shut behind him. The sergeant repaired to his own, slightly tidier desk in the office beyond, removed an envelope covered in thick black pencil from the drawer, and perused the contents with a frown before making copious notes in his own, far neater notebook.

Captain Sarhan removed several bulging files from his chair and dropped them on the floor. He sat down and pushed one of the cups of coffee towards Colonel Barrington, who lifted the small cup and sipped the thick brew, a look of enjoyment on his mustachioed face.

Sarhan lifted his own cup and drained the contents, being careful not to touch the thick sludge at the bottom; he wanted to sleep at some point that week! He put the cup down and sighed. "Not only am I expected to deal with upset tourists and banditry, but now another British traveller has turned up dead in the Nile near Kom Ombo."

Colonel Barrington raised his eyebrows. "Foul play?"

Captain Sarhan shrugged. "Possibly. They are only sending me the corpse because they do not want it. They believe it to be above the abilities of the Kom Ombo office, so why not pass it to me? However, I do not believe it is associated with our investigations; the traveller was not robbed and they still had their documents."

Colonel Barrington smiled as he took a date. "Do we know what his name is?" He paused, consternation on his deeply tanned face. "I take it that it *is* a man? Dashed bad show if an Englishwoman died out here!"

"Yes, it was a man — apparently, he was travelling with his family by airship to the Eridanus Eau de Nil..." He paused as Colonel Barrington made a choking sound, his face turning a worrying shade of purple as he fought to dislodge the date from his gullet. As the older man composed himself, Captain Sarhan sat back and gave him a questioning look. "I take it you recognise the name of the hotel?"

Colonel Barrington removed a large handkerchief from his pocket, pressed it to his streaming eyes, and nodded. "Actually, my dear Sarhan, that is why I am here. I bear with me a request for assistance from the Empire, which may have something to do with the explosions and murders that have been happening in your jurisdiction over the last few months."

○

Sunday 24th
Carandini's Office
11:45am

Miss March knocked on Carandini Bey's office door. "Mr Bey, may I talk with you? We appear to have a small problem."

Carandini looked up from his desk and frowned. "A problem? I already have far too much to deal with, Miss March. It will have to wait."

Miss March shook her head. "I'm very sorry, Mr Bey, but it can't. A sandstorm is approaching. The Eridanus Corporation have ordered us to take every precaution to protect the guests and the buildings."

Carandini gave an exasperated hiss and glared at her from behind his desk. "These buildings have withstood over two and a half thousand years of sandstorms, Miss March!"

His secretary sighed; they always had the same argument every time there was an issue with the peculiar desert weather.

"Yes, Mr Bey, they have. But over the course of those years, the top layer of stone has been eroded and some of the more fragile parts of the structure have been completely destroyed. If people discovered that we allowed similar damage to occur to the guests who stay here, the Eridanus Corporation would remove us both without giving it a second thought. We have to implement our sandstorm protocol to protect the guests, the buildings, and, being rather blunt, our positions."

Carandini scowled and flung himself back in his deep-red leather armchair. "You are, of course, quite right." He groaned and rubbed his eyes. "Give the order to deploy the Simulandro workers and the protective shutters, and send maids to inform the guests that, until the storm has abated, they must stay within the covered areas of the hotel." He sat up and shuffled the paperwork on his desk. "Bloody good thing the corporation insisted on building walkways with removable glass shutters." He turned and gazed out of the large window; the view beyond a perfect Egyptian tableau. He turned back to his secretary. "What time is the storm due?"

Miss March looked at the document in her hand. "At approximately five o'clock this afternoon, Mr Bey."

Carandini rolled his eyes. "But of course! What truly marvellous timing!"

Miss March frowned, the expression somewhat incongruous on her smooth face. "I'm sorry, Mr Bey?"

Carandini looked at her. "Oh...I did not tell you? Oh, yes...the information came in while you were dealing with the Contessa and her issues over breakfast." They shared a mutually supportive look at the memory of the Contessa de Mostada's great upset over the lack of kippers at the breakfast table.

Miss March regarded Carandini thoughtfully. "Judging by

your expression, Mr Bey, this information heralds something worse than a sandstorm."

"I'm afraid so. I received a telephone call from the Aswan police. It appears they have discovered a body in the Nile at Kom Ombo. They believe it to be a British citizen who was travelling on the *Cartouche* with his family." Carandini leant back in his chair. "I'm afraid that it was one of our repeat visitors; Julius van Sloane—" He stopped and frowned as Miss March let out a shocked gasp. "Miss March, are you all right?" As she began to shake, Carandini moved to her side. and guided her into the spare seat by his desk. Hurrying to the door he threw it open and called to a young steward who was passing, "Yiorgos, quickly, a bottle of brandy and a glass. Hurry!"

The young steward bowed and ran down the corridor to the locked cupboard where the brandy was kept.

Carandini left the door open, returned to the shocked woman, and gently patted her hand until Yiorgos appeared with a tray bearing a small bottle of Napoleon brandy, two glasses, and a tray of biscuits. At a nod from Carandini, he placed the tray on the desk, poured two large glasses of brandy and left, closing the door quietly behind him.

Carandini pressed a glass into her trembling hand. "Drink this…it will help."

Miss March took a deep sip of the dark-amber liquid and coughed as the spirit burned its way down. She pushed herself upright and gave Carandini a tremulous smile. "How very embarrassing! I'm terribly sorry, Mr Bey. I'm quite all right."

He frowned. "Are you sure, Miss March? You look quite pale."

She nodded as she took another sip of her brandy. "I'll be fine." She darted a strange look at her employer. "It's just… I've dealt with the Devereaux family before…" She blinked and hurriedly continued. "At another hotel. I'm sorry, Mr Bay…it's just a terrible shock." She looked at Carandini; her eyes intent. "Are they quite sure it *is* Julius — I mean Mr van Sloane?"

Carandini nodded. "Yes, they are. His wallet with his identity papers was found on his body." He picked up the second glass of brandy and sipped it. "The family have barely arrived at the hotel, and I am to be the bearer of terrible news."

Miss March shook her head. "Please, Mr Bey, let me inform the family."

Carandini's eyebrows shot up. "Miss March, that would not be proper. I, as the manager, should carry the news to the bereaved family."

Miss March bit her lip. "It's just…I know the family, Mr Bey. Please let me be the one to tell them."

Carandini considered his secretary's earnest request; having dealt with such situations once or twice in the past, he disliked the emotional scenes when families were given such upsetting news. If his secretary wanted to take the task upon her slender shoulders, that was her choice. He nodded. "Very well, Miss March, I'll leave it in your capable hands. The police informed me that three officers would arrive no later than two o'clock this afternoon. That gives them time to inform the family and leave before the sandstorm arrives." He eyed Miss March. "I was also informed that they will be bringing his body…for identification purposes. They have the documents they found in his wallet, but someone will have to formerly identify him. I trust one of the family will be able to do this?"

Miss March nodded. "Yes…I believe Kiefer will probably be the best to see to that…" Her face turned a shade paler as she pressed her hand to her face. "Poor Margaux!"

Carandini poured her another brandy and sat down

behind his desk, a disquieted expression on his face. "You are a professional woman, Miss March, kindly refer to the family members by their titles and surnames, not their Christian names." He leant back in his chair. "I understand that over the years you may have developed what you feel to be a sense of camaraderie with the family. However, you are an employee in this hotel, and they are a very wealthy, highly placed family. Your emotional connection to them is rather unnerving, and I must ask you, as your employer, to desist."

Miss March stared at him, open-mouthed. As Carandini finished speaking, she snapped her mouth shut and an expression he couldn't quite place flashed across her face, followed rapidly by a dull white light that flashed in both her eyes before it disappeared as swiftly as it had arrived. Carandini blinked as Miss March dropped her gaze and nodded meekly. "Yes, Mr Bey. You're quite right, of course. I don't know what came over me. I shall endeavour to be more professional in my future dealings with the Devereaux family."

Carandini smiled uncertainly. "Very good, Miss March. I trust you will inform the family with your usual skill and grace."

Miss March placed her empty glass on the tray, then stood up and smoothed the front of her linen day dress. "Thank you, Mr Bey. If you would excuse me, I shall break the news to the Devereaux family and inform them of the police request for a formal identification."

Carandini stood up too. "Of course, Miss March. If there is anything they need, please inform me and I'll see it's done."

"Of course, Mr Bey."

As she left his office, Carandini frowned again; Miss March's reaction had been a touch dramatic…he hoped she wasn't getting ideas above her station — that would never do! As he turned his attention to the papers on his desk, he paused; the strange pale glow that had briefly appeared in her eyes must have been a trick of the light…there was no other possible explanation.

He jumped as a knock sounded on his door. He stood abruptly as Darling entered his office. "Yes, Captain Darling. How may I help you?"

Darling smiled languidly. "I need to place a telephone call, Mr Bey. I understand that yours is the only device in the hotel?"

Carandini nodded. "Yes, it is. We insist on a relaxing environment for our guests with no access to such modern paraphernalia."

Darling's smile widened. "I am afraid I must insist, Mr Bey. I need to place an urgent call…" Darling paused, wondering what would be the best way to get Carandini out of his office so he could call Colonel Barrington and confirm the timings for their appointment; he had a sudden flash of inspiration and continued. "…To the Eridanus Corporation."

Whatever he was expecting, the slight blanching of Carandini's face was not it. Darling frowned. "Mr Bey…are you quite all right?"

Carandini's mouth dropped open as he blinked. "Captain Darling, you amaze me. How on earth did you find out about the death?"

Darling covered his surprise with aplomb. He gestured at the spare armchair by the desk, and at Carandini's nod, sat gracefully as his mind flew through the possibility that Carandini had found out the truth about the fracas at Abu Simbel. "Why don't you tell me what you know, Mr Bey? Then I will call the…corporation and clarify the particulars. We need to make sure the information you've received is accurate. I doubt that the Eridanus Corporation would like any misinformation to be disseminated before it's ascertained to be correct."

As Carandini nodded and began to talk, across the hall, Miss March was hurrying to her own little domain. Entering the small but efficient office, she closed the door, lifted the communications tube from her desk, and blew down it. A responding whistle came back almost immediately as a tinny voice spoke at the other end. "Yes, Miss March?"

"Santos, we have been advised that a sandstorm will arrive at approximately five o'clock this afternoon. I need you to deploy the Simulandro staff and the shutters across the entirety of the hotel. Please also send maids to inform the guests of our sandstorm protocol." There was a slight pause, then the tinny voice responded. "Understood, Miss March. We will see to the order immediately."

"Thank you, Santos." She pushed the tube back into its cradle and looked at her reflection in the ornate oval mirror on the wall behind her desk. Frowning at the appearance of her deathly pale skin and unnaturally large eyes, she reached for the chatelaine at her waist and used one of its many keys to unlock a drawer in her desk. Removing a small compact, she applied a light dusting of face powder, followed by a small amount of alkanet salve to her colourless lips. She checked her appearance and added a little of the salve to her cheeks; that was better…she looked a little more human.

A bubble of hysterical laughter welled in her throat. She pressed her hands across her mouth and tried desperately to swallow the sound that threatened to escape. Taking a deep breath, she sat at her desk, unlocked a separate drawer, and removed the bottle of gin she always kept for emergencies. Emptying the glass of water that had sat on her desk since breakfast, she poured herself a double, and drank the neat contents in two gulps. She took several deep, shuddering breaths; feeling more human was not something she had been able to claim for a very long time!

She replaced the bottle in the drawer and locked it again.

Leaving her office, she walked towards the Isis corridor which housed the Devereaux family's collection of suites. Her footsteps quickened as she approached a particular door. On reaching it, she didn't pause to knock, but instead entered quickly and closed the door behind her.

The rooms occupiers; Marguerite, Margaux, Kiefer, and Camillia, stared at her in surprise. Kiefer stood with a frown. "What on earth do you think you're doing, entering without even knocking?"

Miss March shook her head as she looked at Marguerite. "I know why Julius hasn't returned!"

Silence descended and Margaux looked at Miss March with a cold eye. "Why? Was it you, Vanessa? Were you the reason he abandoned me on the airship?"

Miss March stared at the angry woman in shock. "Margaux! I've never thought of Julius as anything other than my benefactor! And I wasn't even on the *Cartouche* when he went missing; I've been here since your last visit. No, Margaux, I'm afraid I have news of Julius — the worst kind."

A muscle twitched under Margaux's eye as she stared at the distraught young woman. When she spoke, her voice was matter of fact. "He's dead?"

At Miss March's nod, Kiefer gave a bark of laughter and shook his head. "Dead again? That bloody idiot! How many more times do we have to tell him to be careful?" He looked at Miss March. "Do you know how?"

She shook her head. "All I know is that his body was found in the Nile near Kom Ombo. The police are coming here at two o'clock this afternoon, and they are bringing his body for formal identification." She looked at Marguerite. "There's something else..."

Kiefer's lip curled into a sneer as he poured himself another drink. "There always is!"

Miss March ignored him and addressed Marguerite. "A

sandstorm is approaching. It will arrive at approximately five o'clock this evening."

Kiefer frowned and looked at his mother. "That leaves us very little time."

Marguerite waved her hand. "It will be fine." She looked at Miss March. "I take it the usual route to the chamber will still be completely accessible."

Miss March nodded. "Although because of the storm, anyone seen in the vicinity of the Chapel of Mandulis will certainly be seen, as there's only one path to it through the hallways. I suggest we go after everyone else has retired for the night."

Everyone turned to look at Marguerite. The matriarch gazed at Miss March. "I concur. I suggest we gather in this suite at three o'clock tomorrow morning." Kiefer pulled a face at the hour suggested, then caught his mother's eye and immediately turned his gaze to the floor as she continued. "We can ensure that all is made ready in time for the full ritual. Now, Vanessa, return to your office."

Miss March looked unhappy at the obvious dismissal, but nodded. "Of course. I'll return." She turned to leave, her eyes on Kiefer, but he didn't even look at her.

As the door closed behind Miss March, Margaux stood, walked to the drinks cabinet, and poured herself a treble scotch. She sank it without a word and poured herself another. Marguerite shared a look with Kiefer, who removed the glass from his sister's hand and drank the contents. "Dearest Margaux, you know what you're like when you drink too much. We really don't want you giving away our secrets, do we?"

Margaux stared at her brother through tear-filled eyes, then laughed bitterly. "What the Hell would you know of me, Kiefer? You know *nothing* of me!" She slapped the empty glass from his hand and ran out of the room. Entering her own suite, she slammed the door behind her, threw herself onto the bed and wept.

Back in Marguerite's suite, Camillia turned her limpid blue eyes to her grandmother. "This is the second time that Papa has died in thirty years; can we bring him back again so soon?"

Marguerite smiled and patted her granddaughter's cheek. "Of course we can, darling — we've done it before. But he must wait until after we have resurrected your dear grandpapa." She looked at Kiefer. "We need Julius' skull. You make the formal identification, Kiefer, that way you can find out where they will be keeping his body."

Kiefer nodded. "I'll see to it. If the police are bringing him here, that will certainly make retrieving it easier."

Marguerite turned to her granddaughter with a smile. "There, my dear. We shall claim your father's skull. After we have resurrected your dear grandpapa, we shall start the process for your father. But remember, my dear child — after we have brought your grandfather back, it will take thirteen moons for us to find all the necessary donors to resurrect your dear father."

Camillia beamed. "Thank you, Grandmama."

○

Thorne and Aquilleia's suite
12:10pm

Aquilleia picked up the leash as a knock sounded at the door. "Enter," she called.

The door opened to reveal one of the hotel maids, who bobbed a curtsy. "Excuse me, Ma'am, but a sandstorm is due to arrive at five o'clock. I am to tell you that the shutters are going up, and for your own safety, you are not to walk beyond them."

Aquilleia frowned. "Do you know how long the storm will last?"

The maid shook her head. "I'm afraid not, Ma'am…it could be a few hours, or a few days."

Aquilleia nodded. "Thank you."

The young maid bobbed again. "Thank you, Ma'am."

As she left, Aquilleia looked at the expectant Labrador and smiled sadly. "I'm afraid you will have to put up with just me again on your walk, Veronique."

A voice came from the bedroom doorway. "I may be up to a gentle meander along the riverside."

Veronique hurtled to Thorne's side and gave a delighted wiggle as she snuffled at his hands. Aquilleia looked at her husband with a concerned expression. "Are you sure? Darling's staying here because of the investigation…we may meet him while we're walking."

Thorne nodded as he walked to her side. "I know. But I was brought into this case because I'm a professional, therefore, I need to start acting like one. I overheard the maid — if there's a sandstorm approaching, we need to take Veronique for a walk before it lands. I need to explain things to Elliott and Giselle." He sighed as Aquilleia wrapped her arms around his neck. "I can never forget the past…but for the time being at least, I need to move past it so I can bring all my effort to bear on the case in hand."

Aquilleia kissed him gently and pressed her forehead against his chin. "We shall deal with whatever happens, my love…it's what we do."

As they clung to each other, a sudden, rattling snore rent the air. They stared at each other before turning to Veronique, who had grown tired of her humans' strange behaviour and decided to work on her beauty sleep. Thorne and Aquilleia shared a look before Thorne took the lead and jingled it. "Come along — walkies!" A brown eye slowly opened and fixed on Thorne. The black Labrador snuggled into the rumpled sheets, and closed her eyes.

Aquilleia grinned at her husband. "You should know better." She walked to the wardrobe, reached into her hatbox, and produced a handful of biscuits. "Veronique...vittals!" The Labrador immediately bounded off the bed and sat by Aquilleia's side.

Thorne raised an eyebrow at the unembarrassed dog. "Everyone has a price, don't they, Veronique? Well, let's head out for this walk and see if we can find Elliott, Giselle, and this unnamed, fluffy ball of murder they've adopted."

Aquilleia laughed as the three of them left the suite and walked down the Osiris corridor into the entrance hall of the palatial hotel. As they entered the huge room, they saw a large number of Simulandro stewards in the process of locking thick glass panels across the wooden arches that ran alongside every corridor and hallway. Just by the main door, four stewards were carefully fitting glass panels across the roof of the entrance hall; each steward taking one side of the heavy panels before lowering them into place. Thorne, Aquilleia, and Veronique turned and made their way to the jetty for a leisurely stroll by the river, as in the distance, a vague yellowing of the sky foreshadowed the approaching storm.

○

The Covered Terrace
1:20pm

Elliott leant across the table. "Shall I pour?"

At Giselle's nod, Elliott dropped a splash of milk and a single sugar lump into one of the fine bone China cups on the table, lifted the matching teapot, and poured a steady stream of piping hot India tea. Taking the proffered cup, Giselle took a sip. "Perfect!"

As they sat in companionable silence, Darling appeared on the corner of the terrace and made a beeline for their table. "Good morning. Have you heard about the sandstorm?"

Giselle placed her cup and saucer on the table and sat back in the rattan chair. "Yes. We understand it's due to arrive shortly before the cocktail hour."

Darling nodded. "I witnessed a sandstorm many years ago; a young gentleman refused to stay inside and was left slightly — well, decorticated, is the only term I can think of to describe it! It certainly wasn't very pretty...and neither was he until his skin grew back!" He turned to watch the Simulandro stewards who were bolting thick panels of glass in place on the hidden metal framework that ran across the tops of the columns. "I can certainly understand why they lock the outer doors."

Giselle frowned. "Won't the glass make the rooms very hot?"

Darling sat down and waved at one of the stewards. "Absolutely. That's why, when you return to your suite, you will see a small device, surmounted by a large block of ice in your room. As the ice melts, it drives a small motor which powers an equally small fan. It works on the same principle as the cooling motors within Simulandro androids, though those are driven by the android's movements, not melting ice. It'll help keep your rooms cool until the sandstorm has passed and they can remove the panels."

He shifted in his chair as the human steward approached and bowed. "Yes, Sir?"

Darling smiled at him. "I'm aware that it's not yet the cocktail hour, but I believe a Martinez would be quite beneficial. Heavy on the gin, if you please."

The steward bowed again. "Of course, Sir."

Darling watched the steward walk into the main building before turning to Elliott and Giselle with a serious expression. "I have some rather unpleasant news which may have something to do with the case."

Elliott raised an eyebrow. "Oh?"

"It concerns one of the Devereaux family; Mr Julius van Sloane. We now know why he wasn't at breakfast on the last day of travel, or dinner the night before." Darling summarised what he had learned from Carandini about the discovery of Julius' corpse at Kom Ombo, and his body's impending arrival with the officers investigating the case. He paused as the steward returned with his drink. Darling waited until the steward was out of earshot before continuing. "Luckily for us, one of the men arriving with the corpse is Colonel Barrington; two birds, one stone. His presence is quite handy, in that our discussion about the attacks on the British travellers can easily be hidden within the investigation into van Sloane's death."

Giselle took a biscuit and nibbled the edge. "Have they any idea how he died?"

Darling sipped his Martinez. "From what scant information I gleaned from Carandini, I don't think so. His body was discovered in the river, but some water-dwelling residents had found him several hours before the humans! When they finally dragged him out of the Nile, he was in a bit of a mess, I'm afraid."

Giselle pulled a face. "How very unpleasant." She paused and caught her husband's eye; they had yet to inform Darling of their suspicions about the terrorist named in the dossier as Egyptian Blue, and the possibility that he could be a necromancer named Caeruleum...and a member of the Devereaux family. "Could van Sloane's death have something to do with the terrorists?"

Darling shook his head. "I doubt it. His death doesn't fit the terrorist's modus operandi; apparently, his jewellery was still on his person, along with his identity documents."

Elliott frowned. "What do you mean by 'identity documents'? His passport? That would be a touch strange...very few travellers wander around with their passport in their pocket or reticule."

Darling smiled. "He was carrying his wallet, which contained several membership cards; gentlemen's clubs, that sort of thing. All in his name."

"Understood." Elliott sipped his tea and darted Darling a sharp look. "Have you seen Thorne? He needs to know about this meeting with the Egyptian police and Colonel Barrington."

Darling shifted in his seat again. "I tried talking with him on the *Cartouche*..."

"And?"

Darling sat back in the rattan chair with a grimace. "It went as well as you would think."

Giselle raised an eyebrow. "Ah! Well, we need Thorne and Aquilleia on this case."

Darling absentmindedly reached for a large slice of seed cake and bit into it. "I am quite aware of that fact." He sighed. "I'll try and talk with him again before they get here."

"Before who gets here?"

They turned as Thorne and Aquilleia appeared by the table. Elliott stood. "Ah, Thorne, Aquilleia…Veronique. Darling was just telling us about a rather interesting twist in our case."

Thorne pulled out one of the chairs for Aquilleia and gave his brother a guarded look as he sat down opposite him. "Indeed? Do tell."

Elliott looked at Darling. "Perhaps you would do the honours, Darling? Your chat with Carandini being so fresh in your mind."

Darling blinked. "Yes, of course." Elliott sat back in his chair and raised his hand to call the steward back; the brothers were finally talking…this called for more tea and cake…and possibly something a little stronger!

Darling waited until the steward had taken their order and left before informing Thorne and Aquilleia of the death of van Sloane and the approaching arrival of Colonel Barrington.

Aquilleia looked at the others. "I had a vision the other night just before dinner…what I saw must have been van Sloane's death."

Thorne looked at her. "Why didn't you tell me?" Aquilleia touched her husband's hand. "Your mind was on other things, my love. It didn't seem important at the time."

Giselle's eyes darted between the brothers. Realising that her friend didn't want to talk about how upset Thorne had been in front of the cause of his distress, Giselle cleared her throat. "What did you see?"

Aquilleia closed her eyes. "I saw a balcony, a woman's back, a black-clad figure, a flash of water…then nothing. Someone disappeared from my sight…someone *had* died. But there was another sound…a strange, distant murmur that didn't quite fade away. It was almost as though someone was moving away from me at great speed, while leaving a permanent echo behind."

Darling took a sip of his Martinez. "Well, he was certainly moving very fast, plummeting, as he was, to his gravity-assisted demise several hundred feet below the *Cartouche*..." He paused at the slight snigger from his brother. The two men looked at each other in silence before Aquilleia continued. "I've heard a similar sound before...coming from Marguerite Devereaux's reticule."

Elliott looked at Thorne. "Ah, yes, there is something else you need to know, old chap...about the Devereaux family."

There was a slight pause as the steward returned with a tray laden with teapots, cups and saucers, cakes, and biscuits, while behind him came a Simulandro steward bearing a tray with two bottles of Champagne and four coupes.

Elliott smiled at the stewards. "That will be all, thank you." He grasped one of the bottles and began to pour, pausing only to offer Veronique one of the oatcakes. "Darling, why don't you tell Thorne and Aquilleia about just who and what the Devereaux family really are? And then we will tell you a little something we discovered about one of the names in the dossier."

Darling glared at Elliott through narrowed eyes. "As you wish." He accepted a full coupe of champagne, and settled back in his chair with a decidedly wicked smile. "Perhaps, after I have done so, you will also inform my brother and sister-in-law about the unexpected and somewhat bloody arrival of a very old friend?"

Elliott raised his glass with a rueful smile as they sat in the warm, Egyptian sun and tucked into the first meal Thorne and Darling had shared for centuries.

○

The Reception
2:00pm

Gaston Cavet entered the reception, stood a few polite feet away from the desk, and waited patiently for the lone steward to finish dealing with the Contessa de Mostada. The elderly and slightly squeaky lady was gesticulating wildly and volubly expressing her concern that she had missed the last post. As the steward patiently explained that she had at least thirty minutes before the postal boat left, Miss March walked out of her office with some files for Carandini, saw Cavet waiting, and made her way to the desk. "Yes, Monsieur Cavet? How can I help you?"

The Frenchman smiled at her and smoothed his moustache. "I wish to leave a private missive for one of the other guests. Would you have the means for me to write such a note, and deliver it?"

Miss March nodded. "Of course, Monsieur Cavet. Please follow me." She led the Frenchman across the reception and into a small room at the far end that contained three writing desks. "There are pens, paper, and envelopes, Monsieur Cavet. If you hand the note in when you're finished, I'll see that it's passed to the guest in question."

"Ah…how organised you are. Merci beaucoup." Miss March left the room as Cavet sat down and composed a short note. He blotted the ink, placed the note in a small envelope, wrote a name on the front, and returned to the reception, where he handed the note to the waiting Miss March. Her smile faltered slightly as she saw the name on the front of the envelope. "I'll see that Mlle Gagnon receives the note, Monsieur Cavet."

"Thank you, Mlle March." He walked back to his suite as

Miss March stared at the note; she needed to see the family urgently — Marguerite would know what to do. She turned at a sudden babble of voices from the entrance to the reception and slipped the note up her sleeve as Carandini Bey entered with three men, two of whom she didn't recognise. She covered her shock at the sight of the third man and forced a smile. "Good afternoon, Mr Bey. I was just about to deliver a note to a guest…is there anything I can help you with first?"

"No, thank you, Miss March. Gentlemen, this is Miss March, my secretary. Miss March, allow me to introduce Colonel Barrington, Captain Sarhan, and Sergeant Jaziri." The three men turned to look at her and bowed.

Miss March nodded to them. "Gentlemen." She caught Sergeant Jaziri's eye and shook her head almost imperceptibly, then turned back to Carandini and lowered her voice. "I understood that Mr van Sloane would be arriving with you?"

Carandini glanced around the quiet reception hall, and leant in. "Mr van Sloane has been taken through the back corridor to the second meat locker. We thought it best that he be placed somewhere out of the way of the guests and the staff…and given the usual weather in Egypt, preferably somewhere cold! Luckily, the second meat locker is not used very often." He turned back to the three men and waved an expansive hand towards his office. "Gentlemen, please come to my office. We can talk privately there."

He turned back to his secretary. "Actually, Miss March, there is something you can do. Colonel Barrington has requested the presence of Mr Caine, Mr Thorne, and Captain Darling at our meeting. Please send someone to inform them that we shall be waiting in my office. After that, kindly apprise the family that the identification will take place at half past two, and arrange for one of the stewards to escort them to the meat locker."

Miss March's eyes widened. "But I don't understand, Mr Bey. Shouldn't the family be told first? And why bother the other guests with this information…?" Her voice faltered at the expression of anger that appeared on Carandini's face. His voice was sharp as he snapped. "That is enough, Miss March! Kindly do as you are told." He turned to the party behind him. "Gentlemen, if you will follow me."

Colonel Barrington and Captain Sarhan followed Carandini down the corridor that led to his office. As Sergeant Jaziri sauntered slowly past Miss March, she hissed under her breath. "We need to talk!"

Jaziri darted a sharp glance at the three men some distance ahead of him, his dark eyes wary as he whispered back. "There should be an opportunity during the identification. I'll be guarding the door." He left her side and quickly caught up with the others as they disappeared inside Carandini's office.

Miss March pulled the note from her sleeve and tapped it against her lips worriedly; it felt as though things were beginning to unravel. She walked swiftly from the reception towards the Isis corridor and paused at the suite door. Remembering the anger on Kiefer's face when she had simply walked in, she knocked and waited. Catching sight of her reflection in the mirror by the door, she hurriedly tucked an escaped strand of auburn hair back into her bun.

After a few moments, the door swung open. Vincenzo smiled at her. "Hello again, Vanessa. Is everything all right?"

Miss March shook her head. "I must speak with Marguerite."

Vincenzo turned to the room and raised his voice. "It's Vanessa…she says she needs to speak with you."

A voice spoke from within, "Let her enter."

Vincenzo stepped back from the door and gestured into the room. Miss March walked past him and paused as

Marguerite looked up at her from the settee, her face and neck covered in a thick layer of green balm. The older woman pulled a face. "With careful planning we can live forever, but the dry heat of the desert can still dry our skin. What's the matter, child?"

Miss March swallowed. "There are three things, Marguerite. Firstly, the police have arrived with Julius' body. The identification is set for half past two, and one of the stewards will collect the person who is performing it. I take it that Kiefer will be performing this duty?"

Marguerite nodded, a look of sadness on her face. "Margaux is currently drinking herself into a stupor in her suite. Kiefer will do his duty by his sister. Continue."

Miss March nodded. "The investigating officials are Colonel Barrington of the Veiled Protectorate, Captain Sarhan of the Egyptian police…and Sergeant Jaziri."

Vincenzo's eyebrows rocketed down across his nose; he looked sharply at Miss March. "What in God's name is Le Noir doing here? Has he said anything?"

Miss March shook her head. "There was no time for a conversation, not with the others there. We've agreed to talk during the identification."

Marguerite closed her eyes with a pained expression and pressed her fingertips to her temple; her slender fingers gliding across the green unguent on her skin. "If nothing else, confirm with him the approved copy of the list. Then we can organise for the most financially viable guests to be separated from their wealth while we're here."

Miss March stared at her. "But, Marguerite, because of the sandstorm, there's no way for their men to secure the travellers and their possessions in their usual fashion."

Marguerite lifted her empty Champagne glass and waved it at her husband. As he refilled the coupe, Marguerite smiled at Miss March. "They can have their men standing by, ready to attack, after the sandstorm lifts. As far as I am aware, there are only two couples worthy of our consideration; the Caines and the Thornes. After being trapped indoors for a day or two by a sandstorm, what could be easier than encouraging them to take a trip on a dahabiya? A few sharp smacks over the head with a blunt object will give us all the time we need to go through their rooms and take whatever we think suitable. We can arrange to share the spoils with the Black Eagle later." She held up her right hand, the large diamond on her ring finger glistening in the gaslight. "Immortality gives us our bodily appearance, and money shrouds it in a glittering cover of social acceptance. It takes a great deal of money to look this fabulous, so we need all the money we can get. Thanks to the deal Kiefer agreed with the Islamists, we are guaranteed a constant supply of wealth — minus a small commission for Le Noir, the Black Eagle, and their cause, as a finder's fee, of course — but only as long as there is a constant supply of wealthy travellers. We need their assistance in sourcing the wealth, and they need our contacts to sell the items in Europe…a perfect example of a symbiotic relationship." She smiled at Miss March. "Now, what was the second issue?"

Miss March took a deep breath and held out the note. "Gaston Cavet gave me this note…it's addressed to Jane."

Marguerite raised an immaculate but green eyebrow. "And you bring it to me, not Jane. Why?"

Miss March swallowed hard. "I have a horrible feeling about him; I think he knows something about the family."

The matriarch nodded as she leant forward and took the envelope. "Very well; but if this is a personal 'je t'adore' note from a man to a woman, I shall leave your punish-ment to Jane's discretion." Miss March blanched at the threat as Marguerite opened the envelope and scanned the note, her face darkening. "It would appear that I owe you an apology, Vanessa. You were quite correct in your fears. Hmm...he mentions that he was in Montmartre when Kiefer suffered his injuries during that little duel...and again when Heathers returned to deal with the two young men responsible." Marguerite sat back in her chair and looked at her husband. "Go and get Jane. Find Kiefer and André and bring them too...we need to have a discussion about what to do with Monsieur Cavet — sooner rather than later!" She sighed and waved her hand. "And the third issue?"

Miss March swallowed. "When the men arrived, Mr Bey told me to bring Mr Caine, Mr Thorne, and Captain Darling to his office to talk with the police."

Marguerite frowned. "But they are guests here. Why on earth..."

Miss March nodded. "It *is* strange. If they're guests, why concern them with Julius' death? Unless—"

Marguerite's eyes gleamed. "Unless there is something more to Caine, Thorne, and Darling than meets the eye!

○

Carandini's Office
2:20pm

Carandini looked at his guests. "Private enquiry agents?" He raised a Mephistophelean eyebrow at Colonel Barrington. "On whose side?"

Colonel Barrington took a sip of his tea and flicked his fly-whisk in an irritated fashion. "The Empire's, of course! Who else is there?"

Carandini and Sarhan shared a glance before the hotel manager gestured at the two other people who had entered the room with Elliott, Thorne, and Darling. Two people whose presence neither he, Barrington, nor Sarhan had expected. "And the…ladies?"

Elliott and Thorne did not bother to cover their amusement as Giselle inflicted the full wattage of her smile on Carandini, who could only blink at the sight of her disarming dimples. "We too are enquiry agents, Mr Bey."

Aquilleia smiled at the faint grumble from the floor. "As is Veronique. We work together on our cases."

Carandini nodded at Darling. "And this gentleman? I can see a familial resemblance to Mr Thorne. Are you all enquiry agents?"

Darling smiled. "Indeed, we are all agents, Mr Bey. Now, to the case in hand. We understand that the body of Mr Julius van Sloane was discovered in the Nile, by the town of Kom Ombo. Do we know exactly how the gentleman met his end?"

Colonel Barrington nodded at Captain Sarhan, who frowned as he sat forward. "Gentlemen, I understand that you are in some way endorsed by the Empire, but I have to say that this situation is quite unusual. I have never been required to bring a private organisation into an investigation. I am rather unsure…"

Elliott reached into his breast pocket, removing a small black leather wallet. "I understand, Captain. Perhaps this will assist?" He handed the wallet to the unconvinced Egyptian, who opened it. His frown deepened as he scanned the identification card within. He returned the wallet to Elliott. "I understand what it says, and I understand that you are here to provide assistance with the case involving the Islamists; but I still don't understand why—"

Darling looked at the dissentient police officer and snapped. "This is becoming quite tedious, Sarhan. We have provided you with paperwork proving that we work for the Empire, and as such, have clearance to work with the Veiled

Protectorate on this particular matter. Both you and Colonel Barrington are bound by your duty, as well as your oaths, to provide us with any and all assistance in this matter! Now; do you know how Julius van Sloane died, or not?"

Captain Sarhan flushed angrily. Thorne took out a pencil and notebook as Sarhan finally responded; his voice clipped and tight. "The examiner believed that the injuries were caused by van Sloane falling into the Nile from a great height."

Elliott caught Thorne's eye and leant forward; they knew from Aquilleia that van Sloane had fallen to his death from the airship, they simply had to nudge the authorities into accepting it as the only possibility. "Possibly from the *Cartouche?*"

Captain Sarhan nodded. "That is their belief."

Giselle looked over the rim of her teacup and joined in with her husband's game of encouragement. "The main question being; did he fall, or was he pushed?"

Captain Sarhan shrugged. "The authorities are not prepared to answer that. However, there are flakes of paint and wood under his fingernails which suggest he was clinging to painted wood shortly before he fell." He paused. "We spoke to the Eridanus Corporation, who sent their stewards to check all woodwork on the airship. Not only does the paint match the colour used by the hotel; a very specific shade of eau de nil, but marks that are consistent with scratches from fingernails were discovered in three areas on the airship. Several are on the woodwork in the bridge, but no guest is allowed in there for security reasons. A few marks were found in the viewing salon, but the windows there do not open wide enough to permit the passage of a guest."

Thorne looked up. "And the third set of marks?"

Captain Sarhan looked at his own notes. "The third set

were on the balcony rail of the suite belonging to the honey-mooning couple; Mr André Devereaux and his wife, Mrs Evelyn Briar-Devereaux."

Silence fell as five people caught each other's eye and tried not to think of the vision Aquilleia had spoken of earlier, or the unexpected presence of Masquelyne. Elliott closed his eyes and groaned quietly — he needed to find his father, and sooner, rather than later!

Thorne caught the narrow-eyed look Captain Sarhan gave Elliott. Thinking quickly, he asked, "And you're absolutely sure they can't say whether van Sloane was pushed or not?"

Captain Sarhan slowly shook his head. "They will not say one way or the other. Between the injuries inflicted by the impact and the post-mortem damage caused by crocodiles and fish, there is no way to tell if any of the marks on his body were caused by an attacker. All they can say is that they believe he was gripping on to a wooden rail on the *Cartouche* shortly before he fell."

Darling looked at his pocket watch. "Ladies and gentlemen, it's almost time for us to attend to the identification. I suggest we head to the meat locker and await the arrival of the Devereaux family."

◯

The Meat Locker
2:40pm

As Carandini led them towards the main corridor, he paused, then turned to the group with a pained expression. "May I ask, ladies and gentlemen, that we utilise the staff corridor? I would prefer to keep the news of Mr van Sloane's death and subsequent storage in the meat locker from our guests. The majority have travelled here for a sumptuous and relaxing holiday, not to be involved in what may turn out to be either a tragic accident or a grubby incident."

Captain Sarhan's eyes narrowed as Colonel Barrington glanced at Darling then turned to Carandini. "Yes, of course. Has a member of staff been sent to collect the person carrying out the identification?"

Carandini led them across the hallway and through a door into a narrower corridor that was bare of both paintings and carpeting. "Yes; the identification will be carried out by Mr Kiefer Devereaux. I sent one of the Simulandro stewards to collect him."

Giselle frowned. "You sent an android?"

Carandini opened a door and paused, a look of irritation on his face. "It was either the Simulandro or Miss March, and I fear that Miss March has been getting ideas above her station regarding the Devereaux family."

Giselle raised her eyebrows. "How so?"

Carandini paused. "Referring to them by their Christian names, becoming emotionally attached. She said she had known the family for years, including when she worked at a previous hotel. I found it all rather embarrassing."

Elliott and the others exchanged glances. "How did the family respond to such familiarity?" Giselle asked.

Carandini led them through the door and down the even narrower hallway beyond. "Oh, it wasn't in front of the family..." He paused again, with a worried look. "At least, not at that time." His dark brows knitted. "Although; that's rather strange..."

Thorne studied him. "What is strange, Mr Bey?"

"Miss March said she knew the family from her time at another hotel, but as far as I'm aware, she's never worked at any other hotel. She came straight to us from working in a private capacity for a countess in Italy…somewhere near the lakes, I believe."

Darling nodded. "Interesting. Thank you, Mr Bey."

"But how could that mean anything—"

"Bey! I've been waiting for over five minutes! I shall inform your superiors when I see them at the club on our return to London!" Elliott's eyebrows lifted a fraction at the audible grinding sound issuing from Carandini's teeth as Kiefer stepped out of the doorway leading to the meat locker and raised an insolent eyebrow. "Who are these dreary looking people?"

As Kiefer saw Giselle, a predatory smile appeared on his face, which vanished instantly as Elliott stepped in front of his wife. "Mr Devereaux? My name is Elliott Caine. We are investigating the death of your brother-in-law, Mr Julius van Sloane."

Kiefer glared at Elliott; his blue eyes snapping with anger. Elliott smiled lazily, his long canines glinting in the lamplight. Kiefer turned and stormed back into the meat locker. Elliott looked at the others, a faint twinkle in his brown eyes. "Oh dear!"

Giselle grinned and tapped her husband on the arm with her fan. "Behave!"

He smiled. "But I'm having so much fun! Ladies, gentlemen, shall we see to the identification?"

As they entered the room, Captain Sarhan addressed Jaziri. "Stand by the door and don't allow anyone to enter. Do you understand?"

Sergeant Jaziri nodded sharply. "Yes, Sir." As the door swung shut, he listened to the introductions being made within and shook his head; in the face of death, everyone was still so very proper! He took up position in front of the door and rocked back and forth on the balls of his feet.

After a few minutes had passed, Miss March appeared

and hurried to his side. She glanced about her before she spoke, keeping her voice low. "About the list; are the targets confirmed as the Caines and the Thornes?"

As Jaziri nodded, she gestured at the closed door. "The Caines and the Thornes are the two couples in there!"

Jaziri nodded. "I recognised their names. So, they are the private enquiry agents sent to assist Sarhan and Barrington?"

Miss March bit at a fingernail. "Yes. And the other man's name is Captain Anthony Darling."

"Another enquiry agent. But he seems to have more sway with the Veiled Protectorate. Barrington was deferential to him, which suggests…"

"Which suggests what?" Miss March prompted.

Jaziri shrugged. "That he has more power than Barrington."

Miss March gave a sharp bark of laughter, which she hurriedly stifled before giving the door a worried glance. "But Barrington's the voice of the Veiled Protectorate in this part of Egypt! He's a colonel — Darling's a lowly captain!"

"I will see what I can discover. They will be finished soon, go quickly! I will contact you later to let you know what I discover."

Miss March hurried away and turned the corner just as the door opened and Darling's head appeared. He looked up and down the corridor before turning to Jaziri. "Is everything all right, Sergeant? I thought I heard voices."

Jaziri spat an uncouth word in the silence of his own mind and adopted an embarrassed expression. "I do apologise, Captain Darling; I was saying a prayer for the dead."

Darling studied him. "Very well. As you were." He returned to the meat locker, closed the door behind him, and folded his arms. His green eyes, so similar to Thorne's, were thoughtful.

Beside him, Giselle and Aquilleia sat on one of the shelves

in silence, Veronique on the floor beside them. They had decided there was no need for them to witness the result of Julius's entanglement with the crocodiles of Kom Ombo, and had instead made themselves comfortable by the door. It also offered Aquilleia the opportunity to listen to the soft murmuring coming from where Julius' lay. As she tried to make sense of the sound, she turned her lavender eyes to the bored-looking Kiefer, who was standing by the shrouded remains of his brother-in-law. He pointedly pulled out his watch and glared at Colonel Barrington. "Let's get on with this, shall we? I haven't got all day!"

Colonel Barrington and Captain Sarhan exchanged glances and the Egyptian officer shrugged. "As you wish, Mr Devereaux." He flipped the cover from the top half of the corpse and intoned in a practiced voice, "Do you, Mr Kiefer Devereaux, confirm that this is the body of your brother-in-law, Mr Julius van Sloane?"

Kiefer's lip curled in disgust as he looked at the mauled remains. "How in God's name can I tell, man? There isn't much left!"

Elliott pointed at a crescent-shaped birthmark on the upper right side of the torso. "Do you recognise this mark, Mr Devereaux?"

Kiefer's mind flew back to the last time they had resurrected Julius; yes, he dimly remembered a birthmark *had* appeared on the torso during the ritual. "Yes...yes, I do believe he had a birthmark..." He caught Elliott's eye and cleared his throat. "I mean, yes, Julius did have a birthmark on his chest." He looked at Colonel Barrington. "I believe this to be the body of my brother-in-law, Julius van Sloane. What happens now?"

Colonel Barrington blinked; he was used to brusqueness, but it didn't usually occur during the identification of a corpse by a family member. He harrumphed. "If, as you claim, this is the body of your brother-in-law, we shall retire to Mr Bey's office to complete some forms, and then we shall take his body back to the morgue at Kom Ombo to prepare him for his return to England."

Kiefer stared at him; this was something he hadn't foreseen. Thinking quickly, he shook his head. "Colonel Barrington, as you will understand, my sister wished to say her farewells to her husband. However, due to her grief, she has taken a sleeping draught and will not wake until much later today."

Colonel Barrington looked aghast. "I must protest, Sir! This is out of our hands. The body must be returned to the morgue in Aswan for the correct storage…" He paused, leant in, and hissed. "It's the heat, you understand? It can do some rather unpleasant things to…" He gestured at the remains. "Corpses!"

Kiefer's eyebrows drew together; he was not used to people refusing him. He spoke through gritted teeth. "Yes, Colonel Barrington, I do understand." He gestured at the cold, lead-lined room they stood in. "This place is as good as any morgue. We are due to return to Cairo at the end of the week, so it wouldn't be for too long."

Colonel Barrington looked at Captain Sarhan. "Well, it is most irregular…" He started as a voice came from the back of the room. "I think it will be quite all right, Colonel Barrington."

They all turned to look at Darling who smiled at Kiefer. "The necessary paperwork can be seen to now, but the return of Mr van Sloane's corpse to the proper facilities can be paused until after Mrs van Sloane has said her farewells to her husband." His smile widened as he looked at Kiefer. "The gentleman won't be going anywhere, will he? After all, we only die once; isn't that so, Mr Devereaux?"

A faint, ugly smile appeared on Kiefer's lips as he looked at the smiling man. "As you say, Captain Darling, as you say."

Colonel Barrington moved forward. "If Captain Darling is prepared to accept this irregularity, who am I to argue? But, Mr Devereaux; if your sister witnesses her husband's final state, it could cause her untold harm. I must insist that you impress this upon her; the injuries inflicted upon her husband mean that she should not look upon him, and instead remember him in happier times."

Kiefer hid an unpleasant smirk; Margaux had seen her husband in far worse states, but that was not for them to know. "I shall inform my sister of your wishes, Colonel Barrington — but when Margaux makes up her mind to do something…" He shrugged.

Darling glanced at Colonel Barrington. "Whatever Mrs Devereaux decides, the body can stay here for a few days, as long as Mr Bey is prepared to accept the presence of a corpse in his kitchens." He turned to Carandini. "It's in your hands, Mr Bey."

Carandini managed a tight smile. "I'm sure it won't be a problem, Captain Darling. I'll have a word with the chef, who I'm certain will understand."

"Thank you, Mr Bey. Perhaps Mr Devereaux would like to accompany Colonel Barrington and Captain Sarhan to your office, for the necessary evils of the paperwork?"

"You mentioned that earlier, Captain Darling," snapped Kiefer. "What exactly is the nature of this paperwork?"

Darling smiled at Kiefer. "Proof of your identity, proof of your brother-in-law's identity; simple things like that. Your passports will suffice, Mr Devereaux. I'm sure you know where they are."

Kiefer glared at Darling, then marched past him, threw the door open and strode down the corridor. Carandini hurried to the door. "Mr Devereaux?" Kiefer turned with a scowl and Carandini smiled politely. "That's the wrong way, Mr Devereaux. If you would care to follow me?" He bowed to Giselle and Aquilleia, then indicated the correct direction.

Kiefer returned, his face an unbecoming shade of puce as Carandini, Colonel Barrington and Captain Sarhan joined him for the walk to Carandini's office. As they made their way down the corridor, they were also joined by Sergeant Jaziri.

As the door closed behind them, Elliott nudged Thorne and gestured at the remains of the head; a pulpy, but obviously skull-shaped mass. "Well, at least we have a positive identification…in spite of his injuries."

Thorne put his notebook in his breast pocket. "Not a very well-mannered one, though."

Elliott shrugged. "We have the full remains, and unlike the case involving poor Valentine Carstairs, we don't have to play the time-honoured game of pin the head on the stump." Aquilleia and Giselle grinned as Thorne sniggered.

Darling leant against the wall, folded his arms, and looked at his sister-in-law. "What could you sense about the people in the room?"

Aquilleia's smile faded. "Kiefer's very good at shielding himself…but, as he's a necromancer, he's had to protect himself from others sensing his thoughts. It might also have something to do with his quite overwhelming sense of his own self-importance."

Giselle nodded. "I'm not psychic, but he's definitely not the kind of man you want to cross, or have take a fancy to you. I very much suspect that he's never heard the word *no* in his life!"

Aquilleia nodded. "Absolutely. With Colonel Barrington, what you see is exactly who he is; a dedicated military man more than capable of spinning a web of death to catch those he considers a danger to the Empire." She smiled. "The main thing on his mind right now, though, other than being concerned for Julius' widow, was his desire for one of his manservant's curries!"

Darling laughed. "And Captain Sarhan?"

"Again, a solid military man; reliable and capable, but irritated by what he saw as Colonel Barrington's willingness to demean himself, by looking to you — in his eyes, a lesser officer — for permission to accept things."

Elliott studied Darling. "I take it Colonel Barrington hasn't told Captain Sarhan of your true position in the investigation?"

Darling shook his head. "It's strictly on a need-to-know basis, and the fewer people who know, the better!" He turned to Aquilleia. "Could you read anything else from them?"

"I think Sergeant Jaziri's hiding something."

Darling's eyebrows lowered. "What makes you say that?"

"He was very…stilted. He seemed reluctant to even look at us. And he hid his thoughts very well, too; I only managed to perceive two words."

Giselle moved forward slightly. "What two words?"

"Al-Aswad."

Giselle blinked. "Al-Aswad?" She looked at Elliott, stunned. "I can't believe it!"

Elliott returned her look. "I don't understand?"

"Al-Aswad is Arabic for 'The Black'. In French, it would be translated as 'Le Noir'!"

Thorne blinked. "You're saying that Sergeant Jaziri is one half of Rouge et Noir?"

Giselle nodded. "It would appear so, yes."

Darling nodded slowly. "In which case, we need to keep an eye on Sergeant Jaziri. Let's not bring it to Captain Sarhan's attention just yet, though…we can use the next few days to see what we can discover." He looked at Aquilleia. "Anything else?

"That distant murmuring sound I heard earlier…when I felt Julius die, but I could still vaguely hear him? I think I understand why. If the family are necromancers, then Julius isn't really dead — well…his body is, but his soul is alive… trapped between the world of the living and the realm of the dead, awaiting his resurrection. That's why I can still hear him." She tapped her cheek thoughtfully. "But that doesn't explain the sound I heard the first night on the airship; Julius wasn't dead then. *That* suggests there may be another family member who was already dead when the Devereaux family boarded the *Cartouche*; someone they brought with them."

Darling nodded slowly. "From what we know of the family, one of their number isn't here; the patriarch, Reynaud Devereaux."

Elliott looked at Darling. "The patriarch? Is he Marguerite's brother?"

"No, her husband."

Thorne frowned. "I thought Vincenzo Prezzo was her husband?"

Darling grinned at his brother. "He is; it takes thirteen moons to resurrect a necromancer. When Reynaud dies, Marguerite welcomes Vincenzo back as her – well, in a duel, I suppose he would be Reynaud's second. It's a very peculiar arrangement, but then the entire family is very, very strange!"

○

The Jetty
3:45pm

Colonel Barrington stood on the jetty and glared at the mechanic, his bristling moustache appearing on the verge of launching a direct assault on the indifferent young man before him. "We need to be in the air within the next hour, or we'll be trapped by the sandstorm! You know she's a temperamental old bird — fix her!"

The mechanic wiped his hands on an oil-stained rag, shrugged, and disappeared back into the engine room of the small but elegant airship that was Colonel Barrington's private air-carriage.

As they waited, Sarhan decided to lay any chance of promotion on the line. "Excuse me, Colonel Barrington, but why do you allow a mere enquiry agent to treat you with such disrespect?"

Colonel Barrington lashed out with his fly-whisk at a particularly slow fly, narrowly missing Sergeant Jaziri, who stepped back hurriedly. "Because that mere enquiry agent is in fact a commander in the British Empire, Captain Sarhan, and as such, outranks me." He looked at the two men with a serious expression. "I trust this will go no further, gentlemen?" At Captain Sarhan's nod he continued. "To use his correct title, Commander Darling is head of an organisation that works sub rosa with our government and whose very existence is referred to in feared whispers. He uses the title of captain because — well, I think it appeals to his sense of humour! They get things done, Captain Sarhan — unpleasant, dangerous, hidden things — and we let them get on with it with minimal fuss, interference, or involvement."

He missed the sharp, calculating look that appeared on Jaziri's face, as Sarhan nodded. "I understand. How do I deal with Commander Darling if he contacts me?"

Colonel Barrington smiled. "The standard operating procedure in these cases is quite simple, Captain; keep out of his bloody way and hope he doesn't contact you again. If he does, give him whatever he asks for as swiftly as possible and pray that's good enough!" Sergeant Jaziri hopped out of the way again as Colonel Barrington made a sudden pointing movement with his fly-whisk and barked, "Mechanic wallah's coming back."

The mechanic grinned and waved at the airship. "Fixed and ready to take you back to Aswan, Sir."

Colonel Barrington smiled widened. "Good man!"

The three men boarded the small craft and took their seats. As the pilot began the procedure for take-off, Colonel Barrington turned to the large cupboard next to him, unstoppered one of the crystal decanters and poured a large whisky. He waved a tumbler at Captain Sarhan, who nodded; after his experiences over the last few hours, the sun was over the yardarm somewhere!

○

The Kiosk of Trajan
4:45pm

In the sweltering heat of the terrace, Maxwell, one of the many Simulandro stewards who worked at the hotel, carefully lowered the final panel into place, inserted the key, and twisted the locking clasps; securing the glass within the metal and wood framework that would protect guests and staff from the approaching sandstorm. As he removed the key, he suddenly realised that the birdsong around him had stopped.

Maxwell raised his head above the temporary roof he had spent most of the day building as the sky in the east darkened dramatically. He watched the changing light with detached interest — a Simulandro was not allowed any other form of thought — as billowing clouds of deep-orange sand approached the hotel. He stood, unhurriedly climbed down one of the columns flanking the Kiosk of Trajan, and walked towards the entrance hall.

As he approached the doorway between the main building and the Temple of Asclepius, the sandstorm exploded around him. Maxwell struggled to stay on his feet as the deadly wind tore through his hair and clothes. The coarse sand abrading his skin as he fought his way past the thrashing palm trees at the edge of the covered terrace.

He finally reached the main door to the entrance hall and hammered at the glass portal. After several minutes, the door was opened by the Simulandro maid, Farasha, who caught the steward as he fell; the clockwork mechanism of his skull and jaw partially exposed by the howling sandstorm that had completely stripped the layers of skin from one side of his face.

◯

Gaston Cavet's Suite
5:55pm

Gaston Cavet raised an immaculate eyebrow and smiled at his reflection; perfection! How could any sensible woman possibly resist? To be sure, some had tried over the years, but they were too few to harm his reputation. He attached his monocle chain and tucked it behind his cravat; his fingers caressing the neatly folded dove grey silk that covered his throat; yes…perfection.

As he admired himself in the mirror, there came a knock at his suite door. Gaston frowned; he wasn't expecting any visitors. He checked his pocket watch; it was far too close to the cocktail hour for any type of assignation…one must allow nothing to interfere with one's aperitif — not even a tryst! With a sigh, he threw the door open with a flourish. When Gaston saw who was standing on the threshold, a delighted smile appeared on his face. "My dear Mlle Gagnon,

I take it you received my missive? I did not expect you to make the approach this evening."

He stepped aside to allow his guest to enter, then closed the door and stroked his moustache as he took in her slender form clad in a perfectly fitted evening gown of blue velvet with gold trim, with matching boots, and reticule. The finishing touch to her elegant ensemble was a hair pin topped with a golden frog. Gaston smiled faintly; such an outfit was most suitable for a lady, but not for a lady's companion.

Jane smiled at him, but humour did not appear in her eyes. "Monsieur Cavet, let us not waste any of our valuable time." She held up the letter. "What will it take for your... curiosity to disappear?"

Gaston raised an eyebrow. "Straight to the crux of the matter, as always, Mlle. Very well. What was witnessed so many months ago could be taken as a trifling little thing... unless of course, one knows about your family — and I know more than others." He spread his hands in a conciliatory manner. "I am sure it's all a mistake which can be dealt with in a few moments of your precious time...and that of your bank manager's! But not right now. It's almost the cocktail hour, and I must insist that the next time you wish to see me about our little...arrangement, you let me know in advance. Now, please allow me to escort you to the cocktail hour."

As he moved towards the door, Jane's smile widened. She reached out and stroked Gaston's smiling face with her hand. He halted and leant towards her; his eyes closing and his lips parting in anticipation of a kiss. With one sharp movement, Jane pulled the long, ornate pin from her hair and plunged it into his eye, forcing the sharp length of metal deep into his brain. Gaston's mouth dropped open in shock, but he made no sound. As Jane wrenched the pin from the wound and stepped back, the Frenchman dropped like a felled oak; his face smashing into the polished marble floor as thick red blood and other liquids slowly spread around his dark head like a halo. Jane's smile finally reached her eyes as she contemplated his corpse; family business done, and done well. Such a shame that Julius had never bothered to follow her lead.

She walked into the bathroom and washed the pin, making sure no trace of blood or tissue remained before she pushed it back into her neatly-dressed hair. Jane looked in the mirror and smiled at her reflection before she brushed a non-existent speck from her flawless cheek and returned to the sitting room.

She cast a derisive look at the man who had tried to blackmail the family; would it be best to hide the body? She looked down at her immaculate evening gown, then at the spreading pool of blood and gore; perhaps not...blood was an absolute nightmare to get out of velvet. She pulled a face as she recalled the number of gowns she had lost over the years. No; far better to leave him where he was — it would certainly be better for her outfit. Jane opened the door and looked up and down the hallway before stepping out of the suite, pulling the door shut, and walking down the Osiris corridor.

As she entered the empty reception hall, she paused, then entered the writing room. She took a notelet and penned a simple missive in Cavet's name stating that he had no desire for either dinner or a supper tray, and was to be left in peace until his breakfast tray was delivered in the morning. Returning to the reception, she checked the hall was still empty before dropping the note on the silver salver that sat on the desk.

With a happy smile, Jane walked through to the bar and the cocktail hour, while in the silence of the Osiris corridor, the Frenchman lay dead in his suite.

○

Monday 25th
The Staff Corridor
01:25am

As the last of the Simulandro stewards finished work and left the kitchens for their shared dormitory, silence fell in the vaulted chambers of the hotel. The silence, however, did not last long, as a black-clad figure, wearing a black mask and carrying a large carpet bag, slid from behind one of the many curtained columns and silently made his way towards the staff corridor and the kitchens beyond. He paused at the end of the corridor and peered around the corner…it was empty; excellent. He hurried down the silent hallway, taking care to make as little noise as possible; Simulandro androids were known for their exceptional hearing, and he didn't feel like explaining his presence to a determined subhuman at that hour of the morning!

After a few short minutes, he arrived at his destination; the doorway to the second meat locker. He turned the handle and winced as the burnished brass made a sharp clicking sound in the heavy, still air. With a gentle push, the door swung open and he entered the cold, windowless room.

Closing the door, he removed the black mask, took a deep breath, and rubbed his face; grimacing at the sensation of his sweat chilling rapidly on his skin. Turning to the shrouded corpse on the makeshift bier, he placed the carpet bag next to the body, opened it, and removed a thick towel and a wickedly sharp knife. He whisked back the thin sheet and looked at the mangled remains; in particular, the thin strip of tissue that connected the head with the body.

Reaching out with the knife, he made a sharp, dismissive movement and severed the narrow cord of flesh. The head of

Julius van Sloane was hurriedly wrapped in the towel and placed in the carpet bag, along with the knife. He looked at the mask with distaste but donned it again before opening the door. Pausing to check the corridor was clear, he stepped into the hallway, closed the door, and silently returned to his suite.

He entered his sitting room, walked straight past the other occupant, and entered the bathroom. Placing the bag in the sink, he stripped off the mask and tossed it on top. He washed his hands and re-entered the sitting room, threw himself into one of the comfortable armchairs, and finally addressed the other man. "I need a drink…make it a treble."

The young man stood, walked to the bar, and poured the drink without a word. He walked to the figure in black and handed them the glass of whisky. "How did it go, uncle?"

Kiefer shrugged as he accepted the glass. "As expected. When collecting the head of a family member, it's usually much easier than harvesting the body parts to resurrect them." He took a gulp from the glass. "Might be wise to check the hall for blood; he started dribbling on the way here."

Linden hurried to the door, opened it a crack, and poked his head through the gap. He turned back. "I can't see anything." He closed the door. "Uncle, I'm concerned. We've never had to deal with being in such close proximity to the authorities before — not while resurrecting a family member! They were actually in the same building as us earlier, and Jane still thought it a good idea to kill Cavet!"

Kiefer sat up and glared at his nephew. "Now you listen to me, Linden. You're only a few hundred years old. What you mean is that *you* have never had to deal with the proximity of the authorities before! *We*, the family, have. Just do what your grandmother tells you and everything will be fine. Now, I'm in need of a bath before the rest of the evening's…or rather, this morning's, events. Fix me another drink." Kiefer stood up, handed his empty glass to his nephew, and began to strip as he wandered back into the bathroom.

As the door closed behind him, Linden stared at the empty glass before turning back to the bar and pouring two large whiskies. He sank one in silence before carrying the other to the bathroom and knocking on the closed door. "Uncle, your drink."

The door opened and Kiefer, now naked, took the glass without thanks. "I'll be half an hour." He closed the door in Linden's face and turned on the taps as his nephew entered his own bedroom, closed the door, and sat in thought in the warm darkness.

○

The Entrance Hall
3:30am

In the strange and otherworldly illumination offered by the blending of the sandstorm and the predawn light, a group of black-robed figures appeared by the doorway leading from the private suites to the entrance hall. Carrying shuttered candle lamps that cast a dim light and bearing a large steamer trunk between them, they made their way down the glass-enclosed hallway towards the Temple of Isis. Their journey taking them past the Temple of Hathor, the Kiosk of Trajan, and the Chapel of Imhotep, before they finally arrived at the entrance to the Chapel of Mandulis.

The lead figure turned to face the rest of the group and pushed back the lightweight black cotton cowl covering their face. Marguerite smiled as she gazed upon the faces of her gathered family, but her smile faltered as she remembered the loss of yet another of their clan; Julius might have been a poseur, a ne'er-do-well, and an adulterer, but he *was* a part of their family, and would be again. Marguerite's lips set and her eyes flashed with a pale light; vengeance would be theirs…as it had always been!

She reached within her cloak and removed a jewelled dagger. Raising the gleaming blade high above her head, she led her family down the covered walkway. As they walked, they were joined by another black-clad figure, who joined Kiefer and walked the rest of the way by his side.

The group entered the Chapel of Mandulis, and walked past the still-vivid frescos, towards the far end of the chamber. Marguerite paused before a hieroglyph of the Ankh, the symbol of life. She held out her pale, slender hand and pierced the tip of her finger with the blade. A glittering bead of crimson appeared on her white skin. She stepped forward and pressed it against the hieroglyph; anointing the symbol with her blood.

A faint white light appeared around the edges of the wall as part of the fresco swung back to reveal a flight of stone steps that lead into a hidden part of the structure's history. For, although the building above ground was that of the Chapel of Mandulis, the warren of chambers and passageways below ground was that of the ancient Temple of Nekroshema…a place of worship dedicated to the sacred Mother of necromancers. Marguerite entered the steep passageway and unshuttered her lamp; the golden light from the candle filling the stone corridor and guiding the rest of the family as they carefully lifted the trunk through the narrow space. As they made their way down the steps, the last of their number closed the hidden door before slowly following the others into the flickering, lamp-lit darkness beyond.

After several minutes of walking, the passageway ended in what appeared to be a solid stone wall covered with a heavily detailed, carved, and painted relief of Nekroshema herself. Clad in a gown of deepest red and seated on a throne of skulls, her deathly white face was surmounted by a mass of dark hair that surrounded her skeletal figure like a black halo. On her lap, clasped in her pale, thin hands, were a golden diadem, a black vial, and a jewelled blade.

Marguerite bowed before the image and again pricked her finger; this time anointing the crown with her blood. As she stepped back, the image of their sacred mother seemed to shift; the dark, deep-set eyes glowing with a sudden white light as the solid stone door slowly pivoted on its hinges and swung open to reveal the inky blackness of the chamber of resurrection.

○

The Chamber of Resurrection
4:30am

The room beyond the door was huge, with a large pool of pale green water placed at its heart. In the middle of the pool was an altar, set on an island of stone and linked to the rest of the chamber by a short, golden bridge; the graceful span a physical reminder of the space between the land of the living and the realm of the dead. The walls were covered with ornate reliefs; their gold, red, and blue pigments still vivid, describing the resurrection process in great detail; the death of the one to be reborn, the reconstitution of their body, the words required for the ritual, and the resurrection itself.

The steamer trunk was carried across the bridge and placed with great care and reverence next to the altar. Marguerite approached the trunk, deftly twisted the six locks and opened the lid; within the trunk, bathed in a golden glow, lay twelve body parts, each placed in its anatomically correct position. The components...including the eyes, and the wounds which bore witness to how they had been severed from their original owners, appeared waxy and bloodless, almost unreal, in the strange light that emanated from the trunk and which enveloped and temporarily protected the body parts from the passage of time.

Marguerite reached into her ever-present reticule and removed the penultimate piece of the macabre jigsaw puzzle; Reynaud's skull. She smiled in delight as the soft murmuring that hovered constantly on the edge of the family's hearing grew louder. "Yes, my darling. Everything's going to plan. Evelyn is still a virginal offering, and she suspects nothing."

The murmuring became more intense. Marguerite frowned, then shook her head. "I don't understand. Only the family can hear your voice in this state; no one else—"

The murmuring became forceful as Reynaud responded violently to his wife's words. Camillia whimpered in pain as the bass voice seemed to crawl inside her head. A slow smile appeared on Heathers' face as he enjoyed the effect his master's voice was having on the younger member of the family. The flickering torch lights twisting his grey, bland features into a frightening mask almost as ugly as the sounds coming from Reynaud's disembodied skull.

Marguerite flinched but continued to listen to her husband's ire, nodding every now and then. "So, there's another who can hear you as well as us? We shall find them, my darling. Rest assured; they will not live long enough to see you resurrected! But now we must start the cleansing ritual."

The bass voice took on what could only be described as a petulant tone. Marguerite smiled knowingly. "Yes, my love, it *is* necessary." She crossed the bridge and carefully placed her husband's skull in the trunk, resting it just above the blood-less wound on the throat of the top half of the torso and between the two pale blue eyes before turning to face the rest of the family. "Let us begin."

The family formed a circle around the pool. Marguerite joined them as they stood, hands raised, palms upwards, and began to chant; the words sibilant and low. As the sound filled the room, the eyes of the family changed from their usual colours to an opaque white. As their chanting increased in speed and sound, the green water of the pool began to move, the surface writhing and twisting as though alive. The chanting became a wall of sound; the words echoing and reechoing against the walls of the chamber until the chant became a form of music in the round…and then, as it reached its zenith, it stopped.

In the unearthly silence that followed, part of the pool slowly rose in a thick ribbon of water. It approached the dismembered form and poured into the trunk like a sentient waterfall, gently enveloping the contents within its watery embrace. The eau de nil of the water and the golden glow from the trunk illuminating the chamber and all who stood within its reach with an eldritch light.

As the water slowly rolled away and returned to the pool, Marguerite crossed the bridge and examined the contents of the trunk; the once-separated body parts had fused together, but the eyes and skull were still uncon- nected. Marguerite smiled; all they needed now was the blood of a virginal offering, and Reynaud would return to her.

She reached out a slender hand and caressed the polished skull and crooned. "Soon, my love…soon we shall be together again." She looked at Margaux. "There is much sorrow for the loss of another of our kin, yet this loss, too, is temporary. Julius will be returned to you." Marguerite's eyes filled with a blaze of white light as she faced the circle. "We shall always return; we shall always be family!"

The blinding light in her eyes was reflected by her kin as the family chanted in response. "We shall always return!"

Marguerite carefully lifted the skull from the trunk and replaced it in her reticule. "We've done all we can for this night. Let us return to our suites and make plans for the next few days."

Kiefer frowned. "We don't have time to waste, Mother! We should kill Evelyn now, resurrect Father, and leave." He flinched as his mother turned her white eyes on him. "We are trapped in a sandstorm, child. It makes sense to wait and bide our time until we are free to leave. Evelyn is not going anywhere, and for the time being, neither are we. Now… back to our rooms; we could all benefit from a little more sleep." She turned and walked back down the corridor leading towards the Chapel of Mandulis.

As the rest of the family followed, one of their number paused by the trunk and placed a gentle hand on the shoulder of one of the family's many victims; a shoulder that would soon become part of his resurrected grandfather. Linden pushed back his cowl and stared at the remains; his face lit by the faint light that still emanated from the trunk. He stood in silence for a moment before closing the lid and following the rest of his family back to the chapel.

As the family left the chapel and made their way down the covered corridor to the entrance hall and reception, a strange blurring appeared around one of the carved images of Mandulis on the wall as the intricately carved god seemingly stepped out of the relief…while leaving his image behind in the stone. The figure paused as a faint golden light rippled across their form, the glow pulsing under his skin as he returned to his usual appearance. Masquelyne brushed down his wings, allowing them to open fully before carefully folding them back; changing always caused creases, but flattening himself completely caused absolute havoc with his wings! He ran a slender finger across the carved image of the ankh, a thoughtful expression on his face. So…blood was the key. Did it have to be fresh? Or could it be taken from an unwilling donor? He smiled; this information was far too good not to share. He consulted his pocket watch; hopefully, the other concerned party would arrive soon…he looked forward to sharing this information with a like-minded person.

Beyond the doorway leading out of the Chapel of Mandulis, a figure sat with a shuttered lantern and watched from a hidden viewpoint as the Devereaux family and their assorted servants retired to their rooms. He paid great attention to the shuffling figure of Sedgewyck, who stumbled slightly as he painfully made his way at the back of the procession. He was assisted by another figure, whose cowl slid back to reveal the pale, expressionless face of Heathers. The hidden figure smiled as he carefully opened one shutter on the lantern, made a note in a small notebook and tucked it back into his breast pocket — perhaps there was truth in the saying that no man was a hero to his valet. He wheeled round at a sudden noise behind him; the revolver out of its holster and in his grip as he came face to face with Masquelyne.

Masquelyne held up a conciliatory hand and smiled. "I have been watching you, as you have been watching them. I have information that may be to your advantage…"

The man looked at him and raised a querying eyebrow. "Oh, yes? I take it you're the person who left a message in my room?" He paused. "How exactly did you get into my suite? I know I locked the door."

Masquelyne smiled lazily. "That is for me to know, friend." He gestured at the gun. "Will you put down the revolver?"

The man shook his head with a wary smile. "Not just yet.

This is most strange. What is it that you think I should know?"

Masquelyne's smile widened, his canines glinting in the flickering light afforded by the other figure's lantern "It involves the Devereaux family of necromancers and murderers." He paused at the man's sudden intake of breath. "Yes, I too know them for what they are. And I know you witnessed a certain...event, shall we say? At Kom Ombo. I also know that you have told no one what you saw. May I ask why?"

The other figure half-smiled. "Who would believe that I witnessed a man throw another off an airship, before seeming to dissolve into the very side of the vessel as if by magic?" He paused, then whispered softly, "I know they have murdered many, so very many, including—" He swallowed hard. "I want justice — and vengeance!"

Masquelyne nodded. "Then you are fully aware of their evil; an evil that must come to an end. I believe us to be on the same side — the side of truth, justice, and retribution. Are you interested?"

The man paused, then tucked the revolver back into its holster. He nodded, a gleam in his eye. "I am very, very interested!"

"Then allow me to share with you what I believe will happen over the course of the next few days..."

The Eau De Nil Hotel and Island

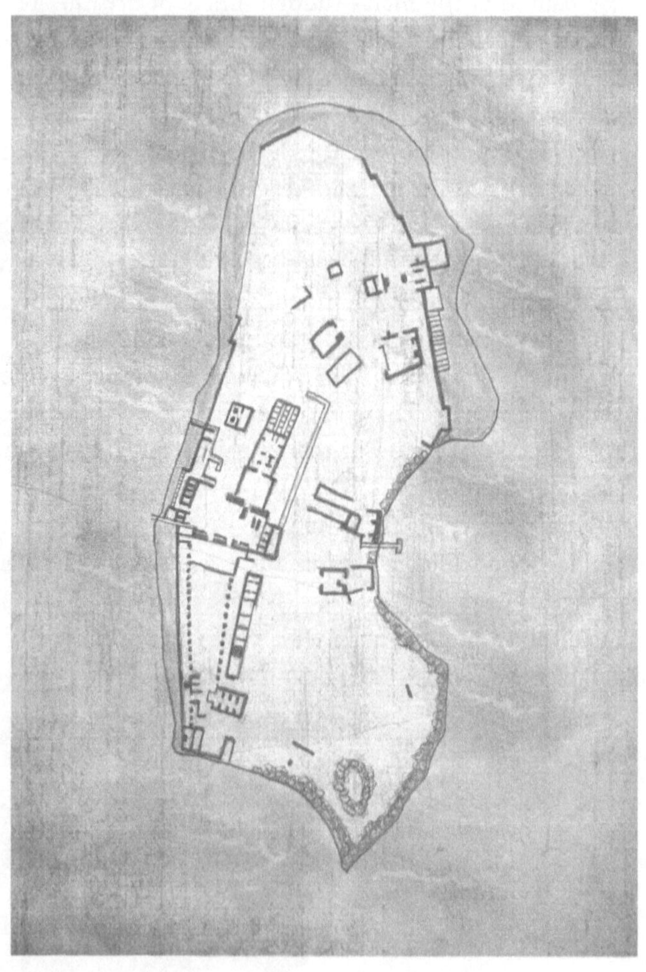

PART
III

The Entrance Hall
5:00am

In the dim light afforded by the flickering glow of a solitary gas lamp, a dark figure walked quietly past the reception desk and through a door marked *Private*. Closing the door behind them, they moved swiftly down the long corridor before they reached the office at the right-hand end of the corridor; the office of Carandini Bey.

Reaching out a gloved hand, they grasped the door handle and twisted, wincing as a loud click echoed in the narrow hall. Their fear of having to deal with a lock was unrealised as the door swung open to reveal the dark room beyond.

They entered the quiet office, closed the door, and unshuttered their lamp. Spotting their target, they sat at the desk, placed the lamp to one side, removed a small screwdriver and a pair of pliers from their pocket, and began. There was a faint snipping sound as several of the wires linking the telephone to the mainland were carefully cut away. They then turned their attention to the telephone itself.

After several minutes of determined work, the figure leant back in Carandini's chair and took a deep breath; part one of their plan was over — now for part two!

○

Gaston Cavet's Suite
8:15am

The steward balanced the breakfast tray and knocked at the door. "Monsieur Cavet. Your breakfast tray, Sir."

There was no answer. The steward frowned; the gentleman in question had stayed at the hotel before and was very particular about his breakfast; the poached eggs would be ruined if they were left too long. He knocked again and waited; still no answer. The young steward shrugged and opened the door. "Good morning, Monsieur—" The word caught in his throat as he saw the body of the French author, lying face down in a mirror-like pool of congealed blood. The shocked young man hurriedly placed the laden tray on the bed, moved to Cavet's side and turned him over — a difficult task, as the dried blood and other matter had set like a deep-red glue, almost anchoring the body to the marble floor. As the steward broke the gory bond and settled the Frenchman on his back, the dazed young man took in the damaged, bloody eye, and the Frenchman's distressing expression of open-mouthed shock.

Feeling his gorge begin to rise, the steward stood and left the room. Pulling the door shut behind him, he all but ran to Carandini Bey's office.

○

Thomas Breton's Suite
8:19am

Thomas blearily raised his head from the down-filled pillow, stared at his travel clock and groaned; why on earth had he set his alarm for such an ungodly hour? Coffee; that was what he needed, and plenty of it!

He rolled over in the fine cotton sheets and tugged at the bell pull that hung by his bed. Reclining against the well-stuffed pillows, he listened to the rapidly approaching feet with pleasure; the hotel might be owned by a grossly bourgeois coterie of capitalists, but at least the staff were good at their jobs.

His smile became a frown as the approaching feet walked straight past his door and continued along the Osiris corridor. Thomas' face immediately settled into the expression he adopted whenever he saw what he believed to be an abuse of power. He thought of it as his 'thinking man of the people' face, while most who knew him referred to it, with varying levels of derision, as his best petulant pout. Thomas yanked angrily at the pull, folded his arms, and waited.

After several minutes passed without the arrival of a steward to take his breakfast order, Thomas grumbled an oath, got out of bed, and pulled his dressing gown on. Tying the cord with an angry flourish, he stomped to the door, threw it open, and stepped into the corridor...where he immediately collided with the tall frame of the hotel manager, Carandini Bey. Thomas glared at him; another bourgeois capitalist — or at least the tool of one!

Before Carandini could speak, Thomas began. "Mr Bey, I am not used to being kept waiting! When I ring for a steward, I expect them to arrive promptly."

Carandini stared down at the angry artist before responding with a rapid-fire stream of Arabic. One of the three stewards behind him, a young man from Alexandria, bit his lip at Carandini's use of several colourful, colloquial terms that ran the gamut from questioning the artist's parentage, suggesting his intellectual capabilities were on a par with those of a squashed melon, and musing over his future viability as a suitable compost for pomegranates. At the end of this stream of invective Carandini bowed smartly, pointed at one of the stewards, and barked a few words in Italian. The young man bowed deeply as Carandini and the other two stewards continued down the corridor and disappeared into one of the suites at the far end.

The young Italian looked at Thomas with a carefully neutral expression. "How may I help you, Sir?"

Thomas frowned at the young man; his inability to understand any language other than English and the basics of ancient Greek and Latin drilled into him years earlier in boarding school had left him incapable of understanding just what Carandini Bey had said…however, his inbuilt paranoia left him absolutely certain than he had been insulted; but quite how, he simply couldn't say. He glared at the steward and barked. "Breakfast! Coffee — black!"

As he turned back to enter his room, Carandini and the two stewards reappeared in the corridor. Carandini's face was pale and set as the three men walked past Thomas without acknowledgement. Thomas frowned as his steward followed them; what on earth was going on? He shook his head and closed the door; hopefully breakfast wouldn't take too long.

He entered the bathroom and began to run a bath. Looking at the array of ornate bottles on the shelf by the bath, he opened and sniffed the contents of each before settling on the bottle labelled *Jasmine Milk*. He poured some of the highly-scented liquid into the tub and watched as bubbles began to appear. Turning to his reflection in the mirror, he prodded the jowls that had started to form on either side of his chin and frowned — perhaps it was time to start growing a beard?

He turned at a knock on the door to his suite. Reentering his bedroom, he bellowed. "Enter!" The door swung open to reveal the young steward, who was carrying a tray. "Your coffee, Sir."

Thomas blinked; that was much quicker than he had expected. He stepped aside and gestured to the steward to enter.

The young man closed the door, placed the tray on the small table by the door to the terrace, bowed again, and made to leave. He paused expectantly as Thomas held up his hand. "Yes, Sir?"

Thomas sat down at the table, and gestured at the coffee pot. The young steward hesitated for a moment before pouring him a cup of the thick coffee.

Thomas watched with a supercilious expression on his face, then spoke. "I demand to know why my call was ignored. I rang twice — twice! — and was ignored on both occasions. Your manager did not show me the courtesy of addressing me in my own language, and the other stewards did not even acknowledge my presence. Indeed, they walked past me to enter another guest's suite and see to their needs instead! Are the whims of another guest more important than *my* needs?" He did not wait for the startled steward to answer; he sat back in his comfortable armchair with evident enjoyment as he continued. "I was invited here by the Eridanus Corporation themselves to create a work of art. They recognise my ability to produce a glowing tribute to their hotel. *They* respect me — but their staff, it appears, do not!"

As Thomas opened his mouth to continue his stream of self-righteous invective, there came another sharp knock at his door. Before he could respond, the door opened and Carandini Bey entered. The manager took in the irate looking Thomas, looked at the young Italian steward and raised an enquiring eyebrow. "È difficile?" *"Is he being difficult?"*

The steward nodded. "Sì, signore."

Carandini snapped his fingers and pointed to the door. "Vai e aiuta gli altri a spostare il corpo nell'armadietto della carne con l'altro. Assicurati che nessuno ti veda e non menzionare nulla di tutto ciò agli ospiti!" *"Go and help the others move the body to the meat locker with the other one. Make sure no one sees you, and don't mention any of this to the guests!"*

The young steward nodded again. "Si, signore." With a smart bow to Thomas, he left the room.

Carandini bestowed a gracious and placatory smile on Thomas. "Mr Breton, I am most terribly sorry for my earlier rudeness." He leant in slightly and fixed a conspiratorial eye on the artist. "I trust I can count on your full discretion?" Before the querulous but now curious Thomas could speak, Carandini continued. "I am afraid that one of our guests has been taken ill. Nothing contagious, I hasten to add, a mere..." A shadow passed across his face. "...migraine, of sorts." He beamed at Thomas; the waxed ends of his mustachios glinting slightly in the gaslight. "Thank you for your understanding, Mr Breton. Do enjoy your breakfast." In one smooth, practised move, he bowed and left, closing the door silently behind him.

Thomas stared at the door with an expression of deep mistrust, then took a gulp of his coffee. "Bloody foreigners!"

On the other side of the door, Carandini smoothed the front of his waistcoat and grimaced. "Bloody arriviste!" He shook his head as he walked back down the corridor towards what had been Gaston Cavet's suite; what a damn mess!

Back in his suite, Thomas' frown deepened as he wondered which guest had been taken ill. The suite in question was obviously the one they had entered, at the far end of the Osiris corridor. As he sat, he became aware of a faint tinkling sound coming from the bathroom — he'd left the bath running! With a muttered expletive, he hurried into the bathroom and turned the water off just as it was in danger of overflowing. Thomas pulled the plug and allowed some of the water to escape before removing his dressing gown and climbing in. He sank into the highly scented water with a happy sigh; a few minutes of soaking and then…to work.

○

Gaston Cavet's Suite
8:45am

Carandini watched grimly as the stewards lifted Cavet's body, placed it inside the large Persian rug that had been repurposed as a means of smuggling the corpse out to the meat locker, and laboriously rolled the thick material around the cold body. Having checked that no part of the dead Frenchman was visible, he snapped his fingers at the three stewards. In unison, they lifted the large rolled-up rug and walked to his side. Carandini opened the door and poked his head around the edge of the gilded wooden frame; the corridor beyond was empty. He stepped out and gestured to the men, who walked past bearing their load. Moving to the front of the strange parade, Carandini led them to the service corridor which in turn led directly to the kitchens.

Carandini entered the bustling room and held the door open as the stewards carried the rug to the meat locker that already contained the corpse of Julius van Sloane. Carandini scanned the corridor. No one had seen them…that was a relief! He turned as the angry-looking chef approached him and gestured at the three stewards with a large knife. "Monsieur, again? I must protest!"

Carandini leant forward and murmured in the chef's ear; within seconds, a sizeable number had been agreed as suitable remuneration for the chef's upset. The placated chef smiled and returned to his lunch preparations as the three stewards placed Cavet in the meat locker and reappeared in the kitchen. One sidled over to Carandini. "We have placed Monsieur Cavet alongside Mr van Sloane, Sir."

Carandini nodded. "Excellent. Return to your duties. If anyone needs me, I shall be in my office." As the steward bowed and left, Carandini also left the kitchens and returned to his office, his brow furrowed in thought; two bodies in as many days…at least they could keep each other company in the meat locker!

○

Carandini Bey's Office
8:55am

Carandini entered his office, pushed the door shut and closed his eyes. What a bloody shambles — and it wasn't even mid-morning! At least van Sloane's death had occurred elsewhere, and could legitimately be omitted from the hotel's ledger of incidents. Gaston Cavet's death, however, was quite obviously murder…and a murder that had occurred within the hotel grounds.

Carandini stood by his desk and frowned; how best to deal with this utter calamity? Perhaps the best place to start was with a telephone call to the Eridanus Corporation's head office? He winced at the thought of the management's reaction to such an appalling piece of news, then shook his head resignedly…it couldn't be helped; he had to place the call, and the sooner, the better. He sat in his chair and reached across his desk for the telephone. As he looked directly at the machine, there was a moment of silence before he realised exactly what he was looking at. His bewildered expression was rapidly replaced by anger, as, without a word, he stood, marched across the corridor, and entered Miss March's office.

The young woman looked up from her typing with a startled expression. "Mr Bey? Is something wrong?"

Carandini gritted his teeth. "Miss March, something is indeed *very* wrong! One of the guests, Monsieur Gaston Cavet, has been found dead in his suite. Not only that, but someone has entered my office and destroyed the telephone!"

Miss March swallowed hard. "Monsieur Cavet? But that's…terrible!" She frowned. "Are you sure about the telephone?"

Carandini waved his hand towards his office. "Please, Miss March, see for yourself."

The secretary stood up and hurried to Carandini's office. She entered, and stared at what had been the telephone; a small collection of brass plates and wires sat where the instrument usually rested. She frowned as she looked at the cut wires. "But there was no reason for—"

Carandini looked at her with a frown. "No reason for what, Miss March?"

Miss March opened and closed her mouth, looking somewhat like a startled fish. "Oh…because of the sandstorm, Mr Bey. We can't leave the island and the police can't travel here, either. There was no reason for someone to damage the telephone. We're trapped, one way or the other."

Carandini glared at her. "Yes, Miss March, we are trapped — with a murderer!"

She blinked and clutched at throat. "A murderer?"

Carandini nodded grimly. "Yes! Gaston Cavet was murdered. Go to your office and lock the door. Don't let anyone in until I return; I know who can help us!" He pointed. "Now, go, and lock yourself in."

Miss March stared at him before returning to her office

and locking the door. She sat down and stared at the wall in dumfounded silence; she knew why Jane had killed Gaston, but not why anyone in the family would destroy the telephone. Unless it wasn't one of them; but in that case, who had done it…and why?

Back in his office, Carandini closed the door and sat in his comfortable armchair. He had absolutely no desire to inform anyone of what had occurred, and because of the damage to the telephone, they would have to wait until the storm had passed before they could inform the police. There was, however, a form of official police presence already on the island. He nodded to himself; he could wash his hands of the entire issue by informing the enquiry agents that, as the face of the Veiled Protectorate, the glory of investigating the murder of Gaston Cavet was theirs alone.

He lifted the communications tube and blew down it. After a few moments, the tinny voice of the communications Simulandro responded. "Yes, Sir?"

Carandini sat back. "Please find Messrs Caine, Thorne, and Captain Darling. Ask them to meet me in the second meat locker as soon as possible; it's a matter of some urgency."

"Yes, Sir." There was a faint click as the tube was hung up at the other end. Carandini smiled grimly; there just might be a way out of this after all!

○

The Temple of Hathor
9:00am

Thomas slammed the wardrobe door shut, gazed at his reflection in the mirror, and fingered the length of material looped around his neck; having to decide between either the magenta or the fuchsia cravats had been an absolute nightmare!

As he collected the supplies he needed for his day's work, the lid came off a tube of Cobalt blue and smeared across his hand; swearing under his breath, Thomas grabbed a rag from his paint box, soaked the corner in linseed oil, and pressed it against the worst of the oily smear. He threw the stained rag back into the box, picked up his easel and bag, left his suite, and walked towards the Temple of Hathor. The ongoing sandstorm made the light almost unbearable, but he had an inkling that he could use it to his advantage. After all, if it had worked for Turner and Monet, it could work for him. He juggled his easel and sketching bag as he walked down the glass-enclosed corridor towards the Temple and cast his artistic eye across the incredible columns that glowed with an unearthly orange light in the swirling haze of the storm outside; stunning…absolutely stunning!

As he approached the temple, he spotted Dr Amicus Mirylees and his assistant Dr Jones, who were sitting on the far edge of the structure. They had been formally introduced at dinner the previous evening, and Thomas had found the elderly man's flat refusal to discuss the British political situation at home and abroad rather rude. Thomas glared at the elderly archaeologist through narrowed eyes as he approached the pair, several ideas spinning through his mind; perhaps the old man could still be of some use? Thomas decided to pretend that the previous evening's somewhat tense discussion had never occurred and approached the two men with a smile. "Good morning, Dr Mirylees, Dr Jones." He waved his paint-stained hand at the view on the other side of the thick glass panels that surrounded them. "Awful weather we're having."

Amicus looked at him over the top of his glasses; he hadn't been impressed with the artist's behaviour at dinner;

however, he was quite prepared to be magnanimous...up to a certain point. He acknowledged Thomas' greeting. "If you think this is bad, why, when I was here back in..." He paused and looked at his assistant and the painter. "Well, let us just say that it was quite a while ago and the storm back then lasted over a week!"

Thomas looked at him with dismay. "Oh, good God! I hope this doesn't last as long — I have work to do!"

Amicus looked at the artist with an eye that was still faintly jaundiced; he had been quite taken aback by the artist's aggressive manner at dinner, and had decided not to engage him in any form of social discourse during the rest of his stay at the hotel. But here he was, and showing no signs of taking his leave. The archaeologist took a deep breath; perhaps to avoid yet another political diatribe, he should ask a question that would encourage the artist to talk about his more favoured topic; namely, himself. "At dinner you said that you are a painter, Mr Breton?" Amicus and Dr Jones shared a look; Thomas' not very self-deprecating declaration of the magnificence of his own artistic ability had been the first thing out of his mouth at dinner...closely followed by a denunciation of the current state of political debate, and a demand that both Amicus and Dr Jones agree with his opinion.

As Amicus and Dr Jones smiled benignly at the artist, Thomas smiled in response; excellent — the first step had been taken, and not by him. He spread his hands in as self-deprecatingly a manner as his ego would allow. "For my sins, Dr Mirylees, for my sins. You stated last night that you were a part of the archaeological dig that discovered this site?"

Amicus nodded, pride on his deeply tanned and lined face. He gestured to the magnificent building. "Yes, indeed. This was amongst my discoveries..." He gazed at the building; his voice trailing off as his mind revisited the glories of the past.

Thomas cast a surreptitious glance at his pocket watch; he was running rather late. As he cleared his throat, Dr Jones stood up and smiled at them. "If you will excuse me, Dr Mirylees, Mr Breton. I must return to the terrace and see how my wife and son are."

Amicus waved his hand. "Yes, yes, of course. Biting insects can be quite unpleasant for a child on their first trip to Africa." He looked at his assistant over the top of his spectacles. "I take it your good lady has the necessary medicines with her?"

"Yes, Dr Mirylees. Caroline has everything required in her nurse's bag."

"Excellent, excellent. Well, off you go, my dear boy."

Dr Jones nodded at Thomas before walking off. Once he had gone, Thomas looked at Amicus. "Nurse's bag?"

Amicus smiled. "Yes. A particularly good find; an archaeological assistant whose wife is also a trained nurse."

"Quite." Thomas decided to take the plunge. "Dr Mirylees, I was wondering if I could ask you for a very special favour?" The elderly archaeologist looked over the top of his wire-rimmed glasses and raised his thin white eyebrows as Thomas hurriedly continued. "I have been engaged by the hotel to create a painting of this magnificent building. Even though I can see her in her pristine glory today, I would rather like to see her as you, and the others in your dig, first saw her. It would enable me to truly touch the essence of this quite remarkable place. Could you assist me in my endeavour?"

The elderly archaeologist blinked; of all the possible approaches he had expected from the querulous artist, this particular one came as quite a surprise. As he gazed at Thomas in silence, the artist feared he had over-egged the pudding. He relaxed as a delighted smile appeared on Amicus' face. "My dear boy, of course I can assist you! I have in my files some of my most treasured possessions; photographs of when we first came to this place, in 1865..."

Thomas stared; photographs? He hadn't expected that; simple, colour-washed sketches were all he had hoped for, but photographs? He nodded encouragingly. "Photographs of the island and this incredible building would be a superb aid to my art, Dr Mirylees."

Amicus returned from his memories with a jolt. "Yes... yes, of course. Now let me see..." He lifted the battered valise that sat by his chair; a battered valise that had seen much duty over many years, undid the scratched latches and rummaged inside; taking care not to mix the carefully filed contents. He pulled out an envelope and squinted through his thick lenses at the spidery writing. "Oh no...not that one." He threw Thomas a conspiratorial look. "A few items we managed to salvage from the library of Alexandria...we discovered the remains of the Mouseion, and within it, several dozen scrolls that were still legible!" He smiled and tapped his nose knowingly. "Some very interesting historical facts and details about many things, including the true origins of the more recent additions to the Abrahamic faiths and their ways of worship — but I shall say no more! Now, where were we? Ah, no...that's my sketchbook from when we first came here." He looked up at Thomas. "We found several marvellously inventive hidden passages all over the site. I made notes about them, but, of course, they won't be of any use to you. Ah, yes...photographs from the 1865 expedition. Here we are." He handed Thomas a thick envelope and closed his bag.

The artist opened the envelope carefully and pulled out the contents: he blinked as dozens of tintypes fell in his lap. His hands trembled as he pored through the collection —

some of the images had even been hand-tinted! He pulled out one sepia-toned image and studied it keenly; a smartly dressed group of men standing in the outer court at the entrance to the Chapel of Mandulis stared back at him, large blocks of carved stone and excavation equipment littering the ground around them.

He held the photograph out to Amicus. "Are these the other people from your excavation?"

Amicus nodded, and pointed to each man in turn. "This gentleman was Mr Richmond Jarvis: it was he who organised and funded the expedition. The young man standing next to him was his assistant, Edmund Street…" Amicus paused as he looked at the image. "Edmund…died just a few days after this image was taken. Such a terrible tragedy for his dear friends, and his family…and of course for his wife — they were married here, earlier that same week."

Amicus' voice trailed off as he remembered the sad events that had led to the premature ending of the dig, and their sorrowful return to England without the amiable young man whose life had ended tragically. He shook his head. "But I digress. Next to Edmund is Joseph Goode, our artist, and the last man is, of course, me."

Thomas nodded as he studied the photograph; could the Chapel of Mandulis be the right building for his painting? Images began to appear in his mind's eye of just what he could achieve using the smaller building as the centerpiece. The Eridanus management had wanted the forecourt of the temple at the heart of the painting, but that image was so common…why, it was even on postcards! If only he could make them see what he could; the rich colours of the chapel before him intermingled with the beauty, the texture, and the eternal grandeur of flawless ruination. The entire image was perfectly finished by the juxtaposition of the utterly remark-able columns with the dark portal behind the men in the photograph; to his artist's eye, it was perfect...and only he, Thomas Breton, could possibly do it justice!

Thomas' heart soared as his artistic thoughts merged with his ego and swept him away on an ocean of verbosity that carried him straight through pretention and into the loving arms of self-indulgent narcissism.

As Thomas floated away with his thoughts, and Amicus focused on the images of his past, neither saw the figure of a man quietly move away from where he had been hiding by the steps of the temple. Instead of using the main entrance, the man walked along the covered terrace to one of the many doors leading to the private suites. Stopping at one, he turned the handle, slowly opened the door, and entered. Closing the door behind them, he smiled; so, the old man had a sketchbook detailing the hotel's hidden passages...how very interesting. Perhaps a visit to the elderly archaeologist's suite during the cocktail hour would be beneficial.

Back at the temple, Thomas suddenly caught sight of something in the photograph that pulled him from his artistic rapture; behind the men was the door leading to the vestibule, and standing in that doorway was a figure that, though faint, was unmistakably that of a woman. Thomas pointed at the image. "Dr Mirylees, who is the woman in this photograph?"

The elderly gentleman glared at Thomas. "My dear young man, it was not that type of dig! There were only gentlemen on the Jarvis expedition, I can assure you!"

Thomas patted his bag and found his magnifying glass. Holding it to his eye, he took in the figure; tall, dark-haired, and, shockingly for the era, garbed in trousers. The fullness of her womanly shape was accentuated by the contrast between her light-coloured attire and the darkness of the doorway she stood in. Thomas looked up from the photograph and saw a strange expression on the older man's face;

he made a conciliatory gesture. "You are of course quite correct, Dr Mirylees. May I borrow this tintype?"

Amicus stared at the younger man, then gave him a sharp nod. "With the sole stipulation that you ensure the hotel knows your painting incorporates elements from my photograph."

"I agree, Dr Mirylees. I shall ask the hotel secretary, Miss March, to draw up a simple contract to that effect…would you find that acceptable?

"That will be more than satisfactory, Mr Breton."

The artist leapt to his feet and offered the elderly archaeologist his hand: Amicus hesitated before accepting it with a slightly stiff smile.

As Thomas left the temple, clutching the photograph like a prize, the strange expression returned to Amicus' face. He opened his valise, withdrew another envelope, and sifted through another selection of photographs before he found the image he was looking for; a copy of the image Thomas had chosen; four men standing in the doorway of the Chapel of Mandulis, and in the doorway behind them, a dark-haired woman. Amicus took out his own magnifying glass and gazed at the figure; nodding slowly as he placed the glass on the arm of his chair. "You were not a part of our dig, but you *were* there." Amicus placed the photographs back in the envelope and gazed across the Nile as his mind turned to a letter he had received several weeks earlier…a letter that had been the catalyst for his return to the place that still held painful memories so many years later. "So, he was right…you have returned to the scene of your crimes. Who now is in your web of death, I wonder?"

○

The Reception
9:15am

Dr Jones left his suite, walked back to the brightly lit reception, and took his place behind an irate Thomas, who, having been informed by the apologetic Simulandro manning the desk that Miss March was currently unavailable, was complaining volubly. After being promised that drawing up the contract between the artist and Dr Mirylees would be the first item on her list once she returned, Thomas grumpily accepted the offer, but not before leaving strict instructions about the breakfast, elevenses, lunch, high tea, dinner, and supper trays that were to be brought to his suite over the next thirty-six hours while he worked on his painting.

As he stalked back to his suite with colours, perspectives, and the pros and cons of whether or not to add people floating around his head, the Simulandro steward turned to look at the archaeologist waiting patiently at the desk and tilted his head to one side. "Yes, Dr Jones? How may I be of assistance?"

"I know it's quite soon after breakfast, but may I order a pot of tea for two and a selection of cakes to be brought to our suite, please?"

"Of course, Sir. What time would you like the tray?"

"As soon as you can, please."

The Simulandro bowed. "As you wish, Sir. Do you require anything else?"

"No, that will be all, thank you." Dr Jones left the reception and headed back towards the hallway that led to the suite of rooms he shared with his wife and young son.

As he turned the corner of the Osiris corridor, he saw

Rex Nympton standing by the door to his suite. The solidly-built American looked quite unwell; his face was pale, and a thin sheen of sweat was visible on his tanned forehead. Dr Jones frowned. "My dear Mr Nympton…are you well?"

Rex looked at the young archaeologist with a relieved expression. "I am mighty pleased to see you, Dr Jones! I understand your good lady is a nurse. Would she have anything for malaria? I had a bout with the damn thing a while ago, and I can tell when it tries to make a comeback."

"Yes, of course. Please, do come in." He hesitated. "I would ask that you please be quiet; our son is unwell. He was bitten by mosquitos, and had quite a bad reaction to the bites. It has made him a trifle…fractious!"

Rex's smiled wanly. "Of course, I quite understand."

Dr Jones opened the door and gestured for Rex to enter. The large, airy sitting room was lit by gas lamps…the light filling the room with a soft yellow glow as the sandstorm continued unabated outside.

Dr Jones closed the door and whispered. "Please take a seat. I'll let Caroline know that you're here." Rex nodded gratefully and sank onto one of the settees as the young archaeologist walked to a closed door and quietly turned the handle. Pushing the door open just a crack, he peered around it and murmured a few words; a voice responded from the room, softer and lower. Dr Jones nodded and carefully closed the door, then turned back to Rex. "My wife will be out shortly."

Rex nodded. "Thank you kindly."

A few minutes later, the door opened and Caroline Jones entered. She was tall and slender, her pale-blonde hair pinned in a tidy bun at the nape of her elegant neck. She smiled at her husband and turned to Rex. "Mr Nympton, I understand that you're feeling unwell?" She looked at him closely; taking in the sweat on his face and the sudden chills that caused his shoulders to shudder. "You believe it to be a recrudescence of malaria? I take it you've had malaria in the past?"

Rex nodded. "Yes, Ma'am. I did some travelling around these parts a few years ago, I came down with it then. This is the third time it's come back, though; damn thing! Uh… Beggin' your pardon, Ma'am."

Caroline smiled. "I've heard worse, believe me. I have some powders that should help." She collected her medical bag from its place by the door, set it on the table, and opening one of the many compartments. She removed a small box of cachets and handed them to the sweating American. "Here; take one now, one with lunch, and one with dinner. I recommend that you drink plenty of tonic water with a touch of gin…for medicinal purposes, you understand? I would also suggest that when you return to your suite, you send for a steward and request very simple lunch and dinner trays for today, equally simple breakfast, lunch, and dinner trays for tomorrow, and spend the next two days resting."

Rex smiled. "Thank you, Ma'am, you're my kind of nurse!" He paused. "Would it be possible to have something to help me sleep, as well, Ma'am? The last time I had malaria I was awake for three days. I really don't need that to happen again." Caroline nodded. "Of course." She opened another compartment in her bag and removed a small box bearing the legend *Dr Morpheus' chloral sachets*. "Take one of these shortly before bedtime. Don't take more than one a night or you'll need more than the help of a nurse!" Rex grinned tiredly. "Thank you again, Ma'am."

As he opened the door to leave, he startled the Simu-landro steward who was standing at the door with a tray. The steward nodded at him before addressing the archaeologist. "Your tea and cakes, Dr Jones."

The archaeologist smiled. "Lovely. Please put it on the table by the settee. Thank you."

Rex nodded as the Simulandro walked past him. "Good morning, Doctor Jones, Mrs Jones, and thank you again."

The young archaeologist smiled. "You're most welcome, Mr Nympton."

Rex left the suite, feeling better than he had when he'd entered. As he walked down the corridor, he failed to notice the strange shadow that skimmed across the ceiling behind him and darted through the wall into the Jones's suite.

○

The Meat Locker
9:25am

As they entered the cold, windowless room, Aquilleia looked at the covered remains of both Julius and Cavet and frowned; something was wrong. She gasped and pressed a hand to her temple as a sharp stabbing pain shot across her forehead. She sat by the door as Carandini gestured to the second shrouded figure and looked imploringly at them. "As I explained to you in my office, he was discovered dead this morning. Judging by his injuries, he's been murdered! So, you see, ladies and gentlemen, we desperately need your help."

Thorne looked at him with a raised eyebrow. "Why us? Why haven't you called the police in Aswan?"

Carandini took a deep breath and drew himself up. "Someone has vandalised the telephone in my office, which is the only line into and out of the hotel." Elliott and Thorne exchanged glances. "I am afraid that, as enquiry agents working for the Veiled Protectorate, you are our only hope of dealing with this in a tasteful manner. Ladies, gentlemen, I beg of you — help me!"

Elliott turned to Carandini. "Would you give us a few moments to talk in private, Mr Bey? Official business, you understand."

Carandini blinked. "Yes, of course. I'll wait outside." He left and closed the door behind him,

Thorne pulled out his notebook with a wry expression. "We don't have much choice, do we? While we're here, we're the face of the Empire and the Veiled Protectorate. It simply wouldn't do for us to ignore a murder in order to enjoy our long-overdue honeymoons, now, would it?"

Aquilleia, her head throbbing from the pain that was working its way towards her eyes, responded from her seat by the door. "Sadly, you are quite right, husband."

Thorne smiled at his wife before turning his gaze to the shroud covering the mortal remains of van Sloane. He paused and stared at the space with narrowed eyes before turning to his old friend. "Elliott, we have a problem!"

Elliott moved to Thorne's side as he carefully lifted the shroud from the corpse to reveal the bloodied, empty space where Julius' head should have been. Elliott looked at Darling. "You need to see this."

Darling joined them in staring at the decapitated remains; a muscle began to twitch in his jaw. "This is obviously the work of the family! No one else would have a reason for this type of desecration."

Giselle nodded. "They've taken the skull; the one part they need to resurrect him."

Aquilleia's eyebrows drew together. "I knew something was wrong when we entered the room. When Kiefer identified Julius, Julius' voice was faint, but it was still in the same room as his corpse. It isn't anymore." She looked at the others. "I can still hear him...just. His voice is almost imperceptible now…but I *can* still hear him. It's here, somewhere in the hotel." She stroked Veronique's head. "As Darling said; his skull must have been taken by one of the family…and that means more murders, to replenish their stock of body parts, and ensure *his* resurrection!"

Darling's face wore a grim expression. "I've had enough of these orders to protect the Devereaux family! I cannot — *we* cannot sit by and do nothing when we know what they are up to and why!"

Elliott turned to Aquilleia. "Can you find out what happened to Julius right before his death, and when his skull was taken?"

Aquilleia frowned. "I can try…but the fact that his head isn't here might make things difficult." She stood by the shelf, gently rested her hands on the decapitated corpse, closed her eyes, and began to hum. After a few minutes she looked at Elliott, silver lights swirling in her lavender eyes. "He died trying to kill Evelyn. He had a knife, and was climbing over the balcony when a dark figure with wings appeared and dropped him to his death. His skull was taken early this morning by a man dressed in black." She sat on the edge of the shelf and took a deep, shuddering breath. "That is all I can see."

Elliott winced. "Then it would appear that I *do* need to talk with my father." He turned back to Aquilleia and gently placed a hand on her shoulder. "I am sorry to ask this of you, but can you try with Cavet?"

Aquilleia pressed a trembling hand to her temple and nodded. She walked to the shelf that held the dead French-man. Thorne stood next to her with a watchful expression as she laid her hands on the shrouded body, and again closed her eyes and began to hum.

Her eyes suddenly flew open, the silver lights filling even their whites, as she backed away from the corpse, shaking her head. "I can't see much—" Thorne caught her as she slowly sank to the floor and carried her to the shelf, placed her in a sitting position and knelt before her, gently rubbed her hands; an expression of deep concern on his face.

Giselle sat beside her friend. "Could you see anything at all?"

Aquilleia swallowed. "I saw one image…a flash, nothing more."

Giselle nodded. "Go on."

"All I could see was an image of a golden frog."

Thorne frowned. "A golden frog?"

Aquilleia nodded. "I believe it was the last thing he saw." She swallowed as a sudden streak of dark red light flashed across her vision; oh, no…not now! She had far too much to do without having to deal with a migraine!

Elliott and Thorne eyed the covered remains of Gaston Cavet as Darling stoked his beard and mused. "A golden frog?" He looked at the others. "Well, we have no choice but to deal with this in, as Mr Bey said, a tasteful manner. It will certainly give us the opportunity to keep an eye on the family."

Giselle looked at the Frenchman's well-dressed corpse. "He is definitely dressed for dinner, but I cannot recall seeing him during the cocktail hour."

Thorne nodded. "Neither can I. That puts his time of death at no later than six o'clock." He stood and ran an eye over Cavet's outfit. "I would say he was killed very shortly before that time…" He reached under the well-pinned cravat and carefully removed a fine galleried monocle. He held it up as it spun gently on its gold chain; the cracked glass flashing in the gaslight. "The placement of the monocle is one of the very last stages to any gentleman's preparations for dinner. I would say that death came no earlier than a quarter to the hour."

Elliott nodded. "So, we have an approximate time of death." He looked at his pocket watch. "I think we should let Mr Bey know our decision about taking on the case. Thorne, let the gentleman in, will you?"

Thorne opened the door. "Mr Bey?"

Carandini entered and looked at them hopefully. "Well?"

Darling stepped forward. "Mr Bey, we will accept this case on behalf of the Empire and the Veiled Protectorate."

Carandini's relief was palpable. "Oh, thank God! Thank you, ladies, and gentlemen. I am most relieved." He frowned suddenly. "I suppose that you would need someone to offer an idea of the possible time of death? I might be able to offer some assistance with that. Let us return to my office; the... odour and the lack of air here is making me feel rather unwell!"

He turned without waiting for a response and walked out of the meat locker. Elliott and Giselle shared a glance as they and the others followed him to his office.

As Giselle and Aquilleia sat, Carandini stood behind his desk, opened a drawer, frowned, closed it, opened the next drawer down, and with an expression of relief, removed the topmost file. Rummaging through the thick wad of papers, he removed a document and held it up with a triumphant expression. "I thought that you might need the assistance of a medical personage — for working out the time of death and other...necessities. We don't have a doctor here at the hotel, but we do have a nurse. One of our guests, Mrs Caroline Jones. She's the wife of Dr Jones, assistant to the eminent archaeologist Dr Mirylees. She might be able to assist you. According to our research, she worked as a nurse in the New London Hospital for Women, then in the coroner's office in Stoke Newington. When she married, she was forced, under the marriage bar, to cease work. However, her husband took a position with the Pondicherry Museum in India, and because nurses with her background were needed, she worked in one of the women's hospitals there. That's where her husband met Dr Mirylees, and they both took a position with him in a private capacity."

Thorne took out his notebook and frowned. "You research your guests?"

Carandini nodded proudly. "We always check the backgrounds of all those who stay with us."

Giselle raised an eyebrow. "Why?"

Carandini smiled and stroked his moustache. "We are the greatest hotel company in the world, Mlle Du'Lac. Accordingly, we insist on only the finest calibre of guest."

Giselle raised an arch eyebrow. "I see. And yet here we are, in your wonderful hotel, with two examples of the finest calibre of corpse currently residing in your second meat locker. Two corpses that have, to all intents and purposes, been created by one or more of your finest calibre of guests."

Carandini's mouth opened and closed several times before his shoulders, along with the waxed tips of his mustache, finally drooped. "As you say, Mlle Du'Lac, as you say."

Elliott cleared his throat. "Mr Bey, though your offer is quite kind, we will not be needing the assistance of Mrs Jones." He looked at the nonplussed manager and lightly tapped his nose. "We have our ways, Mr Bey. Now, we'll need the documents you have made on all the guests currently staying at the hotel. I take it you have similar ones on the staff?"

"Yes, of course." Carandini handed the thick dossier to Elliott, opened a different drawer, and removed another document. "This is the file on our human staff. We currently employ fifty-five humans and twenty-five Simulandro staff."

Giselle frowned. "You don't keep files on your Simulandro staff?"

Carandini shook his head. "There's no reason to. They have no previous history, as they were built specifically for the hotel. They're programmed to carry out their orders and retire to their dormitories at the end of their set working times."

Giselle looked at him steadily. "So, you have no files on them because they have no lives to report on?"

"Exactly."

Elliott heard the sharp note of anger in Giselle's voice and almost imperceptibly shook his head; now was not the time. Giselle caught his look, snapped her mouth shut, and settled back in her chair with a sniff.

Carandini paused; there was one last thing…and it could well be the one that would cause the investigators the most concern! He cleared his throat. "I thank you for accepting the investigation on behalf of the Empire and the Veiled Protectorate. There is, however, a clause to your acceptance of the case, and one that I must beg your indulgence to accept. Due to the nature of our business; international reputations, shareholders, and the possibility of terrible reviews in the newspapers…" As Carandini's voice trailed off, Elliott looked at him from under lowered brows; his expression ominous. "Go on, Mr Bey." Carandini spread his hands. "May I please request that when the other guests are informed of the, ah… incident, you imply the unfortunate Monsieur Cavet met his death…by his own hand?"

Thorne's eyebrows shot into his hairline. "You want us to lie to the guests about our investigation?"

Carandini shook his head firmly. "Not at all, Mr Thorne. No, instead, I would like you to…" He paused as he tried to choose the right word.

Giselle looked at him with a sardonic expression. "I believe the term you are looking for is 'fudge', Mr Bey. You want us to avoid using the frightening word 'murder' around your paying guests, and to wave around the possibility of an act of self-destruction as the cause of death…am I correct?"

Carandini looked embarrassed as he nodded briefly. "Yes, that is what I am asking…what I am *begging* you to do, Mlle Du'Lac."

Giselle looked at him with a raised eyebrow. "Did Monsieur Cavet have any family, Mr Bey? The reason I ask is that they might become rather upset at your slandering their family member when it finally comes out that he was, in fact, the victim of a particularly violent act of murder."

Carandini looked pained. "I understand, Mlle Du'Lac. Monsieur Cavet has — I beg your pardon — *had*, no family. Please, don't misunderstand me…I have no desire for you to lie to the other guests. All I ask is that you be a little circumspect in informing them of the precise nature of Monsieur Cavet's death."

Elliott Looked at him steadily. "Falsely claiming that Cavet's murder is a suicide will make our attempts to solve his death a trifle difficult, Mr Bey. Investigating a murder gives us the right to scrutinise our fellow guests for possible motives, enter their rooms, and search their belongings. Investigating a suicide does not."

Carandini hugged the file to his chest. "I understand, Mr Caine, but please…I beg you, do your best."

Elliott shared a glance with the others; at the faint nods from each of them, he turned back to Carandini. "In the current circumstances, Mr Bey, we have no choice but to acquiesce to your request." He held out his hand. "May we have the file on your human employees?"

Carandini handed him the documents with a relieved expression. "Thank you, Mr Caine, Mlle Du'Lac, Mr Thorne, Madame Aquilleia. I cannot tell you how relieved I am."

Elliott looked at his friends. "I suggest we return to our rooms to refresh ourselves, then reconvene in our suite at half past ten. We can go over the files Mr Bey has so kindly furnished us with." He turned to Carandini. "We shall see what we can discover, Mr Bey. Good morning."

As they left his office, Carandini closed the door behind them, returned to his desk and sat down with a groan. He shook his head wearily; the Eridanus Corporation were quite generous with their wages…but nothing was worth this level of stress!

○

The Entrance Hall
12:55pm

Kiefer entered the reception, saw Carandini and Miss March talking, and with supreme arrogance raised his voice to interrupt their conversation. "Miss March? My family and I wish to book an excursion to one or two of the neighbouring islands once the sandstorm has blown over. I trust you can organise this?"

Miss March darted a quick glance at Carandini, whose perfectly blank expression appeared a trifle wooden as he turned and stalked back into his office. "Of course, Mr Devereaux." She turned to the Simulandro steward who was manning the reception desk and handed him a document. "This is the document that Mr Breton requested. Please see that it's delivered to him immediately." At the sharp nod from the android, she turned back to Kiefer. "If you would care to come into my office, Mr Devereaux, I can make the booking for you."

Kiefer shook his head. "I don't know the names of the islands. Come with me to the Temple of Augustus, and I'll point out the ones we wish to visit."

"Very well, Mr Devereaux. If you would please wait here,

I'll get the necessary forms." She entered her office, returned almost immediately bearing a clipboard, and followed Kiefer down the corridor that led to the restaurant. Passing through the French doors, they entered the glass covered terrace and headed towards the far side of the island. They walked past the swimming pool before reaching the furthest point on the island; the ancient Temple of Augustus, which now housed the hammam. As approached the temple, they were unaware of the strange, shadowy movement that followed under the ground behind them.

Kiefer reached the raised dais that afforded a glass-encased view of the strait between the island and the mainland, and paused to take in what little he could see through the billowing yellow haze beyond the glass panels. He turned and scanned the covered walkway they had taken; no one had followed them, as far as he could see. He grasped Miss March's wrist and pulled her against him, pressing a not-unwelcome kiss against her soft lips. She smiled up at him, her usually pale skin slightly flushed. "Why, Mr Devereaux! If Carandini Bey sees us, I'll be struck from the company!"

Kiefer grinned. "If he tries, I'll kill him. We need you here, Vanessa." He kissed her again. "Now, first things first…we know that Caine, Thorne, their wives, and Darling are enquiry agents working with the Veiled Protectorate." A faint opaque light appeared in Kiefer's eyes as he continued. "I don't like having such an obvious presence of the law this close to the family, and I have a plan to remove these unexpected irritants from our lives; we'll follow our original plan to rob and kill the two couples and simply add Darling to the tally…and that will be the end of them. It will also be the end of this particular shopping expedition, because, according to Hammad's list, there are only two guests here with pieces of jewellery worthy of our attention; the female enquiry agents, Giselle Du'Lac, and Aquilleia Aquileisi." Kiefer gave a sharp bark of laughter. "Two attractive birds with one very heavy stone!"

Vanessa frowned slightly at his remark, and touched his arm tentatively. "I would like to add someone to the list, Kiefer. I think the Contessa de Mostada might make a suitable addition…and rather a healthy contribution to our coffers." At Kiefer's frown, Vanessa hurriedly explained. "I know that she isn't on Hammad's list; she entered Egypt by a different port, so he missed her. However, her jewellery is quite spectacular, of exquisite quality…and rather plentiful!"

Kiefer nodded slowly. "Add her as a mark." He paused, a deeply unpleasant expression crossed his handsome face. "The women enquiry agents might also bring us an extra bounty; I think they should both make a special, one night only appearance at the slave market across the border…" His lips widened in a cruel smile. "One with hair like flame and skin like milk, and the other with lavender eyes and hair like a raven's wing — they'll both bring a very good price!

Vanessa gazed at Kiefer; there was something on her mind, but she hesitated before voicing her concern. "Kiefer… should we be worried about Julius' death?"

Kiefer gave a bark of laughter. "That dithering great dolt? No, he probably died from realising his sheer uselessness and fell from the airship!"

Vanessa smiled uncertainly. "He certainly isn't the usual type of person the family usually attracts!"

Kiefer nodded as he played with a wisp of her red hair. "It may well be a while before we get around to reanimating dear Julius — he's a complete waste of time, money, and body parts!"

"Margaux might complain."

Kiefer shrugged. "Let her! When Father isn't here, I'm the voice Mother listens to, and I think it's high time we put Julius out to pasture!"

Vanessa's eyes widened. "But he's a member of the family! Reynaud will return in the next few days. Surely, he will—"

Vanessa flinched as Kiefer's eyes flashed with a blinding white light. He gripped her wrist. "Don't ever question my position in the family, Vanessa! I said it will happen, so it will! Father will take my side in this — Mother will make sure of it!"

Vanessa twisted in his grip. "Kiefer, you're hurting me!"

Kiefer laughed. "You've never complained before!" He let go of her wrist with a mocking smile. "Now, you have the list. When the sandstorm has passed, we'll strike." Kiefer paused. "If we kill the husbands first, that will leave Du'Lac and Aquileisi alone, and that will certainly make kidnapping them easier. We can keep them in the ritual room until the private air-carriage comes for us; as humans, they won't be able to open the doors to escape. Then we can leave this boring place, pop across the border to sell them, and be on our way back to civilisation within a few hours." A scheming expression appearing on his face. "It might also be an idea to hide the corpses of their husbands, the friend, and the dog, in the ritual room with them…that should terrify them into silence, and it'll keep the authorities busy looking for five people they will never find." He grinned. "Now, out of interest, has anyone caused a fuss over Cavet's death?"

Vanessa, rubbing her wrist, shook her head. "Bey has managed to keep his death hidden from most of the other guests, but he informed Caine, Thorne, their wives, and Darling."

Kiefer glared at her. "That's all we need. Have they worked out when he was killed?"

Vanessa nodded, looking worried. "Apparently, they have ways of working out the time of death without any assistance from a doctor; they know he was killed shortly before the cocktail hour. I only found out a few minutes before you came into the reception."

Kiefer's eyes filled with white light as he again seized her wrist. Vanessa screamed in pain; her delicate bones cracked under the superhuman pressure from his fingers as he glared at her. "What bloody use are you, Vanessa? We pay you in immortality for your assistance in keeping the family one step ahead of the authorities, you useless whore!" He threw her to the ground and paced, muttering under his breath. "I need to keep this from Mother—" He halted and turned his burning white eyes on Vanessa, who flinched back, her damaged wrist cradled against her chest. Kiefer took a deep breath. "We need more information about what they know, sooner rather than later!" He glared at her. "You've become lax in your dedication to the family, Vanessa — you must prove yourself worthy of our gift! Now, what else do you have to tell me?"

Vanessa wiped her eyes and took a deep breath. "Bey will make an official announcement this evening at dinner. He'll inform the guests of Cavet's death, but it'll be couched in such terms so as to appear to be a case of suicide. The enquiry agents know that it isn't...they know that it's murder, but they have accepted his request to investigate Cavet's death, sub rosa...it was the only way Carandini would allow them to investigate. I believe they'll send word to Colonel Barrington when the sandstorm dies down."

Kiefer's dark eyebrows lowered as he stared at her. "That bloody old fossil! I can deal with him." Suddenly, his eyes widened. "There's another old fossil here; Mirylees! Of course!" He looked at the bemused Vanessa. "You were between resurrections at the time; Mirylees was part of the dig when we came here to resurrect Heathers back in 1865." He smirked. "One of the men on the dig became the final offering. He was a bachelor of sorts; perfect as the virginal sacrifice. Mother had to woo him with an offer of marriage before he allowed her anywhere near him. Needless to say, his wedding night did not go according to plan!" He snorted with laughter as he remembered the night, so many years earlier, when his family had murdered Edmund Street to resurrect their faithful valet.

As he reminisced, Vanessa watched him fearfully; she loved Kiefer…but she was also afraid of him. "Kiefer, why did the family destroy the telephone? I could easily have prevented any calls getting through to the police."

Kiefer stared at her, then spoke in a soft voice which made her flinch. "What? What has happened to the telephone?"

Vanessa looked up at her lover and whispered, "It was destroyed last night…" She cowered as Kiefer's face darkened with rage. He strode away from her and stood with his back turned, fists clenching. When he turned to her, his eyes were entirely white. She lowered her gaze and stared at the floor as she raised her quavering voice. "You mean…it wasn't the family?"

Kiefer closed his eyes and took a deep, shuddering breath. When he finally opened them, he spoke as though addressing a child. "Why would we destroy the telephone, Vanessa? We needed it to organise a private air-carriage to take us to Cairo after we resurrect Father."

Vanessa face was imploring as she held out her uninjured hand. "Kiefer, I'm afraid! Something's conspiring against us! Given the closeness of this investigation, is it sensible to continue with our plan to rob and kill the enquiry agents?" Kiefer stared at Vanessa as she continued to speak, her voice shaking as the words tumbled from her mouth. "Perhaps we should ignore this particular inventory and wait until after the investigation is over. If they find stolen goods in our possession, or anything else that could incriminate us, it will destroy our arrangement with Hammad and his movement — and they aren't nice people to cross, Kiefer! We can target the next set of guests after we have resurrected your father and the family have left; what do you say?"

Kiefer stared at her in stunned silence, his wrath building at the sheer audacity of a human woman believing that she knew better than he about how to deal with their current predicament! His lips peeled back from his teeth in a feral snarl as he violently slapped her hand away. "I want Caine and Thorne dead, you stupid bitch! I want my money! I want their jewellery! I don't give a damn about the bloody Islamists, or their creed! They are the means to an end, and the end is money! More money for me…and more money for the family! If they try to move against us, they will discover an enemy more than capable of destroying them, *and* their precious cause!" He jabbed an angry finger at the cowering woman. "And I want that bloody redheaded bitch and her friend sold for a good price! See to it, Vanessa. Remember; you're only a part of this family while you're of use to us, regardless of what Mother says!" He stormed away, his back ramrod-straight as he marched along the covered corridor and back to the hotel.

Vanessa watched him until he had disappeared, then sat up with a pained sob. Using her good hand, she made shaky notes about the nonexistent trip she would have to show to Carandini when she returned to the office. She stood up and cried out at the sudden, jarring pain in her arm. Her knees threatening to give way as she looked at her broken wrist through tear-filled eyes; she couldn't explain away such an obvious injury, she would have to ask Marguerite to heal the broken bones before she could return to her office. She bent carefully, keeping her broken wrist pressed to her chest as she picked up her clipboard and began to walk back to the main building.

As she walked past the hammam and down the path that would lead her back to the hotel, there was a sudden movement as Linden silently stepped out from behind one of the covered columns and stared after her, his face troubled. He had overheard enough of the conversation to be deeply concerned. He knew of the family's agreement with the Islamists, and it *had* served them well, but Kiefer's lust for domination and money was rapidly becoming unmanageable. Linden leant back against the column and shook his head; he desperately needed to talk with his grandfather... Kiefer was out of control, and Linden was honest enough to admit that, as much as he loved his grandmother, when it came to Kiefer, he was her favourite child and she allowed him to take great advantage of that fact. Only their grandfather had the power to bring him to heel...and for the family's sake, that day would have to come sooner, rather than later.

○

The Reception
1:30pm

Masquelyne locked the door to the room he had taken for his unauthorised stay at the hotel, stood by the narrow bed, and made his way towards the reception as only he could. Taking a deep breath, he gently shook his wings until they hung loosely from his shoulders to the floor, then he raised them to wrap around his body; the gossamer thin skin became flushed with soft, pulsing colours as his wings enveloped him, covering him, from crown to toe, like a living shield. Masquelyne closed his eyes and slowly sank into the ground; as his body merged with the stone, he opened his golden eyes...his vision taking on the shimmering haze it always did when he utilised this particular part of his gift. The silky sensation of his body moving through cool stone eased as his head became fully covered by the marble tiles on the floor. As he settled to a suitable depth, he began to move fluidly through the stone; an almost imperceptible shadow under the terrace floor the only sign of his passing.

As he approached the reception, his shadow slid up one of the many columns and he stepped out from within the carved stone. His wings settled into the semblance of a light-coloured duster across his shoulders as he leisurely opened the door and entered the main building.

As he rounded the corner, he walked straight into one of the four people standing there. "Oh, I do beg your pardon—"

Thorne blinked. "Masquelyne?"

Masquelyne stopped dead. "Shadavarian?"

The sudden silence was broken as Veronique launched herself at Masquelyne, whose pale face split in a wide smile as the ecstatic Labrador leapt up at him and licked his face. He held the dog close and rubbed her ears. "Xenocyon! How is my favourite battle hound?"

Thorne grinned. "She is doing very well, Masquelyne." He darted a quick look around the empty reception. "But here, her name here is Veronique."

Elliott looked at his father, his eyes both worried and exasperated. "I'm glad we found you, father. We need to talk before Darling sees you…a little something to do with just how Julius van Sloane took a short, vertical jaunt from an airship and landed in the middle of a dinner party for a bask of crocodiles!"

Masquelyne opened his mouth, paused, and nodded. "Yes…I do believe that I owe you an explanation. Perhaps we should adjourn to somewhere a little more private?"

Thorne held up his hand. "There's something I need to do first." He embraced his friend's father. "It's lovely to see you again, Masquelyne." He turned and held out his hand to Aquilleia. "I'm sure that you remember my wife, Aquilleia."

Masquelyne nodded, a smile on his lips as he kissed Aquilleia's hand. "How could I possibly forget the Flatworld Witch? How are you, my dear?"

Aquilleia smiled as she kissed his cheek. "I'm very well, thank you, Masquelyne." She darted a quick glance at her husband. "Aside from what I believe to be the beginnings of a migraine." At Thorne's worried look, she patted his hand. "It should be fine."

Giselle looked at Elliott. "I suggest that we retire to our suite for our discussion. That should guarantee us privacy."

Masquelyne smiled at his daughter-in-law. "In that case, I'll travel to your suite in such a way as to not draw attention to my presence."

Elliott nodded. "Very well, father. You do know where our suite is?"

Masquelyne nodded. "Of course." He stepped back into the shadows afforded by one of the many columns in the reception, wrapped his wings around himself, and sank back into the ground.

Elliott and the others made their way through the empty reception where Thorne paused and handed Veronique's lead to Aquilleia. "I might just see about ordering a tray of drinks. I'll meet you at the room." He disappeared through the door at the far end of the reception as Aquilleia and Veronique followed Elliott and Giselle to their suite.

As they were settling themselves into the collection of velvet-covered settees and armchairs by the large window, Masquelyne's head suddenly appeared in the centre of the floor. He rose, shook out his wings, and bowed to Giselle and Aquilleia. "Ladies."

Aquilleia released Veronique from her lead and joined

Giselle on one of the settees. "It's been so long, Masquelyne… too long."

Masquelyne nodded as he settled himself into one of the armchairs. "A great many things have happened since last we met…" His face darkened slightly. "Not all of it good, I have to admit…"

Giselle smiled as she carefully arranged her skirt. "One way or another, our lives *are* rather entertaining, aren't they? I don't mind excitement, mystery, or danger…I really rather enjoy it. It's certainly far more entertaining, however, when one doesn't have to wade through piles and piles of dratted files!" She waved her hand at a large pile of paperwork on one of the tables.

Masquelyne took in the files with a raised eyebrow. "Something to do with the case?"

Giselle nodded. "Apparently, the hotel keeps dossiers on all its guests and staff…well, the human staff at least. Carandini Bey graciously gave us the files for a little light reading. Bearing in mind the calibre of guest, I expected, or rather, was hoping for, a soupçon of scandal, but aside from the artist Breton cheating on his examinations at Cambridge, there wasn't really anything too unseemly, or that would have a bearing on the case. Luckily, because the files are all about money and social position, the notes on us were rather…limited in scope, shall we say? Elliott, enquiry agent; me, singer; Thorne, enquiry agent; Aquilleia, psychic; Veronique, housetrained." She grinned at the faint whine that came from the insulted Labrador.

Masquelyne's eyes were guarded. "Anything else…about the other guests, I mean?"

Giselle frowned. "Not really." She picked up several of the files. "The guests are all listed in order of their income; wealthiest first. As you would expect, the Devereaux family are in first place. They're all lumped in as one entity, and are described as 'an attractive and socially superior family. The hotel's idea of the perfect guests'..." She looked at her father-in-law with a raised eyebrow. "The Eridanus Corporation really didn't look too closely, did they? The Contessa de Mostada is second, and is described as a 'wealthy, excitable, and pernickety widow, of superb quality.' Surprisingly enough, the third guest is Thomas Breton. He is, apparently, an 'ill-mannered narcissist, a self-proclaimed Marxist, but also a fairly decent artist, trying desperately to pretend that he comes from poverty to better suit the art set in London.' His parents own a sizable estate in Dorset, and they pay him a handsome income every year to support his artistic leanings." Giselle held out the file to Masquelyne who looked at the sum mentioned and raised his eyebrows. "A very handsome sum, indeed!"

Giselle nodded. "The four of us are next on the list. Then it's Gaston Cavet. I know that he's dead, but I do so love being nosey. He's described as a 'wealthy bon vivant and celebrated author of impeccable gallic stock'."

Masquelyne looked at Elliott and grinned. "It sounds as though they're describing a stew!"

Giselle giggled as she skimmed through the pages. "I've lost my place...oh, here we are. Dr Mirylees is 'ancient, fussy, and extremely particular.' His assistant, Dr Jones, and his wife and child are dismissed as 'not the usual type of guest.' The American, Rex Nympton, is last on the list, and is as he himself has already described; a 'Jack of all trades' who is now the Pinkerton agent for Texas."

She dropped the file back onto the pile and picked up another ream of paper. Her smile disappeared as her expression darkened. "But this document...this is really quite grim! This is the hotel's file on the human staff. The Eridanus Corporation refers to them as 'Liveware'." Giselle's lip curled in disgust. "The women are all listed by their appearance, and the men are all listed by the speed of their work. Their files contain nothing about who they actually are as people... nothing at all!" Giselle dropped the papers onto the table. "There's also a document in this file that I don't think Carandini Bey meant to include. It details a commission, from the Eridanus Corporation, to the company who manufacture Simulandros. In it, the Eridanus Corporation placed a sizable order for multiple Simulandro staff to be created, programmed, and delivered to the hotel; android and gynoid, serving staff, and security...far more Simulandros than we've seen since we've been here. I don't know where they could keep them...unless, once they arrived, they were sent somewhere else..." Giselle's voice faded slightly as she thought. She shook her head and continued. "I digress. In this document, the Eridanus Corporation actually refer to their human and Simulandro staff as 'Liveware and Synthware'." Giselle looked nauseated. "Liveware and Synthware! They're so used to treating their Simulandro staff like non-humans, they've actually started to treat their human staff like Simulandros." She paused as the suite door opened and Thorne entered the room. He was followed by two Simulandro androids, each one bearing a sizable tray loaded with champagne, caviar, blinis, cake, and a meaty bone for Veronique.

The androids set out the light repast, bowed, and left the room as silently as they had arrived. Elliott poured several glasses of Champagne and handed one to Giselle who took a deep breath, accepted the drink, and helped herself to a large slab of sponge cake.

Masquelyne accepted a coupe of Champagne and looked at his son over the rim of the glass, his eyebrows raised. "So...what was it that you wanted to talk about?"

Elliott returned his father's arch look with one of his own. "You know very well, father!"

Masquelyne grinned. "Very well. Getting straight to the

point; yes, I admit to killing Julius. In my defence, I hasten to say that it was very much his own fault. He was armed with a knife and he was waiting on Evelyn's balcony with the sole intention of murdering her."

Thorne sat next to Aquilleia, pulled a notebook and pencil from his breast-pocket, and began to take notes.

Aquilleia nibbled at a caviar-topped blini. "What were you doing there?"

A faint flush touched Masquelyne's pale cheeks. "I was keeping an eye on Calliandra...I mean, Evelyn."

Elliott noted the use of his mother's name in silence and looked at his father with a guarded expression. "What happened, father?"

Masquelyne shrugged. "He was sitting on the balcony waiting for the moment to strike, so I chose the correct moment and struck first. I picked him up and looked him in the eyes..." He sat back, a thoughtful look on his pale face. "You can measure the character of a man by looking in his eyes."

Thorne looked at him, his pencil hovering over his notebook. "Then what did you do?"

Masquelyne shrugged again and took a sip of his champagne. "I dropped him over the rail."

Elliott swore under his breath. Thorne failed to maintain a neutral expression as he looked at his friend's father with an approving nod. "That must have come as quite a shock to Julius!"

Masquelyne raised his glass, a faint smile on his lips as he remembered the events that had taken place on the airship's balcony. "It was indeed; an unpleasant and quite fatal shock. I regret to say that his life ended far too quickly to be a just punishment for his crimes. His impact on the surface of the Nile, however, did add a touch of insult to injury, as he became both an offering to Sebek, *and* an hors d'oeuvre to that particular deity's followers. It was quite interesting watching the waters of the Nile turn red; quite Biblical, in fact." His golden eyes flashed as he looked at his son. "But I want it on record that the subsequent death of Gaston Cavet was not my doing."

Elliott nodded, his fingers plucking at his beard. "Do you know who was responsible?"

Masquelyne shook his head. "All I can say is that it was not I."

Elliott sat back in his armchair and took a sip from his own coupe. He watched as Masquelyne helped himself to the caviar and blinis. "Father, you aren't a guest at this hotel, are you? We never see you in the bar or the dining room. Where are you staying? How are you getting food?"

Masquelyne took a slice of cake from one of the dainty plates on the table and smiled. "As Giselle has already pointed out, the hotel employs many Simulandro workers. After their working program is finished for the day, they return to their quarters until the following morning. At the very back of beyond...on the farthest most corner of this island, there's a small building that contains one room for the androids, a second room for the gynoids, and a very small bedroom and bathroom where the Simulandro technician stays when he is servicing the workforce. The technician isn't currently in residence, so, I'm staying in his room." He took another sip of his drink and sat back with a smile. "During the evening, I utilise my gift and make my way through the hotel; quite literally, in fact! To the kitchens, where I am afraid that I am forced, due to my trying circumstances, to purloin food and suitable beverages..." He paused and looked at his loaded plate and Champagne coupe with a wicked grin. "...from their usual place of storage."

Giselle hid a smile as her father-in-law placed both his plate and coupe on the small table next to him and spread his hands in a placatory gesture. "And with that, my lords and ladies, I hereby rest the case for the defence."

Elliott sat forward; a deep green light in his eyes. "But to what end, father?"

Masquelyne looked at his son; the humour dropped away from his eyes and was replaced by coldness. "I am simply staying here to keep an eye on Evelyn, and to make sure that when the Devereaux family try to kill her; and they will try… I will be there to prevent it." He picked up his coupe. "She is to be their final victim. Despite all their planning, there was one thing they couldn't foresee; the sandstorm. They will not dare make a move against her until the sandstorm is over and they can leave the island without drawing attention to the new face in their midst; that of Reynaud." He sipped his drink, his eyes distant. "That, my son, is when I will answer to no master; not the Empire, not the Espion Court, not Darling, not even you. I will do whatever I have to, to prevent them from killing Evelyn."

Giselle sat forward. "And after she is safe? What will you do then, Masquelyne?"

Masquelyne looked at his daughter-in-law. "That is up to Evelyn, not me. The choice of staying a human, or returning to Astraea with me is entirely her choice…as it should be."

Giselle's eyes narrowed. "And the Devereaux family? What of them?"

Masquelyne smiled; a cold, steady smile. "When I know that Evelyn is safe, if any of them still draw breath, I shall wipe them from the face of the Earth. It's not a matter of if, but when."

Marguerite And Vincenzo's suite
1:30pm

Vanessa tucked the clipboard under her arm and raised her uninjured hand. She winced at the sharp pain in her broken wrist as she knocked at the door of Marguerite and Vincenzo's suite. The door was opened almost immediately by Vincenzo, who looked at her damaged wrist and raised an eyebrow. "Kiefer?"

Vanessa nodded silently. He stepped out of her way and gestured towards the main bedroom. "Marguerite is resting. I will let her know you are here."

He disappeared into the bedroom as Vanessa stood by the door and tried not to move her arm too much. She turned at the sound of tutting from the chaise longue by the terrace door. Marguerite's companion, Violette, smiled as she wagged her finger. "No one likes tattletales, Vanessa — especially not the mothers of men who like breaking women's bones." She lay back on the chaise and stretched voluptuously. "Kiefer learned his predilections from both his parents. Who do you think taught him all he knows? It certainly wasn't me!"

Vanessa glared at the smirking young woman. "Mind your tongue, Violette! I know who and what you are. I have spent the last five hundred years serving the Master and Mistress; they need my assistance in keeping their connection to this place and our other resurrection sites secret. In spite of the Master's attraction to you, *you* are utterly replaceable; *I* am not! Remember that, and you will live a far happier and longer life!"

Vincenzo reappeared at the door and paused as he became aware of the change in atmosphere; he looked at the two women through narrowed eyes. "Vanessa? Marguerite will see you now."

Vanessa swept into the bedroom, pointedly ignoring the now open-mouthed Violette, and closed the door firmly behind her. Violette continued to stare at the door with a look of rage on her smooth face — no one had spoken to her in such a way for years! She caught Vincenzo's eye; the handsome young Italian grinned at her and bowed in a mocking fashion as he left for a game of cards with André in the bar.

In the dimly lit room on the other side of the bedroom door, Vanessa's ire towards Violette dissolved into mute silence as Marguerite approached her. The matriarch's eyes blazed with a blinding white light as she touched the younger woman's injured wrist; Vanessa bit back a sharp cry of pain as she felt and heard the broken bones knit together under her skin. As the sensations stilled, Marguerite returned to her armchair, sat down with a sigh, and raised an eyebrow. "So, tell me, child; a lover's tiff, a too-passionate game, or anger?"

Vanessa paled; no one could keep secrets from Marguerite for long…not even Kiefer. She leant forward and in a low murmur began to explain everything that had happened by the Temple of Augustus.

Back in the sitting room, Violette sat and seethed. She had to admit that the odious Vanessa was quite correct; her connection to the family was tenuous and solely based on the Master's penchant for requiring occasional additional company in the marital bed, but Marguerite was also accommodating in that sense…as was Vincenzo, and Violette was firmly of the belief that a companion should always be willing to bend to both Master and Mistress. Violette tapped an immaculately manicured fingernail against her lips; with a little thought, it might be possible to remove the irreplaceable Miss March — after all; all things, even good things, generally come to an end.

The door to Marguerite's bedroom opened and Vanessa appeared. Violette's eyes narrowed; the secretary looked far too happy and relaxed for her taste. She darted a sharp glance at Vanessa's wrist; the once-injured joint was now obviously healed and hung lightly by her side.

Vanessa gave Violette a contemptuous glance and left the room with a dismissive sniff, closing the door none too gently behind her. Violette scowled at the door; enough was enough — that whey-faced bitch had to go!

Vanessa, ignorant of Violette's burgeoning plans, continued to the reception where she dropped the clipboard with the arrangements for the Devereaux family's non-existent trip onto her desk, then crossed the hallway to Carandini Bey's office and knocked on the open door. He looked up from the document he was reading. "Yes, Miss March."

Vanessa gave him a pained smile; one she was well practised in using. "I have the information for the trip for the Devereaux family, Mr Bey. I'll see to it shortly." She delicately pressed a pale hand to her temple. "Would it be acceptable if I took a few moments away from my desk? I'm afraid that I have the beginnings of a migraine."

Carandini frowned slightly; he was quite aware of his secretary's migraines...they were, thankfully, few and far between, but had on more than one occasion rendered her incapable of seeing to her duties for several hours. "Yes, of course, Miss March. Take as long as you need." Vanessa smiled wanly. "Thank you, Mr Bey."

She turned and made her way to her private rooms in the staff quarters. The journey took several minutes, as her suite was situated in a group of low-lying buildings tucked away on the far side of the terrace, carefully hidden from the view of paying guests...and prying eyes.

Approaching her rooms, Vanessa selected a key from the chatelaine at her waist, unlocked the door, and entered the small suite. She closed and locked the door, and pressed her back against the cool wood with a tired sigh; what a God-awful mess the day had become!

Reaching out to turn up the gas lamp, Vanessa covered a yawn as the golden light filled the small room. Turning towards her bed, she stopped abruptly at the sight of the unexpected and extremely unwelcome guest sitting on her settee. Vanessa's breath caught in her throat; blinding white lights filled her eyes as she fearfully pressed herself against the door and stared in abject terror at the silent visitor. Her heart pounding in her ears, she turned to look the chest of drawers next to her; stretching out a shaking hand, she grasped one of the china ornaments, turned to face the unwanted guest, and let the curio fly from her hand.

The scabrous-looking black and white cat ensconced on her settee dodged the china knick-knack that smashed on the floor scant inches from where it sat, stared at her in an insouciant manner, and licked its chops; the small pile of bloody fur on the neatly embroidered cushion next to it testifying to the good lunch it had recently enjoyed.

Vanessa reached for another china ornament. "Oh, do get out, you repulsive thing!" As the second missile flew through the air, the now angry cat bared its teeth and hissed; Vanessa's mouth opened in a silent scream of agony as the noise violently penetrated her skull; the sibilant sound and harrowing pain rising in volume and intensity inside her body until she could feel them reverberating in her very bones. She fell to her knees and wept; pressing her hands desperately against her ears as the cat continued to show its displeasure by arched its back and hissing again, before it turned and casually sauntering out by the French doors, in search of another light snack.

As the cat left, Vanessa slowly lowered her hands, crawled to the French doors, and closed them with a whimper. She stood shakily, using the door handle as support; the rending pain had ceased, but her bones still felt incredibly weak. She moved unsteadily to the settee, pushed the cushion the cat had used as a plate out of the way, and curled up until the worst of the weakness had passed.

Turning to look at the mess next to her, she grimaced as she used her handkerchief to scoop up the pathetic remains of the rodent dispatched by the hotel's resident mouser. She walked back to the French doors, threw the corpse into the nearest potted plant, and closed the door before the cat could return; of all the gifts the family had given her, an over-whelming repulsion of cats — which was enthusiastically reciprocated — had to be the most unexpected and ridicu-lous...but the rest of the family had exactly the same fear.

Vanessa sighed in relief as she locked the French door. She cast a despairing glance at the ornate cushion the cat had used as a plate; it looked quite ruined. Perhaps the hotel laundry could salvage it? She sat wearily on the edge of her bed and took off her boots, then removed her jacket, chate-laine, skirt, and blouse, and began to undo her corset. She looked at the clock; it was just a little past two o'clock now. She smiled tiredly as she tugged at her corset's tight laces; thanks to yet another of her terribly convenient migraines, she would have plenty of time to overcome the aftermath of her unwanted encounter with the hotel's cat. She paused as she loosened the final lace; perhaps a soak in a nice hot bath was in order?

Vanessa took a deep breath as she dropped the whalebone and linen corset on her bed rapidly followed by the rest of her undergarments. She gave her ribcage a much-needed scratch before taking a simple blue peignoir from the wardrobe and draping it round her shoulders. Tying the belt around her slender waist, she poured herself a small glass of sherry, and sat at her dressing table. Her lip curled as she thought back to the barbs she and Violette had exchanged in Marguerite's suite; Violette was a tart, and they were always easy to replace. The Master was set in his predilections and had always been easy to accommodate; as long as the girl was willing, pretty, young, prepared to both indulge *and* participate in the family's penchant for murder, mutilation, and resurrection, and had the carnal appetites of an alley cat, he was happy. Vanessa smiled as she sipped her sherry; if the vacuous Violette tried to cause any problems, she would discover just how easily replaceable her sort was.

Vanessa placed her glass next to her jewellery box, opened one of the drawers in the dressing table and pulled out a locked writing case. Retrieving her chatelaine from the bed, she selected the smallest key on the shortest chain, unlocked the case and removed two books. Opening the thicker of the two, she uncapped her fountain pen and paused; no…she couldn't face writing the day's events; the memory of Kiefer breaking her wrist was far too fresh in her mind. She pushed her diary and the accompanying thoughts aside, opened the second book and perused the ledger's neatly recorded contents with a satisfied smile; details of the family's victims in Egypt marched in double-entry perfection across the pages; names, dates, personal possessions taken and sold, the cash amounts raised, and the account the funds had been paid into. She turned to the second half of the ledger; her smile faded slightly as she looked at one of the names in the 'payments for services rendered' lines and realised that she had not settled that particular account. She frowned as she hurriedly made a note to see to the payment as soon as the storm had passed; the last thing the family needed was for one of their more volatile go-betweens to turn on them due to an unpaid bill.

Vanessa closed the book, finished the last of her sherry, and stood with a sigh; it was definitely time for a relaxing bath. Crossing the room, she opened the door to her private bathroom and reached into the dimly lit chamber to turn up the gas lamp. As her fingers groped across the wall for the switch, she let out a sudden cry of shock as a strong hand reached out from behind the door and grasped her painfully by the wrist. The low gaslight cast long, flickering shadows as the figure lunged out of his hiding place in the bathroom, gripped Vanessa by the throat, and slammed her head violently against the wall.

Brightly coloured lights exploded behind Vanessa's eyes. Reeling from the blow, she lashed out with both her fists; the extra strength given to her by the family's gift causing her attacker to grunt in pain and fall to his knees. She ran to her dressing table; her hands reaching for her chatelaine as the man climbed groggily to his feet and stumbled after her. Vanessa bit back a sob of fear as she darted to the door and fumbled with the key; her shaking fingers finally setting the key in the lock as the figure paused briefly by the bed to rip one of the silken tiebacks from the curtains. As Vanessa turned the key and desperately pulled the door open, the man took on a sudden burst of speed and ran at her. Swinging his fist in a vicious right hook, he punched her savagely in the back of the head; the force of the impact having the dual effect of slamming the door shut and smashing her face into the solid wooden panel.

Vanessa fell to the floor, her head spinning as a bloodied lump began to appear over her right eye. She pushed herself to her knees and shook her head to try and clear her vision as the dark figure walked back into the bathroom and collected the weapon he'd left there. Returning to her side, he slapped her desperate hands away, pushed her onto her back, and knelt on her chest; lifting her head, he deliberately cracked it twice against the floor. He leant over the now unconscious woman, and tied the silken cord around the top of her arm. He waited until the veins in her arm became engorged, then, with the empty syringe he had brought with him, carefully injected an air bubble into her vein. He leant back against the door and watched in silence as the method he had chosen took its course, and the unconscious woman's breathing finally stopped.

He closed his eyes, and rubbed his face; another one to check off the list. Leaning forward, he removed the cord, then repeatedly jabbed the syringe into Vanessa's wrist until it was covered with dozens of red marks that looked like insect bites. He smiled grimly; that was exactly the effect he had hoped for. He straightened her body; ensuring her peignoir covered her modesty, before folding her hands neatly across her breasts. When she had been laid out to his satisfaction, he stood, walked to the drinks cabinet, poured himself a large sherry and raised it towards Vanessa's carefully arranged corpse. "I do hope that you understand, my dear, it was entirely personal."

He drained the glass and placed it on the table. Noticing the two books, he picked them both up and flicked through the pages, his eyes widening at the names and payments in the ledger. He tucked the books under his arm and carefully propped a small, hand drawn calling card against the jewellery case; the image on the card was that of a simply drawn flying insect.

As he reached for the door handle, he saw the chatelaine hanging from the lock. Lifting the beaded clip, his eyes widened as he looked at one of the keys that graced it; a skeleton key…how very useful!

With a smile he palmed the chatelaine and left the suite, closing the door carefully behind him; all that was needed was to return the hypodermic syringe before Mrs Jones knew that it was missing.

○

Thorne and Aquilleia's Suite
1:50pm

Aquilleia stood in front of the bathroom mirror and applied a little salve to her lips. She paused as the sudden coldness that signified the beginnings of a vision began at the base of her spine. She sat on the edge of the bath and took a deep breath as two images slowly appeared in her mind's eye; a hypodermic needle, and small, red marks…almost like insect bites. As she focussed on the vision, she let out a sharp gasp of pain as her psychic observation was violently interrupted by a stabbing sensation that started in her left temple and spread rapidly across her forehead. Dark red lights appeared in her eyes, mingling with the silver and temporarily robbing her of her sight, as the full force of the migraine struck. Aquilleia stood blindly; holding her hands out before her, she stumbled into the sitting room, fighting waves of nausea as she whispered. "Thorne? Thorne…are you there?"

Thorne, who had been standing by the French doors watching Veronique snuffle around the potted plants on the covered terrace, dropped his coffee cup and ran to Aquilleia's side; scooping her into his arms, he carried her to the bed and placed her gently on the silken coverlet. He knelt by her side helplessly as she pressed her hands to her head and whimpered in pain

Veronique, having heard the commotion, appeared in the doorway and hurried to her mistresses' side; sitting next to Thorne she worriedly pressed her broad black nose against

Aquilleia's hand as Thorne whispered softly. "My love…what can I do?"

Aquilleia swallowed and whispered softly. "Nothing. It should pass on its own…they usually do." She reached out blindly towards him. "I had a vision…before the migraine."

Thorne caught her hand. "What did you see?"

"A hypodermic syringe. There was something else…but that was when the pain began, so I can't be sure. I think it might have been…insect bites."

Thorne lent towards the bedside cabinet and tugged at the bellpull. Almost immediately, there came a light tap at the door. Thorne raised his voice as much as he dared. "Enter!"

The door was opened by Farasha whose bright blue eyes took in the scene; her Simulandro programming ran rapidly through several scenarios before deciding on the one that held all aspects of the tableau before her. She looked at Aquilleia and whispered. "A migraine, Madame?"

At Aquilleia's pained blink, Farasha looked at Thorne. "I shall return with everything required, Sir." As the door closed silently behind her, Thorne turned back to Aquilleia and pressed a gentle kiss on her palm. "A very knowledgeable and thorough maid." After little more than a minute had passed, a soft tap came again at the door which opened before Thorne could call out. Farasha reentered the room carrying a tray which bore a bottle of champagne, two coupes, a small plate with two dry biscuits, a tiny sherry glass, and a small glass bottle marked 'laudanum'.

Farasha opened the bottle, carefully measured a miniscule amount into the sherry glass, and pressed it into Aquilleia's hand. "Take this, Madame…it will help with the pain."

Aquilleia's blind eyes looked towards Thorne. "What is it?"

Thorne raised his voice. "Laudanum…a very small dose."

Farasha nodded. "Just enough to take the edge off the pain and enable you to rest, Madame."

Aquilleia sipped the liquid and sank back into her pillows as Thorne tucked the coverlet around her. Farasha silently opened the bottle of champagne, poured two coupes, and placed them on the tray. She turned to Thorne. "Will there be anything else, Sir."

Thorne looked at his wife who gestured 'no'. Thorne turned to Farasha and shook his head. "No…no, thank you. That will be all."

Farasha blinked at his politeness. "You are very welcome, Sir." She bobbed a curtsy, and left the room as silently as she had arrived as Thorne turned back to Aquilleia.

"I'll stay with you."

Aquilleia took a deep breath. "I'll be fine, my love. You need to tell Elliott and Giselle what I saw. We both know it means there has been another death." She pressed her hand to her temple as the pain rippled across her head. "But because of this damn pain, I can't see or hear who it is!" She closed her eyes as a wave of nausea hit her. "Please tell Elliott and Giselle that I'll be fine…I just need to rest my mind for a while, that's all."

Thorne looked concerned. "Very well, my love. I'll take Veronique with me. Please try to rest. I'll be back as soon as I can."

Aquilleia managed a pained smile. "I know."

◯

Marguerite and Vincenzo's Suite
2:00pm

Kiefer stared at Marguerite in outrage. "I most certainly will not apologise to her! She's a human, Mother…I can treat her as I choose! Since when have we ever treated humans as our equals? They are good for nothing more than either a pet or a sacrifice."

Marguerite fixed Kiefer with a gimlet-eyed glare. "I really don't care what you think, Kiefer! Vanessa is an integral part of our family…she left her humanity behind her a very long time ago in order to join us. We need her to act as our go-between. But if you insist on abusing her, she will, at some point, decide that not even *you* are worth the pain! Now… find her and apologise. I don't care what you have to do to placate her, just do it!"

Kiefer stared at his mother, his mouth opening and closing like a goldfish. He finally snapped his mouth shut, turned on his heel and stalked from the room leaving a cloud of muttered expletives in his wake.

O

Miss March's Private Rooms
2:10pm

After looking for Vanessa in the reception and discovering that had taken to her rooms with a migraine, Kiefer angrily walked out to the staff quarters. As he approached Vanessa's door, he paused and fiddled with his cufflinks as he wondered just how he had managed to get himself into his current situation. He glared at the ceiling as his ire rose at his predicament; a necromancer with more than four thousand years of life, the grandson of Nekroshema herself, having to debase himself to a mere human…the bloody shame of it!

He turned his baleful stare on the door; could he simply ignore his mother's order, retire to the bar, and wait things out? Surely anything was better than degrading himself further? He took a deep breath; no, his mother would find out if he failed to carry out her demands…she always found out. He gritted his teeth and knocked at the door. "Vanessa? It's Kiefer. May I come in?"

He stood and waited, but received no response. He frowned; that was unusual. Vanessa was always accommodating to him, even after his more physical outbursts. Kiefer knocked at the door again, then tried the handle. As the door swung open, he strode into the room and stopped dead on the threshold. He hurriedly closed the door before turning back to stare incredulously at Vanessa's body. He walked to her side and looked down at his lover's neatly arranged corpse; taking in the massive bruise above her eye, the blue tinge to her lips, and the multitude of tiny red marks all over her wrist with rising anger. He coldly prodded at her shoulder with his leather-shod toe, but there was no response. His lips peeled back from his teeth as he ran his fingers through his oiled hair. "Bugger!"

He bent and lifted her slender hand; it was still warm. He dropped it to the ground with a grimace of distaste. He paused; could the person responsible still be in the room? His eyes filled with a white light as he turned and entered the bathroom; it was empty. He returned to the small bedroom and stood next to his dead lover. His petulant rage needing a victim, Kiefer kicked out viciously at Vanessa's body before he turned and left the room.

As he strode angrily back to his mother's suite, myriad thoughts ricochetting inside his mind, but one above all held sway; Mother was not going to be happy!

○

Marguerite and Vincenzo's Suite
2:20pm

Marguerite stared at her eldest son blankly. "Dead? How?"

Kiefer took a gulp of his whisky. "It looked as though she had been struck across the face, but her lips were blue... almost as though she had been smothered. There were also red marks around her wrist."

Marguerite's dark eyes narrowed. "Marks? What kind of marks?"

Kiefer shrugged and poured himself another drink. "I couldn't really say, Mother." He frowned as he thought back to what he had seen in Vanessa's room. "They looked more like insect bites than cuts."

Marguerite sat back in her chair. "You know what must be done. Collect Vanessa's head and dispose of her corpse in the river. The less the Caines, Thornes, and Darling know about this the better!"

Kiefer stared at her. "But, mother...the sandstorm!"

Marguerite waved her hand dismissively. "You know that I can heal any injuries you may incur..." She looked at him with a glint in her eye. "Even broken bones! Now, you have important work to do, so you can miss the choosing of the stones. Go and see to Vanessa, and bring her skull straight back here."

Kiefer knocked back the rest of his drink and left the room, slamming the door behind him as he made his way angrily back to his suite to gather the things he needed.

Linden looked at his grandmother. "But, surely, Mr Bey will realise that she's gone missing?"

Marguerite shook her head. "It's of no matter. With a touch

of my enchantment, I will have Bey eating out of my hand and believing everything I say. Leave him to me." She smiled grimly. "Now…to business. We need to resurrect Reynaud by dawn tomorrow. Violette, get the bag." Her companion nodded and disappeared into her room. She returned swiftly bearing the little velvet bag which she held out in turn to each family member. As the penultimate stone was chosen, she returned to her seat and took the last stone from the bag.

There was a pause before André held up the black stone with a raised eyebrow. "I see that it's my turn to take the stage." He finished his drink. "I do believe that I shall take my beloved for a walk under the covered terrace; there's a lovely spot just beyond the Kiosk of Trajan, where the view of the river is quite stunning…and, curiously enough, there is also a doorway that is easily opened for those with the strength to do so! The Nile is quite beautiful, and the crocodiles do so enjoy a light high tea."

Violette opened the small wooden box, removed two items, and handed them to André. He accepted the knife and crystal vial with a vicious smile, stood and bowed to his mother. "I shall return shortly."

○

Evelyn and André's Suite
2:45pm

André entered the dimly lit room and approached the bed. His smile widened unpleasantly as he looked down at the unconscious Evelyn who lay prone on the silken coverlet. Using the family's gift of enchantment to make her accept his proposal of marriage and to make her sleep during most of their time together had made his life so very much easier.

Actually having to talk with Evelyn had started to get on his nerves two days after they had first met!

He walked to the French doors and drew back the curtains. Opening the doors, he stepped out onto the covered terrace and cast a quick glance up and down the enclosed walkway beyond; empty...excellent!

Re-entering their suite, he left the French doors slightly open, sat on the edge of the bed and leant forward; his eyes filled with an opaque white light that slowly turned a faint pink as he used his enchantment to bend his wife's will. "Evelyn? Evelyn...it's time to wake up, my dear. As your eyes open, you will feel the overwhelming desire to go for a walk by the side of the Nile..."

He sat back, his eyes returning to their usual colour as Evelyn's eyelids began to flutter. She opened her eyes and looked up at André who smiled and pressed a kiss on her hand. "My darling, are you rested?"

Evelyn looked up at her husband with a slightly bemused expression. "Have I slept again? I feel so strange."

André effected a look of gentle concern. "You had another of your migraines, my dear. You've suffered so many over the last few weeks. When we return to London, perhaps you should see a doctor?"

Evelyn sat up slowly and pressed a hand against her cheek. "I was having such a strange dream..." She stopped and darted a flustered look at her husband; a light flush infused her cheeks as she turned away from him and reached for the glass of water on the bedside table; her thoughts turning back to the dreams she had...dreams of a man with burning yellow eyes.

André watched her expectantly as she took another sip of water; any moment now...

Evelyn turned back to him and gestured towards the French doors. "I know the storm is still raging, but would it be possible to take a gentle walk...I feel that I've spent so much time sleeping I've lost my chance to see much of Egypt."

André caught her hand and pressed a light kiss to her wrist; his smirk hidden from her sight. He sat back. "Of course, my darling. Shall I call Jane to assist you in dressing?"

Evelyn withdrew her hand from his grasp and snapped. "No! I do not require the assistance of my former companion." She laid no particular emphasis on her use of the word *'former'*, but André heard it...loud and clear. His eyes flashed angrily. "Evelyn__"

"No!"

André blinked at the sudden sharpness in his wife's voice as she pushed him away, stood, and walked to the door. She turned to look at her husband with cool grey eyes. "I've given Jane her notice, André, and that is the end of the matter. I have made do with the use of the maids here in the hotel, but when we return home, I shall send word to Barber asking her to return to my service. Now, please send for the maid to assist me."

She turned from André without waiting for a response and entered the bathroom; closing the door non too gently behind her. André sat on the edge of the bed and ground his teeth; Evelyn's contempt for Jane was utterly beyond the pale...and her burgeoning independence was, quite frankly, unbecoming in a human woman whose sole purpose was to appear pretty and vapid on his arm, accept his council with humility, and then be drained of her hearts blood. André's lips thinned; the level of disrespect he was expected to accept from nothing more than a rich, pretty, and socially acceptable brood mare was insupportable! Next time a virgin offering was required, they could damn well find a young child and be done with it...no more marriages!

He stood up angrily as the sound of running water came

from the other side of the door, then paused in mounting anger as he heard the unmistakable sound of the key being turned in the lock. Blinding white lights of rage filled his eyes as he realised Evelyn had locked the door between them. André stormed to the bathroom door and ripped off his cravat; winding the silken material between his fingers until it resembled a paisley-print garotte; sometimes, the best solution was the one closest to hand!

As he raised his foot to kick the door open, he staggered backwards, dumbstruck, as Masquelyne suddenly emerged from the solid wall between the bathroom and sitting room…his body gliding through the stone as though through water. Stepping away from the wall, his wings arranged themselves silkily around his shoulders as he fixed the stunned necromancer with an icy glare.

André's eyes widened in fear. The twisted paisley cravat fell from his nerveless fingers as the two men stared at each other; each passing second becoming more and more oppressive. Then, with a guttural snarl of rage, Masquelyne leapt. The impact of his attack propelling the two men through the half open French doors and into the stone-flagged walkway beyond. The doors crashed violently against the walls; ricocheting back with the force of their passing, before slamming shut as the two immortals battled each other across the covered terrace.

André grasped at the strong fingers that gripped his throat and desperately tried to peel them away. As he fought to break Masquelyne's steely grip, he realised with sickening certainty that his opponent could easily match his own immortal strength. His mind spinning, André fell back on the deceptive tactics that had long served the family; enchantment, and a plea to human compassion, empathy, and mercy. He released his grip and held out a beseeching hand, the opaque white of his eyes touched with pink as he employed the family's gifts with full force. His eyes shone with tears he had always found easy to fake as he begged. "Please! Why are you doing this?"

Masquelyne smiled grimly, his hands still gripping André's throat. "Your gift of enchantment doesn't work on me, necromancer." His smile widened at the look of shock that appeared on André's face. Masquelyne nodded. "Oh, yes, I know exactly what you are. You ask me why I am doing this?" His eyes narrowed; the golden lights swirling violently within. "It is a husband's duty to love and protect his wife… not murder her father then plot to murder her to resurrect his own patriarch!"

With a snarl of fury, Masquelyne lifted André by his lapels and threw him through one of the thick glass panels that protected the terrace. The sound of breaking glass was met by the whistling scream of the sandstorm; the almost overwhelming sound filling the covered walkway as André fell backwards and lay stunned on the glass and sand-strewn marble flagstones beyond.

André's lips peeled back from his teeth in raging desperation; he knew he couldn't possibly defeat his opponent; whatever the man was, he was far too strong. There was only one option available. He leapt to his feet, glared at Masquelyne. "Damn you!" He ripped his handkerchief from his pocket, pressed it to his face, and ran into the raging sandstorm.

Masquelyne paused by the shattered panel, his yellow eyes narrowing as he watched the panicked necromancer disappear into the swirling sand. A sudden thought came to his mind. He turned away from the damaged window, a faint smile playing on his lips.

André ran through the storm as though the hounds of Hell were chasing him. He reached the far side of the Kiosk of Trajan and pressed his back against the stone wall; his breath rasping in his throat as realisation dawned that, for the first time in his life, *he* was the prey. Fighting against his rising panic, he turned and carefully peered around the edge of the wall; whatever the man was, he wasn't there. He turned back, leant against the wall, and took a shuddering breath though the handkerchief; his eyes watering as the sandstorm flailed at his face and hair. He turned to look through narrowed eyes at the closest portion of the covered terrace; yes…there was a door in one of the panels; he could force it open and be back in his mother's suite within a few minutes.

As André took a step forward, two pale hands suddenly emerged from the stone wall behind him and gripped his upper arms; pinning them to his sides as Masquelyne, his face cold and set, but his eyes glowing with a terrible golden light, emerged from the wall and wrapped his wings around the gibbering necromancer. André screamed in fear and turned desperately within his grasp, coming face to face with the implacable Other who stared back at him; an expression of glacial rage on his face. As he tightened his grip, Masquelyne's lips peeled back in a snarl; the necromancer's fear was not enough…the punishment had to be greater. He took a shuddering breath and allowed his rage to manifest. André stared in horrified disbelief as Masquelyne's face began to change; his pale skin becoming a dull, leathery green, his face stretching…teeth elongating and becoming sharper, as the wrathful Other took on the appearance of one of the denizens of Sebek.

André's sanity, already hanging by a thread, finally failed him. In mindless terror he flailed at the creature before him, but to no avail. Masquelyne's arms tightened around him as he began to move backwards; dragging the screaming necromancer inexorably into the stone wall. As he felt the warm stone move through his legs and torso, André's screams became higher; a shrill, piercing, seemingly unending squeal, that was mockingly echoed back by the whirling maelstrom of the storm above him, until, suddenly…he stopped.

Masquelyne looked down into André's darkening eyes. "For Emmerson Briar, and for Evelyn…my Calliandra."

Masquelyne took a deep breath and changed back into his usual appearance. He released his grip on the dead necromancer, turned his back dismissively, and travelled back through the stone, to the covered terrace. Reaching the French doors that led to Evelyn's suite, he entered cautiously; hearing the faint splashing sounds coming from the bathroom, he stepped back into the covered terrace, drew the curtains, and quietly closed the doors. He brushed himself down before he again sank into the ground; there was someone he urgently needed to talk with.

○

Marguerite and Vincenzo's Suite
2:45pm

Kiefer entered his mother's suite and kicked the door shut behind him. Dropping a heavy hessian sack on the floor by the settee, he silently helped himself to a large whisky.

Marguerite looked at the bag, then turned to look at her son. "That was quick. Were there any issues?"

Kiefer drained the glass, and poured himself another. "That rather depends on your idea of 'issues', Mother. Luckily, her rooms were on the far side of the island, so there were no witnesses to see me enter her suite…" He paused and looked at her silently.

Marguerite frowned. She sat back in her chair and narrowed her eyes. "What are you trying to say?"

Kiefer shrugged. "I retrieved her head. But before I could dispose of her body in the Nile, I heard someone moving around in the rooms next to hers. What with discretion being the better part of valour, I thought that I should leave before I was seen."

Marguerite stilled. "So, where is her corpse?"

"Well, I certainly couldn't carry out your request without being spotted, so I left it where it was, and returned here with her head."

Marguerite pressed her lips together. "Damn!"

Kiefer mockingly raised his glass. "To Vanessa; she was occasionally useful in life, but a bloody nuisance in death!"

○

Carandini's Office
3:10pm

Carandini looked up as one of the Simulandro stewards knocked on his door. "Yes, Kemp?"

"I regret to inform you that there has been a breach of the covered terrace, Sir."

Carandini sat forward sharply. "Have any of the guests been injured?"

Kemp shook his head. "Not that we know of, Sir. It was brought to our attention by one of the guests; Mrs Jones. She was taking her usual walk around the terrace with her perambulator and saw that the panel had been damaged."

Carandini stood with a frown. "Where was the breach?"

"Directly outside Mr and Mrs André Devereaux's suite, Sir."

Carandini's frown deepened. "And they heard nothing?"

The steward shook his head. "We have spoken with Mrs Devereaux, and she informed us that she had been in the midst of her ablutions for quite some time. He husband had been in the suite with her, but had obviously left before the incident had occurred."

Carandini nodded. "Very well. Miss March kept a set of keys that open the locks on the covered terrace panels. You'll need those to undo the section that needs replacing. They should be in the top drawer of her desk." He looked out of his window and grimaced. "The winds are still quite strong. Send Maxwell to replace the panel. There's no point in losing another Simulandro when he's already been damaged. After that's been done, start the paperwork to arrange for him to be collected for deconstruction and for his replacement to be sent as soon as the storm has passed. "Carandini sighed as he sat back in his chair. "It's a shame, but it would cost far too much to have his skin replaced. Far better that he be sent for scrappage. As one of the more recent Silver models, I'm sure they'll be able to reuse most of him." Kemp bowed and left the room as Carandini turned back to his paperwork.

Kemp crossed the corridor and entered the silent office. He opened the top drawer and paused. The whirring sound grew louder as he blinked rapidly; the keys were not where they should be. He closed the drawer, returned to Carandini's office, knocked at the door, and cleared his throat. "I regret to report that the keys are not in Miss March's office, Sir."

Carandini's frown returned. "They should be there…" He paused. "Ah, yes, Miss March had a migraine and retired to her room for a few hours rest. She may well have taken the keys with her on her chatelaine." He looked at Kemp with a sharply raised eyebrow. "I don't think Miss March would be very happy in we disturbed her in the midst of a migraine, do you?"

Kemp cleared his throat. "No, Sir. Very good, Sir. Is there another set, Sir?"

"Yes, yes, there is. In the safe in Miss March's office." He wrote a set of numbers on a piece of paper and handed them to the Simulandro. "Here is the combination. Destroy it after you have retrieved the keys. After Maxwell has finished replacing the panel, return the keys to me. That will be all. Thank you, Kemp."

The Simulandro bowed and left the room. As he walked down the corridor, a shadow swept unnoticed across the ceiling behind him.

○

The Covered Terrace
3:20pm

Maxwell pulled the leather and glass goggles down over his eyes, taking care not to catch the damaged skin and exposed metal on his cheek. He picked up the heavy wood and glass panel and nodded at Kemp, who opened the door to the covered terrace and swiftly stepped out of his way. The Simulandro steward watched Maxwell enter the sand-filled passageway before hurriedly closing the door as the sound of the sandstorm filled the bar.

Kemp turned and gestured to the maid who was standing behind him. "Farasha, sweep up the sand and ensure that Maxwell retires to the dormitory to await transportation for deconstruction after he has replaced the panel." He turned and left the room, missing the strange expression that crossed Farasha's face. She stood by the door and watched through the small pane of glass as Maxwell walked down the sand-strewn terrace towards the French doors that led to the Devereaux suite,

As Maxwell arrived at the broken panel, the full force of the sandstorm hit him. He rocked slightly on his heels as he found his balance, then began the task of replacing the broken panel. With swift, efficient movements, he unbolted the damaged frame and moved it to one side. He looked at the shattered glass and paused; a faint line appeared between his eyes as, for the first time in his existence, he felt curiosity; the glass was far too thick to be easily smashed. He turned his gaze from the broken panel out into the swirling sandstorm that still raged across the open terrace and his frown deepened. Lifting the new panel into place, the whirring sounds coming from his skull speeding up as he thought about what could possibly have damaged the thick glass.

As Maxwell continued his work on the panel, beyond the covered terrace, on the other side of the Kiosk of Trajan, someone else was involved in a far more unsavoury task. Hidden from the Simulandro's keen sight and hearing by the roaring storm, a sandblasted figure, clad in tweeds, and with his head swaddled in gauze to protect his eyes from the sand, calmly removed a sharp penny knife from his pocket and began to saw at something that protruded from the wall before him. Patches of sweat appeared on the gauze that covered his face, as the yellow stone of the wall became streaked with crimson rivulets.

After a few minutes had passed, he gathered his bloody trophy, wrapped it in a towel he'd brought from his suite, and walked through the storm towards a section of the covered walkway that was furthest from the distant Simulandro. Approaching one of the door panels, he removed the chatelaine from his pocket, unlocked the door panel and entered the corridor…closing and locking the panel behind him. Pausing to make sure he was alone; he removed the gauze from his face and made his way down the corridor towards the main building.

Entering through the main door into the reception, he tucked the bundle under his arm and walked with confidence past the steward manning the desk and continued towards the suites on the Isis and Osiris corridors.

Moving silently towards one door, he pressed his ear against the wood and listened; the faint sound of voices could be heard.

He straightened and looked up and down the silent corridor; it was empty. He unwrapped the bundle, took a small piece of card from his pocket and forced it into André's gaping mouth. Holding the sandblasted head by its oiled hair, he took a deep breath, then with one violent movement he threw the door open, flung the head into the room, and pulled the door shut before running manically back to his own suite. He entered the room, hurriedly closed the door behind him, leant back against it, and drew in a shuddering breath.

He turned slowly and pressed his ear against the door, hearing nothing, he frowned; people *had* been in the room... he'd heard them. He stood and pressed his hand against the door before turning and walking to the drinks cabinet in the corner. He poured himself a large brandy and downed it; it had been quite kind of Masquelyne to tell him of the manner of André's death...he could only hope his little pictograph was clear enough for the family to understand. He poured himself another drink and sat by the French doors, a bleak smile playing about his lips; war had now officially been declared.

◯

Aquilleia and Thorne's Suite
3:30pm

Aquilleia woke with a start; the images flashing through her mind's eye jostling for position with the red flashes that, though fading in intensity, still streaked across her sight. She sat up slowly as the visions faded and pressed her hand against her forehead with a groan; the worst of the migraine appeared to be over, but the occasional twinge of nausea remained.

Pushing back the bedclothes, she shivered as the cold air came into contact with her skin; the ice block fan in their room was extremely efficient at bringing the temperature down…perhaps a touch too efficient! She blinked slowly and rubbed her cold hands together; perhaps a warm bath was in order?

Aquilleia stood slowly. Pulling her peignoir around her shoulders, she wandered into the bathroom and turned on the taps. Pouring in a large quantity of rose-scented bath oil, she sat on the edge of the bath and thought about what had woken her; laudanum always slowed her ability to receive a vision, so what she had seen had happened far earlier… possibly more than an hour. She took a deep breath as she focussed on her vision; images of a paisley-print cravat, swirling sand, and cold yellow eyes…

She bit her lip; another had died…and again, Masquelyne had been present.

○

Marguerite and Vincenzo's Suite
3:45pm

In the sitting room, Marguerite, Kiefer, Vincenzo, and Violette's in-depth discussion about their return trip to London came to an abrupt halt as the suite door was violently flung open, hit the wall, then swung back and closed with a slam.

Violette watched, dumbstruck, as André's head sailed

through the air towards her before landing with a sickening, wet crunch by her feet. As the head settled on the Persian rug, leaving a bloody trail of gore on the knotted wool, she stared into the blank, dark eyes and drew in her breath to scream. Kiefer's hand suddenly clamped down over her lips. He pulled her backwards and hissed in her ear. "Be quiet, you stupid bitch! If you scream, everyone in the hotel will want to know why!" He released his grip and glared at her as he took out his handkerchief and wiped his fingers. He turned to Marguerite who was standing by the settee; an indecipherable expression on her pale face as she stared at her youngest son's decapitated head.

Kiefer's eyes narrowed. "Mother?" He raised his voice. "Mother!"

Marguerite turned her face towards him, but her wide eyes were still focussed on André's head. Kiefer strode to her side and slapped her across the face. Blinding white lights filled her eyes as she instantly reacted and returned the slap; her greater strength knocking Kiefer to the floor. He shook his head and managed to raise himself up on one knee. He looked up at his mother with an unpleasant smile as he wiped the blood from his split lip. "I thought that would bring you back!" He stood and stalked to the door. Opening it, he stood in the corridor and looked up and down the empty passage. He reentered the suite and closed the door, shaking his head. "There's no one there. Either they ran the length of the corridor, or..." He stopped and gestured to the door.

Vincenzo nodded slowly. "Or their suite is on the same corridor as ours."

Kiefer looked at the head and grimaced. He glared at Heathers. "Brandy! And make it a double!"

As Heathers poured the drink and handed it to him,

Vincenzo nudged André's head lightly with his foot. "There appears to be something in his mouth…"

Kiefer snapped his fingers. "Heathers, see to it." The silent manservant obediently stepped away from the bar and crouched down by the head. Reaching into the gaping mouth, he removed the piece of card and placed it on the table. Kiefer leant over the image and frowned. "It looks like a crocodile…" His voice trailed off. He looked at his brother's head, then turned back to his mother. "I don't understand."

Marguerite pinched the bridge of her nose tiredly. "That much is obvious, Kiefer!" She sat back in her chair with a tired sigh and gestured to her youngest son's head. "Heathers, see to André. Place his head with that of his father." As the manservant saw to André's removal, Marguerite picked up her Champagne coupe and took a sip. "We now have the additional problem of not knowing where André's body is. If the killer has hidden it, that would make our lives far easier…but we can't be sure. So, just in case, we will need to devise a suitable response if the authorities find his body before we leave." She held out her coupe to Kiefer who gritted his teeth and grudgingly refilled his mother's glass. She looked up at Heathers as he reentered the room. "Heathers, go and tell the others that we need them here…we need to make the choice." She paused. "I will tell Jane about André. Just tell them to come here immediately." She turned her head and addressed her bruised companion. "Violette, fetch the bag."

○

Marguerite and Vincenzo's Suite
4:10pm

Jane sat by the gory stain on the Persian rug and dabbed at her eyes with a wispy handkerchief as a sullen-looking Violette made her way around the room with the velvet bag before returning to Marguerite's side and pulling the final stone from the pouch. She opened her hand, glared at the black stone before spinning violently on her heel and throwing it at the far wall. Marguerite, whose face was set and implacable, sighed. "You know the rules, child. The one who chooses the stone—"

Violette screamed. "No! Don't you see? She's killing us!"

Kiefer rolled his eyes and sat back in his armchair. Throwing his leg over the armrest, he raised an eyebrow as he sipped his drink. "Keep your voice down, harridan! Now…who do you think is killing us?"

Violette pressed her hands to her cheeks. "That bitch Evelyn! It has to be her — there's no one else!"

Kiefer shared an amused look with his niece. "I doubt very much that Evelyn is capable of murder, not least because André was keeping her under control at all times. But someone on the island is definitely enjoying themselves." His voice dropped as he murmured, "I wonder…I wonder who it could be?"

Marguerite shrugged as Heathers refilled her coupe. "It doesn't matter right now. We shall resurrect those we have lost, and then we shall hunt down those who have harmed us…and we shall entertain ourselves in the process!"

Linden looked at his grandmother with revulsion. As he saw her gloating, exultant cruelty mirrored on the faces of

his family, his stomach turned. "Excuse me, I have to…
excuse me!"

As he bolted, Kiefer addressed his sister. "What's wrong
with your pup, Margaux?" An ugly light appeared in his eyes.
"Perhaps he needs someone to show him how we really play;
should I pay him an educational visit?" He smirked at her. "He's
yet to experience what it's actually like to die and pass into the
liminal space to await resurrection. Perhaps a little light death,
followed by thirteen moons in the Abyss and a resurrection
ritual would loosen him up a little…what do you think?"

Margaux stilled. She looked at her brother steadily.
"Linden is young by our standards. He has yet to understand
what it is to truly be a part of this family; to live forever and
witness death without end." She took a deep breath and fixed
a gimlet eye on her smirking sibling. "Having a dedicated
sadist in the family has proved useful in the past. I've turned
a blind eye to your predilections when they were of use to
the family…but I will not allow you to threaten my son." She
stood up; blinding white lights appeared in her blue eyes as
she addressed her brother. "If you even attempt to carry out
your threat to murder my son, I promise you here and now
that by the time I am finished with you, there will be nothing
left of your skull to resurrect; you arrogant, ignorant, petulant, repugnant, infantile, spoilt excuse for a man!"

Kiefer leapt to his feet. White lights filled his eyes as he
screamed. "How dare you speak to me like that! I should have
left you to rot when the Inquisition took you__" He broke
off and darted a wild look at his mother.

Margaux stared at her brother, her face as pale as her
eyes, as she nodded slowly. "It *was* you — I thought it was.
You gave me up to the Inquisition, knowing what they would
do to me."

Marguerite waved her hand at her daughter. "Water

under the bridge, my dear Margaux. The Inquisition was such a long time ago, and we *are* family, after all. Now, forgive your brother, and let us continue with the work at hand; the resurrection of your dear father."

Margaux looked at her mother, her face blank. "Forgive him? After what they did to me? I finally discover that the Inquisition's torture of my body and mind was enabled by my own brother, your son, and you tell me to forgive? No, Mother, I think not. I will make sure that Father knows exactly what Kiefer did to me as soon as he is returned to us." She turned her head slowly to look at her now equally pale brother. "I will never forgive you, Kiefer, and neither will Father." She walked out, closing the door quietly behind her.

Kiefer looked at his mother, his rage giving way to uncertainty and fear. "She won't tell Father, will she?"

Marguerite shrugged. "She might." She stood up and patted her son's cheek. "My darling child, you know you are my favourite, and Margaux is your father's. Your dear Papa will punish you as he sees fit when he returns, and there is nothing you can do to prevent it."

She turned away from her now terrified eldest child, saw Violette chewing a fingernail, and slapped her hand. "Stop biting your nails, Violette — it makes your hands look ugly." She sat back in her armchair with a sigh and closed her eyes. "Well, one saving grace is that Evelyn didn't witness anything that could attract any unnecessary attention. And if we kill her soon, we won't have to inform her of André's death. I really couldn't bear to deal with a human display of hysterics right now." She opened her eyes and looked at her tearful companion. "The quicker Evelyn is dead, the better for the family. Now, Violette, you have been chosen. Evelyn is alone in her room — take the blade and the vial and see to it."

Violette glared at her mistress; her eyes full of tears. She stormed to the ornate box on the sideboard, removed the jewelled knife and vial, and ran from the room; slamming the suite door as she went. As she rounded the corner of the corridor, she collided with the solid chest of Rex, who put his hand out to steady her. "Well now, darlin', slow your hustle." He caught sight of her tears and frowned. "Are you all right, Ma'am?"

Violette scowled through the watery veil that covered her eyes and slapped his hand away. "I'm perfectly fine, you hideous American! Leave me alone!"

Rex's usually benign blue eyes hardened. He took a step back and touched his forelock with a sardonic expression. "Well now, thank you for your kind words, Ma'am. You have a lovely day too."

Violette watched him enter his suite and close the door before giving voice to a dismissive sniff and stalking to her own rooms. She entered and slammed the door with extreme force, threw the blade and vial onto her bed, pressed her forehead against the cool wood and allowed her tears to fall. No one had ever threatened the family like this…indeed, no one had ever managed to kill two members of the family so close together, let alone three. Violette pulled out her handkerchief and pressed it to her eyes. She had been with the family for nearly four hundred years; Reynard Devereaux himself had rescued her from becoming a starving peasant's meal during the Great Famine. She had been offered food, shelter, and a family of sorts, and she had willingly accepted the price they asked in return without fear or barter.

Violette straightened slowly and pressed her hand against the door. Marguerite was an amusement, but Reynard was her life; she would do whatever it took to bring him back, Violette took a deep breath and looked at the heavy, ornate ring on her index finger; crafted from onyx and silver, it had been a gift from Reynard, who had in turn been gifted the ring by Lucrezia Borgia in 1507…for services rendered. A slow smile appeared on Violette's tear-streaked face as she realised how she could serve her master.

She hurried to the bathroom, splashed her face with cold water, and applied fresh powder. She returned to the sitting room, tugged the bell pull and waited.

After a few short minutes, there was a deferential knock on the door. Violette raised her voice. "Enter."

A very young maid appeared on the threshold. "Yes, Ma'am?"

Violette studied the ring on her slender white finger with a smug smile. She addressed the maid without looking at her. "I need a bottle of Champagne and two glasses — hurry!"

The maid bobbed. "Yes, Ma'am." She returned a few minutes later, bearing a tray with a bottle of Champagne in an ice-filled silver bucket, two crystal coupes, a plate of almonds, and a plate of sweet biscuits. Placing the tray on the table by the window, she opened the bottle, and paused as Violette spoke. "Inform Mrs Evelyn Briar-Devereaux that I wish to speak with her immediately." The maid bobbed again and left, pulling the door closed behind her.

As Violette sauntered to the table, she was unaware of the rippling shadow that had appeared on the ceiling above her. She sat and poured two glasses of champagne. Opening the top half of her ring, she carefully sprinkled a measure of the pale, powdery contents into one of the coupes and watched with narrowed-eyes as the powder dissolved into the champagne; she had used the poison many times before...the lower the dose, the longer the victim took to die. She pursed her lips in thought, and then emptied the rest of the powder into the sparkling wine; better safe than sorry! She smiled as she stirred the liquid with the caviar spoon, imagining how the afternoon and evening would play out; the simpering bitch would drink the poisoned Champagne and die, enabling Violette to stab her in the heart and fill the sacred vial with her blood. Then, Reynaud would return, and, as the one who had taken the final blood offering, she would be the one to receive the glory of her master's affection. Violette settled back in her chair, closed her eyes and smirked; perfection!

As she sat and daydreamed, the shadow above her darted across the vaulted stone ceiling and down the wall before finally coming to a halt beside her. Masquelyne silently stepped out from the wall, switched the Champagne coupes, and then stepped backwards; dissolving back into the stone without a sound.

There was a light tap on the door; Violette's eyes snapped open. "Enter!" She sat up with a vicious smile, which vanished as the maid reappeared alone and bobbed a curtsy. "An it please you, Ma'am, Mrs Briar-Devereaux has a migraine and is too unwell to leave her room. Will there be anything else?"

Violette stared at the maid; why was nothing ever easy? She leapt to her feet, her face twisted with fury. Picking up the plate of almonds, she hurled it at the maid, who pressed herself against the wall, wide-eyed. Violette caught up the plate of biscuits and ran towards the terrified girl, who bolted as the plate sailed through the air, trailing biscuits and crumbs, and smashed against the wall.

Violette kicked the door shut, punched her hand violently against the wall, and vented her rage in a silent scream as the stone crumbled under her fist; why? Why were the fates seemingly working against them to protect an insignificant and naïf piece of human flesh that would die anyway; wrinkled, grey, and withered, after living a meaningless, mundane, and fleeting life?

She rested her head against the cool stone and took a shuddering breath; she needed to calm down...letting her temper control her was not the answer. Reynaud had always said that planning with coldness was far better than reacting in anger. She nodded slowly; the taking of the final offering needed cold planning…not violent rage.

Violette turned to look at the two Champagne coupes. She walked slowly to the table, picked up her glass, and raised it in a toast. "For you, *my* Reynaud!" Taking a deep draft of the sparkling wine, she sat back in her chair and rested the coupe against her cheek; if the grieving widow was in no state to see her now, she certainly wouldn't be dining later. Perhaps a visit during the cocktail hour would be best? Everyone else would be in the bar, which would give her enough time to enter Evelyn's suite, stab her, place a few drops of her blood in the vial, and leave without being seen.

Violette laughed, her small white teeth gleaming in the gaslight; it was so simple as a plan…it was bound to work! Perhaps that was why Julius and André had failed: they had tried to be creative, when all that was needed was a quiet moment, a dark room, and a sharp knife.

She drained the last of her Champagne and threw the glass into the empty fireplace. Collecting the vial and the knife from her bed, she tested the blade's razor-sharp edge with a vicious smile. Dropping them into her reticule, she looked at the clock on the mantle; there was still time for her to have a rest before she had to dress for dinner…and visit Evelyn.

Placing her bag on the dressing table, she sat on her bed and lay back with a sigh. As she settled into her pillows, her eyes suddenly widened and her smile froze. She put a tremulous hand to her throat; something was wrong — very wrong! As she tried to take another breath, a series of violent spasms suddenly gripped her throat. She clawed at her neck in panic; her short, sharp nails gouging into her flesh as she began to choke. She fell off the bed and stumbled towards the door, her face turning purple as she struggled to breathe.

She fell to her knees and beat at the door with her clenched fist; her strength splintering the wood in her desperation.

The door suddenly opened and a face appeared: a face she recognised. Violette held out her hand, imploring them for assistance, but her relief turned to horror as the face smiled a slow smile. "Well, my dear, you *are* in a bit of a pickle, aren't you?" He entered the room and closed the door behind him. Eying the heavy ring on her finger, he tutted. "Those Borgias!" He raised his eyes and looked at the room; taking in the full coupe on the table and the shards of the other glass in the fireplace, before raising their voice. "It might be an idea if we let her know why, before she departs."

As Violette's vision began to dim, she blinked as part of the wall seemed to move towards her. Before her horrified, unbelieving eyes, the approaching mass changed into the figure of a man with wings; a man whose golden eyes gleamed coldly as he stared down at her. "You and your family of murderers should have known better than to rely on a poisoned cup…it's all too easy to switch glasses."

The man who had opened the door smiled as he held up a small piece of card, removed a fountain pen from his pocket, and drew a simple pictograph. "Poison is indeed a woman's weapon. It's certainly a great leveller for abused women who have no other option against strength, power, and violence. But in this case, my dear, *you* are the one whose strength, power, and violence, has been laid waste by its properties.

Violette made a final, hideous choking noise as she fell sideways on the marble floor, her sightless eyes gazing at the wall.

Masquelyne collected a tooth mug from the bathroom, then returned to the sitting room. He and his companion sat at the table and finished the bottle of Champagne as they discussed the remaining players in their game of vengeance and justice.

○

Thorne and Aquilleia's Suite
4:45pm

Aquilleia sat up in her scented bath as images suddenly appeared in her mind's eye; a Champagne coupe, a heavy ring, and the roughly drawn image of a skull and crossbones. Feeling a sudden wave of nausea, she hurriedly climbed out of the bath, knelt by the toilet, and retched. She pushed her wet hair out of her eyes and drew a shuddering breath; she recognised the ring as one she had seen on the hand of Violette Donnadieu; Marguerite's companion.

Aquilleia stood slowly and reached for her towel; that was the second vision of death she had witnessed in little over an hour; migraine or no migraine, she had to find Thorne.

○

Marguerite and Vincenzo's Suite
4:50pm

Marguerite sighed and studied her nails with a thoughtful expression. "Perhaps I should get a manicure? I can't possibly be reunited with Reynaud with my nails in such a state."

Vincenzo stared at his wife, an expression of amused disbelief on his handsome face. "Marguerite, someone is killing the family, *our* family, one by one, and you're worried about your fingernails? Aren't you just a little concerned?"

Marguerite stood and ran a slender finger down her husband's cheek. "My darling Vincenzo, death is not something we fear…you should know that by now. We have overcome its limitations for millennia. Members of our family have died and returned more than five hundred times. Over the years, I have been murdered on no fewer than twenty-eight occasions…" She looked at him archly. "Three of those deaths were at the hands of my dear husband, Reynaud." A faint smile played about her lips at the memory. She caught the skeptical look on her young husband's face. "Vincenzo; we are immortals…we feel things differently from humans." She smiled at him. "Don't worry, my darling husband. If the killer takes your life, we shall bring you back. It only takes a year to return one of our own to life." She patted his cheek. "Sadly, I'll have to resurrect André and the others after Reynaud — I cannot possibly be accused of favouritism! So, it might take a few years to get to you. You *do* understand, don't you, darling?" Marguerite continued without waiting for Vincenzo's response. "But you are quite right; we must deal with whoever is making our lives uncomfortable. Something permanent and possibly a touch uncivilised! I will talk with Heathers. He can be *very* uncivilised when he wishes; and that is usually because we have told him that *we* wish it!"

Vincenzo winced; he had borne witness to several of Heathers' incivilities over the years…the most recent had been in Montmartre. The silent valet's propensity for extreme savagery, and the resultant barbaric deaths of the two young men who had provoked the wrath of the family, was not something he wished to dwell on.

He walked to the drinks cabinet, and poured himself a generous whisky; he was in desperate need of a massage, a steam, and a bath; preferably in that order. He sat back in his chair. "If you're going to have a manicure, then I'm going to the hammam."

Marguerite regarded herself in the mirror and smoothed an immaculate eyebrow. "Of course, my darling. Now, I must have a little tête à tête with Kiefer before the cocktail hour. With Vanessa dead, we've lost our helper here, which means there's no buffer between us and the management." She sighed. "One is loath to admit it, but perhaps a simple murder is required; nothing ornate or special, just pure simplicity, speed, and efficiency. Hopefully, Violette will succeed where Julius and André failed." She glanced at the clock on the mantlepiece. "We're running out of time; Evelyn must die, and she must die within the next few hours." Marguerite leant across the arm of the chair and kissed him. "Now, my darling, do be careful, but remember; if the killer takes you from us, we *shall* bring you back."

Vincenzo looked at her with a faintly mutinous expression. "I'll just have to wait a few years in Hell first."

Marguerite laughed; her small white teeth glittering in the gaslight. "Hell doesn't exist, my dear child! It's an empty threat, used as a form of control by those who wield power over humans. You of all people should know that! You have rested in the liminal spaces before…you know what awaits you there; peace and serenity."

Vincenzo stared at his drink. "Nothingness isn't peace, Marguerite."

Marguerite sighed. "I can't deal with you when you like this, Vincenzo." She opened the door and paused as he suddenly raised his voice. "Call the steward for me, will you?" Marguerite smiled, tugged the bell pull, blew him a kiss, and left.

Vincenzo closed his eyes and massaged the bridge of his nose. In spite of his frequent and animated attempts to enlighten her over many years, Marguerite still had a complete disregard for the implacable nature of death; but he had been born human…he knew just how relentless, remorseless, and uncompromising it could be.

A deferential knock sounded at the door. Vincenzo finished his drink. "Enter."

The chief steward entered the room and bowed. "Yes, Sir?"

Vincenzo refilled his glass and flopped into his armchair, throwing his leg over the arm. "I require the immediate use of the hammam and a masseuse. See to it, will you?"

The steward bowed again. "Of course, Sir. If you care to go to the hammam now, I will send word for the masseuse to be there when you arrive." He left, closing the door silently behind him.

Vincenzo sipped his drink, then closed his eyes and rested the glass against his forehead; what a damnable mess! He tossed back his whisky, climbed out of the armchair and entered the bedroom. He rummaged through his wardrobe for his dressing gown and smiled as he slid his arms into the dark-blue silk; he might lose his place in Marguerite's bed for a while, but he would give up his position in the family over his dead body! His smile widened at the irony, but it was true; even if he had to wait several years to be resurrected, it was a price worth paying. To dress in fine silks and linens instead of the harsh cloth of the clergy, which would have been his fate had he stayed with his kith and kin in Puglia, was a far better fit to his temperament. In the face of the murders, the blood, and the rituals, even witnessing his blood kindred wither and die, if someone had offered him a way to travel back in time and change his decision, he would have made the same choice; he would always choose the family.

Vincenzo tied the silken cord around his narrow hips, collected his preferred massage oil and a large towel from the bathroom, and sat on the edge of the bed to pull on the thin leather slippers he always wore to the hammam. He opened the French doors and entered the covered court-yard, his feet slapping on the marble as he walked down the wide stone steps to the covered terrace. In the distance, the swimming pool could just be seen through the swirling yellow sand that continued to howl around the island, and beyond it, the gleaming stone buildings that housed the hammam.

After several minutes, Vincenzo arrived at the covered terrace beside the swimming pool; the most recent addition to the hotel's facilities and usually a very pleasant one to visit during the heat of the day. The uncovered pool's usually limpid water was stained an ugly shade of yellow, as the storm whipped its surface into foam and deposited sand in the once-inviting depths.

Vincenzo walked past the pool to the studded door of the hammam. He pushed it open and frowned; there was no masseuse waiting for him in the small, tiled room. He walked in, slamming the door behind him as he dropped the bottle of oil and his towel on one of the three massage tables, and opened the door to the small room that housed the steam bath. That too was empty, but hot steam billowed copiously from the pipes along the far wall. Vincenzo smiled; the ancient ways were usually the best, but modern plumbing ensured a constant production of temperature-controlled steam.

He returned to the massage room, walked to the cool room at the far end, and opened the door; again, there was no masseuse. Vincenzo scowled; damn the man! Well, he wasn't going to wait any longer! Disrobing, he dropped his dressing gown next to the oil, toed off his slippers, and entered the steam room. Closing the door, he sat in the enveloping heat with a happy sigh, closed his eyes and relaxed.

As Vincenzo dozed in the steam-filled room, a sudden, heavy rattling sound came to his ears. Opening his eyes, he frowned as he saw a shadow flitter across the door's small frosted window. Sitting up on the marble bench, he addressed the figure; a note of sharp annoyance obvious in his voice. "It's about time you arrived!" I've been waiting for over five minutes! He walked towards the door and pushed; but the door didn't move. He leant forward, pressing his eye to the small window, but could see nothing through the treatment on the thick glass. He pushed angrily against the door, which stubbornly refused to yield. "If this is your idea of a joke, it's in very poor taste!"

A calm voice spoke from the other side of the door. "I can assure you, Mr Prezzo, this is no joke. You don't know me, but I believe you knew my dear brother, Wilton. He was one of your wife's many victims; chosen as an offering to ensure the resurrection of her first husband, Reynaud."

Vincenzo became very still. His breath caught in his throat as the voice continued. "I considered sparing you, because you weren't in London when my brother was murdered. But then I realised that you, much like all the others who marry into, or work for, the Devereaux family, don't care about the trail of blood and grief you leave in your wake. You may not have been there, Mr Prezzo, but your unwavering support for the family means that the grief and loss I suffer every day will happen to others, again and again, until the entire Devereaux family is removed from existence. As you willingly married into that evil clan, you too must be erased to ensure that no more innocents die; to ensure that no more innocents are made to suffer the pain that *I* have endured for so many years."

The figure walked past the now heavily chained door and dropped a small piece of card onto the massage table next to Vincenzo's towel. He approached the largest steam pipe and again studied the diagrams next to it. He slowly twisted the temperature valve to maximum heat, then turned the main steam pipe handle firmly to the left; opening the vent to its fullest, and allowing the maximum amount of scalding steam to enter the locked steam room.

Vincenzo stared at the approaching cloud in horror as he

realised his fate. He shouted in Italian, slamming his fist against the small window; the thick glass cracked, but it refused to break as the figure on the other side of the barred door continued. "The Devereaux family wouldn't even allow me the comfort of supporting my mother, my wife, or my infant son. My mother died of a broken heart after Wilton's death. Marguerite attempted to kill me, and when she failed, she murdered my wife and child, and framed me for their murders to ensure that she would inherit my brother's estate. Yes, Mr Prezzo, your beautiful, immortal wife murdered a six-month-old babe in arms, along with his mother, who cradled him as they were killed. I fled for my life, abandoning my name and my family's wealth — it was the only way I could hunt the Devereaux family down like the bestial wretches they are! You married into a covey of evil, Mr Prezzo — and for what? Money? Position? Power? Those privileges have abandoned you now. In the name of justice and retribution, you are exposed to me. As judge, jury, and executioner, I find you as guilty as those who murdered my family. I leave you to suffer your fate, the heat of which will continue indefinitely, as you spend eternity burning in Hell!"

He left the hammam with a smile as the steam cloud filled the small room and Vincenzo started to scream.

◯

Thorne and Aquilleia's Suite
5:10pm

Aquilleia laid out a simple outfit on the bed, dropped her corset next to it, and tugged at the bell pull. As she waited for the bell to be answered, she pulled on her undergarments, draped her peignoir around her shoulders, and sat at the dressing table. Lifting her hands to begin the task of pinning her hair, a cold sensation started at the base of her spine. Aquilleia's lips parted; not again! She blinked as images crowded into her mind; a pair of leather slippers, a thick white cloud, and a voice crying out; *'Basta!'*. She shivered as the visions faded, and yet another voice became distant.

She looked up as a gentle knock came at the door. "Enter." The door was opened by Farasha, who stood at the threshold and inquired in a low voice. "Yes, Madame? How may I be of assistance?"

Aquilleia stood slowly and gestured at the clothes on the bed. "I need you help me dress, please, Farasha. I also need to know where my husband and our friends are at this precise moment in time."

Farasha entered the room and closed the door behind her. "Mr Thorne, Mr Caine, and Mlle Du'Lac are in Mr Darling's suite, Madame. I took them a tray of tea a short while ago."

As the maid collected the corset from the bed and began the task of lacing her in, Aquilleia thought about the speed of her last few visions; no wonder she'd suffered a migraine! But at least now, she knew the identities of those she could no longer see.

○

Violette's Suite
5:15pm

Kemp smoothed his waistcoat and knocked at the door. "Miss Donnadieu? It's the head steward. I'm afraid that I must talk with you." After several long and silent seconds had passed, he again knocked at the door and leant forward; his sensitive hearing could detect no sounds coming from the other side of the door.

He sighed; even though he had been made for his position, he never quite knew how to deal with guests who abused the staff…he simply couldn't understand why they thought it a proper or acceptable thing to do. He grasped the door handle and turned it. As the door unlatched, Kemp breathed a sigh of relief; at least the door wasn't locked *this* time! He allowed himself an eye roll at the memory of the last time a guest had attacked a member of staff at the hotel… the ensuing ruckus had been quite mortifying for Mr Bey. The lady in question had taken a knife to Farasha over the Simulandro maid's perceived lack of care in lacing the not insubstantial lady's corset. Luckily, Farasha had managed to escape with minor damage…the guest, however, had locked herself in her suite and thrown a fit of hysterics. Kemp shook his head; he could still hear her shrieks of rage, demanding that Farasha be returned to her for 'suitable chastisement'. In response to her categoric and shrill refusal to unlock the door, Mr Bey had ordered Maxwell to open the door…and Maxwell had certainly put his back into it! The guest had, for her trouble, ended up on the receiving end of a solid wooden door that had been kicked off its hinges by an enthusiastic and unusually angry Simulandro steward; it was a mistake the guest only made once.

A thoughtful expression appeared on Kemp's usually impassive face; the events of that day had led to Maxwell being placed on limited duties that involved minimal contact with the guests. He sighed; at some point, the management were going to realise that Maxwell and Farasha were unusually close…impossibly close, considering their programming.

He shook his head, pushed the door open, and stopped on the threshold; his blue eyes taking in the prone body of a woman lying on the floor. In spite of her swollen and purple countenance, Kemp's recognition program swiftly identified her as Violette Donnadieu, He closed the door, knelt by her side, and checked her breathing, which he almost immediately ascertained was not in evidence. He sat back on his heels and looked at the small piece of card on her chest; the image it bore, was that of a skull and crossbones.

○

Kiefer and Linden's Suite
5:15pm

Kiefer sat back in his armchair. "We must hurry, Mother. If we perform the ritual to resurrect Father tonight, we can return to Cairo as planned, and leave for Italy from there."

Marguerite nodded. "We'll need transport…it might be worth setting up a meeting with one of the human stewards. We'll need an airship as soon as the sandstorm dissipates. A few Egyptian pounds in the right hands should get us a suitable vessel. But right now, I want you to find my husband and tell him to return to our suite. Then I want you to check on Margaux."

Kiefer smirked. "Getting him used to being on a short leash, are you, Mother?"

Marguerite fixed him with a cold stare. "Do as you're told, Kiefer. Vincenzo was going to the hammam. Find him. See that Margaux is safe, and then organise the airship to Cairo."

Kiefer's eyes flashed angrily. He stood and walked to the door. At the threshold, he turned to his mother, gave her a mocking bow, and left.

○

The Hammam
5:25pm

Kiefer entered the steam-filled massage room and frowned; the massage room shouldn't be steamy…and why did it smell like someone had been cooking pork? He jammed the main door open, walked to the temperature valve, and turned the steam off. As the room cleared, Kiefer saw that a chain had been looped through the handle of the steam-room door and secured with a padlock.

Walking over, he snapped the lock, removed the chain, and pulled the door open; leaping backwards as Vincenzo's swollen corpse landed at his feet.

Kiefer's lip curled in revulsion as he looked at the remains of his occasional stepfather; the once-attractive Italian's long brown hair was plastered in thick wet strands against his blistered skin; his dark eyes rendered almost invisible by the raw, swollen folds of his eyelids. Kiefer bent to look at Vincenzo's hands and grimaced; the usually immaculate fingernails were torn and bloodied. He turned and looked at the inside of the steam room door where bloody tracks and gouges in the woodwork showed how Vincenzo had clawed at the heavy door in a desperate attempt to escape.

Kiefer ignored the grumbling complaints coming from the inside of his step-father's skull and glowered at the swollen corpse; how the hell would he explain this to Mother? She had given him two tasks; find Vincenzo and check on Margaux — and so far, things were not going very well!

Kiefer tapped his foot angrily as another thought occurred to him; if the authorities found yet another member of their family dead, it would cause even more trouble. He scowled; there was only one possible way to protect the family!

As he turned to the door, the ominous grumbling from the skull swelled. Kiefer turned back to Vincenzo's body and held up a warning hand. "Yes! I know...I'm dealing with it!"

Kiefer turned and hurried back to the entrance hall. Hopefully, given that it was fast approaching the cocktail hour, no one else would want to use the steam room before he returned. He entered the reception; taking care not to be seen by any of the stewards who were hovering around the corridor between the dining room and kitchens, and strode down the corridor to his suite. Entering the cool room, he opened the small black leather trunk that always accompanied him on his travels, and removed one of the many Damascus steel knives that were strapped to the inside of the lid. He also collected one of the hessian bags normally used for collecting body parts from unwilling donors. Placing the blade in the bag, Kiefer opened the door, and checked the corridor was empty before hurriedly returning to the hammam. As he approached the building, he looked around; no one else seemed to be in the vicinity. He entered the hammam, and closed the door. Dropping the bag and knife on a table, he moved Vincenzo's corpse into a more suitable position, took out the knife, and with one clean slice of the razor-sharp blade, severed his stepfather's head. Taking a swift step back from the thick, dark red blood that oozed from the gaping wound, he wrapped the head in a towel and bundled it into the bag.

Kiefer placed the bag by the door; ignoring the muffled complaints coming from the skull, and moved to stand by the large window at the far end of the room. The sandstorm was still active, but its rage seemed less fierce; he could at least now see the Nile as the storm-teased river continued on its journey just a few feet away from him.

He threw the window open, and stepped back as swirling clouds of yellow sand filled the room. Kiefer waved his hands in front of his face and ground his teeth; the sand would be obvious on his clothing and in his hair. Once he returned to his suite, he would have to bathe and change, and that would make him late for the cocktail hour. He turned back to Vincenzo's corpse with a scowl, removed his jacket, rolled up his sleeves, and picked up the bath towel that the unknowing Vincenzo had left on the massage table. Throwing the large towel across the stump where his step-father's head had been, he grasped both the corpse's wrists with one hand and dragged the decapitated corpse across the room to the window, where he threw it into the Nile.

Kiefer turned back to the room and using several of the towels, mopped up as much of the blood as he could with what he had to hand. He hissed an oath as a miniscule amount of blood spattered onto his sleeve; he should have found Heathers and told him to deal with it...there was a reason why they employed staff!

When he had finally finished, he threw the blood-soaked towels into the Nile, closed the window, and heaved a deep sigh; well, that was that! Hopefully, Mother would understand. Now all he had to do was organise an airship, check on Margaux, and then they could gather the rest of the family, resurrect Father, and leave.

○

Darling's Suite
5:25pm

Darling groaned as he looked at the list of deaths. "Julius van Sloane, Gaston Cavet, and now, according to Aquilleia's visions, Vanessa March, André Devereaux, Vincenzo Prezzo, and Violette Donnadieu! When in God's name will it end?"

Aquilleia held up the piece of card that had been left on Violette's breast. "That's a very good question. These killings seem to be in the name of a certain God...or at least, in the name of his plagues."

Darling raised an eyebrow. "Pray explain."

Aquilleia settled back in her chair. "Let's start at the beginning; the first death was that of Julius. When he fell into the Nile, his body turned the river red. Next, Gaston Cavet was stabbed in the eye with a very long, thin piece of metal, something much like a long hairpin, and I've seen Evelyn Briar-Devereaux's companion, Jane Gagnon, wearing an ornate hairpin topped with a golden frog; remember, I had a vision of a golden frog being the last thing Cavet saw. Miss March had what seemed to be multiple insect bites around her wrist. And the card left with Violette Donnadieu is the universal sign for poison."

Darling frowned. "What are you suggesting?"

Aquilleia smiled. "When I was reborn here, it was to an extremely religious Catholic family." She counted on her fingers. "Water turning to blood, a plague of frogs, a plague of biting insects, and pestilence. What would that suggest to you?"

Thorne sat forward. "It would certainly explain the strange calling cards that were discovered near some of the bodies. Each card bears an image symbolic of one of the Biblical plagues." He frowned. "But the cards only started with the third death; that would suggest..." He trailed off, looking at Elliott with a slightly panicked expression as his friend shot a quick look at Darling; they still hadn't informed him of Masquelyne's admission of guilt in the death of Julius. Elliott covered his friend's mistake speedily. "Which would indeed suggest that the deaths of both Julius and Cavet were not their work. This particular killer started with the third victim." He paused and looked at Darling. "If victims one and two were killed by someone else…you do realise what that means?"

Darling groaned and rubbed the bridge of his nose. "Two killers!" He frowned. "That would suggest a remarkable coincidence in two killers both choosing methods of murder that match the Biblical plagues." He sat back with a brooding expression. "Unless, the second killer was biding their time… perhaps they witnessed one of the murders, and saw an interesting and rather macabre means of throwing any investigation off their scent.

Aquilleia nodded. "It might be a touch worse than you think. Because of what I saw in my visions, I believe that Jane Gagnon is the person who killed Cavet." She sat back with a faint smile. "So, three killers!"

Thorne frowned. "Right. Well, that's one murderer identified." He looked at Aquilleia with a slightly helpless expression. "But that won't get us very far with the authorities. We can't tell Colonel Barrington that we've identified one of the killers because you had a vision proving it! How do we arrest her? There's no actual, physical proof. And even if we did arrest her, there's nowhere we can hold her that she can't break free from…she is, after all, a necromancer."

Giselle shrugged as she stroked the blissfully unconscious kitten sprawled across her lap. "We're all trapped on this island until the storm has finished. She's trapped with us."

Darling nodded. "Yes, but what if she kills again?"

Aquilleia shook her head. "I don't believe that she will. I think she killed Cavet because he threatened the family."

Elliott sat back in his chair and tapped his fingers against his chin. "Tell us everything you saw in your visions."

Aquilleia sat back in her chair and gathered her thoughts; she had already decided not to tell the others of one image, that of Masquelyne's eyes, until after she had had the opportunity to speak with Elliott privately. She took a breath and began to explain the images that had appeared to her through the afternoon. As she finished, she threw up her hands. "That's why I believe the killer...the one who is targeting the Devereaux family, is using the legend of the Biblical plagues as methods of murder. What I saw in regards to the two missing deaths; those of death by animal attack and that of the plague of boils suggests that the two people who have been murdered are André Devereaux, and Vincenzo Prezzo."

Giselle frowned. "Why them?"

Aquilleia poured herself another cup of tea. "In the vision I had with the sandstorm, I saw a paisley-print cravat...it was one I had seen on André earlier this morning. In the vision with the billowing cloud, I heard a man's voice crying *'Basta'*. That's the Italian word for *'Enough'*...that was Vincenzo." She took a sip of her tea. "I think that André was killed out in the storm, and that Vincenzo was killed in the hammam."

Thorne took a biscuit. "But how does that tie in with the Biblical tale?"

Aquilleia paused. "With André, I can't be sure...unless a wild animal was a part of the attack. But with Vincenzo, the last thing he saw was a cloud of steam rushing towards him."

Thorne shook his head. "I still don't understand...how did you go from a plague of boils to the hammam?"

Aquilleia grimaced. "A plague of boils would be very difficult to recreate...unless one had the ability to cause such harm magically. But boiling someone in steam? That *could* be done. And there's only one place on the island that could be used to inflict such a death."

Thorne looked down at his half-eaten biscuit and placed it back on his saucer with a slightly nauseous expression. "The hammam."

Aquilleia nodded. "Hmm. Bearing in mind that I believe Vincenzo was boiled to death, rather than inflicted with pustules, that suggests the killer has a rather dark sense of humour, but also, luckily for us, no arcane abilities — and that implies that they're human."

Elliott and Thorne exchanged glances as Darling tapped his lips with a thoughtful expression and mused. "Killing the family according to the Biblical plagues of Egypt. It *is* novel, I'll give him that."

Elliott frowned as he registered Darling's words; he turned to look at Darling. "You said 'it *is* novel, I'll give '*him*' that'…who is '*him*'? If you have information that would assist us, Darling, please share it."

Darling grimaced. "Ah, you have me!" He took another sip of his tea. "Very well. Due to a previous case involving the Devereaux family, I believe I already know the true name of our killer. I believe it to be a gentleman by the name of Barrett Cushing. His brother, Wilton Cushing, married Marguerite Devereaux in 1878 and was, I believe, one of the family's many victims."

Elliott sat back; his eyes watchful. "Go on."

"In the spring of 1878, Wilton Cushing met and married Marguerite Devereaux in a whirlwind courtship. Shortly after they were married, Wilton took ill, and soon died. The cause of his death was described as consumption. The death certificate was signed by a local doctor, who died in a carriage accident shortly after his patient."

Giselle raised an eyebrow. "How opportune."

Darling nodded. "Cushing was buried quickly, with no funeral and no wake. His friends were quite horrified at his widow's lack of seemly conduct, and organised a wake without her. She, unperturbed, left for the South of France within a week of his death. Shortly after his burial, the police received a report that someone had broken into the Cushing family crypt and mutilated Wilton's body. They were beginning the investigation when a gentleman presented himself at the police station and declared that *he* had broken into the crypt, but the body was already mutilated when he opened the coffin."

Giselle shook her head. "But why would someone break into a stranger's crypt?"

"He wasn't a stranger, Giselle. It was Wilton Cushing's brother, Barrett. He saw the damage that had been inflicted on his brother's body and insisted that his brother had been murdered by inhuman fiends — and he certainly wasn't wrong! He went to the police, the judiciary, and his local Member of Parliament, all of whom told him that he was skirting dangerously close to a one-way trip to Bedlam for putting such fantastical suggestions before them — namely, that a family of ungodly monsters had murdered and mutilated his brother. Thank you, my dear." This last was addressed to Aquilleia as she handed him another cup of tea.

Darling took a sip, and continued. "The politician actually did threaten Barrett with incarceration in Bedlam, refusing to countenance the idea that such a prominent and financially generous family could be anything other than upstanding members of the community." Darling's face became somber. "Barratt Cushing disappeared shortly after that, and remains missing to this day."

Giselle raised her voice. "What was his profession?"

Darling smiled at her over the gold rim of his cup. "He was an actor."

"So, you're suggesting that Barratt Cushing, realising his fears sounded like the ravings of a madman, decided that if he couldn't have justice, he would make do with vengeance... then disappeared and planned his revenge in hiding?"

"That is indeed my thought."

Giselle took another sip of her tea. "If he was an actor,

there might be photographs of him in costume — have you found any?"

Darling nodded. "We were only able to find one photograph. If my memory is correct — and I possess a very good memory — it was a trifle difficult to make out the features of the actor under the make-up." He sat back. "It was an image of a man dressed as a Grenadier Guard....the only photograph we could find was from his performance in Gilbert and Sullivan's *The Sorcerer* in 1877, the year before his brother died."

Giselle nodded. "Rather apt. How old did he appear in the photograph?"

Darling considered. "As I recall, he was approximately twenty-one when the image was taken, so he would be closer to forty-five now. But as an actor, he would be gifted in using stage make-up to change his appearance." Darling's eyes gazed into the distance as he remembered the case. "I believe he's here in Egypt. Wherever the Devereaux family are, so will he be."

Giselle tapped her chin. "Well, the only men of around forty-five here are Carandini Bey, Dr Jones, Rex Nympton, and possibly Thomas Breton."

Darling's green eyes twinkled at her. "Remember what I said about using stage make-up? Are we entirely sure about Dr Amicus Mirylees...or even the Contessa de Mostada?"

Giselle sank back in her chair with a groan.

Elliott looked at Darling. "Did Wilton Cushing have any other family?"

The gentle humour left Darling's face. "That is where things become far, far worse. His mother, broken-hearted, died just a few weeks after he was murdered. Barrett was married, with an infant son. Shortly after he began investigating the Devereaux family, his wife, Sonia, and their child were murdered in their home in London." Darling shook his head. "We were meant to believe that Barrett had gone mad with grief for his brother and killed them. But the leader of the Espion Court knew that to be false."

Aquilleia looked at her brother-in-law. "Who was the leader of the Court at the time?"

Thorne raised his voice. "Darling has been leader of the Espion Court for over three hundred years."

As they all looked at him, Darling shrugged under their scrutiny. "Sometimes we help, sometimes we hinder...it usually depends on the person asking for assistance. Because of the Devereaux family's...unusual status and the accusations against them, the Espion Court was brought in to investigate. Shortly after, I received a letter from Barrett..." Darling paused. "I have absolutely no idea how he managed to discover who I was, or how he came about my address. He explained his fears and requested my help. I knew what the family were, of course, and I knew they were pretty much untouchable because of their connections within government and high society."

A muscle twitched in his jaw as he continued. "Then Barrett's wife and son were found dead. He was accused of their murders and disappeared." Darling's lip curled in anger. "I knew it was the family; I simply couldn't prove it! And I knew I would never be granted the authority to deal with them permanently. The unfortunate and deeply ugly truth is that even the Espion Court can be overruled if an interested party in a position of power has a quiet word with our Ruler!"

Darling looked at them with an exasperated expression. "Our King is a good man at heart...but he's far too easily swayed by certain devious individuals who know how to appeal to his desire to be kind! It's one of the many reasons why I prefer that human governments know nothing about us...or, indeed, about any of the other branches of Crypto-

Anthropos. A family of necromancers who can resurrect and reanimate the dead would hold massive sway with any susceptible human politician, businessman, socialite, or warmonger. Any amount of money could be asked in return for a semi-eternal life, or a constant supply of unthinking minions who kill to order, and certain people would willingly pay until their funds dried up — then, of course, without being resurrected in time, so would they!"

Darling took a sip of his tea. "So, knowing the family for what they were, I rebelled as much as I could with what little authority I had at the time. I refused to serve Barrett Cushing up to the family for their entertainment! I insisted that there was no evidence to suggest that he was guilty of the murders of his wife and son. I ruled that Wilton Cushing and his brother's wife and child had been killed by person or persons unknown. I filed the necessary documents with both the Empire, and the Espion Court, and ensured the investigations into both Barrett Cushing and the Devereaux family were closed." He sighed. "Unfortunately, that left the family at large to continue their schemes. I resented the fact that the Espion Court was ordered to watch the family and protect them from harm. I found and *still* find the family's crimes against humanity and those like us impossible to ignore. But there were some who refused to allow Barrett Cushing justice. Now, it appears that they must instead accept his revenge."

Elliott settled back in his chair. "And you firmly believe that Barratt Cushing is behind the murders here?"

Darling shot Elliott a sharp look. "I do. Elliott, I have no love for the Devereaux family. However, I *have* been tasked to protect them, and I've failed in quite a spectacular fashion! In order to ensure my future survival in the Espion Court, I must at least discover their killer. Whether or not he's brought to justice is quite another thing."

Elliott looked at him quietly. "Or, as we said earlier; killers."

Darling waved his hand carelessly. "Well yes. If as Aquilleia has said, Jane Gagnon killed Gaston Cavet, there are quite obviously two other killers, Barrett Cushing being one..." He looked at Elliott's expression; a faint frown appearing between his brows as he slowly lent forward in his chair. "What are you not telling me?"

Elliott took a deep breath and continued to look at Darling.

Thorne rolled his eyes. "Just tell him, Elliott! My brother may be many things, but after what he's told us about Barrett Cushing, he *will* understand."

Darling looked at Elliott over the rim of his tea cup as Elliott cleared his throat and began. "The first death, that of Julius van Sloane...was caused by my father."

Darling choked on his mouthful of tea. His teacup clattered as he dropped it back into its saucer. "I should have known! That bloody idiot!" He looked at Elliott with an exasperated expression. "I suppose he told you why?"

"That my father believes Evelyn Briar-Devereaux to be the reincarnation of my mother? Yes, I do. He also told us what he'd discovered about the Devereaux family."

Darling pulled out his handkerchief and mopped at his waistcoat. "He *is* correct. Evelyn is your mother — or rather, Calliandra, the woman she was in Astraea, is your mother." Darling sighed. "I suppose I should explain, though your father has probably already done so. After centuries of searching, your father finally found Evelyn in London a few years ago. He recognised her immediately, but she was an innocent child...only fourteen years old, and he couldn't bring himself to approach her. He spent years trying to work up the courage to do so. After Evelyn was presented at her debutante ball, André Devereaux whisked her off her feet and asked her to marry him." Darling shook his head. "That nearly killed Masquelyne; after finally finding her, to lose her again? He was beside himself. He contacted me and asked for my thoughts. Knowing what I did about the family, I suggested he keep an eye on the gentleman in question; if anything of an unsavoury nature occurred, it could be used to prevent the marriage." Darling sighed. "Unfortunately, something did happen, but far too late to prevent the marriage."

Elliott and the others shared a glance; they had heard this from Masquelyne, but it was nice to have it all officially confirmed.

Giselle sat forward. "What happened?"

"Earlier this year, just a few days after the wedding, Masquelyne was following André and Kiefer as they returned home from their club. The Devereaux family home in London is just a few doors down from the house that Evelyn's father bought the newlyweds as a wedding gift. It was quite late, and as they arrived, they were met by Julius, and Vincenzo. Masquelyne thought that quite odd; it was very late...why talk in the street when there were two comfortable houses within a few dozen yards that were at their disposal? As they stood, a carriage pulled up...a carriage driven by the Devereaux family manservant, Heathers. The men boarded the carriage, and made their way to Abney Park Cemetery, closely followed by Masquelyne. When they arrived, they removed a rolled-up rug from the carriage and carried it to an open grave. They unrolled the rug, revealing the mutilated body of a man, which they then threw into the grave, before leaving. Oddly enough, their behaviour roused Masquelyne's curiosity!" Darling looked at Elliott with a faint smile. "You know what your father's like when something piques his curiosity — nothing can stop him until he discovers all! Your father watched them leave, and then disinterred the corpse. The man's right eye had been taken and he had been stabbed in the stomach, but he was not as dead as his killers would have liked. My friends, that poor soul was none-other than Evelyn Briar-Devereaux's father; Emmerson Briar."

Thorne dropped his now blunt pencil onto the table next to him, pulled another from his pocket, and continued scribbling.

Darling took another sip of tea. "Before he died, Briar told Masquelyne his fears about his son-in-law's family. In an attempt to assuage them, he had hired a private enquiry agent to look into the Devereaux family. That very morning, the agent had informed Mr Briar of his findings, namely that the family were involved in murder most foul, and ungodly rituals involving the corpses of their victims." Darling shook his head. "Briar's mistake was in being an honest and fair man. He went to their house in Mayfair and informed them he would have his daughter's marriage annulled. He was attacked by Kiefer, and bundled into the rug by Heathers. Kiefer and André left the house and created an alibi for themselves by going to their club for the evening." He darted a sharp look at Elliott. "Before he died, Briar also revealed something rather salient about his daughter's marriage…which I will not divulge in mixed company."

Giselle raised an auburn eyebrow. "Would it have something to do with the fact that the marriage has, so far, been unconsummated?"

Darling blinked. "Yes. The final sacrifice must be a virgin offering. Indeed, Briar was quite insistent about sharing that information. An annulment on the grounds of an unconsummated marriage would mean his daughter's safe return to society, untouched by any whisper of disgrace."

Giselle nodded. "So, the family chose their victim and

kept their virginity safe in the only way they could in this era — by marriage."

"Exactly. Although, for Masquelyne, that knowledge had an altogether different connotation." At Giselle's understanding nod, he continued. "The enquiry agent had managed to overhear various conversations, within the house in Mayfair and elsewhere, and realised why the family needed Evelyn. She was the final piece in their diabolical scheme — they needed the heart's blood of a virgin to resurrect Marguerite's husband, Reynard Devereaux."

Aquilleia spoke first. "But how on earth did the enquiry agent deal with the horror of what he'd discovered?" She paused. "He *was* a human, I take it?"

Darling nodded. "Oh, yes. He was a man of very strong faith; to him, everything in life was a battle between good and evil...a fight between God and the demonic, so that is what he took the family to be; demons."

Aquilleia looked thoughtful. "He wasn't wrong!" She frowned. "Marguerite *was,* married to Vincenzo Prezzo... surely he would have had something to say about his wife's dead husband returning from the grave and reclaiming his place by Marguerite's side?"

Darling shrugged. "I suspect he was prepared to turn a blind eye to murder, mutilation, bodysnatching, and a spot of musical bedmates in exchange for eternal youth." He placed his cup and saucer on the table. "Stepping away from his paramour and becoming a lesser member of the extended family may be a bittersweet pill to swallow...but I am sure the expensive playthings he will still be able afford will help mitigate his woe...somewhat."

Thorne grinned as he continued to make notes. "Don't be a bitch, Darling!" His brother blinked and grinned back. "Yes, dearest!" The two men smiled at each other.

Giselle and Aquilleia shared a look as Elliott contemplated Darling over steepled fingers. "What of the private enquiry agent? Surely, he realised that what happened to Mr Briar was no accident?"

Darling spread his hands. "On the same night Briar was murdered, the agent was also killed. His offices were razed to the ground in a blaze that destroyed several neighbouring buildings. One never crosses the Devereaux family and lives to speak of it." He sighed. "Briar died of his injuries shortly after revealing his sorry tale to Masquelyne, whom he begged to protect his daughter. Masquelyne of course agreed, and Briar went to his eternal rest a somewhat happier man than he had been at the beginning of his evening. Masquelyne left his body in the open grave, where it was later discovered by a nightwatchman. The truth of Briar's death was kept very quiet…especially from Evelyn. It appears that the family decided a belated honeymoon in a country where travellers sometimes find the climate, food, and the native flies, a touch deadly would be the best place to complete their ritual and bring their patriarch back to the family bosom. The death of a young Englishwoman in such climes would not be the first of its kind — and around the Devereaux family, I very much doubt that it would be the last!"

Thorne looked up from his notes. "This particular family's bosom sounds more and more like a nest of vipers!"

Giselle looked at the clock over the mantle. "Oh, look at the time! It's almost the cocktail hour."

Darling checked his pocket watch. "Bearing in mind Aquilleia's visions, I think we should find the various family members who have disappeared from her sight. I suggest that we check on the hammam first." He looked at his brother. "Shall we?

There was a short pause before Thorne nodded and placed his notebook and pencil on the table. "Good idea. He turned to Aquilleia. "You've already witnessed Vincenzo's death…there's no need to witness the scene of the crime a second time. We'll deal with this if you and Giselle take Veronique and prepare for the cocktail hour. We can discuss what we discover over a bottle or two of champagne; what do you say?"

Aquilleia smiled at her husband. "That sounds like a good idea to me." She turned in her chair as Giselle placed her teacup back in its saucer, stood, and looked at her friend. "Let's retire to our suites for a brush-up, then walk down to the bar. Who knows what else has happened while we have been sitting here?"

Aquilleia nodded. As she stood, a shiver started at the base of her back, working its way up her spine. She turned to Thorne; silver lights swirling in her lavender eyes. "There has been another death!" She winced at the sudden sharp pain that stabbed across her temple. "I can see a cocktail shaker, a golden frog, and an ice pick!"

Elliott and Thorne locked eyes; the memory of their case in Marmis Hall flooding back at the mention of the implement that had been used to kill Lord Scott-Brewer.

Darling looked at Aquilleia, his green eyes sharp. "The same golden frog that Jane Gagnon used to kill Gaston Cavet?"

At Aquilleia's pained nod, Darling looked at Elliott and Thorne. "Her suite's on this corridor."

Thorne gestured towards Aquilleia who shook her head faintly. "I'll be fine."

Giselle scooped the sleeping kitten from her lap, moved to sit next to her friend, and settled the grumbling young cat on one of the plumped, velvet cushions. "Veronique, Pusskin, and I, will stay with Aquilleia. Go…quickly!"

○

Jane's Suite
5:32pm

Jane sat up on her bed and wiped the tears from her face. She entered the bathroom, turned the hot water tap on, and poured a large quantity of attar of roses into the running water. Walking back into her bedroom, she tugged at the bell pull and waited. At the sound of the knock at her door, she raised her voice. "Enter."

The door was opened by a slightly harried looking maid who bobbed a swift curtsy. "Yes, Ma'am?"

"I need a maid to help me dress. I expect her to be in my suite at six o'clock exactly."

The maid bobbed again. Yes, Ma'am."

As the door closed quietly behind her, Jane sat at her dressing table and set out her jewellery for the evening; a gold and ruby necklace, matching earrings, and her beloved golden frog hairpin which she removed from its case and placed next her jewels. She looked at her reflection in the polished mirror and frowned at the pale face that looked back; in truth, she didn't feel hungry; either for food, or for company, but her place in the family meant that sometimes she had to do things even if she didn't want to. She sat up and straightened her shoulders; André would expect her to represent him, and she would never let him down!

She stood and wrapped her arms around her body to try and force some semblance of warmth into her slender frame as she paced; her body as agitated as her mind. Her satin slippers pressing into the deep pile of the Persian rug by the bed as her mind refused to leave its contemplation of the last few months that she had spent with André; valuable time they had been forced to share with that simpering sacrifice,

Evelyn! How could André have stood it? How could he have spent so much time with that insipid, holier-than-thou cretin? Time that would have been far better spent with her; his true love…and actual wife.

Jane stamped her foot and swore. Now look where the fool's plans had led him! It would be more than two years before he could be returned to her, the imbecile! Jane spat another uncouth word, which only those who recognised Ancient Greek would understand, and glared at the drinks tray in the corner; usually, she only drank with André; her eyes again filled with tears — two years, at least!

She stormed to the tray and began to mix a cocktail. A double measure of gin went into the steel cocktail shaker, followed by the juice of a violently squeezed lemon and two large lumps of sugar. Jane eyed the glass and added another sugar lump, then opened the lead-lined cupboard that held a large block of ice, removed the ice pick from its holder, and began to chip slivers of ice for her drink. As she hacked at the block of ice, she was unaware that the curtains at the door to her private terrace had begun to move.

A silent figure stepped from behind the curtains and crept towards her, the Persian rug muffling the sound of his footsteps as the unsuspecting Jane continued to hack at the lump of ice. As she raised the pick one more time, he seized her wrist. Jane turned with a gasp as a back-handed blow knocked her to the floor and sent the ice pick flying.

Her attacker knelt beside her and watched her breathing; excellent…unconscious, not dead. He considered the ice pick with a frown; a perfectly acceptable instrument for murder, but quite unsuitable to the purpose at hand. Turning his head, he saw the block of ice in its lead-lined container; ice? How opportune. He nodded at the perfect symmetry as yet again, the fates smiled down on his plans.

Pulling on his gloves, he arranged the unconscious

woman's body; placing her hands neatly across her breasts, and smoothing the creases out of her gown, before turning back to the ice cupboard. Reaching in, he gripped the block of ice, lifted the heavy weight high above his head, and brought it down firmly on the unconscious woman's skull.

Taking a step back, he cast a critical look at the resultant injury and frowned thoughtfully before lifting the ice block and repeating the blow three more times.

He dropped the block of ice next to Jane's corpse and removed a piece of card from his pocket; he paused to consider, then drew a simple image of a snowflake which he placed next to the corpse.

Taking out a small sketchbook, he flipped through the intricate drawn and richly coloured pictures before pausing at one particular image he had found earlier. Holding the book open, he walked to the far wall and stood before one of the ornate columns that stood on either side of the bathroom door. Looking at the book, he ran his hand over the carved images on the stone column before he found the one he was looking for. Pressing his hand firmly against the image of the Ankh, he stepped back as part of the floor in front of him slowly opened to reveal a set of stone steps leading down into the darkness. Removing a candle and a box of matches he'd had the presence of mind to bring with him, he lit the candle, and raised it above his head. Peering into the secret passageway he paused to listen, but could hear no sound coming from the silent depths. Taking a deep breath, he stepped into the dark corridor and made his way to his next, long overdue appointment.

○

Camillia's Suite
5:36pm

Margaux shook her head, her blue eyes flashing. "I don't care, Camillia! Regardless of what my damned brother thinks, our family is in danger! Now, lock this door behind me." She turned and slammed the door behind her as Camillia, sullenly locked the door, threw herself into the chair next to her dressing table and pouted; Mother could be such a bore at times! At least Uncle Kiefer and Grandmama could be entertaining…and Grandmama *had* promised to bring back Papa.

She lifted her finger and stopped the tear that slid down her pale cheek; poor Papa…it would be several years before she saw him again. As the glowing gaslight caught the teardrop on her finger, Camillia's eyes widened at the shimmering lights of orange and red in the crystalline liquid. She turned to the large jewellery case on her dressing table, avarice in her pale-blue eyes; it wouldn't hurt, and no one was there to see…

She pulled the crocodile-skin case to her, slid back the locks, and opened the lid; glittering gemstones of every hue, in settings of every valuable metal, winked at her from the black velvet within. Camillia removed a large ruby pendant in an ornate gold setting and held it to the light; the flawless, multi-faceted gem reflected the gaslight with a radiance all of its own.

She sighed happily; the benefits of being part of a family of immortal necromancers lay not only in taking the life essence from their chosen victims, but also in acquiring their wealth. Her eyes widened in delight as she replaced the pendant and removed an exquisite set of diamond and platinum cufflinks. As a woman who valued things over people, and jewellery above everything else, she was very happy with her life. Even with the sudden, unexpected death of her father, things could have been much worse; after all…she could have been born human! She held the cufflinks up with a smile; a peal of silvery laughter cascaded from her bow-shaped lips as the diamonds flashed in the light. "Pretty things." She cooed. "Such pretty things."

"I agree."

Camillia spun around in her chair and stared in shock at the dimly lit man standing in her bathroom doorway. She threw the cufflinks onto the dressing table and stood up with a glare, wrapping her dressing gown tightly around her slender body. "How dare you enter my suite! I didn't hear you knock."

The man walked to the door that led to the outer hallway and turned the key. "That's because I didn't use the door."

Camillia's mouth fell open as he walked towards her and she finally recognised him. She moved to the other side of the dressing table, putting as much space as she could between them. "What do you want?"

He paused at the table, picked up the cufflinks and held them to the light, in a mockery of her own actions moments before. "They *are* lovely, aren't they? My mother thought so, when she bought them for my brother."

Camillia's pale eyes widened. "Your…brother?"

The man nodded. "Wilton Cushing; one of your family's many, many victims." The figure dropped the cufflinks back on the dressing table and offered her a mocking bow. "Allow me to introduce myself; Barrett Cushing, at your service…or not, as the case may be! I have spent years following your family, learning your habits, discovering just what you are. Years of concealment — but finally, my family will have justice!"

Camillia stared at him; the whites of her eyes visible around her pale iris. "It was you? You killed Papa and the others?"

Barrett laughed softly. "I will admit to the deaths of most, but not your father. Although I did witness his death, which set in motion certain ideas." A smile touched his lips. "I was always good at planning things, even with very little advance warning. Wilton said it was my strength. Whereas he always made spur-of-the-moment decisions that he would later regret...like marrying your inhuman grandmother."

White lights flashed in Camillia's eyes as she tossed her head defiantly. "I'll scream, and then you will be as dead as your brother!"

Barrett Cushing closed the lid on the jewellery box, picked it up by its handle, and advanced towards the young woman. "I think not. You value these trinkets more than the lives of those you kill. You think it your right to steal lives and things. You think them a part of you...allow me to assist you with that belief!"

Camillia's eyes widened in disbelief. She turned with a gasp and ran to the door that led to the private terrace, but Barrett followed her. Swinging the crocodile skin case with all his strength, he struck the back of her head and knocked her to the ground. Barrett grasped the dazed but conscious necromancer by the neck, turned her over, and dragged her back to the table. He opened the jewellery box and upended it; rings, pendants, and chokers tumbled across the floor next to him. He grasped a fistful of the precious stones and began to force the jewellery into her mouth...piece by piece.

After several minutes, he stood up and looked at his handiwork. Camillia's blue eyes were wide open, gazing blankly at the far ceiling; her mouth was also open, the smooth jaw almost unhinged from the amount of jewellery he had crammed into her throat and mouth to suffocate her.

Barrett looked at the single item left in the jewellery case; a platinum and emerald tiara. He smiled humourlessly; with the best will in the world, he couldn't fit that in her mouth. He took the diadem and placed it on the dead woman's head. He pushed himself to his feet and entered the bathroom, pausing to look at himself in the mirror. He nodded at his reflection before splashing cold water on his face. He dried his face, walked back into the sitting room, and removed his brother's cufflinks from the dressing table. As he slid them into his breast pocket, he heard a distant gong and smiled; the first bell for the cocktail hour. Unfortunately, he would miss it; there was yet another important task for him to see to before dinner.

He removed another piece of card from his pocket, drew the simple outline of a locust, and threw the card on the floor next to Camillia.

Fishing the candlestub out of his pocket, he lit it, and left by the same secret passageway he had used to enter Camillia's suite. As he decended the dark steps, however, he took a different route; a route that would lead him, not back to Jane's rooms, but to the suite of yet another unsuspecting member of the Devereaux family.

○

Darling's Suite
5:40pm

Giselle refilled her friend's teacup and placed it on the table. "Drink this. I've added more sugar than you usually have."

Aquilleia gave her friend a smile of thanks as she lifted the teacup and saucer and took a sip; closing her eyes as she savoured the taste. She placed the cup back on the saucer with a sigh. "Perfect." She looked at Giselle with a slightly embarrassed expression. "You didn't have to stay with me, Giselle…I would have been perfectly fine on my own."

Giselle sat down opposite Aquilleia and shrugged elegantly. "To be honest, the more I discover about the Devereaux family, the less inclined I am to assist in either the investigation *or* their protection. They *are* rather vile!" She sat back in her chair and paused to tickle the kitten who, having been evicted from her comfortable nest on Giselle's lap, had decided to sulk on the cushion next to her. "But I must admit that I find the case rather intriguing. I wonder what Elliott, Thorne, and Darling have found in Jane's suite?"

Aquilleia took another sip of her tea. "If my vision was correct…and they usually are, a very dead necromancer."

As the two women smiled at each other, Giselle's smile faded as Aquilleia's teacup began to rattle in her saucer; the fine China clattering in her suddenly shaking hands as Aquilleia's eyes again filled with silver lights. She looked at Giselle, her voice less than a whisper. "There's been another…"

Giselle knelt by the chair and removed the teacup from her friend's hand. "What do you see?"

Aquilleia blinked slowly; her eyes, now completely silver, moved sightlessly as she focussed on what she could see in her mind's eye. "A ruby pendant, a pair of cufflinks, and a jewellery case."

Giselle frowned as she considered the surviving members of the Devereaux family. "Jewellery…Camillia has a love of jewellery. Is that who you can see?"

The silver in Aquilleia's eyes became tinged with lavender as the vision began to fade. She blinked rapidly and took a shuddering breath. "I…I'm not sure. Possibly."

Giselle stood. "I'll find the others. Veronique, stay and protect your mistress."

She squeezed her friend's hand and hurriedly left the

room as the kitten sat up on its stuffed plinth and padded across to Aquilleia's lap. Veronique settled herself on the rug and stared at the suite door; her usually limpid, chocolate brown eyes touched with a faint red glow as she guarded her exhausted mistress.

○

Margaux's suite
5:43pm

Alone in the large suite of rooms, Margaux glared at the door that stood between her and what remained of her family and stifled a sob; she knew they could bring Julius back, but that it would be so very long was almost too much to bear. She would have to wait until his resurrection for the opportunity to slap his face and tell him that she wanted a divorce!

Margaux pulled a dainty handkerchief from her sleeve; it wouldn't be the first time Julius had avoided discussing their marital issues by getting himself killed! She patted her eyes, and blew her nose thoroughly; the ensuing sound resembling an approaching herd of irate elephants. She dropped the sodden handkerchief into the little wicker basket that served as a laundry bag and bit her lip; Julius was such a thoughtless dolt! She stumbled to the drinks cabinet and with a mulish expression, poured herself a treble measure of single malt whisky, and gulped the contents.

Gripping the decanter and her drink, she sat heavily on the edge of her bed, refilled the glass, drank it, and poured herself another. She placed the decanter on the bedside table, leant back against her pillows, and gazed sightlessly at the far wall as she sipped her drink.

After several minutes of determined drinking, a frown appeared on Margaux's tear-streaked face; she felt...strange.

Margaux blinked slowly and shook her head, but the groggy feeling persisted. She looked at the half-empty decanter; whisky didn't usually affect her *this* quickly! She raised her eyes and gazed blearily at the room, which appeared to be swinging from side to side like a ship in a storm. As she lifted her empty glass and pressed the cold crystal to her cheek, Margaux's eyes suddenly rolled back in their sockets. The glass fell from her hand and rolled across the Persian rug, as her limp body slid off the bed and folded into an ungainly heap on the floor.

In the ensuing silence, there came a faint scratching sound, followed by the grating rasp of stone grinding against stone, as one of the carved marble columns at the far end of the room slowly pivoted to reveal a secret passage…and the dimly lit figure of Barrett Cushing bearing a flickering candlestub.

Barrett entered the suite, placed the nearly extinguished candle on the floor, and knelt beside Margaux. He pressed his fingers against her throat; good…she was still alive.

Sitting back on his heels, he glanced at the floor-length eau de nil silk curtains hanging at the windows, then looked back at Margaux as a slow smile appeared on his face; perfect!

Moving to the windows, he ripped the curtains down, carefully folded the slippery material, and placed it on the bed. Turning to the wardrobe, he opened the doors and rummaged through the contents before spotting an empty carpet bag. He placed the curtains in the bag, dropped a small card onto the bed, and returned to Margaux's side, where, seemingly without effort, he lifted the unconscious woman and swung her across his shoulder. Collecting the bag, he entered the secret passageway just as he heard someone knock on the outer door to the suite. Barrett swiftly pulled the hidden lever and closed the door to the passageway as, in the room beyond, Kiefer opened the suite door and entered the now empty room.

Kiefer spotted the half-empty decanter by the bedside and smirked; Margaux was nothing if not predictable!

Closing the door behind him, he placed the bag with its questionable contents on the floor, and called out. "Margaux? It's time we had a little discussion, sister-mine!" His smirk broadened into an unpleasant smile as he tilted his head to one side, awaiting Margaux's response. In the silence that followed, Kiefer paused to wipe his finger along the top of the bookshelf by the door. He looked at the smidgen of dust on his finger and grimaced; pulling out his handkerchief, he wiped his finger and continued. "Mother and I are not at all happy with your behaviour, Margaux..." Kiefer's eyes narrowed; his smile was replaced by a scowl as he realised that his expected audience was not there. He strode to the bathroom door, and flung it open — empty. He entered the unused servant's bedroom; his sister wasn't there either. He stood in the centre of the suite and glared at the corners of it as though they were deliberately withholding his sister's location.

His fists clenched in anger as he spat. "Margaux, where are you?" He gritted his teeth; bloody woman! "Whatever you may think, my dear sister, this is not amusing, and the outcome of this ridiculous charade will not be pleasant for you! I don't have a sense of humour, Margaux...as well you know!"

Kiefer's handsome face darkened even more as his threat was met with indifference by the inanimate contents of the room. He spat an obscenity and stalked towards the door. Throwing it open, he glanced back; his eyes narrowed as he suddenly realised that, although the artfully swagged pelmet was still present and correct, the curtains that should have hung beneath were missing. Frowning, Kiefer closed the door, collected the bag that contained Vincenzo's head, and walked towards the denuded windows. He looked up at the empty curtain rail and spotted a thin strand of torn eau di nil material peeking out from under the pelmet. Kiefer stood by the French doors and scowled; there had been three things on the list his mother had given him, and he had failed at two of them. He was not looking forward to explaining the last few events to his mother!

He yanked the French door open, entered the covered terrace, and paused; it was empty…excellent. He really didn't need to meet anyone while bearing his current and rather bloody baggage.

○

Margerite and Vincenzo's Suite
5:46pm

Kiefer walked quickly to the French door that led to his mother's suite, stopped, and carefully peered around the edge of the door; his mother was alone, standing at the drinks cabinet, with her back to the French doors. He took a deep breath, entered the room, closed the door, and cleared his throat. "I have good news, and bad news, Mother."

Marguerite looked at him; her face set. She picked up her glass, sat on the settee and waved her hand at him. "Bad news before good."

Kiefer placed the bag on one of the armchairs. "I have found Vincenzo."

Marguerite's eyes dropped to the bag next to her son; her eyebrows lowered. "Elucidate!"

Kiefer winced at the flatness in her voice. He moved to the drinks cabinet and poured himself a large brandy. He turned back to his mother, took a deep breath, and began his explanation.

When he had finished, there was an ominous silence. Kiefer looked at his mother and decided to give her the good news. "But I *have* found someone who can provide us with an airship."

When she did not respond, he frowned and continued. "He says the storm should blow itself out earlier than expected…within the next few hours, actually, which gives us a time frame. He'll have the vessel ready and waiting to leave by ten o'clock this evening."

As the silence became oppressive, Kiefer bit back an exasperated sigh; his mother could go for weeks without talking to someone if she believed they deserved her silence. He shrugged. "Fine." He went to the drinks cabinet, picked up the brandy decanter, then turned to his silent mother and held it up. "Can I get you another?"

He ducked as an empty tumbler suddenly smashed into the wall beside him. He stared at the glittering shards of glass, then turned to his mother and bellowed. "What the hell was that for?" He flinched back as her eyes flashed with white light. Marguerite gestured at the bag and hissed. "You dare to ask me that? After what you did to Vincenzo?"

"Mother, I didn't kill him — not this time, anyway! He was like that when I found him! I thought getting rid of the body and bringing back his skull was the best thing to do, given the current circumstances!"

Marguerite wrapped her arms around her slender frame, closed her eyes and sighed. "So many are gone…it will take years to free our family and bring them back." She looked at Kiefer. "And what about Margaux? Have you spoken to her yet?"

Kiefer took a deep breath. "Not yet, no. I went to her

suite, but she wasn't there. I'll go back and see if she's returned."

Marguerite shook her head. "I'll come with you. I can't stay here and do nothing. I'll pack later"

Kiefer opened the door and, as his mother walked past him, gave her a mocking bow. Entering the corridor, they stopped as they saw several stewards standing outside Jane's room. Marguerite and Kiefer shared a look as they walked down to the suite.

Arriving at the door, Kiefer snapped his fingers at one of the stewards. "What's going on? One of our family is staying in this suite. I insist you tell us what's happened!"

As Kiefer took a step towards the steward, Carandini Bey appeared in the doorway. "Mr Devereaux, I am afraid that there has been another tragedy. Your sister-in-law's companion, Mlle Gagnon..."

Marguerite's eyes widened as she let out a shocked gasp. "No, not Jane!" She tried to look past Carandini. "Please, I must see her—"

Carandini held up his hand. "No, Madame Devereaux, I must insist...what lies in that room is a scene of such horror that I cannot permit a lady of your sensibilities to bear witness—"

Marguerite pushed him aside and stopped dead on the threshold. She blinked as she took in the amount of blood that had pooled around Jane's head — or rather, what little there was that remained of Jane's head — and that had soaked into the thick Persian rug like a deep-red halo. Her eyes flickered as she saw the large lump of bloodied ice. "Her...her skull! Oh, God! How will we be able to—" She shot a wild look at the other men standing in the room. "I am sorry, I shouldn't be here."

She paused as Carandini once more held up his hand. "I am afraid that I have more terrible news for you, Madame

Devereaux. Your companion, Mlle Donnadieu, has also been found…dead."

Marguerite stared at him, her face deathly pale. "Where is she?"

Carandini looked at Darling who nodded faintly. "She has been placed with the other bodies in the meat locker, Madam. They will shortly be joined by Mlle Gagnon."

Kiefer appeared at his mother's side and took in the contents of the room with a cold expression. He held out his arm to his mother, who accepted it without a word as she allowed her son to escort her from the room.

Elliott raised his eyes from the unpleasant sight of Jane Gagnon's corpse and darted a look at Carandini who was standing in the doorway. He looked at Thorne and waggled his eyebrows as he murmured. "We were interrupted by Aquilleia's vision…it might be an idea to pop over to the Hammam and see if what was suggested previously has actually occurred."

Carandini caught part of his *soto voce* remark and looked at him with a concerned expression. "Is everything all right, Mr Caine?"

Elliott bit his tongue; some humans had rather good hearing…rather too good, in his opinion! He addressed Carandini with an affected sigh. "I just wish that we had more people to help us with this case, Mr Bey."

Carandini looked at him sharply as an idea suddenly occurred to him; a seemingly innocent offer of help could rid him of a certain steward who was no longer of use to the hotel. "I might be able to assist with your request, Mr Caine."

Elliott raised an eyebrow. "How so?"

"Maxwell, one of our Simulandro stewards, was injured by the sandstorm…nothing that would harm his workings, but his skin was damaged. …" Carandini spread his hands. "The Simulandros must have a certain…perfection in their appearance, you understand? The skin could be replaced, of course, but the cost would be astronomical, so I arranged for him to be removed for deconstruction. But if he could be of assistance in your investigation, I am more than willing to sign him over to you for as long as you would require his services."

Elliott looked at Carandini; a faint green tinge appeared in his brown eyes. "You will sign him over to me...for as long as I require his services?"

Carandini looked puzzled. "Yes...if he would be of benefit to your investigation."

Elliott nodded; a slight smile playing about his lips. "I accept your generous offer."

Carandini walked towards the door. He paused at the threshold. "The only problem I can foresee, is Farasha."

Darling looked at him with a raised eyebrow. "Farasha? Why?"

Carandini looked a little uncomfortable. "It may sound strange...but they appear to have become fond of each other."

Elliott frowned. "Why should that be considered strange?"

Carandini shrugged. "They're Simulandros, they're not programmed to feel closeness or friendship. Their sole purpose is to work."

A green light burned in Elliott's eyes. "Then we will take Farasha as well. Giselle has required a maid for quite some time. Two birds with one stone."

Carandini frowned. "I don't think that the Eridanus Corporation will accept—"

Elliott cut him off. "Both or neither, Mr Bey." He smiled as a sudden thought arrived. "You could inform them that the private enquiry agents who are investigating the case are prepared to accept both Maxwell and Farasha in lieu of payment. That way you have saved the company a rather sizable expense."

Carandini stared at him before nodding slowly. "Yes…yes, of course. I'll see to it. If you will excuse me, gentlemen…it appears that I have two Simulandros to find and remove from our books."

As he turned to leave the room, Elliott called out. "Mr Bey? When you have found him, please send Maxwell to the hammam and ask him to wait for Thorne."

Carandini nodded. "Of course."

Thorne nodded. "I'll go there now." He paused as Giselle suddenly appeared in the door. She nodded at Carandini's polite bow as the manager left and hurried to her husband's side. "Aquilleia has had another vision of death. She thinks it was Camillia."

Thorne gripped her arm. Is Aquilleia all right?"

Giselle nodded. "As well as can be expected, but she's very tired. She's never had so many visions in such a short space of time before…no wonder she had a migraine!"

Thorne turned to look at Elliott and Darling, before he could speak, Darling raised his voice. "Go to your wife. I'll go to the Hammam, if Elliott and Giselle check on Miss Devereaux."

Thorne nodded and hurried out of the room. Giselle took in the injuries to Jane's skull with a grimace. "That looks extremely deliberate." She looked at Elliott. "Was there another card?"

Elliott nodded and held up a piece of card that bore the image of a snowflake.

Giselle looked at the drawing and pursed her lips slightly. "A snowflake. That can symbolize cold, ice…or a plague of hailstones." She looked at Elliott and Darling. "Aquilleia was right; the killer *is* using the biblical plagues to wreak their revenge upon the Devereaux family."

○

Marguerite's Suite
5:55pm

As they entered her suite, Kiefer tightened his grip on his mother's arm. "Stay calm, Mother…"

Marguerite took a shuddering breath. "Calm? I've been calm. Two or three deaths…that's manageable. But now… after what this lunatic has done to our family? I've tried to stay calm, but it will take years to get our family back!"

As Kiefer steered his mother inside and closed the door, Marguerite shrugged off his hand and glared at him with tear-filled eyes. "Did you see what they did to her skull? I don't know if she can be resurrected with that…that damage!"

Kiefer stalked to the drinks cabinet, poured two large whiskies, drank his in one mouthful and handed the other glass to his mother, who took it with unseeing eyes as she sat on the edge of the settee. "Oh, Kiefer…if we can't bring her back, how will André deal with her loss?"

Kiefer shook his head. "We'll deal with that if we have to. Take heart, Mother. We resurrected Margaux with a crushed skull once, remember? She returned to us with no loss of function or ability." Kiefer poured himself another whisky. "She merely felt an overriding desire to shop at the House of Worth for a sturdier hat!"

Marguerite fixed him with a cold stare. "Several members of our family have been killed by someone who seems to have a vendetta against us, Kiefer. I was far less worried about the deaths of Julius and Vanessa, because we've dealt with such events before. I was calm even in the face of André's death. But in destroying Jane's skull, this killer has shown that they have some knowledge of what we are — and how to destroy us — and I find that terrifying!" Marguerite took a steadying sip of her drink. "I hope you're right about Jane. But we still need her skull…" She grimaced. "We usually boil them clean, but the soft tissue seemed to be the only thing holding it together! That will make it awkward to pack." She looked at her son; the white light shimmering in her eyes. "We need to finish the ritual, resurrect your father, gather our resources and leave. I think we should go directly to the villa in Italy. Once there, we can set about resurrecting the others." She sighed. "It's not ideal, but the secondary ritual chamber there will have to suffice; its powers are lesser, and the ritual takes much longer, but I don't think we should return here for a while."

She took another sip of her drink and looked at her son. "I'm sorry about Vanessa, Kiefer."

Kiefer frowned. "Why?"

Marguerite looked at her son with a faint smile. "You really aren't all that bothered by her death, are you?"

Kiefer shrugged. "She had her uses, Mother."

"Yes, she did. She organised the right rooms at the hotel to facilitate our particular needs. It might be difficult, but hopefully we can bring her back and have her reinstated in the hotel at some point in the distant future."

Kiefer gave a bark of laughter. "She's dead, Mother, and the humans will find out about it pretty damn soon! How on earth can we reinstate her after they've seen her corpse?"

A distant light appeared in Marguerite's grey eyes. "One of two ways; I can alter her appearance during the resurrection ritual. She's a human familiar, so it will be quite simple to achieve. Then she can reapply for her old position as her own sister or niece. If Carandini tried to interfere…well, accidents *do* happen, and new managers are easy enough to find." She took a sip of her drink. "Or, we simply wait until the humans who are currently employed by the hotel have all died. Either way, we shall return."

The Hammam
6:10pm

Darling stood in the entrance to the hammam and glared at the empty room, taking in the damage to the door and the heavy smell of cooked pork with a wrinkled nose. He turned back to the massage room, looked at the window at the far end of the room and noted the sand that covered the floor underneath. He sighed; someone had obviously tried to remove the evidence of what had occurred in the damp rooms, but the traces were obvious for those who knew what they were looking for.

Darling shook his head and walked out of the hammam. He looked up as a Simulandro steward appeared in the dimly lit covered walkway and stopped before him. "Mr Darling? Mr Bey has informed me of a change to my orders. I have been sent to assist Mr Thorne, Sir. My name is Maxwell."

Darling took in the damage to the Simulandro's face. "Thorne had to check on another line of inquiry, so I'm afraid that you'll be assisting me, Maxwell."

Maxwell bowed. "Very well, Sir." He hesitated. "I was instructed to inform Mr Thorne about one or two things that have occurred in the last quarter of an hour, Sir; should I inform you instead?"

Darling noticed the unusual hesitation in the Simulandro's demeanor. He nodded. "Yes. Please do, Maxwell."

The Simulandro looked relieved. "Very well, Sir. In which case, Mr Caine and Mlle Du'Lac went to check on Miss

Camillia Devereaux as agreed, and they can confirm that she too is dead."

Darling closed his eyes and rubbed the bridge of his nose; another one! He would be lucky if he had a job to go back to on his return to the Espion Court! "Thank you, Maxwell. Where was Miss Devereaux found?"

"In her suite, Sir. Mr Caine said that he and Mlle Du'Lac would be informing Mrs Marguerite Devereaux of her granddaughter's death…" Maxwell paused and consulted his pocket watch. "…at this very moment, Sir. And that, if you wouldn't mind, Sir, they would like you and the others to meet with him in their suite of rooms at your earliest convenience." The steward paused; his blue eyes faintly curious. "From Mr Caine's demeanor, Sir, I believe that he has discovered something else of benefit to your investigation.

Darling took in the Simulandro's unusual inquisitiveness with an unreadable expression. He turned and gestured to the building behind him. "There's evidence to suggest that another member of the Devereaux family was murdered in the hammam, Maxwell. Please see that no one enters this building. I'll send another steward to take over from you in a few hours' time."

The steward straightened. "Very good, Sir. But it's quite all right, Sir…I don't need to rest. I shall stay here until relieved.

Darling nodded. "Then I'll take my leave of you. Thank you, Maxwell."

The steward bowed again. "Sir."

Darling walked away from the hammam with a thoughtful expression; there was something very strange about Maxwell that had piqued his own curiosity; the Simulandro's obvious interest in their investigation, though a touch inhibited, seemed far more human than artificially programmed. Indeed, Simulandro's were never programmed to be curious…if they were, it would spell disaster for many of the governments, businesses, and private homes that employed them to provide nothing more than polite, deferential, and invisible slave labour. He turned to look at the Simulandro, who was now standing with his back to the hammam door; yes…intriguing!

○

Elliott and Giselle's Suite
6:20pm

Elliott looked up from his chair as Darling entered the room. "Ah, I see that Maxwell found you."

Darling nodded. "Indeed, he did. A most interesting character. He has curiosity, and that's not usually programmed as standard." Darling sat on the settee and looked at Elliott with a raised eyebrow. "I understand that you've discovered another dead Devereaux? The family certainly aren't having a very nice holiday here in Egypt!"

Elliott grimaced. "The fragrant Camillia. Yes…that was a rather disturbing discovery." He explained the method of murder to Darling, who winced.

Elliott gestured to the table next to the settee. "When we returned to our suite, these were waiting for us."

Darling looked at the items on the table; two books, a jewelled knife, and a crystal vial. "He raised his eyebrows. "And what are they?"

Elliott poured two coupes of Champagne and placed one on the table next to Darling. "The books are Miss March's diary, and what appears to be a highly detailed ledger. Giselle used her gift and managed to have a short discussion with Abditivus about the knife, the vial, the sandstorm, and the destruction of the telephone. With regards to the weather and the infernal device, he's asked that we continue to keep him informed of the situation via Giselle." Elliott sipped his champagne. "He believes the knife to be one of the Blades of Nekroshema; the Being considered by many to be the Mother of necromancers. It's the weapon they use to take the blood offering from their final victim. The vial is the vessel used to catch and contain the blood used in the resurrection ritual." He looked at Darling with a grim smile. "I don't know who delivered the items, but I think that we could hazard a guess!" At Darling's nod of agreement, Elliott continued. "As for the books; the ledger mentions names, codenames, payments, and dates...in particular, certain dates that tally with dates pertinent to our investigation. Two of the codenames mentioned are 'Black Eagle' and 'Le Noir'...but the ledger also gives their real names." He handed the books to Darling. "You might be surprised, but I rather doubt it." He took out his pocket watch. "My message reached you, so hopefully, Giselle, Thorne, Aquilleia, and Veronique should be arriving soon. I think perhaps we wait until after they arrive to continue this discussion."

Elliott and Giselle's Suite
6:26pm

Thorne gently tucked the blanket around Aquilleia before turning back to the items on the table. He fixed his monocle, opened one of the books, and studied the names. "So, now we know who Le Noir and Black Eagle are." He looked at his brother. "How much access to the police files on the Islamists does Sergeant Jaziri have?"

Darling grimaced. "As Captain Sarhan's sergeant in the

Aswan office, he has much the same access as Sarhan, with no questions asked."

Thorne continued to peruse the ledger. "And this man, Officer Amin Hammad…is he a police officer?" he handed the book to Aquilleia who read the names with interest.

Darling sat back in his armchair with a scowl. "No! He's the bloody steward at the Eridanus desk of the Cairo Aetherdrome!" He shook his head angrily. "It's glaringly damned obvious when you see it all on paper; a watcher at the aetherdrome, checking the travellers for the richest harvest, assisted by a police officer who can fiddle the information on what was stolen." He rubbed his eyes. "But it still doesn't tell us who the masterminds are! Miss March and Kiefer were obviously willing participants in their murderous plans; Miss March had a mind for organising and Kiefer likes money." He glanced at Elliott. "Jaziri and Hammad are fair game, but I believe that they are just middlemen. We need the people at the top; the ones who are using the money to fund their dastardly plots against the Veiled Protectorate and the British Empire, dammit!"

Elliott poured five sizeable coupes of Champagne and handed them round, then sat down in an upright armchair. "There *is* a way of gathering that information…"

Darling looked at him suspiciously. "What way? Pray tell, Caine, what have I missed?"

Elliott took a sip of his drink and looked at Darling, his brown eyes thoughtful. "We were invited here because the Espion Court is usually beyond the ken of the government, yes?"

Darling nodded. "Yes. The average politician is far too naïve to understand what we are, where we come from, or what we are capable of. It's the ones who *do* know about us that we need to watch out for!" Darling's green eyes narrowed as he looked from Elliott to his brother and back again. "Again, what have I missed?"

Elliott placed his coupe on the table beside him. "Do you remember the Marlow-Glass case?"

Darling frowned in thought, then sat back in his chair. "Of course. Lord Marlow-Glass was a very highly placed member of society who had a penchant for the murder and mutilation of little girls. In the end, it fell to the Espion Court to deal with him, as, due to his familial and political connections, he couldn't be touched—" Darling paused and looked at Elliott, aghast. "Surely you aren't thinking about contacting Fellithropos?"

Elliott picked up his coupe and sat back. "The Espion Court have used his services for many, many years. When it comes to unearthing information that people refuse to offer up willingly, he's exceptional at getting them to…open up, shall we say? He's an excellent agent."

"He's an obscenity! Have you forgotten what he did to Marlow-Glass when he finally found him?"

Thorne looked at Darling with a raised eyebrow. "Squeamish, brother? Fellithropos is a highly valuable, suitably mutable member of the Espion Court. Surely the fact that he carried out the sentence which the Court had passed on Marlow-Glass is not an issue?"

Darling snapped his teeth together and stared at his brother in silence. He placed his hands on the table between them and leant across it; his voice clipped and matter of fact. "The problem was not the sentence of death, Thorne, it was the manner of execution. I am very much in favour of the death sentence for crimes such as those committed by Marlow-Glass. However, knowing that he was executed by a member of the Espion Court, who used his gift of Otherness to change his mouth into that of a lion to rip the criminal apart…that, brother, is a step too far!"

Aquilleia blanched and took a healthy gulp of her champagne; she had heard many strange tales about Fellithropos, the Other who had a great hatred for abusers of women and children. He was the Espion Court's final port of call when dealing with either those from whom the Court needed immediate information, or predators who were so highly placed that they were deemed untouchable. He ensured that no such presumed protection ever lasted for long…but then, neither did his victims after his unusual interrogation techniques! She looked at Darling. "Was the manner of Marlow-Glass' execution your sole concern in that particular case?"

Darling took a deep breath, knowing that, regardless of his words, he had already lost the argument. "It was."

Aquilleia held up the diary. "We now know there's to be another raid on a British garrison, but we don't know which one. Le Noir and the Black Eagle, however, do. Fellithropos has proven his worth in the past by encouraging those who refuse to answer questions in a timely fashion to speak…ah, sooner, rather than later, shall we say?" She looked at Elliott and Darling. "The Empire has allowed us carte blanche… remember the document? 'With finality and speed'? We know these men will be sentenced to death for treason, anyway. Can Fellithropos be encouraged to carry out the executions without too much…theatre?"

A faint smile flickered across Elliott's face. "I am sure it can be encouraged!"

Darling held up a hand in surrender. "All right! All right! I know when I'm beaten!"

Giselle gave him a bright smile as she stroked the kitten who had once again taken up residence on her lap. "Excellent. I'll contact Abditivus immediately."

Darling sipped his drink. "Very well. Please inform him about our concerns, and that I request Fellithropos travels to Egypt immediately to engage in a spot of interrogation germane to our case. After the necessary information has been gathered, the two men in question are to be…untheatrical dispatched with finality and speed." He sat back on the settee. "I believe that the name he prefers to be known by in this realm is 'Villiers Locke'. He lives in Astraea, so he should get here quite soon." He drained his coupe, a faint smile playing around his lips. "I doubt very much that these murderous villains will be at all prepared for the arrival of the Patchwork Gent."

○

Aswan
Colonel Barrington's Office
7:35pm

A slow, deliberate knock sounded at the door. Colonel Barrington looked up from his sheaf of papers and frowned. He wasn't expecting anyone at that hour; even his secretary had gone home! He leant back in his seat. "Enter!"

The door opened and one of the largest men Barrington had ever seen entered; nearly seven feet in height, with a thick shock of silver-white hair that hung past his broad shoulders, the man paused in the doorway and smiled. A shiver ran up Colonel Barrington's spine at the sight of the man's slightly too-wide mouth. He stood up sharply and nodded. "Yes? Who are you?"

The man sat, without invitation, in one of the two armchairs in front of the colonel's desk. He placed his attaché case on the floor, then peeled off his fine, dark red leather gloves and slapped them across his knee. In a deep and husky voice that oozed like treacle touched with a faint Cockney accent, he addressed the military man. "Colonel Barrington, my name is Villiers Locke. I've been sent by the

Espion Court to assist the Veiled Protectorate with a case that appears to be somewhat…awkward."

Colonel Barrington sat back and looked at him warily. "I can assure you, Mr Locke, that the Veiled Protectorate is more than capable of investigating her own cases."

Villiers made his hands into a steeple and looked at the colonel over his knitted fingers; a faint smile appeared on his full lips as he raised a quizzical dark eyebrow. "Is it really?"

Colonel Barrington frowned, then leant forward. "Who did you say sent you?"

Villiers's smile widened. "Commander Darling of the Espion Court."

Colonel Barrington blinked. "Oh!" He shot the man a sharp look. "I trust you can prove that?"

Villiers leant forward, placed the attaché case on his lap, opened it, and withdrew a single sheet of paper which he handed to the suspicious colonel. "Here is proof of my identity from the Espion Court."

Colonel Barrington's eyebrow climbed with every line he read, until it was well up his forehead. He placed the document on his blotter and looked at the man opposite with a quiet air of resignation. "It seems to be in order, Mr…Locke. What can I do for you?"

Villiers fixed his thickly lashed hazel eyes on the colonel. "The people I work with have discovered the identity of two men they believe to be part of the Islamist group targeting travellers in Egypt."

Colonel Barrington sat up, his moustache bristling. "Marvellous! We must inform Captain Sarhan. I shall send for him immediately."

Villiers held up a hand as he reached for the telephone. "Please, Colonel Barrington, don't place that call just yet. The two men work in positions valuable to the Islamists; they have access to certain pertinent information. They act as bridges to pass that information to those who arrange the robberies and murders. I need to approach the second man before he realises that we know what part he plays in this malign scheme."

Colonel Barrington stared at him. "Positions that give them access to information…and you are asking me not to call Sarhan?" At Locke's nod he slowly sat back with a pained expression. "Please don't tell me it's Sarhan. He's far too good a man to lose."

"It isn't Sarhan."

Colonel Barrington took a deep breath and looked at the document on his blotter. "What do you need?"

Villiers opened his case and removed another document. "I've already interviewed one of the two men; he worked for the Eridanus Corporation at the Cairo Aetherdrome. He gave me some information before he…left, but I must speak with the second man. That's why I'm here, Colonel Barrington. This is the man I wish to interview." He pushed the document across the desk.

Colonel Barrington looked at the name and sighed. "Rotten apples — and one rotten apple spoils the barrel!" He looked at Villiers. "If it means ending this bloody mess, do what you have to do." He averted his eyes as Villiers sat back and smiled broadly, his mouth appearing to have slightly more teeth than was usual.

"Thank you, Colonel Barrington; I truly appreciate your support."

○

Aswan
Captain Sarhan's Office
7:45pm

Sergeant Jaziri looked up from his paperwork and leapt to his feet as two men entered his office. "Captain Sarhan…" His voice trailed off as he looked past Sarhan to the massive man who closed the door and leant against it with a leisurely smile. Jaziri stared at the smiling man before turning back to Sarhan who fixed him with a steady gaze. "Sergeant Jaziri. Certain matters have been brought to our attention. This gentleman needs to talk with you. Please sit down."

As Sergeant Jaziri sat warily back in his chair, Sarhan moved to stand by the desk; he stopped abruptly as Villiers stepped in front of him. "I work better alone, Captain Sarhan. Please close the door on your way out."

Captain Sarhan looked at him sharply. "I don't like this Mr Locke. This is *not* how we do things here!"

Villiers placed his bag and hat on Jaziri's desk and stood opposite the now unnerved Sergeant. "You are quite correct, Captain Sarhan. It's *not* how you do things here. It's also not how the Empire does things; it is, however, how *I*, and the people that I work with, do things. In agreeing to my presence, both the Veiled Protectorate and the Empire have agreed to *my* way of business. Now; please leave us."

Sarhan glared at Villiers in anger, then turned on his heel and left the room; closing the door not too gently behind him. As the slamming sound died down, Villiers slowly turned to look at Jaziri. The silence became oppressive as the two men stared at each other for several long minutes before Villiers leant forward, placed his hands on the desk, and smiled toothily. Sergeant Jaziri's mouth dropped open in horror; he shot back in his chair and stared, wild-eyed at the sight of Villiers' impossibly wide grin.

Having received the reaction he wanted, Villiers sat in the chair opposite the now terrified man, and leant back; a faint flicker of dark red in his gleaming hazel eyes. "Now, Sergeant Jaziri…tell me about the information you gleaned for the Devereaux family and the Islamists. Tell me about the innocent men, women, and children you robbed, raped, murdered, and sold."

○

Marguerite and Vincenzo's Suite
7:45pm

Marguerite looked up as Kiefer entered the room. "Have you found Margaux?"

Kiefer shook his head. "No. She isn't in her room, and she's not at dinner, either."

Marguerite wrapped her arms around herself. "We must find her!" She closed her eyes and turned back to the window.

Kiefer scowled at the back of his mother's head; she always became maudlin when more than three of the family died in a year. He poured two large whiskies, walked to his mother's side, and held a glass out to her. "We'll find Margaux, Mother. She's probably drinking herself into a stupor somewhere in the hotel. We'll collect her before we leave. Now, a toast; to the family — our family — and its continued resurrection."

Marguerite looked at him silently, then accepted the glass and raised it. "The family." She took a sip, then calmly threw the rest of her drink in his face.

Kiefer's blue eyes filled with a blinding white light. He

stood deathly still, liquid dripping from his dark face as he looked into his mother's equally white eyes. He took his handkerchief from his breast pocket and wiped his face. "You obviously believe that I deserved that. Are you quite finished?"

Marguerite threw herself into one of the plush armchairs and held out the empty glass. "Get me another drink!"

Kiefer took the glass, refilled it, and handed it to his mother, who was gazing through the window. "I would have liked to see Vincenzo one last time, Kiefer. You should have come and told me what happened."

Kiefer scowled. "For God's sake, Mother! It's not like you haven't lost a husband before!"

Marguerite glared at her son, the white light in her eyes fading. "You know nothing of love, do you, Kiefer? You are spoilt, selfish, and utterly immoral. " Her face softened a little. "You remind me so much of your father…it's one of the many reasons why you're my favourite." She sipped her whisky. "We're running out of time. I need the skulls; Camillia's, Violette's, and Jane's. There's no time to do it cleanly — just get them, and then go and get Evelyn. Everyone should be at dinner, so that gives us plenty of time." Her eyes became distant. "I want a few words with that precious brat before we take her essence. Tell Linden, Heathers, and Sedgewyck to meet us at the chamber and bring only what they need to return to Rome." She paused and tapped her fingernail against her lip thoughtfully. "I think it would be best if we used the secondary entrance to the chamber, the one that leads from what is now the Simulandro dormitory, not the main door from the Chapel of Mandulis…we don't want any witnesses to our dragging Evelyn to her impending doom! Now, if the airship will be ready for ten o'clock, the ritual must start no later than thirty minutes before then; that will give us time to collect the heads, find the others, and gather what few items we need to bring with us while also giving us time, in those thirty minutes, to resurrect your father, and give him a few moments to gather himself before we leave for the jetty. I'll meet you by the ritual chamber at half past nine." She paused and shook her eyes with a sigh. "If we haven't found Margaux before we leave, we'll have to leave her to find her own way to Rome. She should be fine…she's dealt with such things on her own before…as well you know!"

Kiefer smiled a slow, ugly smile. "Finally!" He left his mother's rooms and headed to his suite for a knife and another hessian bag. He threw the door open and stalked towards the leather trunk. He ran a cold, knowledgeable eye across the various blades within before selecting a viciously sharp knife with a very thin blade. The cuts had to be precise so that all the parts would match up; Camillia would thank him for it later.

He grabbed a spare handkerchief, a large carpet bag, and another hessian bag, and shoved them inside the trunk. Kiefer paused by the drinks tray and poured himself a double brandy. Knocking the drink back in one, he took the decanter into the bathroom, emptied the brandy down the sink, refilled the decanter with water, and tucked it next to the bags in the trunk. Opening one of the drawers in his dressing table, he removed his passport and tucked it into his breast pocket; along with the trunk, that was all the packing he needed to do! With a vicious grin, he lifted the chest by one of its handles and effortlessly wheeled it out of his suite, pausing only to close the door as he made his way towards the second meat locker.

Arriving at the room, Kiefer paused and looked around him; the hallway was empty and silent. He grasped the handle and pushed; the door didn't open. Kiefer gritted his teeth; someone had locked the door! He gripped the handle and with deliberation, sharply twisted it while leaning against the door; the crunch of splintering wood echoed in the marble-lined corridor as the door finally opened. Kiefer quickly entered the meat locker, placed his trunk by the wall, and pushed the damaged door closed…utterly unaware that behind him, a worried eye was watching him through a keyhole.

As the door to the meat locker closed, the door directly opposite opened and Linden stepped out; an expression of deep concern on his youthful face. He pressed his eye to the keyhole in the meat locker door and flinched as he watched his uncle go about the business of gathering the skulls.

Linden backed away from the door; a thousand thoughts ricocheting in his mind. He hurried to his grandmother's suite and entered without knocking; the room was empty, but he could hear the sound of running water coming from the bathroom. Closing the door, Linden rested against it and closed his eyes; nearly all the family were gone, taken by a killer who knew their weaknesses…a killer who was determined to push them to the brink of extinction and beyond for their crimes.

He heard his grandmother moving around in the bathroom and winced as he heard her talking to herself about what she would do to Evelyn before taking her heart's blood; she was obviously in no mood for second thoughts or reconciliation! Linden ran a shaking hand though his hair — it had to stop…it had to stop, or the family's overwhelming desire for money would be the cause of their ultimate, permanent, demise. The few that remained must regroup and start again.

As he opened the door to leave, a faint murmuring sound arrived on the edge of his hearing. Linden froze; his eyes darted around the room before coming to rest on his grandmother's reticule, and the large hessian bag next to it.

As Linden stood by the door, his face became pale but

determined; there was one more death...a death that was necessary to serve the family...but then, it had to stop.

○

The Second Meat Locker
7:55pm

Kiefer stood by the shelf and gazed at the jewellery spilling out of his dead niece's mouth; that was quite handy...with one cut, they would have both Camillia's skull and most of her jewellery collection. He removed his jacket, rolled up his sleeves, and proceeded along the same lines as he had with Vincenzo. Taking great care to ensure he missed the jewellery crammed in her open mouth, Kiefer made one swift movement with the blade and severed his niece's head.

As her head came away, he frowned; something was wrong. He bent over the headless corpse and peered into the open wound; more jewellery was clearly visible in her throat. He stood up with a huff; this was going to take far longer than he had anticipated! With a curl of his lip, he dragged his niece's body onto the floor and set to work.

After several unpleasant minutes, the meat locker floor resembled more that of an abattoir's than the clean and tidy cold room it had earlier been, as, with a flourish, Kiefer pulled the final item of jewellery from Camillia's chest cavity and frowned at the state of his hands. He then turned to Violette and Jane and continued his bloody task. His work finally done, Kiefer placed the heads neatly side by side on one of the shelves, put the bloody jewellery in the hessian bag and glanced around the room looking for something to wrap the heads in; he smirked as his eye fell on a sheaf of butcher's paper.

Wrapping the heads in the thick sheets of greaseproof

paper, he removed the decanter of water from the carpet bag and replaced it with the heads; tucking them carefully neck side up into the spacious bag, along with the hessian sack containing the jewellery.

Kiefer removed the stopper from the decanter and poured water over his hands, rinsing the worst of the blood away. He wiped his knife with his spare handkerchief and placed the knife and the decanter in the bag, then placed the entire package in the trunk. Rolling down his sleeves, he pulled on his jacket, checked his pocket watch, and grimaced; they were running out of time, but after the events of the last thirty minutes, he desperately needed a wash. He could just imagine his father's face if he welcomed him back smelling like a charnel house!

○

Linden and Kiefer's Suite.
8:28pm

Entering the room, Kiefer closed the door, pushed the trunk against the wall, made his way to the drinks cabinet and poured himself a large whisky. He turned as the French doors to the covered terrace opened and Linden walked in.

As he saw his uncle, a sudden, panic-stricken expression crossed Linden's face; his left hand moved rapidly to cover a slightly damp, rusty coloured patch on his waistcoat.

Linden paused to gather himself and saw the trunk by the door. He nodded at it as he poured himself a similarly sized brandy. "What's in the trunk?"

Kiefer knocked back the whisky. "Camillia, Violette, Jane, and part of Camillia's jewellery collection. We're moving the ritual to within the next hour. The sandstorm will have dissipated enough to enable us to leave. I've already chartered an airship to take us back to Cairo. Pack only what you can carry in a carpet bag and go to the ritual room through the doorway in the Simulandro's dormitory." He poured himself another drink. "I need to tell Heathers and Sedgewyck to meet us there." He sniffed at his sleeve and made a face. "Gods, I need a bath!" He looked at his nephew through narrowed eyes. "Have you seen your mother?"

Linden looked at him sharply. "No…no, not since lunch. Is something wrong?"

Kiefer smiled humourlessly. "I can't find her…and I've looked everywhere." He shrugged. "It's of no matter. Get your things and go to the chamber."

Linden stared at him. "But…we can't leave Mother behind!"

Kiefer finished his drink. "Your grandmother is of the mind that if Margaux isn't at the airship in time, she can make her own way back to the villa in Rome. Serves the stupid bitch right for threatening to tell father about…" Keifer's voice trailed off at the thought of his father discovering that he had abandoned his sister to the Spanish Inquisition so many years ago. A dark look crossed his face as he lent back against the drinks cabinet and again refilled his glass. "Just do as you're told, Linden. Gather your things, and go to the ritual chamber."

Linden stared at his uncle and shook his head. "I can't leave Mother." He looked at Kiefer before suddenly blurting. "Uncle…we have to change."

Kiefer stared at him. "What?"

Linden swallowed hard and continued. "The family…we have to change. We've strayed from what we were. The One who gave us power over life and death, Nekroshema, how would she react to our addiction to murder? To wealth and society? Our need for humans to rent a form of our immortality for money? We debase ourselves for trinkets when we can have it all! Uncle, we've fallen too far. We should kill because we have to…not because we like it! We need to return to the old ways."

Kiefer looked at Linden steadily. "The old ways?"

Linden nodded. "Yes! Nekroshema's gift millennia ago made us demigods…sharing that gift with humans, even in a weaker, more temporary form, lessens us. We can rise above our need for mortals and the fickle desires of their society… we can return to our glorious past!"

Kiefer continued to look at his nephew. "And how would we return to our glorious past, Linden?"

Linden, so relieved at hearing what he wanted to, missed the dangerous note in his uncle's voice. "We return to the villa in Rome. We contact all those who have received the gift of extended life from us, and we order them to gift their positions of power to us, or the gift will be ended. We own Kings, Queens, Emperors, Prime Ministers, Presidents, warmongers, businessmen, and so many others! Uncle; we can rule the world! Let's talk with Grandmama…I'm sure that, together, we can convince her that now is *our* time — the family's time — to take full control of the human world."

Kiefer looked down at his glass thoughtfully. There was a moment of silence as he drained the contents before, with a violent lunge, he threw the empty glass straight at his nephew. The glass hit Linden fully in the face; the crystal shattering on impact and tearing into the skin around the terrified younger man's eye. Linden flinched back from the brilliant white light that flashed into his uncle's eyes, but before he could escape, Kiefer picked him up by his lapels and slammed him into the wall; the stone cracking under the force of Kiefer's strength. Linden writhed against his uncle's grip as Kiefer lent into his nephew's face and spat. "We already *are* the power, Linden…we already control the humans. We tell them what we want, when we want it, and how, and they obey. There is no need for us to involve ourselves in the daily woe of politics, religion, or work…we have no need to bore ourselves with such inconsequential details. We simply live, and enjoy the trappings of our gift, position, and wealth, while they do as we say."

He released his grip on Linden's lapels, returned to the drinks tray, and refilled his glass. "We keep a few necessary humans between us and the work so that they feel they still have an amount of power…a small amount, I grant you, but still more power than those who reject us. And, due to this thoughtfulness on our part, such humans are even more wretchedly grateful for the bounty with which they are blessed. Who are you to take such gifts away from them, Linden?"

Linden stared at his uncle; his eyes almost unnaturally wide. "You're quite right, Uncle. I'm sorry. I'll collect my things and meet you in the ritual chamber. What time did you say?"

Kiefer smirked. "That's better, Linden. The airship will be ready for us at ten o'clock. Gather your passport and what few things you can carry and be ready in the ritual chamber no later than half past nine…that will give us plenty of time to resurrect Father and escort him safely to the jetty." He waved his glass. "If you want to make yourself useful, go and tell Heathers that we won't be needing him for the ritual. He's to guard the doorway that leads from the ritual room to the jetty and await the arrival of the airship." Kiefer pulled a face. "He tends to get rather emotional when Father returns…the last few occasions have been quite embarrassing and I have absolutely no desire to deal with him when he behaves in such a fashion!" He made a shooing gesture with his hand. "You may go."

Linden stared at him before turning slowly and entering his bedroom. He returned almost immediately with a small carpet bag. He looked at Kiefer. "I'll travel in what I am wearing. Do we need our robes for the ritual?"

Kiefer paused; his mother had not issued any instructions on that issue, but he was damned if he was going to admit that to Linden! "Yes, bring your robes. And hurry!"

Linden gathered his robes and tucked them into his bag. He walked to the suite door, opened it and paused to look back at his uncle. Kiefer glared at him. "What? If you have something to say, Linden, say it. I still have to deal with Sedgewyck, and bathe, and I don't want to waste any more time than I have to!"

Linden opened his mouth and paused; he'd tried…at least he'd tried. He shook his head. "Nothing, uncle…it's nothing. I'll go and find Heathers." He left the suite, closing the door silently behind him.

○

Elliott and Giselle's Suite
8:35pm

Aquilleia sat on the settee and ran a gentle hand across Veronique's silky ears; the migraine that had arrived earlier had obviously been a warning of the sheer number of deaths that had been approaching. She sighed and rubbed her eyes; she had never received so many visions in such a short space of time…she was exhausted!

As she smoothed Veronique's fur, her hand paused; a tremor began in the base of her spine as a series of blindingly fast images appeared in her mind's eye; a falling glass, darkness, and billowing eau de Nil silk.

Veronique sat up and whined as Aquilleia's eyes rolled back in her head and she slumped into the corner of the settee.

The door to the suite opened and Giselle walked in. She gave a horrified gasp as she saw the unconscious Aquilleia and hurried to her side. Aquilleia's eyes fluttered as Giselle gently patted at her face. "Aquilleia? Aquilleia! Can you hear me?"

Aquilleia pressed her hand against her forehead and moaned softly. "There has been another! Another of the family has been killed."

○

Heather and Sedgewyck's Suite
8:35pm

Kiefer dragged his trunk to the suite Heathers shared with Sedgewyck and entered the rooms without knocking. He stopped on the threshold at the unexpected sight of the silent butler standing not three feet from him. Frowning, Kiefer closed the door, looked into Sedgewyck's pale eyes, and waved his hand in front of the butler's face; as ever, no one appeared to be in! He gave a bark of humourless laughter; if his actions in hiring another to harvest the final offering had caused this separation of Sedgewyck's body and spirit, it was perhaps a good thing that Budaiwi and his associates had failed in killing Evelyn. If his father had returned in such a state, his mother would never have forgiven him, and her wrath, though never inflicted on him in the past, was more than strong enough to override whatever motherly instincts she had. Kiefer shuddered; he had, perhaps, been quite lucky there!

He bent forward and bellowed. "Sedgewyck! It's time to leave." he looked at the unresponsive butler and threw his hands in the air. "Fine! Have it your way! We're leaving. You can stay here, and good bloody riddance to you!"

Kiefer turned, still spitting words under his breath as he collected his trunk and left the room, slamming the door behind him. As the harsh sound faded, Sedgewyck's rheumy blue eyes flickered.

○

Evelyn and André's Suite
8:38pm

Kiefer paused outside Evelyn's suite and looked up and down the gas lit corridor; he could neither see, nor hear any approaching footfalls. Satisfied, he pushed the door open and entered the dark room. Pausing to turn up the gaslight, he closed the door and turned to look at the prone, nightgown-clad figure on the bed. An unpleasant smile played about his lips as he approached the sleeping Evelyn.

He placed the trunk containing the heads next to the bed, placed his hands on either side of Evelyn's shoulders, leant forward, and breathed in deeply as he looked at Evelyns restful face; he had hidden it well, but it had been a source of great personal irritation that André had been chosen to marry Evelyn when he had wanted her for himself. Even after he had expressed his desires in no uncertain terms to his mother, she had still taken André's side; pointing out that the last time Kiefer had married a sacrifice, she had died several weeks before the final offering was due to take place; an early death that had been due, no doubt, to his tender ministrations. He had never been allowed to forget that he had very nearly ruined Margaux's resurrection. They had managed to find an emergency replacement by sending Vincenzo to hover around a convent school wearing his Priest's weeds; one of the younger girls had felt safe around a kindly man of the cloth;

a terrible mistake in one so young, but her innocent naïveté had certainly benefited Margaux!

Kiefer grinned at the memory before turning his attention back to the delectable sight before him; such a shame there was not enough time for him to properly enjoy his sister-in-law's company before the ritual. His eyes filled with an opaque, pink-tinged whiteness as he stroked a finger down Evelyn's pale cheek. "Evelyn…you will listen to my voice. You will do as I tell you, without question. When you awaken, you will stand and walk with me, quietly, and without argument. You will obey me. Now, awaken!"

As Evelyn's eyes fluttered open, Kiefer grinned. "Good morning, my dear sister-in-law! Now—" He stopped dead as Evelyn's eyes widened in horror as she saw him. She pushed herself across to the far side of the bed and pulled one of the pillows protectively across her breasts. "Kiefer! What are you doing? Get out of my room!" She stood, still clutching the pillow like a shield as she stared at him from the other side of the bed; her eyes wide in fright. "Where's André?"

Kiefer's eyes narrowed; he'd not expected this. Due to her being under André's will, she should have been far more malleable and willing to acquiesce to his orders…obviously the power of André's gift had begun to fade after his death.

He took out his pocket watch and scowled; there was not enough time to put her back into her trance using *his* voice rather than André's. Kiefer paused and ran through a few different scenarios in his head…none of which ended well for Evelyn, but there was only one that meant she would be in the ritual chamber with them as his mother had requested. He snapped his watch shut and smiled viciously at Evelyn. "I'd like to introduce you to my father, Evelyn…but I'm afraid that you won't live long enough to witness his resurrection!"

With frightening speed, he lunged across the bed and savagely backhanded Evelyn across the face; the force of the blow slamming her against the wall, and rendering her unconscious. As she crumpled to the floor, Kiefer stood over her and slapped her face; an expression of sadistic enjoyment on his face as he brought her back to the edge of consciousness. "No sleep for you, bitch! It's not going to be that easy." He shook her violently. "Come on, Evelyn. Your evening isn't over yet, my dear sister-in-law! You need to be awake for what happens next!" He picked her up, casually threw her over his shoulder, collected his trunk, and left the suite.

○

Margaux's Suite
8:42pm

Elliott looked at Thorne. "I really wish that Aquilleia was wrong on the odd occasion!"

They turned as Aquilleia and Giselle entered the room. Aquilleia gave a small laugh. "So does Aquilleia!"

Thorne hurried to his wife's side and guided her to the dressing table chair. Kneeling beside her, he pressed a gentle kiss on the palm of her hand.

At the sound of a faint cough, they all turned as Carandini Bey appeared in the doorway. Elliott looked at him with a raised eyebrow. "Yes, Mr Bey?"

Bey swallowed hard as he tried to keep his mind averted from the sight he had just witnessed in the meat locker.

"I regret to inform you..." He paused, swallowed again, and shook his head. "The bodies in the second meat locker... someone has desecrated them!"

Elliott looked at him sharply. "Desecrated? How?"

"They've been beheaded! And one of them...Camillia Devereaux, I believe, has been quite horribly mutilated! One of the human kitchen servants discovered the...removals.

She screamed so loudly that I was afraid she would rouse the guests at dinner!"

Thorne pursed his lips. "Things are definitely escalating."

Darling looked at his brother with a raised eyebrow. "Not known for overstating things, are you, Brother?" He turned to Carandini. "Place a Simulandro guard on the door to the meat locker; no one is allowed in or out without our permission. Find the rest of the family and bring them to this suite immediately. Please also send a Simulandro to replace Maxwell at the hammam, so that he can join us."

Carandini nodded; his face ashen as he left the room. Thorne closed the door behind him and turned back to the others. "Barrett Cushing is quite determined to pick off the family one by one. What a bloody mess!" he looked at Elliott and gestured to the bed. "Another card. What symbol does this one have on it?"

Elliott reached out and turned the card over. "Three black circles." He looked at Aquilleia. "Where would that fit in with the plagues of Egypt?"

Aquilleia looked at the card thoughtfully. "Three days of darkness. The penultimate plague."

Thorne looked up. "That would suggest that there have been more deaths than we thought…or, perhaps, the killer has taken those he wanted and has left the rest?""

As Aquilleia was about to answer, Carandini reappeared in the doorway. "I have spoken with the Simulandro stewards; they can communicate with each other far faster than I can. They report that Mrs Marguerite Devereaux's room is empty — as are the rooms of her son, Kiefer Devereaux, her daughter-in-law, Evelyn Briar-Devereaux, and her grandson, Mr Linden Devereaux." He frowned. "Strangely though, their butler, Sedgewyck is still in his room, and Mr Julius van Sloan's valet, Heathers, was just seen walking through the reception and towards the covered terrace by the Kiosk of

Trajan. Your message has been sent to Maxwell, Mr Caine; he will arrive shortly."

Elliott nodded. "Thank you, Mr Bey."

As Carandini closed the door behind him, Thorne turned back to his wife with a quizzical look. "You were going to say something about my suggestion that perhaps the killer has killed more than we know, or has taken those he wanted and will leave the rest?"

Aquilleia sighed. "I've seen all the deaths that have occurred. Most of the family are dead. As far as I can see and hear, only Marguerite, Linden and Kiefer remain of the blood family." She looked at Elliott. "I can also confirm that Evelyn is still very much alive."

Elliott nodded; an expression of great relief on his face. "Thank you." He looked at Thorne. "We need to find the rest of the family."

Thorne raised an eyebrow. "Well, bearing in mind we don't know where they are, that might be a tad tricky!"

Darling grimaced. "Indeed." He paused. "Sedgewyck is the weakest link in the family's chain." He looked at Aquilleia. "I understand that you're weary from your visions, but would you interview him? He doesn't seem threatening. In fact, he appears to be quite fragile."

Aquilleia looked at Giselle and nodded. "I think a light discussion with a very elderly gentleman is all that I'm capable of right now."

Giselle nodded. "We'll take Veronique and Ailuros with us."

Darling blinked. "Ailuros?"

Giselle shrugged winsomely. "It was the most suitable name I could think of for a pretty black kitten. It's one of the many names of the Egyptian Goddess, Bast, also known as 'the Devouring Lady'. Giselle looked rueful. "Quite suitable considering all the food she eats!" She nodded at her husband as she and Aquilleia left the room.

As the door closed, Elliott's face darkened. "I don't like this at all!" He gripped the handle of his sword stick and hurried to the French door that led to the covered terrace.

Thorne frowned. "Do you think the surviving members of the family are trying to escape?

Elliott opened the door and paused. "No, Thorne — I am very much afraid that there is about to be another murder! The murder the Devereaux family had planned since the beginning of their current trail of death and mayhem; the murder of my mother!"

○

Sedgewyck and Heathers' Suite
8:50pm

Giselle knocked on the door to the rooms that were shared by the family's manservants and called out. "Sedgewyck? It's Giselle Du'Lac and Madame Aquilleia...may we come in?"

After a long period of silence, the two women looked at each other; an unspoken agreement passed between them, and Giselle turned the door handle. As the door swung open, they entered the room and stopped at the sight of the room's sole occupant. Sedgewyck was still standing where Kiefer had left him; his arms hanging loosely at his sides and his head bent so far forwards that his chin was resting on his chest.

Veronique padded up to the motionless butler, prodded at his pale hand with her nose, and whined. She turned to look at her mistress, then back at the servant.

Giselle walked to the butler's side and peered up into Sedgewyck's face; the butler's eyes were open, but blank. She passed her hand across his eyes, but received no response. She shook her head. "I think we should leave—" She turned to Aquilleia and broke off as she saw the sudden expression of horror on her friend's face. "What is it? Aquilleia...what is wrong?"

Aquilleia swallowed, silver lights swirling in her lavender eyes. "Heathers and Sedgewyck! I know now why I couldn't see them..." She turned wide eyes on Giselle and gestured at the silent servant. "I can't see them because they're both already dead!"

Giselle's eyebrows shot up. "Dead?" She eyed the immobile butler. "He's a touch slow, but he still looks in remarkable health for a dead man. Dead in what sense?"

Aquilleia reached out a trembling hand and touched Sedgewyck's face, then recoiled. "He was offered the gift of long life for his eternal servitude to the family. He is a revenant...one who died, and was returned. He exists solely to serve them."

Giselle again waved her hand across the butler's unseeing eyes. "What of Heathers? Is he the same?"

Aquilleia shook her head. "I can't see what he is...not yet. All I know is that he too is dead. I'll try to see more."

There was a sudden crash as the door was flung open and a ball of spinning white and blue light flew in, and then halted, revolving in mid-air between the two women. A voice, hollow and faint as though it came from many miles away, spoke. "They promised me immortality. It was gifted many times, but on the last occasion, the gift failed." Flashes of red appeared on the ball's swirling edges. "I will help you destroy the family — on one condition."

Giselle looked at the ball of energy with a guarded expression. "Name your price."

The glowing orb filled with angry, seething light. "Free me from my chains."

Aquilleia looked from the ball of light to the silent body of the butler. "You want us to kill you?"

The ball of energy slowed in its spinning. "I am already dead! I want you to free me from the corpse that I am bound to."

Giselle turned to the butler's physical form. "You agree to help us, and go against the family you have served?"

The light moved in a way that Giselle recognised as a nod. "Yes."

Aquilleia looked at it with a quizzical expression. "May I ask why?"

The glowing ball that was the last remnants of Sedgewyck's consciousness pulsed. "They say that no man is a hero to his valet — I cannot speak for Heathers, but I can confirm that this is very true for his butler! I have witnessed enough evil to last many lifetimes; lifetimes I have lived through. I willfully — nay, eagerly — accepted that others, even innocents, would die to give me a life that was not mine to live. I realise now how far my greed allowed me to fall. I must be released from the chains that bind me to this earth, and allowed to face my fate in the realm beyond."

Giselle looked up the swirling light and gave a sharp nod. "Agreed." She frowned. "If, as my friend say, Heathers isn't the same as you, then what is he?"

The ball of energy swelled slightly, then diminished. "He is…different."

Giselle's eyes narrowed. "How?"

Faint yellow flashes appeared at the outer edges of the ball. "When last he was resurrected, something occurred… something far worse than what happened to me—"

Giselle turned as Aquilleia let out a sharp hissing sound. She stepped back at the sight of the swirls of silver light that filled Aquilleia's eyes. "What is it? What can you see?"

"Heathers isn't a revenant, Giselle, he is a lich! A lich! Thorne, Elliott, and Darling are in terrible danger!"

The two women left the room at a run and raced down the corridor, followed by Veronique, a spinning ball of light, and the slow, shambling figure of Sedgewyck's physical form.

○

Entrance Hall
8:50pm

Elliott, Thorne, Darling, and Maxwell stepped out of the front door and paused under the portico to look at the covered walkways that spread out from the entrance hall to all four corners of the island. As they stood and scanned the area, Maxwell spotted Heathers. The dissipating storm was still casting swirls of sand beyond the glass panels of the covered terrace, but the gas lamps within the walkways afforded enough light to show the distant form of the valet on the walkway that ran alongside the lone building and towards the door that led to the jetty.

Maxwell coughed slightly and addressed Elliott. "Sir?"

Elliott turned. "Yes, Maxwell?"

The Simulandro gestured at the rapidly moving figure. "I believe that is Mr Heathers, Sir."

Elliott nodded. "Thank you, Maxwell." He raised his voice above the wind and called out. "Heathers? We need to talk with you."

The distant figure turned. Heather stared at Elliot silently before turning away and disappearing past the temple.

Thorne raised one eyebrow. "Well…dismissed thus!"

Elliott nodded grimly. "After him."

They hurried down the pathway; Darling and Elliott in front, and Maxwell bringing up the rear with Thorne. As they made their way towards the stone structure, the Simulandro looked at Thorne. "I understand that my contract with the hotel has been terminated, and that I have been transferred to Mr Caine's household, Sir."

Thorne nodded as they reached the edge of the Kiosk of Trajan. "Yes." He looked at the Simulandro. "They were going to terminate you completely."

Maxwell smiled faintly as he gestured to the still exposed mechanics of his face. "Because I am damaged?"

Thorne gave a short bark of laughter; his eyes turned to his brother. "Aren't we all?"

Maxwell nodded; a frown on his pale face. "There is something that I need to mention, Sir…"

Thorne looked at him as they walked. "Farasha?"

Maxwell blinked. "Yes, Sir."

Thorne nodded. "Carandini Bey mentioned that the two of you are close. He's agreed to terminate her contract and transfer her with you. Don't worry, Maxwell…you'll be together."

Maxwell took a deep breath; an expression of relief crossed his face before rapidly disappearing. "Thank you, Sir; that was what I wanted to know." He gestured at the distant valet. "Now, Sir…before we catch up with the gentleman, is there anything that I need to know?"

Thorne took his revolver from his pocket and checked the chamber. "Yes, Maxwell…actually there is quite a great deal that you need to know—"

Thorne's explanation was suddenly cut short as they rounded the corner of the temple and came face to face with Heathers. The stony-faced valet lunged at Darling and delivered a vicious kidney punch that sent him sprawling. Turning on Elliott, he swung a massive blow that struck Elliott across the back of his head, knocking him to the ground. As Thorne ran to Elliott's side, Heathers grasped him by his lapels and launched him through the air and into the side of the temple. Thorne landed at the feet of the stunned Simulandro who lent towards him and enquired. "May I assist you, Sir?"

Thorne took a deep breath. "Yes, Maxwell, you may!"

Maxwell helped him stand and smoothed his lapels. "There we are, Sir…good as new."

"Thank you, Maxwell."

Thorne turned to look at the unconscious Elliott, and Darling who was still sprawled on the ground, clutching his ribs as, with an evil grin, Heathers turned his back on the injured men, and began to walk towards Thorne and Maxwell; his gait becoming faster with every step.

Darling sat up, and clutched at his ribs with a groan of pain. He stared at the figure that was now speeding towards his brother; he was too far away to help! He bellowed at the Simulandro. "Don't just stand there, man! Hit him!" Maxwell looked at Darling with a concerned expression and shook his head. "I can't harm a human, Sir…it goes against my instructions!"

Darling stared at the Simulandro and swore. He looked at Thorne, closed his eyes and concentrated; his outline seemed to blur as, behind Thorne and Maxwell, in the shadows of the temple, a figure — a perfect, mirror image of Darling — suddenly appeared and stepped out of the dark space As Heathers reached Thorne, Darling's double pushed Thorne out of the way; taking the massive blow that had been meant for his brother. He grunted in pain as he threw the valet against the wall of the temple. Heathers, his eyes now filled with a burning red light snarled at him; his thin lips peeling back from his teeth as he pushed himself upright and shrugged off the blow. Darling's double grinned at him and insolently crooked his finger at the valet. Heathers' eye's narrowed in rage; he turned away from

Thorne, Elliott, and Maxwell, began to walk towards the grinning double.

Maxwell stared at Darling and his double. "You're not human…are you, Sir?"

Darling pressed his hand against his ribs and winced. "No, Maxwell…I am not!"

Maxwell gestured at the advancing Heathers. "I take it that the gentleman with abnormal strength and glowing red eyes is not human either?"

Darling nodded painfully. "You are quite correct."

Maxwell nodded thoughtfully. "So…my instructions would not apply to him?"

Thorne helped his brother stand. "No, Maxwell…they would not."

Maxwell nodded slowly. "Thank you, Sir."

The Simulandro suddenly launched himself through the air. Sailing over the double's head, he landed on Heathers' chest, both hands gripping the valet's lapels. As Heathers fell backwards, Maxwell grasped his right arm and with almost no effort, ripped it free from Heathers' torso. The Simulandro stepped back and looked at Heathers, who looked at him and the bloodless limb with interest before backhanding Maxwell across the face. Heathers watching the stunned Simulandro fall backwards before once again turning back to the groggy but now conscious Elliott, Thorne, Darling, and the still grinning double.

The men turned as a sharp retort exploded across the covered walkway as Veronique, Aquilleia and Giselle, her pearl-handled revolver pointing dead at the centre of Heathers chest, suddenly appeared at a run. Elliott's dazed eyes widened as he saw a ball of red light pulsing violently above his wife's head. Giselle looked at him and pointed at the energy. "It's Sedgewyck…he's promised to help us." She gestured at Heathers. "He's a lich!"

Elliott looked at Heathers, stood, and slowly backed away, as the valet pressed his broad, flat fingers against the dull brown patch that had appeared in the middle of his chest. He looked up at Giselle and hissed before disappearing in a flurry of fur and rage as Veronique leapt at him. The enraged battle hound changing into Xenocyon as she soared through the air and smashed into the undead valet; her teeth and talons ripping into undead, bloodless flesh as she savaged the raging lich. As her teeth snapped inches away from his throat, Heathers caught Xenocyon by the scruff of her neck and threw her against the stone wall. Rendered unconscious by the violent impact, she began to change back into Veronique. At the sight of her silent form sliding down the wall, Thorne let out a roar of rage and ran at the valet. Heathers' smile widened as he easily deflected Thorne's blows, wrapped the fingers of his left hand around Thorne's throat, and almost casually began to squeeze.

Aquilleia ran towards her husband; ripping her revolver from her reticule as Thorne grasped at the fingers crushing his trachea. Elliott, Maxwell, Darling, and his double reached them first; the men raining blows down on the lich. Heathers shook the now purple Thorne and looked at them through crimson eyes; his face twisted suddenly as an ugly wet sound came from his throat. Giselle stepped back in revulsion as she realised that he was laughing.

Giselle dropped her reticule to the ground and again raised her revolver. As the dainty pouch landed heavily, the small black kitten, roused violently from her sleep, stalked out of her perfumed bower in irritation and gazed at the scene before her with feline insolence. As his red eyes alighted on the kitten, a different sound altogether came from Heathers' throat as he released Thorne and raised his hands to try and block the young cat from his sight. The kitten stared at the lich; deep in her mind a memory stirred…a memory of the old days.

Covering the distance between them in bewildering speed, Ailuros launched herself at the cringing lich. As the kitten's claws dug deeply into the flesh of Heathers' face, the valet let out an inhuman screech of pain. Ailuros leapt gracefully away from the screaming servant and padded back to the reticule, where she sat and began to groom her paws. She looked at Heathers before turning away with a disdainful sniff, as Heathers began to rot.

Time that was not his to have rapidly caught up with the screaming lich as bloodless flesh and sinews slid from his bones like pieces of brittle driftwood, and crumbled to dust around him.

In the sudden stillness that followed, the kitten leapt gracefully onto Giselle's shoulders and began to purr. Giselle ran a gentle hand across the smooth, black fur. "Well done, Ailuros, oh, very well done!"

As they stood and stared at the small pile of dust, a soft shuffling sound came from the temple. They turned as the body of Sedgewyck appeared and made its way slowly towards them.

The ball of energy moved to float above the butler's head and pulsed. "Remember your promise?"

Giselle nodded sadly. "I remember."

"Then keep it; kill my physical form, and release me."

Giselle raised her revolver and pointed it at Sedgewyck's chest. "I'm so sorry."

"You have no need to be. I am the one who is sorry. I stole life. I give mine to you freely."

Giselle looked at the ball of energy. "Are you ready?"

The energy pulsed. "I have been ready for many years."

Giselle closed her eyes; opening them she looked into Sedgewyck's pale face and pulled the trigger. The butler fell backward, his body landing almost without a sound. Giselle knelt next to him as the ball of energy floated above; soft shades of blue, purple, and white began to appear at the edges as his life energy began to fade. Sedgewyck's voice came again, this time from his physical form as he whispered softly. "Thank you."

Giselle sat back on her heels, tears streaming down her face, as Elliott took the revolver from her and held her tightly.

Thorne slowly pushed himself up with a hoarse groan. "Is everyone all right?" Aquilleia flung her arms around him as Veronique got to her feet and staggered to his side. As Thorne rubbed his bruised throat. Darling nodded at his double who walked up to him, turned, and took one step backwards; his body sinking into Darling's.

Darling looked at his brother and took a deep breath. "This may not be the right time, Thorne…but then, I don't think that any time would be! There's something I need to tell you, something that I fear will make you hate me more than you already do, but I must tell you." Darling took a deep breath and winced as his cracked ribs expressed their outrage. "It's about our father…and the night he died."

Thorne stilled. "Go on."

Darling shifted slightly. "That night…when you found me sitting next to his body…I told you that I had allowed him the gentleman's way out; that he'd killed himself."

Thorne nodded slowly. "Yes."

Darling shook his head; his eyes filled with tears. "He didn't kill himself, brother…*I* killed him."

Thorne's eyes widened in shock. He stared at his brother as Darling continued; the words pouring out of him in a torrent. "I found him that night. He was elated, in a state of utter euphoria about what he'd done…laughing about his 'offering' to Filicidae. I asked him what he meant…that was when he told me that he'd willingly murdered our mother and presented her blood to the abomination to garner its approval."

Aquilleia gently placed her hand on Thorne's shoulder, her face deathly pale as Darling continued. "The horror I felt was beyond anything I've felt before or since…even the times that he hurt us paled into nothing as I listened to him bragging about what he'd done to Mother. I told him he had to face justice for his crimes. He laughed! He was jubilant that he would be given the opportunity to brag about his actions before the King. He went into the bathroom to wash and change; as I sat and waited for him, I was numb, utterly numbed by what he'd done…" Darling's voice trailed off. He looked at Thorne with a haunted expression. "I snapped. I entered the room…he was lying in the bath." Darling's face twisted at the memory. "He was laughing…he was so proud – proud of murdering our mother!" Darling took a deep breath. "His feet were resting on the edge of the bathtub…I grasped his ankles and pulled. He sank under the water…and I held his feet until he stopped moving."

Silence descended around the group, broken only by the soft sound of Aquilleia's sobbing as they listened to Darling's confession.

Darling raised his head, desperately trying not to look at Thorne as he whispered. "Please don't hate me, brother…"

Thorne, his face covered in tears, enveloped his brother in a crushing embrace. "I don't hate you…you did the right thing, the only thing."

Darling wiped his face with a shaking hand. "I wish I had told you sooner…but I couldn't find the courage."

As Thorne, Darling, and Aquilleia sat in silence, Giselle wiped her eyes and took her husband's hand. "Thank the Gods it's over."

Elliott shook his head; a deeply worried expression on his

face. "It isn't over yet." As the others looked at him, Elliott looked at them. "Where are Marguerite, Kiefer, and Linden? And, rather more concerning to me…where are my mother and father?"

◯

The Chamber of Resurrection
9:05pm

Marguerite raised the lantern above her head and glanced back at her son as they made their way down the stone passageway towards the hidden chamber. Kiefer caught his mother's expression and grinned viciously as he dragged his ever-present trunk behind him with one hand, while also keeping a firm grip on the stunned Evelyn, who was slung, like a sack, over his shoulder. Evelyn's face was deathly pale except for the huge bruise that had started to form around her left eye and cheek where Kiefer had hit her; the dark red contusion obvious on her almost translucent skin.

Kiefer's smile widened; in a few short moments, and one fell swoop, they would finally be reunited with their patriarch, and be rid of a prissy and unwanted interloper. Kiefer shook his head; although it had served them well, the family's strategy of marrying the final offering to guarantee their purity had very nearly destroyed them. In the future, when they needed a virginal sacrifice, simply targeting an innocent child, rather than choosing an adult, and utilising marriage as a guarantee, would be a far safer option!

Entering the ritual room, Marguerite placed the reticule containing Reynaud's skull and the large carpet bag beside the door. Turning, her gaze fell on the locked trunk containing the host body parts for Reynaud's resurrection, and a smile appeared on her alabaster face; soon, soon it would all be over, and Reynaud would be back by her side.

As she let out a relieved sigh, her gaze moved to the altar and her smile froze; there, in the space meant for Evelyn, lay a shrouded figure, tightly wrapped from toe to crown in eau de Nil silk. Across the figure's middle, the shimmering blue-green material was stained an ugly red, while at the feet of the figure, sat four canopic jars, each bearing the image of one of the four sons of Horus; human, jackal, baboon, and falcon. Rivulets of deep crimson streaked the sides of the overflowing jars; the uncontained gore surrounding each of the stone urns with sticky, glassy, dark red pools.

Marguerite stared at the bloody figure before slowly raising the lantern above her head, dread flooding her senses as she approached the still form.

As he looked at the bloodied silk, Kiefer suddenly remembered the missing curtains in Margaux's suite. He sat the trunk next to his mother's reticule and stared, fascinated, as she reached a trembling hand towards the covered face and slowly began to unwrap the silken bandages.

As the material fell away, Marguerite gave a sudden sob. "It's Margaux!"

Kiefer dropped Evelyn unceremoniously to the floor, walked to his mother's side, and looked down at his sister's face; Margaux's pale blue eyes stared back at him sightlessly as he curled his lip. "Well...at least we know where she is. We can collect her head and take her with us after we've resurrected Father." He lifted his sister's body from the altar, taking care not to get any of her blood on his waistcoat. Positioning her next to the trunk, he removed the canopic jars and placed them by her side. Lifting Evelyn, he replaced his sister's corpse with the living body of their final offering. He looked at his mother with an expectant expression. "Mother...shall we begin?"

Marguerite nodded and wiped her eyes. She stood by his side, as, on the altar, Evelyn moaned softly. As she opened her eyes, confusion appeared on her face as she tried to move and realised that her hands were tied. Feeling the throbbing pain in her face, she pressed her hands to her injured cheek, and winced. She froze as she saw Kiefer grinning down at her.

"Hello again, precious. I suggest that you don't try to get too comfortable…you won't be here for very much longer!" He stepped back and paused. He opened his pocket watch and looked at his mother with a frown. "I wonder where Linden is? I distinctly told him to be here."

Marguerite smiled unpleasantly at the terrified young woman on the altar; her eyes glittering with tears and visceral hate as she shook her head. "It's of no matter. After his words to you challenging how our family have ruled the humans for millennia, he's nothing more than a traitor!" She waved her hand at the terrified Evelyn who was trying desperately to undo the rope that bound her hands. "We will see to the return of your father, and then we shall deal with those who have turned against us." She removed the sacred knife from her robe and held it before her. "Let the resurrection of your Father, Caeruleum; the beloved son of Nekroshema, begin!"

Kiefer bowed to his mother and walked towards the trunk. He stood beside the ornate sealed box containing the body parts that would carry his father through his next incarnation and waited for his mother's sign.

She raised the knife high above her head. "Pert em hru!"

Kiefer echoed his mother: "Pert em hru!"

A shiver started at the base of Evelyn's back and slowly crawled up her spine. She paused in her attempts to free herself from her fetters. The sensation climbed to the nape of her neck and set her hair on end as the chamber was enveloped in a thick, unnatural silence. She looked at Marguerite, whose eyes had become entirely white. Evelyn's own eyes widened in fear as she looked at Kiefer, whose usually dark-blue eyes now mirrored his mother's.

Marguerite felt the rising energy fill the room. She smiled and held out an ornate key to Kiefer. "Unlock the trunk."

Kiefer turned to the trunk with a smile; finally! As he lent to open it, he paused; a sudden, deeply disturbing thought had occurred to him. He turned back to his mother with a frown. "Mother?"

Marguerite stared at him; her dark brows lowering over her eyes as she hissed. "What?"

Kiefer gestured towards his sister's corpse. "How did Margaux's killer get her body into the ritual chamber?"

Marguerite stared at him; an expression of horrified understanding appeared on her face as she turned to look at Margaux's body. "They must have used Margaux's blood to open the door..." Her voice trailed off as Kiefer whispered. "So, where are they now?"

As the two stared at each other in sudden fear, Evelyn caught a movement out of the corner of her eye as a shadowy form darted across the wall of the chamber. The strange outline seemed to shimmer as it moved along the wall; blurring and coalescing, before it stilled, and leapt clear, as the winged form of Masquelyne suddenly appeared in mid-air and landed into the midst of the chamber's stunned occupants.

Masquelyne caught Kiefer by the throat and slammed his forehead into the necromancer's face. Kiefer's nose disappeared in a bloody explosion as Masquelyne continued his raging onslaught by raining multiple blows at Kiefer's injured head. The dumbfounded necromancer tried desperately to fight back as Masquelyne slapped away his attempts, grasped him by his lapels and threw him violently across the room. Kiefer hit the far wall and lay stunned before he hurriedly pushed himself to his feet and wiped the back of his hand across his bloody nose. Masquelyne walked around the altar and looked down at Evelyn; a muscle twitched in his jaw as he took in the massive bruise that covered the left side of her face. "Calliandra...what have they done to you?"

Evelyn mutely shook her head as he removed a jewelled blade from his pocket and cut the ropes binding her wrists. Suddenly, the events of the last few minutes proved too much for her, as her eyes rolled back in her head and she slumped across the altar.

Masquelyne pressed his fingers to Evelyn's throat. Relieved to find a strong pulse, he turned to Kiefer and Marguerite and smiled, his long canines flashing in the flickering light of the lantern. "Good evening. Please, allow me to introduce myself. My name is Gabriel Masquelyne, I am an immortal, and you, Kiefer and Marguerite Devereaux, are both guilty of the murder of, amongst others, my wife's father."

Kiefer sneered. "Wife? we don't know your wife...and how dare you attempt to__" He stopped as Masquelyne laughed softly. "You cannot escape your crimes, Devereaux." He gestured to Evelyn. "Her true name is Calliandra, and she is my wife. I have searched for her for many, many years... and now, if she will have me, I will take her home."

Marguerite's mouth dropped open. "How dare you! She's André's wife."

Masquelyne raised an eyebrow. "I think you mean that she is your son's widow." He smiled at her gasp. "Evelyn and I were married many lifetimes ago, and no one, especially not a family of degenerate necromancers, will come between us!"

Kiefer's face twisted into a snarl, his eyes filling with white light as he pulled a wickedly sharp blade from his belt.

"Mother! Kill her and resurrect Father; I'll deal with this bloody human!"

Masquelyne's smile widened. "I am no human, whelp! I have lived longer than you — longer even than your father Reynaud. Far back in time, before he was known as Caeruleum…before he became the origin for the myth of Osiris…when he was merely Nekroshema's youngest and most spoilt son." Marguerite gasped as Masquelyne continued. "Oh yes; I know who, and more importantly *what* you are — a family which resurrects itself by murder. But your bloody reign is over!"

Placing the jewelled blade; the same knife he had taken from the corpse of Budaiwi, on the altar next to Evelyn, Masquelyne turned back to Kiefer and crooked his finger at the raging necromancer. "Come along, brat…I don't have all day!"

Marguerite backed away as Kiefer let out a bellow of rage and charged at Masquelyne; blinding white light flashing from his eyes as he gripped Masquelyne's throat and attempted to throw him across the room. As he braced himself to lift, he stopped dead; it was like trying to lift a mountain! He stared in horror at the lazy smile that curled across Masquelyne's face and exposed the amused Other's overlong canines as Masquelyne grasped Kiefer by the throat and launched him into the air. Kiefer let out a strangled shriek as he suddenly found himself, once again, sailing through the air before landing, flat on his back, several feet away. Kiefer sat up and shook his head. He looked at Masquelyne with a horror-struck expression as he realised that the winged man was too strong for him.

On the other side of the room, Marguerite had also suffered the same realisation. She picked up her reticule and the bag of skulls, pulled a plain blade from within her robe, and with a shaking hand managed to prick one of her fingers. She hurried to the far side of the room where she pressed the bloody finger against one of the glyphs on the wall. As a secret passage opened, she turned back to face her son; her eyes were full of tears and rage as she screamed. "Kill him! Kill him, Kiefer…I shall resurrect you!"

Kiefer mouth dropped open in shock as the secret panel closed behind his mother's rapidly disappearing form. His eyes darted back to Masquelyne whose grin widened as he shook his head sighed. "Maternal abandonment…it certainly explains a great deal about your family's behaviour!" He ducked as Kiefer threw one of the canopic jars at him. As the stone jar smashed against the wall behind him, Masquelyne looked at the spilt contents with a grimace. "We'll…when the gentleman who killed your sister decided to move against your family, he certainly dedicated himself to the role!" He turned back to Kiefer. "Now…where were we?" He ducked again as another of the canopic jars was thrown towards him. He wagged his finger at the rattled necromancer. "Now, now, Kiefer…this is becoming quite unseemly! How would the sister you abandoned to the Spanish Inquisition feel about her entrails being thrown about like confetti?"

Kiefer gaped at him. "How do you know…" He stopped as Masquelyne laughed softly. "I am an Other…I am also one of the omniscient beings, Kiefer." The necromancer's eyes widened in shock; the omniscient beings were both a part of, yet separate from, immortals. He began to inch backwards as Masquelyne walked steadily towards him. "I know many things about you and your family, boy. I know what you allowed the Inquisition to do to your sister, I know about your abuse of Miss March…" A muscle ticked in his jaw as he continued. "I also know that you murdered Calliandra's father, and disposed of his body in Abney Park Cemetery. Your family have committed crimes beyond anything a mere human could effectuate, and I, and my accidental partner in crime, find ourselves in the rather enjoyable position of being the ones who will finally bring to an end to your family's soulless, barbarous, and bastardised form of existence!"

A soft voice came from the altar. "He murdered my father?"

Masquelyne turned to look at Evelyn who had pushed herself into a sitting position on the stone plinth. He nodded. "Yes. Kiefer was the one who made the killing blow. I found your father as he was dying. He told me what had been done to him, and by whom. I promised him that I would protect you from harm…" Masquelyne looked at Evelyn; his yellow eyes swirling with golden lights. "Just as I made you that promise when we were married so many years ago."

Evelyn stared at Masquelyne. As she opened her mouth to respond, her eyes widened; she flung out her hand in warning as she let out a piercing scream "No!"

Masquelyne spun back to face Kiefer as the enraged necromancer lashed out and delivered a massive punch to the side of Masquelyne's head. Masquelyne fell to one knee as Kiefer rained blow after blow down on his head and neck, leaving Masquelyne bloodied. Kiefer's eyes burned with a blinding white light; a vicious, rictus grin appeared on his face as he focussed his strength and raised his clenched fist one last time.

As the final blow descended, he rocked on his feet as Evelyn launched herself at him. He turned and caught her by the wrist, laughing at her sharp cry of pain. His laugh stopped abruptly as Evelyn, her pale face filled with hate, raised her other hand high and plunged the Blade of Nekroshema directly into his heart.

An unnatural silence descended as Kiefer stared, dumbstruck, at the jewelled blade embedded in his chest. He looked at Evelyn, her clear grey eyes stared into his as she leant towards him and hissed. "For my father!"

As the jewels in the hilt began to pulse and shimmer with light, panicked realisation filled Kiefer's face. He staggered backwards as the waters that surrounded the altar began to writhe and dance; long, thin tendrils of blue-green water rose from the pool and reached towards him like spindly tentacles. Kiefer screamed impotently as he wrenched the blade from his heart; but it was too late. The power of the blade had already begun to work its way through his body. Deep, bleeding wounds began to appear across his neck where his skull had been repeatedly placed against the torsos of those who had died to give him resurrection.

Kiefer's shrill screams echoed within the enclosed chamber as the eons of life that he had stolen from others began to flee from flesh and bones that were not his. His clothes became saturated in blood as the energy that crafted the joins between the stolen limbs failed, and his body began to separate. The thin, bloody gashes appearing across his arms and legs repeatedly lacerating his skin as the body parts rebelled finally against their servitude to the creature that had taken them and revelled in them as living trophies of his family's crimes.

Masquelyne stood and reached out to Evelyn, who moved to his side in silence. They watched in fascinated revulsion as Kiefer's dying screams became ugly, wet gurgles, that suddenly ceased as the wound between his head and neck ripped wider, severing his vocal cords. As the energy tore through the last shred of skin, Kiefer's head fell to the floor with a dull thud.

Masquelyne took a deep breath; it was done! He had kept his word to his partner in crime, and his own plans were complete. It was time for them to go home. He turned to look at Evelyn and whispered, "Calliandra!"

Evelyn's grey eyes widened — she knew that name! She gazed at the man with golden eyes as she reached out and touched his face. "I know you..." She shook her head. "I remember you; you were at my mother's funeral. I know we met at the masquerade in Venice, but I knew I'd seen you somewhere else..." She looked at the remains of Kiefer. "What were they? Where is André? Oh, I feel as though I'm going quite mad!"

Masquelyne shook his head. "You're not going mad; all will be revealed." He glanced at Kiefer's corpse. "But not here." He paused; his yellow eyes tentative. "Will you come with me, Calliandra? I need to inform a certain person that Kiefer is dead, and that Marguerite escaped. There is much you need to know, Calliandra, and I promise that I will answer all your questions..." An expression of trepidation appeared fleetingly across his face. "And then I shall ask you an important question. I promise you that I will honour your answer...whatever it is." He held out his hand to Evelyn who stared at it for several seconds, before she tentatively reached out and took it. A faint expression of relief appeared on Masquelyne's face as he led her tenderly from the crypt.

After several minutes had passed, a grating sound came from the tomb as the heavy door to the secret passage was slowly pushed back, as Marguerite appeared, clutching her knife, her reticule, and the heavy carpet bag. She saw Kiefer's body, dropped the bags by the doorway, approached her son's remains.

As she knelt next to him, her eyes widened in horror as she saw the Blade of Nekroshema and realised what had happened to his body. Marguerite sat back on her heels, covered her face with her hands, and screamed in loss and rage; she knew what a wound inflicted by the Blade of Nekroshema meant to a necromancer; utter death, without the possibility of return, but she had to hope that with the right approach, and with a suitable offering, Nekroshema would allow the resurrection of her youngest son's eldest child. She choked back a sob as she picked up Kiefer's head and placed it in the carpet bag.

Collecting the Blade of Nekroshema from where Kiefer had thrown it in his dying spasms, she tucked it carefully into the side pocket in the carpet bag, relieved to note that the heads were still silent; their distant grumbling had ceased in the shocking moment of Kiefer's death. She set the bag next to Margaux's corpse, knelt on the floor, gritted her teeth and began to cut through her daughter's neck. Ignoring the sounds and the blood, she worked quickly. When the decapitation was complete, she put Margaux's head in the bag with the others and fastened the latch. Picking up the key from where she had dropped it in her panic, she walked to the trunk which held the body parts for Reynaud's resurrection.

As she looked at the trunk, she realised that the lock was damaged. A horrifying thought suddenly entered Marguerite's mind. She threw open the lid and recoiled; it was empty!

Marguerite turned and scanned the room, her eyes wild. Other than the passage she had hidden in, there was nowhere the limbs could be. A bubble of hysterical laughter suddenly escaped her; she bit the back of her hand to stop it, tears streaming down her face as she realised she would have to resurrect her entire family completely on her own. Marguerite straightened up and drew a shuddering breath which gradually became steadier; she had faced worse in her life...temporary loneliness was manageable when the alternative was accepting the permanent loss of those she loved.

She looked at the dark passageway that led up to the hotel; perhaps the other route would be safer? Marguerite removed her fitted jacket, knelt by the edge of the pool, and splashed clean, cold water on her face, hands, and the blade; the sacred waters washing away her children's blood. Standing up, she pulled her jacket on and fastened it.

Tucking the knife into her waistband, she picked up her reticule and the carpet bag with her left hand and grasped the handle of Kiefer's trunk. Taking the lantern in her right, she entered the secret hiding place within the tomb. Once inside, she placed the lantern on the floor, pushed the lever that closed the lid, collected the flickering lamp, and began to walk through the dark passageway.

Finally arriving at the distant door, Marguerite pricked her finger with the blade she had used on her daughter and placed her bloodied hand on the wall before her; slowly, the panel of stone began to pivot as the hidden panel opened in the outer wall of the Kiosk of Trajan. She took a deep breath of the still-dusty air; the sandstorm had dissipated enough for her to see clearly to the other side of the island. But there was only one thing she wanted to see, and there it was; the small private airship waiting for her at the end of the jetty.

○

The Airship
9:35pm

As the stone portal closed seamlessly behind her, Marguerite hurried across the silent, sand-damaged gardens towards the airship; hopefully, the boy Kiefer had bribed earlier would be there, and prepared to do what they had paid him hand-somely for; carry her and what remained of her family to freedom.

She gripped her reticule and the carpet bag tightly; all that was left of her family resided within those two bags and the trunk. Once they arrived at Cairo Aetherdrome, a touch of enchantment and a few Egyptian pounds handed to the right people should ensure no interference from zealous customs officers; explaining the presence of several decapitated heads in various stages of decomposition and the freshly severed heads of her son and daughter might prove a touch difficult; answering questions about displaced body parts was always so awkward.

She hurried along the path, her tear-filled eyes darting here and there, searching for any threat, but all seemed clear. She reached the jetty, where the airship sat idle at its dock, the soft flicker of a gas lamp visible in the wheelhouse. Marguerite took a deep breath and hurried towards the vessel; she could now hear the contents of the carpet bag murmuring; their voices clamoring to be heard over each other as they moved within their material confines.

As she arrived at the gangplank, the young man Kiefer had paid earlier appeared in the doorway of the wheelhouse, nodded at her, and pointed to the covered sitting area to the aft of the vessel. As she boarded and headed for one of the well-cushioned benches, the young man turned his attention back to the jetty.

Marguerite arranged her tweed travel dress around her and settled in for what promised to be a fairly tedious journey. She knew the airship was one of the fastest light craft available, capable of travelling at eighty miles an hour, but they were over five hundred miles from Cairo, which meant a journey of many hours, she sighed; beggars couldn't be choosers, and it had to be Cairo. She should arrive in the capital in time for breakfast at the Shepheard's Hotel before a swift flight on to Rome. She glanced at the wheelhouse; she should be in time…if the dratted boy started the engine!

She placed her reticule on the seat next to her, tucked the carpet bag next to the trunk, and headed for the wheelhouse, her heels tapping a sharp, staccato tattoo on the stained wooden deck. As she raised her slender hand to knock on the closed door, the engines suddenly sprang into life and a faint thrum began. That was better!

Marguerite returned to the aft sitting area, unaware that she was being watched from the jetty. Several yards away from the moving airship, the young man smiled as he counted the thick bundle of Egyptian pounds he had received for his work; part of his new-found wealth had come from Marguerite's son — but a great deal more had come from the gentleman who was now piloting the airship.

The small vessel rose from the water and began her slow, steady climb. Marguerite looked over the side and allowed herself a relieved smile. Certain of their plans had indeed failed, but there was still hope for the family's survival. A year of solitary work in Italy and her dear husband would be as good as new. Then they could focus on resurrecting the rest of the family. Perhaps, if Nekroshema was kind, Kiefer would be first, then André, then Margaux, and then the baby of the family, little Camillia. Marguerite's smile hardened; then they would find Linden and persuade him to return to the family fold…or face the consequences of his insolence.

As she sat, considering the possible ways of dealing with her grandson's treachery, Marguerite suddenly realised that the airship was leaning to starboard. She looked over the side of the vessel; the craft had not yet set sail for Cairo, but was instead describing a lazy circle around the island. What was the idiot doing? She leapt to her feet, grabbed her reticule, the carpet bag, and the trunk, and hurried to the wheelhouse. Pushing the door open; she stopped dead on the threshold; an expression of sudden fear appearing on her face as she looked at the room's sole occupant.

The man piloting the airship grinned lazily from behind the wheel. "Why, good mornin', darlin'. I did not expect to see you travellin' at such an ungodly hour, and certainly not without the companionship of your lovin' family. I *am* sorry for your losses, Ma'am. Losing so many of your kith and kin who've been with you so very, very, *very* long, must have caused you great distress, Mrs Devereaux…or may I call you *Mrs Cushing*." Marguerite's eyes widened in shock at the unexpected use of one of her many married names.

The humour in Rex Nympton's eyes vanished as he looked at her, and when he spoke again, it was in a clipped, educated, English accent. "Shall I refresh your memory, Madame Devereaux? In 1878, you married Wilton Cushing, by that Yule he was dead, ostensibly of consumption, and his body interred in the family vaults. On New Year's Eve his crypt was broken into, allegedly by resurrectionists; rather an amusing term, all things considered, and his body was discovered…mutilated." A muscle twitched in Rex's jaw. "The lower part of his torso was never recovered."

Marguerite flinched, and Rex smiled as he saw her fear. "I was the man who broke into his crypt and discovered the truth of his death. Allow me to introduce myself, Madame. My name is Barratt Cushing. You and your family murdered my brother Wilton and used his remains cruelly, in a barbaric ritual to resurrect yet another member of your grotesque family!"

Marguerite shook her head as she backed away. "You are insane! No police officer or judge would ever give credence to such ramblings—"

Barrett threw back his head and laughed, his white teeth gleaming in the gaslight. "I can assure you, Madame, that I am very much aware of that." His face became rueful. "The time I wasted trying to get someone — anyone — to listen to me, to make them understand what you and your family were capable of… The years of laughter and derision were far easier to deal with than the pity."

He looked at her, hatred burning in his blue eyes. Then he took a deep breath and smiled. "After being told by my terribly supportive Member of Parliament that I was buying myself a one-way ticket to Bedlam if I persisted in my accusations, word reached you that I would not allow you to get away with my brother's murder, and it was then that you played your final and most obscene card…you murdered my wife and child and made the police think that I was guilty of their deaths, to ensure that you alone would inherit my brother's estate." Barrett leant towards her, his gaze steady. "But I managed to escape, fleeing the country I loved. I reinvented myself — as an actor, I found that the easiest part… but the loss of my mother, brother, wife and child still burned within me!"

Marguerite opened her mouth, then closed it again. She stared at him silently as he continued.

"You and your hell-bound kin disappeared from London after claiming my brother's estate. I followed you through the social pages; a benefit of living in the civilised West, which values the vapid, the false, and the greedy, while decrying the spirited, the real, and the altruistic. I watched you and your family for years, and then I finally realised that there was a pattern to your machinations. One of your number would be injured or seemingly fall ill and disappear …and then they would reappear, as if by magic, none the worse for wear, thirteen full moons later. This was confirmed to me when Kiefer was badly injured during a duel in Paris. Shortly before his untimely demise, his opponent swore to me that he had shot him in the heart and it was confirmed by the young man's second. Duels are illegal, even in Paris, so until the Sûreté ceased their enquiries, both young men decided to retreat to the darker side of the city, away from the long arm of the law. A few days later, both young men were found, in an unpleasant state — eviscerated would be the best word, I suppose — in a grubby back street in Montmartre." Marguerite swallowed as he stared at her.

Barrett paused; a hard light in his eyes. "Thirteen full moons later, your family decamped to this particular hotel, where, after a few days, Kiefer reappeared at your side, a little unsteady on his feet, a little forgetful, but none the worse for wear. It does, after all, take a little time to get over the sudden shock of residing for a year in the darkness of the Abyss and then being resurrected back into the light here." He wagged his finger at her and tutted. "Not very clever, my dear. Considering the deathly state of Kiefer the last time he was seen by witnesses, there is only one possible way to explain his sudden reappearance. But that explanation was impossible — incomprehensible! I could not seek justice in the courts, so instead I sought it in the realm of vengeance!"

Marguerite closed her eyes, willing his relentless voice to go away, but he continued, remorselessly.

He smiled suddenly. "I forgot to mention; I managed to have a very pleasant little chat with your grandson earlier today. He was surprised that I knew what you were. I knew that he had nothing to do with the murders of my family, because my investigations revealed that he was in France at the time. I gave him a choice; to fight and die by your side… or to live a full life, and die without resurrection. It would appear that he chose to become human." He looked at her, his face set. "Searching for the truth of what your family are has almost destroyed me. But after twenty-three years, my vengeance is nearly complete."So, now, Marguerite Devereaux, you alone stand between my murdered brother, wife, and child, and peace — theirs, and mine!"

Marguerite stared at him; her eyes huge in her pale face. "You killed my family?"

Barrett smiled deprecatingly. "Not all of them, I regret to say. The reward for killing Julius, André, and Kiefer must go to someone else. Dear Violette was poisoned by her own ring. But Julius' death, and the subsequent death of Gaston Cavet, gave me the idea." He raised an eyebrow. "I take it that Cavet's death can be attributed to a member of your family?"

Marguerite lifted her chin and glared at him. Barrett shrugged. "I witnessed your esteemed son-in-law falling to his death from the *Cartouche*. As his body landed in the Nile, it turned the river red. Then poor Cavet was stabbed through the eye. I remembered seeing Jane wearing an ornate hairpin topped by a golden frog, and of course, the man was French after all, so I thought…*I wonder*, and then, *how apt*; the first two plagues of Egypt! Why not continue the theme?" His smile twisted as he leant forward. "May I ask a personal question? What did you think about Margaux's mummification? I was rather pleased that I managed to pleat the material. It looked very neat, don't you think?"

Marguerite's breath hissed between her teeth as she stared at the man who had destroyed her family. "You bastard! Do you think a wayward human will stop us from returning? We have enslaved your kind since time immemorial, and we shall continue to do so!" She gazed at him with an intolerably proud expression. "I will resurrect my family and—"

Barrett held up an admonitory finger. "I am afraid that will only work if one of you is alive to resurrect the others."

"*I* am alive, and I *will* bring back my family!" Marguerite frowned as the murmuring from the bag grew inside her mind; the voices sounded almost panicked. She brushed the sounds aside. "We have been running the world of your pathetic species for thousands of years. We created the legends of Isis and Osiris, and many, *many* others! We shall still be here long after the world of Man has died…" Her expression became one of gloating cruelty as she stood tall, her eyes filling with white light tinged with pink. "Unlike your brother, wife, and son, *we* are eternal — and my family *will* return!"

Barrett laughed softly. "I'm afraid not, my dear." He lunged suddenly towards her. She heard a strange, hissing click as a knife slid from its holster on his forearm and appeared in his hand. Marguerite's eyes widened as the razor-sharp blade pierced her breastbone and ran her through.

Rex pulled the blade free and Marguerite fell against the bench. He removed his handkerchief from his breast pocket and wiped the blade before returning it to its holster.

Marguerite blinked and raised a hand to her chest. Her full lips parted as she touched the bloody material over her heart. Barrett straightened his collar and smiled down at her. "One of the many things I spent good money on was learning how to destroy the forces of evil. You can die, just like a human; the only difference is that you can be resurrected; but only if there is a member of your family left alive to do so…and now that your grandson has abandoned you to your fate, that means your death will be eternal. Now, if you will excuse me, I need to see about the grand finale. You stay here, my dear…I'll be right back."

Marguerite held out a pleading hand as he picked up the carpet bag and reticule. "No! They're my family! You can't…"

Barrett's smile disappeared. "Your family's bloody actions over the millennia of your existence have proven you to be both inhuman and inhumane. Therefore, Madam, your concern for the welfare of your family is of *no* concern to me." He opened the carpet bag and looked at the contents with disgust, then held it open for Marguerite to see. "Say goodbye to your family!"

Marguerite fell at his feet with a scream as he stalked out with the bags and the trunk. She shook her head disbelievingly; this couldn't be…if she died, her family could never be resurrected!

Barrett placed the trunk by the wheelhouse door, and climbed the ladder that led to the gasbags above. He sat on the edge, placed the reticule and carpet bag next to him, then pulled a cigar from his breast pocket and lit it. Hearing a sound, he looked down; Marguerite was on the ladder, several rungs below him. She placed a bloodied hand on the lower rail and looked at him beseechingly, the pink tinge in her eyes lessening as the material of her blouse became saturated with her own blood. "Please! You can't do this! My family have existed for thousands of years — you can't take them from me!"

Barrett studied her, his face grim. "You murdered my brother, my wife, and my son. You caused the death of my mother. You have killed countless others; good men and women, and innocent children...people who could not be brought back from the land of the dead — and you expect me to show *you* mercy?"

Marguerite stared as Barrett suddenly smiled. "Very well. I will show you and your family mercy — the same mercy that you showed my family and all the others you murdered!" He took a long draw from the cigar, blew a smoke ring, turned, and stabbed the smouldering tip into the nearest gasbag.

The explosion was massive. An incredible sound rent the evening sky and illuminated it with brilliant blue light. Marguerite could only gaze in impotent horror as death; cloaked in vibrant eau de nil flame, exploded around her.

○

The Entrance Hall

As the debris started to land, partly in the Nile, and partly around the terraces of the hotel, Elliott, Giselle, Thorne, Aquilleia, Darling, Maxwell, and Veronique stood quietly by the entrance to the reception and watched the fireworks. As Elliott turned to the injured Darling, who was being assisted by his brother, the young man from the airship approached them, he bowed deeply to Elliott and held out a package. "A gentleman said 'give this to the one with the walking cane' He also asked that I inform you that a lady and a gentleman have left the island, and will contact you soon. He said that you would know of whom I speak." He bowed again, then walked away as Elliott looked at Giselle with a relieved expression. "I don't know how they managed to leave, but I'm very glad to hear that they have!"

He opened the envelope and scanned the letter. He held it out to Darling. "I believe you need to read this...it's from Barrett Cushing." As Darling took the letter and began to read, Elliott gestured at the burning debris. "A very explosive clan, the Devereaux family."

Thorne nodded as part of the airship's propeller shaft landed with a thud several feet away and embedded itself into one of the sand-covered flower beds. "Indeed."

"She should have known better than to return here."

They turned to look at Amycus Mirylees who was standing by the door to the entrance hall. Elliott shared a sharp look with Thorne. "I beg your pardon, Dr Mirylees?"

The ancient archaeologist waved his hand towards the burning wreckage of the airship. "Marguerite Devereaux...it was she and her family who were ultimately responsible for the deaths committed here; was it not?"

Darling gave him a guarded look. "What makes you say that, Dr Mirylees?"

Amicus gave a humourless laugh. "Death and misery followed that woman just as surely as night follows day." His pale eyes narrowed as he looked at Elliott. "I will tell you this much. Many years ago, she married...and murdered, my good friend, Edmund Street. He was a kind soul...and, as such, an easy target for so malevolent a creature. For reasons that are too painful for me to explain, even now, after all these years, Edmund desperately wanted to be accepted by society, and he believed that having a wife…even one married after such a scandalously short engagement, was the way to buy the acceptance he craved." Amicus shook his head. "When he died, I knew she was guilty, but I could prove nothing…it was merely a feeling." He looked at Darling. "She *is* dead, I take it?" The others looked at Aquilleia who gave a faint nod. Amycus caught her gesture and a genuine smile appeared on his lined face. "I am pleased that she has received her punishment for the crime she committed; it was long overdue, mind you, but justice has finally been done."

He turned away, opened the door, and entered the entrance hall as a tear fell from his eye and ran down his cheek. He took a letter from his breast pocket and reread the final few paragraphs as he walked back to his room. The letter had been sent to him before he had booked his trip to the island. In it, the sender had detailed their plans for Marguerite Devereaux and her family. Amycus smiled grimly as he walked; the offer of witnessing the destruction of the one who had killed his dear friend had been far too sweet a dish to refuse. Arriving at his door, he tucked the letter back into his pocket and closed his eyes. "You can rest now, dearest Edmund…it is done. And to you, Mr Barrett; thank you for being the hammer of justice."

Back on the covered terrace, Elliott and the others watched in silence as the remains of the airship's balloon envelope fell slowly through the air; the smouldering red cotton becoming glowing fragments that landed on the limpid waters of the Nile before sinking into the depths.

Darling held up the letter. "It *was* Rex Nympton. A shame I won't be able to thank him in person; his actions have certainly lessened the number of necromancers on our books!"

Elliott looked at him. "Somehow, I don't think the deaths

of the Devereaux family will be well received by those who used their gifts of immortality."

Darling nodded gloomily. "No. The Espion Court should have known that protecting such creatures would lead to this state of affairs."

Thorne frowned. "Brother, you *are* the Espion Court!"

Darling looked slightly embarrassed. "In mitigation, I was advised to protect them by several members of the Astraean Royal family, the Empire, the civil service, and one or two members of society's finest. I now realise that I should never listen to suspiciously young-looking men and women who work in, or for, the government…or who are well placed in society — they obviously have a hidden agenda!" He huffed again. "What a bloody mess! The paperwork will be an absolute nightmare."

"I might have an idea about that," said Elliott.

Darling looked at him, a hopeful yet wary expression on his face. "Oh, yes? What do you have in mind?" He held up an admonitory finger. "Bearing in mind that your last great idea was to send Villiers Locke to deal with Hammad and Jaziri. I'm pretty sure he'll ignore my orders not to eat them."

Elliott smiled. "Then perhaps this will give us a way out."

They all turned in surprise as a sudden scream rent the air behind them. The Contessa de Mostada, dressed in a deeply unbecoming mustard peignoir trimmed with garish pink marabout feathers, stood on the hotel steps, and proceeded to give them her very best impersonation of an alarum clock.

Giselle approached the wailing woman and, as the Contessa took a deep breath to continue her aural assault, slapped her across the face. The shocked older woman gazed up at Giselle as the younger woman took her hand. "Contessa, back to your suite; I suggest a tray of caviar and Champagne for your nerves. Off you go." Giselle gently pushed the squeaking Contessa back through the door, turned to her husband and gestured to the covered terrace, where several people had pushed the doors open to watch the remains of the airship burn. "I suggest we go somewhere a touch more private to finish this conversation."

They entered the reception and made their way towards the Isis corridor. As they walked through the bar; Aquilleia, Thorne, and Darling paused to grab several bottles of champagne, glasses, a plate of caviar for Ailuros, and a plate of biscuits for Veronique, before they continued to Elliott and Giselle's suite.

Entering the cool room, the others sat down as Thorne and Elliott poured Champagne and passed out the coupes. Maxwell paused to look at the glass being offered to him, before accepting it with a hesitant smile. Aquilleia held one of the oatmeal biscuits out to Veronique, who gave it a suspicious sniff before deciding it was better than nothing and wolfed it down. Thorne sat down beside his wife and removed a notebook and pencil from his breast pocket as Elliott sat in the armchair by the terrace door and continued where he had left off.

"The reason we were originally sent here was to investigate several terrorist attacks, robberies, and murders committed against British and European travellers. In the course of our investigation, we found information suggesting that Miss March and Sergeant Jaziri were the agents known as Rouge et Noir. They passed information on certain guests to the terrorists; Miss March was well-placed in the hotel and Sergeant Jaziri, as a police officer, could change official documents about what was stolen." He shook his head. "We may never know how many they killed or how much was taken to fund the terrorists. We also know that Officer Hammad at the aetherdrome was Black Eagle, and Kiefer was Caeruleum."

Darling frowned. "Why Kiefer?"

Elliott sat back in his chair. "We dealt with a necromancer many years ago who bore the same name, and I suspect he was part of the Devereaux family. I think he was here at the hotel, and, even though we never saw him. He was the family's guiding light, the ultimate reason for the marriage of Evelyn and André, and morally responsible for the murder of Evelyn's father." Elliott paused. "When one of the family dies, the surviving kin have to resurrect them. In order to do this, they collect body parts to bring them back. Evelyn's father was missing an eye; the penultimate part required for the ritual to resurrect. All that was needed then was the heart's blood of a virginal sacrifice."

Giselle spoke, her face pale. "Evelyn."

"Exactly. So, the family came here..." He paused. "There must be a place on this island that they used for their rituals. A place we haven't yet found." He looked at Thorne. "Remember that damn great trunk? The one Kiefer was so concerned about in London?"

Thorne nodded. "Of course! It must have contained the parts for a resurrection — it was certainly big enough!" He looked at Elliott through narrowed eyes. "But whose? The family were all here."

Elliott shook his head. "The family *were* all here, but not in the way you think. The body parts for the resurrection were stored in the trunk, but the family would never leave the most important part of a necromancer to sit alone in the dark. The one piece that follows them through every single resurrection is their skull." He looked at Darling. "I think Caeruleum was ever-present within the Devereaux family, and responsible for the murmuring Aquilleia heard. His skull was in his wife's reticule, awaiting resurrection. I believe that Caeruleum was Reynaud Devereaux, Kiefer's father."

Giselle's lips parted. "His father? Of course!"

Elliott nodded. "The odds of two necromancers bearing the same name lessen drastically if one is the child of the other. I think Kiefer took on his father's mantle when the older Devereaux was between bodies, for want of a better phrase, and continued the family business until his father's return."

Aquilleia looked up from feeding Veronique. "But why? What did the family have to gain from facilitating terrorism?"

Giselle looked at her friend. "Money." Think of their lifestyle; high society, houses and villas in England and Italy, and the servants to run them. They would need thousands a year to live such a luxurious life. All the victims were robbed of extremely valuable items. It would have been easy for the family to find buyers within their network of highly placed, influential friends — especially those who needed to keep the family happy to ensure their own repeated resurrections."

Elliott stood up, a strange expression on his face. "In the light of certain appearances — and disappearances — I shall throw myself on your mercy. Two people have reappeared during this case; including one whom I have never really met, but they mean a very great deal to me." Faint green lights appeared in his eyes, and Giselle gently placed her hand over his.

Elliott cleared his throat and took another sip of champagne. "I suggest we inform the authorities that our investigations led us to this conclusion; given the available facts, the Devereaux family were behind the terrorist outrages and the accompanying murders and robberies. As for the murder committed aboard the *Cartouche* and the others at the hotel..." He paused, a conflicted expression on his face. "I have never shirked in a case in my life, but all I want is to ensure that the authorities never discover my father's part in this. After so long, he and my mother deserve peace."

He gave an exasperated sigh. "My father has his own moral code, and, *yes*, I know he dropped Julius from the airship. but he has admitted killing him because Julius was trying to murder Evelyn. I believe — *I hope* — that is the only death which can be laid solely at his door. The other deaths were mostly the work of Barrett Cushing…with or without my father's support." He groaned and rubbed the bridge of his nose. "We don't even know if Barrett Cushing is dead or alive!"

Aquilleia spoke from her place on the settee, where she was stroking a now sleeping Veronique. "He's dead." The others turned to her. "I felt his death…it was a release. He's gone to be with his wife, his son, and his brother."

Thorne looked at his wife. "It's a shame; I rather liked Rex Nympton, even though he technically didn't exist. Well then, case solved." He paused; his green eyes troubled. "But there may be a problem. I haven't seen Linden for a while, and we don't know where Marguerite or Kiefer are. If we say they were assisting terrorists to support their expensive lifestyles and they reappear after we've sent in our report, that could make matters a touch tricky!"

Aquilleia shook her head. "I believe that both Marguerite and Kiefer are dead; I saw flashes of their deaths; Kiefer's death was…unpleasant, and permanent. Marguerite died aboard the airship. I can no longer see or feel them…nor can I hear the skulls. As for Linden, I haven't seen his death…he may simply be too far away for me to hear him."

Thorne turned back to Elliott. "Can we really get away with lying to the Espion Court *and* the Empire about Masquelyne's part in the death of Julius van Sloane? Bearing in mind that the leader of the Espion Court is sitting right here, listening to us?" He gestured towards his brother.

Elliott nodded; his face serious. "Yes, I believe we can. The authorities will be terribly embarrassed when they discover that a family they sheltered and pandered to, actually supported a terrorist uprising against the Empire while under the protection of both the Espion Court and the very Empire they were conspiring against. That alone should mean the immediate closure of the case, to be filed where it will never again see the light of day. If any of the Devereaux family do reappear, they may well find that their hold over high society, the Empire, and the Espion Court, is at an end." His expression was anxious; a look Giselle had never seen from him before. "I must protect my father and the woman who holds my mother's memories. I ask you, as my friends… will you help me?"

Giselle again reached for her husband's hand. "I will."

Thorne nodded, his green eyes understanding. "Did you really think you had to ask?"

Aquilleia smiled. "I will."

Maxwell took a sip from his coupe; his vivid eyes widened at the taste and the bubbles. He looked at Elliott and nodded. "Of course, Sir."

They all turned to look at Darling, who shifted in his seat and winced. "Given what the family were and what they were capable of, justice of one kind or another was bound to find them, and sooner rather than later." He looked at Elliott. "I concur. We must take into account the discovery of a certain young woman who needs to rediscover her memories; both of who she was, and who you, Phoenixus, and Masquelyne are to her. For the sake of the innocent, I agree."

A sudden loud knock at the door was met by a volley of barks from a startled Veronique, who leapt off the settee and ran to the door, hackles bristling, accompanied, not entirely unwillingly, by the small black kitten, Ailuros, who was clinging like a limpet to the agitated Labrador's neck. Thorne opened the door and raised an eyebrow. "Is everything all right, Mr Bey?"

Carandini Bey pushed past Thorne and glared at them all, then pointed a long, trembling finger at Elliott. "You are the agents for the Empire — do something! Murders, decapitations, animal attacks, and now exploding airships! Mr Caine, I beg you, solve this case, so that my hotel can return to the quiet opulence she is celebrated for."

Elliott smiled. "It's quite all right, Mr Bey. I am very pleased to say that the case is solved."

Carandini blinked. "Solved? You've solved all the murders?"

Thorne grinned at him. "Every last one."

Carandini rocked on the balls of his feet, a beatific expression on his face. "Excellent, excellent." He leant forward conspiratorially. "Who was it?"

Giselle smiled. "Mr Bey, we must inform the authorities first."

Carandini looked rather disappointed. "Oh yes, of course." He paused; his expression concerned. "Have you arrested them yet? Are we still in danger?"

Elliott shook his head. "There is no danger, Mr Bey." He shared a glance with the others before turning back to the manager. "Those responsible for the deaths have perished."

Carandini looked out at the still-burning remains of the airship and nodded slowly. "No one could have escaped such an inferno." He sighed. "That poor, poor family. One of our stewards has informed me that the destroyed airship was hired by Kiefer Devereaux to take his family to Cairo. He must have been on board." He cast his eyes to the heavens, missing the look the friends shared at this piece of news. "So many funerals for poor Mr Devereaux to arrange."

The room stilled. Darling recovered first. "*Which* Mr Devereaux, Mr Bey?"

Carandini blinked. "Why, Mr Linden Devereaux. I saw him earlier today, when he informed me that he had ordered a private air-carriage to take him to Cairo to oversee his family's funerals." Carandini shivered. "Such a tragedy for a young man." He paused and frowned slightly. "But I can't understand why he didn't wait for the airship his uncle had ordered…"

Faint green lights appeared in Elliott's intent brown eyes. "How did he arrange an air-carriage when your telephone isn't working, Mr Bey?"

"Mr Devereaux didn't use the telephone, for obvious reasons. Once the storm began to abate, he hailed one of the boats that fish these waters and paid them to carry his message to the air-carriage company."

Giselle shared a worried look with Elliott. "When does the air-carriage arrive?"

"It already has, Mlle Du'Lac. It came for Mr Devereaux shortly before the airship exploded."

The green lights in Elliott's eyes intensified. "Is Mr Devereaux still on the island?"

Carandini shook his head, a frown on his brow. "No, Mr Caine, as far as I'm aware, he's gone."

○

The Leaving
Tuesday Morning
9:00am

The *Cartouche* landed gracefully in the water and settled against the wood and stone of the jetty while her crew carried out their duties; setting out the walkway and loading the luggage belonging to what remained of the hotel guests. Due to the events that had taken place at the hotel, there were no new guests to disembark from the *Cartouche*. Instead, the passengers journeying to the island were specialist cleaners, under strict orders to leave no trace of the deaths that had taken place at the sumptuous hotel.

Elliott, Giselle, Thorne, Aquilleia, Veronique, and Darling, boarded in an irritated mood. Their plan to explain the killings would still stand with the authorities, as long as Linden didn't cause a fuss. Hopefully, he would take the opportunity for a quiet life, free of the murder and mayhem that had followed his family. That was not to say that the Espion Court wouldn't be keeping a far closer eye on the surviving member of the Devereaux family. Darling had already begun to draft an order to the effect that those who had previously supported the family, whether in government, society, or the Espion Court herself, were to be considered persona non grata, and any attempts to utilise the remaining Devereaux scion's more questionable abilities were to be nipped in the bud.

As the airship began preparations to leave, Maxwell and Farasha stood side by side next to the rail. Maxwell looked at Farasha, "I'm glad that you chose to be here...with me."

Farasha looked at him; a gentle expression on her face. "So am I."

Maxwell looked at her, then hesitantly reached out and took the smiling Farasha's hand.

On the starboard side of the craft, Elliott and the others stood and watched the fishing vessels that had emerged after the sandstorm. If they had taken the time to walk to the port side, they may have seen a young man sitting on a stone bench, watching the airship begin her manoeuvers for take-off.

The young man picked up the sodden, singed carpet bag which he had rescued from the bank of the river. A distant grumbling rose from the bag as he stood on the bank of the Nile and watched the *Cartouche* rise into the air. He turned to the doorway in the wall behind him, and called out. "They've gone."

Footsteps echoed from the long corridor that led to one of the many hidden passages that led to the ritual room. A manicured hand gripped the edge of the door and a man stepped into the bright sunlight. Obviously older than Linden; tall and well-built, with a thick shock of silver-grey hair and painfully bright blue eyes. The man joined Linden to watch the airship disappear into the cerulean sky.

The older man spoke. His voice, touched with a slight French accent, was husky, as though it had not been used for a while. "You say the man responsible for the deaths of our family is himself dead, but there are others who know our secret?"

Linden nodded. "Yes, Grand-père. Four private enquiry agents and a government man; Elliott Caine, his wife Giselle Du'Lac, Abernathy Thorne, his wife Madame Aquilleia, and Captain Anthony Darling."

"Only the five? Bon! That will make things far easier. The fewer who know of us, the better." The older man looked at his grandson. "Before we leave, we need to find the rest of the family." He gestured at the grumbling carpet bag his grandson was carrying. "Your grandmother's voice is not there…neither are the voices of Camillia, Jane, or Violette. We must find them. We must also tidy what needs tidying. We shall always need this place, so it makes sense to leave no trace of our presence, n'est-ce pas?"

Linden smiled, and re-entered the chamber of resurrection. He began to clean the room, his mind replaying the events of the last few hours. After his eye-opening conversation with Rex Nympton…or rather, Barret Cushing, earlier, he had found himself in his grandmother's suite, staring at her reticule, and had made the decision to attempt his grandfather's resurrection himself.

Linden had taken the skull and entered the chamber of resurrection before his grandmother and Kiefer. He had smashed the lock on the trunk, placed the reassembled body on the altar, positioned his grandfather's skull above the collection of body parts, and, in a sudden moment of panic, had left the chamber for a walk, hoping for a sign that his dreams for his family's future were right. Not far from the chamber's secret entrance he had spotted a child playing by the banks of the Nile; the five-year-old daughter of one of the hotel's human staff. Linden had a choice to make...the choice that Barrett had offered him; would he choose humanity, or his family? As he watched the little girl play by the river, he had made his choice.

He had found the resurrection ritual much like the murder of the little girl; quite straightforward to perform, even as a solo act. Carrying his unconscious grandfather's body from the ritual room to the safety and quiet of one of the many other rooms hidden within the Temple of Nekroshema had taken some time, but it had been needed; the first few hours after resurrection had to be peaceful to allow the resurrected necromancer time to readjust to their return from the Abyss.

Linden closed the lid on the empty trunk and turned to the larger items which required disposal. He rejoined his grandfather a few moments later, carrying several pieces of Kiefer's body, and threw them into the Nile. He repeated the journey again, then did the same for Margaux's corpse, and for the fourth and final time, with the body of the little girl.

He collected his bag and a small case and returned to his grandfather's side. Turning to the older man, he held out the case. "A gift for you, Grand-père." Reynaud took the case and opened it to reveal ivory chess pieces with mother-of-pearl and brass inlays and an ebony and ivory board. He turned to his grandson. "Exquisite!"

Linden smiled happily. "I saw it in the suite of one of our…financial backers, a few months ago. I hoped you would like it."

Reynaud smiled back. "It is a perfect gift, Linden. Now, signal the fishermen to continue to search the Nile; my beloved Marguerite is here somewhere. After we find her and the others, we shall leave by boat for Aswan, then travel to Rome, and see to the resurrection of our family." As he looked at his grandson, a strange expression flashed across his face, and was gone before Linden saw it. "After that, Linden, we shall take our rightful place as rulers in this world…and we will start by placing a high price on the heads of Mr Caine, Thorne, and Darling…and their wives!"

The two men shared a look, the vibrant blue of their eyes replaced by opaque white; life was about to become even more interesting for the departing enquiry agents.

○

Venice

In a warren of higgledy-piggledy terracotta-tiled buildings and narrow alleys that seemed to meander for miles but lead nowhere, Luca slowly walked down a narrow alley, paused by one of the many doors that lined the dim passageway, and removed a large key from his pocket.

Marizza looked up as the door to her perfumed prison was opened. The strange man with the wheezing voice stood on the threshold, looking at her. A soft clicking and whirring emanated from his chest as he took a deep breath.

"Mlle Dimitrova, the Toymaker will see you now."

THE END

ABOUT THE AUTHOR

Rhen Garland lives in Somerset, England with her folk-singing, artist husband, 4000 books, an equal number of 1980's action movies, and a growing collection of passive-aggressive Tomtes.

"I thought when I finally started writing that my books would be genteel "cosy" type murder mysteries set in the Golden Era (I love the 1920's and 30's for the style, music, and automobiles), with someone being politely bumped off at the Vicar's tea party and the corpse then apologising for disrupting proceedings. But no, the late Victorian era came thundering over my horizon armed with some fantastical and macabre plotlines and planted itself in my stories, my characters, and my life, and would not budge."

I enjoy the countryside, peace, Prosecco, and the works of Dame Ngaio Marsh, Dame Glady Mitchell, John Dickson Carr/Carter Dickson, Dame Agatha Christie, Simon R Green, and Sir Terry Pratchett. I watch far too many old school murder mystery films, TV series, and 1980's action movies for it to be considered healthy.